Antonia
Saw
the
Oryx
First

ANTONIA SAW THE ORYX FIRST

A Novel

by

Maria Thomas

◁ ◇ ▷

SOHO

Library of Congress Cataloging-in-Publication Data
Thomas, Maria, 1941–1989
    Antonia saw the oryx first.
    I. Title.
PS3570.H5735A5   1987   813'.54   86–31570
ISBN 0–939149–90–7

Manufactured in the United States of America

To my mother Aïda Thomas
and to
my late father Robert R. Thomas

ONE
◁◇▷

Like an African, the white doctor came to work on foot, along a road that lined the port of Dar es Salaam. She would tell people that it was only because her car was in for repairs. She made a joke of it: the car had been laid up almost two years waiting for a part. But the aberration, since no one white ever walked in Africa, and the notoriety it caused, pleased her in ways, even if the walk did not.

Down in the throng, she looked at backs, tangent and overlapping, condensing light into negative spaces between curves made of jawbone, neck and shoulder, of arms bent and gesturing. Cars avoiding pits and holes in the road jammed her into ditches. Children ran in and out trying to get ahead of her. To see the white face better. Although they knew her, saw her every day, they still mobbed her, still begged for shillings.

She approached the hospital from the west. Heavy walls cut from stone and a red tile roof, set in a widening spread of trampled grass and parking lot, in a circle of old mangoes like green domes planted for the shade. She could see the wide corridors and porches where patients waited. It had always been the "natives'" hospital, ponderously efficient, with British nursing sisters tending to it. Now, with less attention, it was not so much falling apart as it was calcifying like tartar on neglected teeth. There was talk that the Swedes (or Norwegians) were planning to build a new wing. They would bring in plate glass and fluorescent lights, things that would break and never be replaced.

Dark shelters and makeshift verandas were already

crowded with patients. Around the old dried fountains, people who had spent the night were shaking their cloths, turning sheets back into shawls or umbrellas against the heat, patterns like butterfly wings fluttering down to the mud.

Her first patient was a boy, an adolescent who had a swelling on his abdomen the size of a grapefruit. One of the rural hospitals had sent him to the capital for surgery and they gave him to her. Someone had shoved into an envelope the wrong set of records, which said the patient had an ectopic pregnancy. It could have been a statue that she examined, carved from such soft wood that she expected splinters. He held his hands at his sides and stared at his mother. For some reason he had been given a whole-blood transfusion, or so it seemed. His mother said, "They changed his blood. His was dirty and no good." Like oil in a Ford.

Throughout the day she saw a host of women patients who wouldn't tell her specifically what was wrong. As she went on asking questions and poking, they went on saying, "Yes, yes . . ." to everything until it looked as though they had pain all over.

"It would be easier to be a veterinarian. Then you wouldn't get so confused." She heard Paul Luenga, come into her examination room to watch her. He held his stethoscope loose in his hand, at his side like a weapon. The remark was sarcastic and meant to catch her in a black thought. But he failed. She faced him, like a reflection; a split second before he turned and left. He was her supervisor now, the director of the hospital, nothing more to her; she let him go without a word. Despite the way he held the stethoscope. Despite his tone. The nurses, of course, had heard all the rumors about her and Luenga and were arranged on the sidelines listening. And the patient, innocent, who had had an operation but didn't know what for. "They took something out," she said, "but I am still sick."

She had ordered coffee at midmorning but had no chance to drink it. It sat on her desk until a skin of milk formed over the surface, a white ring on the edge of her cup that she called the Milky Way. She drank it finally at the end of the day, room temperature and too sweet for the late afternoon when she wanted the pungency of tea. Too heavy. She would have liked to have been transported to a coffee shop someplace else, someplace achingly clean that served espresso, crisp and biting, in tiny cups. A place of antiseptic mirrors and chrome-framed prints advertising historic art shows, names like Miro, Klee, Rothko that came back to her as easily as the taste for fresh cheese and good bread. She was always shocked when she flew north to a European city, as though she were being tossed into the future, not the present, though it was all part of her past.

She hung her lab coat on a hook. There was a triangle of torn pocket keeled over, an isolated shape in the folds of cloth. Melancholy, her fingers walked along the surface of her mahogany desk, across the top of a stranded wheelchair, against the wall, touching the stacks of unfiled medical records yellowing with age. Outside her window, patients dispersed and then regrouped like herdforms clustered around a village at night.

There was enough of the day left that she didn't go home, but walked instead along a lane behind the hospital toward the sea. The sky and tide were swept back over flats of sand and mud, expanses that dwarfed the structures on the land: the palms, the seawall, the jetties stretched into the empty space all made into small, inconsequential things. There were no people around save two old women steaming something in an oil drum using driftwood sticks for fuel. The doctor watched them. They had clams, very large and thick shelled. Like mussels, these were covered with weed and barnacles, but when they opened there were bright orange gills and long blue-black necks. The clams, the women told her, had been ordered by an Italian man. Each week he came and bought as many as they could supply.

"To *eat* them!" This was hilarious, explaining everything about Italians. "Yes," they repeated in unison, "to eat them."

It made the doctor laugh as well. She left the women then and wandered out on a jetty. Rock pools were full of tiny red and turquoise starfish, bristling urchins, crabs that ran displaying single purple claws. She was someone who made the most of solitude, which had, for her, a stretch and opportunity: moments that could drift away from time and space like this one on a siphoned beach. If she were to stand there as the tide came in, she, too, would be at the bottom of the sea with these creatures.

Even as she watched the tide turned and soon the water was touching the jetty. She took some in her hand and tasted it. Seaweeds that had been limp against the rocks began to move as if touched by wind, reached out and seemed to pull water in around them. The two women working on their clams were echoes of that sway. She saw them dip and bend. Soon their customer arrived in his white sedan. His movements, in contrast, were fast and jerking, and he left slamming his car door and revving his engine as if his speed, his noise, could make a difference. Which, for the doctor, was surely more hilarious than the eating of clams.

Four Indians on a motorbike passed her as she started walking home. Sikhs: the man wore a blue turban and a white shirt. A woman sat in front of him, a bunch of gathered cloth. Their two boys rode behind, standing, tossing their heads, annoyed by their bound hair. Later, the doctor passed them, not far along, huddled around the machine, the man kneeling and the woman dusting off her boys, arranging their hair. The heat was starting to be oppressive. A crow swooped from a rooftop and landed on a wooden porch rail. Another joined it; the porch was full of cardboard cartons. Then the Indians came by again, the family of Sikhs, and when she turned to look, there were five of them, a baby suddenly held on the woman's lap, as if she had given birth in the interval. The incident fixed the day in her mind, ready to figure time the way Africans did: as the space between events.

When she found her friend Brian McGeorge on her doorstep, she was aware again of time that was named by event: she hadn't seen him since the rains. He was pale from London, where it might have been winter, and looked as though he came from another planet in his Panama hat, his tropical suit, silk tie, Italian shoes. He bought and sold coffee now instead of growing it the way his family had done. It was the only way, he said, that he could be there and here. "I've worked it out," he said, "so that I have the best of both worlds."

He hated his job: the paperwork, governments, import duties, border controls. His true vocation was photography. He produced one book after another—stark titles and brilliant prints. He loved the stunning nomads (Masai *morani* painted up for their first lion kill, covered with beads), old white men left in Africa, big cats, sweeping empty beaches, stretches of savanna, acacia, baobab. A book of his was always there collecting dust on the doctor's coffee table. *Warrior!* about the rites of passage among the Masai. In private, McGeorge called it *Lost Foreskins and Lion Pelts.*

She told her cook Charles there would be two for dinner and brought her guest a beer while he flipped through his own book making unbridled sounds of admiration. Inside her house, he peeled off his tie and jacket, flung off his shoes, like a creature shedding useless skin. When he finished, spread out on her couch, he became familiar again, her old friend, who came, as always, at intervals, according to seasons passing in other hemispheres.

"The beer's not very cold," she warned. "My fridge isn't getting any younger either. It's a museum piece. I pray over it. I make sacrifices to it."

He sighed, "Each time I come back the beer is worse. But cheers anyway." He was holding up a page for her to see, pointing, smiling. *Morani* warriors with black triangles painted up their legs. The small red plumes on their spears meant they were going after cattle rustlers. All romance. All nostalgia. Africa.

He had some local gossip she had missed. "Bruce's kids, you know, came down from U.K. and found the old boy in bed with *three* black girls. And the old missus not cold in 'er grave." He hooted and clapped, so that Charles, thinking he was being summoned, came in with two more beers. It was the way Charles had of begging time while he stretched things in the kitchen. An aura of onion clung to him like a universal condition. "You're a doc, Tony. What do you suppose has taken over for Bruce's liver? Whatever it is, I want one."

He took prints from the briefcase, for his latest book, to show her. *Hippo!* Pictures taken from a cage he had lowered into rivers and lakes. The animals were even more improbable hanging there under water than when they lolled or grazed up on land. Delicate-skinned, they only came to shore at night. They were rarely seen out of water unless you got up early, expressly for that purpose and just as the sun rose, and found the beach where they had piled against each other wallowing in mud. They were animals that ran on cue, diving from high banks into deep pools. McGeorge had a picture of one, a hippo in the air, a belly flop. He loved it. His head dipped. He had thick blond hair smoothed back. His fingers combed into it. He preferred to wear it dusty, shaggy, trailing on his collar. Now it was clean and freshly cut. He would rearrange it, the hand brushing, loosening it all, a transformation going on before her very eyes. She referred to his London Dr. Jekyll as an allergic reaction. He was better as the tousled naturalist, a Mr. Hyde gone bush.

Wildlife hung on as assurance in their Africa. The national treasures. Rome had the Colosseum, France the Eiffel Tower. Here there were elephant, lion, giraffe. The most available resource: you didn't have to mine it or move it away to sell it. Funny how people remained amazed, as though they only half believed the stories of striped horses, thought ostriches and warthogs a bag of photographic tricks. Like oryx—with horns so straight and balanced that in profile one eclipsed the other—rare, white, giving rise to tales of unicorns. Everyone had his own stories after a safari. The elephant story. The lion story. There were still white men with warm beer around campfires who talked about "buff." Antonia had hers about a ranger in Rwanda who chased a bull elephant from their camp by clicking a couple of stones together: the tiny sound, the huge animals, ears flapping as they ran, the laughter of their party. And her lion story. Where had it been? When? Perhaps Nyasa, far to the south. She would have been thirteen or fourteen. There had been a brushfire, trees burned bare and etched black into a landscape washed wintery white by the moon. She was fascinated, thinking this is what it must look like in North America when the trees go bare, like this ruined place. She stood holding the tent flap open to it . . . each pebble, each charred branch, each blade of dry grass . . . and turning saw a lioness. Right there. They felt each other's breath they were so close and held each other's eyes as if intelligence could pass between them, though neither one was afraid. The cat stepped by the tent, brushing the canvas with her tail. Beyond the camp she took on the color of the moon, a luminous blue.

"And what now, McGeorge, after *Hippo?*" She knew his sequential list of titles, one for each species, one for each tribe, for places with well-known melodic names like Olduvai, Serengeti, Kilimanjaro. Endless, she thought, and beautiful and safe.

"Well," he said, "there's this chap, Peppermill, counting elephant for World Wildlife. We've got *National Geo* for an article. Then Macmillan is lining up for a book. I've thought of calling it *Census.*" He grinned. "There's my American girlfriend who writes." He pulled his hair down in his eyes now.

"Counting elephant?"

"From a plane," he said, "not door to door. You do it on a grid."

At dinner he got maudlin on some wine he pulled out of the same briefcase and complained about the way things had changed in such a short time. "It was the Garden of Eden, Tony," he said, "God's own." He sighed. "Only the perverse bugger has given it to the wrong people . . ." sounding like a fallen angel himself, just expelled from Paradise, full of spite and regret.

So she said, "I believe in history enough to know you can't tell the right people from the wrong ones until it's too late for those caught in the middle."

"Like you?"

"And you." She had her finger pressed in the soft rim of a candle (Charles's attempt at elegance.) It was almost out; a sputtering bit of wax flowed into the chipped teacup that held it. She blew but failed to snuff it.

"You're a defeatist," he told her. "You'll end up all twitter and bisted."

Looking at the candle, her hand on it, nothing left but a black speck of wick, a last flame choked and a thin filament of smoke, she thought it was not defeat, her life here. More like a contract she had made before the real costs were known. She was developing a capacity to drift on events as they came, as though her sense of right and place were all in a state of flux and her surrender to the flow a form of victory in itself, the character of expatriate life now that there were no solid empires holding things up. Nothing but a chaos of international politics that had no root in what was real. She believed there was still a bargain to be made, a deal, a way to catch up with what had been taken from her own history.

Antonia Redmond had been born in Africa. Her father, William, had come out to Tanganyika in 1938 from Cornell University to develop a strain of coffee resistant to berry disease. His young wife, Olivia, followed him a year later, believing that once the work was done they would go home to the States, even after William bought land at the foot of Mount Kilimanjaro and put in his own coffee, even as he began to construct his house. He started with four small rooms, low to the ground, and a wide veranda, facing the mountain where he extolled the views. If his wife was miserable, he believed it wouldn't be for long. He had a powerful faith in landscape; and in the mornings when the mountain was out, he made her sit and admire the snows, bringing coffee for them before the servants arrived. He felt the resonance of its beauty as a distinct physical sensation, and thought that she, though her eyes were closed in defiance, would absorb this euphoria.

After Antonia's birth, Redmond's house began to grow, formed from a series of verandas and courtyards that connected the rooms, all of them facing Kilimanjaro, as if Bill Redmond would go on building until he circled the mountain. The original four rooms became two (Antonia's bedroom and theirs) to which he added a sitting room and a walled-in patio where Olivia could take the sun without any gardeners noticing. Next he built two huge living rooms with vaulted ceilings and thatched roofs. The walls were stone and the fireplace so big that his dogs could sleep inside it while the fire burned. As these rooms filled with his trophies, he built more. When there were parties the house looked like a string of lights woven through the trees.

When Antonia was six or seven they moved her to the

other side of the living rooms into her own wing, which she liked because whenever she wanted, she could go sit in her maid Amina's room and not bother about going to bed. Life in Amina's room was somehow fuller. She liked the food better, the bland mash of corn and the milky, sugary tea, wild leaves cooked like spinach, gristly hard meat boiled and salted. She ate sour fruits or custardy sweet ones, spitting the pips around her in designs. The quarters behind their house, the houses where her father's laborers worked, and the village that sprang up between their farm and the one next to it was where Antonia lived her early life, and even after it became impossible for her to go innocently, as her mother used to say, "down where the Africans live," her memory was easily triggered by a smell or a sound to call up images from her past as a small girl hunkered in a circle with others.

She could have been a lonely, dreamy child but she sought the company of her father, tagged after him, and picked up from him an idea of how she wanted to be. Sometimes she was allowed to go with him and the men who were his friends when they hunted on safari, trips that remained in her memory as stories with no sequence, filled with danger and excitement.

Her first trip was to the Selous to hunt elephant, upstream along the Ruaha to where it broke apart, seven fingers reaching through swamp. Near the camp, there was a baobab tree bigger than any she had seen since. She still told people, "I saw a huge baobab once in Selous." One of her father's friends told her that it would take sixteen men with arms outstretched to span its trunk. He said it must have been at least two thousand years old. This impressed her; even then she saw how old that was. He told her, "Inside the tree there are gallons of water. Elephants break into baobabs during droughts, but here, because there's a river, the trees are never broken and they grow into giants." Which of her father's friends had he been? A man who talked about "God's works" as she sat on his knee.

There were the porters, too. She went with them in boats on the river. She saw how the morning sun made the river look like milk by day. At night, like blood. Sayid, her father's man, a Somali, knew how to row. The other porters, local people from the jungles, Bantus, fumbled and dropped the oars. Sayid, laughing, made them swim after their mistakes among hippos and crocodiles. He took her into his joke, making her laugh, too. Later she understood how he had despised Bantus and was ashamed in retrospect.

The bark of a baobab is oily, shiny, like the smooth iridescent skin of melons. She and Sayid had found a deep cave in its side. He left her in the dark and came back with a tiny deer, a dik-dik. They fed it from their fingertips. Sayid's body was dry, brown, and thin. He had a bush of hair in which he kept things like knives and sticks for drawing pictures in the sand. The Bantus were black and wet, heavy men with short-cropped hair or shaved heads. They looked much stronger than Sayid and had to carry everything. Sayid would not carry. He went bare chested, a wrapper around his waist. His best color was red. Around his neck were leather pouches and amulets; he said these were for protection against evil. Inside were little pieces of paper with sayings from the Koran. He had three black strings around his waist to save him from his enemies. The Bantus wore clothes like white men, walking shorts and shirts. They liked belts. They liked neckties. They liked wristwatches. They wished they had shoes. Sayid liked mirrors.

Sayid rowed, leaning forward, pulling back. His arms seemed longer when he rowed. In the swamp there were giant palm trees that had no tops. The men were frighteningly small moving among them, specks in their boats or on the banks as they hunted. Even the elephants, miniatures, like toys, a line of them on a thin bridge of land; they could have been the tendril of a vine, reaching across linked trunk and tail, an arabesque of tusks. The trees rose.

Her father and two men were on the shore. They had their guns. One waved. Her father turned and motioned for Sayid to stop his approach. He pulled in his oars. She put her feet under the rills of water that slipped from them. There was an elephant where the river bent. It tossed mud on its back with its trunk. Sayid told her it was a male. The females, he said, are never alone. Her father and the other men disappeared. When she asked Sayid where they had gone, he told her to be quiet. Soon the elephant left the water. He scratched his back against a tree. It made her laugh to see such a big thing with an itch. She heard the shot, saw him spin around and fall.

Up in the baobab tree, legs dangling from a branch, she sang a song she had learned from Sayid. The words were Arabic; she didn't know what they meant except he said it was a song about eggs. He walked from the camp calling for her. First he looked in the cave. No, she tricked him, kept very silent, bursting on her branch. Then she dropped a piece of hard candy from her pocket on his head. He climbed up to meet her and they sang together. Then they went up even higher. From there they looked into a valley spiky with the necks of giraffe. Sayid said, "Look, there, hiding behind them is a lion." But she didn't see it.

At night they could hear it roar.

She went with the Bantus along the edge of the river to fish for catfish. She was the one with a new fishing pole and reel. They fished with sticks and strings, but they caught the fish, not her. They tried to teach her how to say words in their language and she did to make them happy. One of them carried her on his shoulders. She pressed her hands into his hair and held on to it like sponges. He knew which mushrooms they could eat and which ones were poison. But Sayid refused to eat a mushroom. He would not eat fish either; he said fish were snakes.

She watched the Bantus hack the tusks from the elephant. Her father and the other hunters stood around smoking and talking. Mr. Norton's elephant. The flesh turned bright red as it released blood, turned deep pink and then white. They rocked the tusks, three men, until a terrible cracking broke them away.

Her father called them dentists. The other men laughed. After they got the tusks out, Mr. Norton's man, Okello, put them on his head. They were all laughing now and smoking cigarettes. Okello walked in a foolish way and made them laugh even harder. There was a deep puddle of thick elephant blood. Sayid lifted her to his shoulders. His hair was softer than the Bantus' and full of surprises. She found a piece of hard candy in there. By then the Bantus had begun to cut up the elephant, strips and chunks of meat to dry in the sun and take home. Her father gave them salt.

Sayid showed her where hyena babies had been tucked

between the roots of the baobab in a small cave of their own. They looked like puppies but had rounded ears. Then she and Sayid ate a roasted rabbit he had killed with his spear. He also had an orange which they shared.

"Why do you say a fish is a snake, Sayid?"

"Because it has skin like a snake. Where are its lungs?"

"Fish don't have lungs, silly."

"There, you see. I'm right."

She made a collection of feathers and arranged them on the table in her tent. A circle. The smallest feathers went in the center and the biggest around the edge. Opening the tent flap she let a triangle of light fall on the decoration there. The colors shone. It looked like a giant flower. One of the Bantu porters was afraid of it. He asked Sayid about it. He said such things were dangerous. The others began to complain until her father told her to take the feathers down. Sayid was laughing as he watched her, saying there was no end to the foolishness of Bantus.

At night in her father's tent the white men drank whiskey or they sat out at a table and watched the river until it was too dark to see anything. There were the voices of men. There was a smell of raw ivory and trophy heads, soapy and rotting. She leaned her elbows on the table and asked her father if they could stay and live on the Ruaha forever.

In the villages as they went home, they heard about a fever. Not malaria. Sayid was frightened. Mr. Norton said they ought to get away as quickly as they could, away from the people and the river. But her father said it was his vacation and he would not be hurried. They camped for three or four nights. She didn't have a tent on those nights but slept, instead, in her father's tent. During the day, they had to walk for miles. Sometimes she dawdled behind with Sayid to pick up beetles, to chase moths. One night, near a village, her father told her to sleep in Sayid's tent.

Was there a moon? Or was it firelight, this light she remembered? Were they outside? Or were they inside? A small hut full of smoke? Gourds on the walls. Blankets on the floor, beds made of string. People lined around the edge of a room on low stools. A woman crying, holding a child, a boy, Antonia's size. He was too big for her lap and his feet hung over and touched the floor. Was he dead? She was somewhere watching, holding Sayid's hand.

The *mganga* was a huge man. He wore colobus monkey skins over his shoulders, the monkey tail fell down his back. At the top of each bare arm was a thick clump of red hair. Beads hung over his face from a crown. He carried a rattle, a bag of animal horns. He was speaking in a soft voice lifting the boy from his mother's lap, carrying him gently to the bed made of strings. He was singing, chanting. The mother stopped crying. She watched as he held a knife against the red coals in the fire. His spit sizzled on the blade. He made a cut into the boy's eyebrow. Blood ran over the boy's face. The *mganga* was smiling, talking to everyone. He made another cut. Sayid picked up Antonia and carried her away. Did she see the red lightning then in the sky or only remember it years later when she came back to the Ruaha to vaccinate during the epidemics? Why had Sayid brought her to that house? Was it the night she had stayed in his tent? She could remember the woman who left her father in the morning. Yawning. Stretching. Hitching a cloth up over her breasts.

Years later when she traveled as a doctor to rural clinics in these places, she thought it was the way a pilgrim went to shrines on a religious quest, to claim, to affirm as much as to ask favor. She shared her father's belief in the power of landscape. Private as her own desires, revealed in the freedom of her memory of what she thought was paradise, she heard her own voice say, "Oh, Daddy! Let's just stay here and live forever and ever!"

Her father had never questioned who he was or whose land he had taken, though history eventually did and seemed to demand in return some ritual of purification, or even simple amends. He was one of those who believed that Africans and white men would eventually get on side by side. As Antonia grew up, the men who came to see him, at night in his study, began to be men with black skins and whenever she stopped to listen, she would hear the word *independence* in conversations held behind the closed door, and their plans for the future.

As an adolescent Antonia was boyish and had her reddish hair cut very short. Her best friend then was Brian

McGeorge, whose family, English, raised coffee on the slopes to the west of her father's. He called her Ant when they first met because she occasionally had the look of one, he said, and because at the time she kept a city of them between two plates of glass. He went to boarding school in England, which made him worldly and established their friendship as a pattern of intervals, while she was taught "in country" as the Americans called it, by missionaries, in a row of white stone buildings that faced another mountain. Meru, a lush blue cone that gave itself to her mornings and faded in the hazes of her afternoons. She climbed Meru with McGeorge every year when he came on school holidays, and Kilimanjaro, though not always to the top because he was only there during the season of bad weather, June, July, August, what they called "summer" in deference to the season those months contained someplace else. After the first climb, she never cared about reaching the ice. She preferred to stay at thirteen thousand feet in a region of mists, which seemed gray and unfeatured from the distance but was alive with giant plant forms, freaky versions of the small succulents and ferns that grew below. Things that had never died, she imagined, since the beginning of time.

Now McGeorge was the only white man from those days whom she occasionally saw; everyone else was gone, their property taken from them by decrees and nationalizations, the country made to follow some idea of socialism that involved hating everything it called "Western" as if the world were flat and Africa was located down the middle without a direction of its own. East, West, North, South, were terms that began to have queer meanings after independence. Her father's house in the hills was turned into a school where Swedish volunteers taught local girls how to weave and make pottery. The coffee was left to grow wild and the bushes were now tall and weedy. Farmers like Redmond used to shade their coffee under tall poplars; but later the cultivation changed and the big trees were banded to kill them and leave the coffee in the sun. It gave an eerie effect, now, those neglected fields and the gray skeletons of the dead trees.

Now Antonia lived in "housing," different, she told people, from a house. The development was called

Kinondoni and was planned and built by foreigners for the swelling numbers of bureaucrats and government employees like doctors. Hers was in a row of ten identical units—living room, bedroom, kitchen. She had European plumbing which meant water inside, a tub, and a flush toilet. It might have been East Germans who designed the place. Or Bulgarians. There was that socialist feeling to it, low-cost slabs and siding, cement blocks, a dull geometry meant to level off advantage. Ironically, there were no common things, only gray buildings stranded on a flat of sand. From a distance the settlement looked half finished, out of funds; whole sections were nothing but marked-out plots scraped away by bulldozers and left to grow weeds. The asphalt that was to cover the roads had never arrived. In the rains, red mud washed over everything. What she enjoyed about the place was the feel, among the rote houses, of village energies breaking into what the planners had tried to organize away. Mud and cardboard shelters were invading the crosshatch of streets. Doorways had been hacked and turned to face other doorways. Spreading families slept under awnings made of woven reeds, and at night, from around the edges where the squatters lived in huts of rag and plastic bags, you heard Makonde drumming. Not so long ago, Antonia herself had joined the mood there and, in a fit of whimsy, had painted her front door a deep violet. Her neighbors called it *"maridadi,"* very fancy, and followed suit, until bright doors bloomed all over Kinondoni like flowers in a slum.

Before McGeorge left town to go count elephants, he took Antonia to dinner, a pilgrimage of sorts, to the Marina Club, a place on the beach. In their day, the club had been exclusive. An Austrian woman famous for her cakes had cooked there. The coffee farmers and their families came down each year for conferences and fun. She and McGeorge had both lost their virginity out on those dunes and to each other, a fact Antonia would have liked to forget. He made it impossible, insisting they go out there as though it were a shrine. It had been a howl a few years ago: now it seemed like any other religious task, fraught and embarrassing. Her recollection was that they had made love several times after that, thinking of it as practice, though they hadn't been sweethearts. The first time was nothing but silly, after which he floored her by looking so amazed, as if he had seen God or had become God. All she wanted to say was, "Is that it?"

She remembered driving to the club especially on nights when there was no moon and the only lights were the thin shafts of car beams struck into the bush. It was like driving in a tunnel save for the lacy crossing of sticks and vines woven on the spot by those needles in the dark. The place held a solid glow around it like a halo, flickering and disappearing as the road dipped and turned. Then it became a darkened shape: the rooms, the dining hall, the long dancing pavilion. Her father always made it a point to arrive late, breaking into that first-night cocktail party like the hero of the hour. He was the one who brought the iced champagne in a metal box.

In those days she didn't mind the heat, didn't even notice it. There were no air-conditioning units then. There was, instead, the luxury of lying naked on fresh crisp sheets each night—and if you took an afternoon nap, the linens were changed again, twice, three times a day if necessary—under a net, opened at all sides to the breeze. Each day sheets dried, iridescent, in the yard near the kitchen: you could see them from a hill behind the club, enormous white rectangles, so unexplained they might have been put there by lost Martians trying to signal outer space. The rest was all green and blue, irregular shapes of land and sky and sea. No one lived on the beach then and the huge tourist hotels of the sixties had not been built.

Africans, McGeorge said, didn't seem to matter then. They were the shadows behind you cleaning up, washing thousands of sheets and dishes, hands bringing you things, carrying your stuff. They were as cute as babies as they were awkward as adults. Until, one summer—Antonia must have been sixteen—the wife of one of the waiters brought her baby to the dining room. She came so shyly, almost as though it weren't important at all, and she stood there on the edge and watched them all eat, holding the screaming infant. Startling: the women were always hidden away in the quarters. You only saw them as they trudged the road to town or washed the endless sheets. A few of the diners could see that the child's arm was burned badly, swollen purple, the outer skin had peeled off and underneath there was something so red, so misshapen. There was so much pus, green, and the fingers had turned black.

Elsa Burton, who was British, ran to the woman and for some reason, Antonia followed. They went right to Mrs. Burton's room. Wet bathing suits were strewn, and towels, a smell of cologne.

"Get me some hot water. Now. *Fast,*" she shouted at the stunned girl.

Antonia went to the kitchen. Big kettles bubbled on charcoal braziers. She bent over and filled a saucepan. A small girl was watching her, picking fruit parings from a bucket and nibbling on them, scraping a mango skin with her teeth. As Antonia looked up, the child, in shame, ran away. When she got back to the room with the hot water, Elsa Burton had the burned baby down on the bed.

"We'll have to remove the hand, my dear," she told Antonia. And she did.

Now the hotel was run by the Ministry of Tourism, though no tourists ever came there. A busload from the Russian embassy appeared on Sunday afternoons to eat tough grilled meat and bounce around in the warm sea. When the northern border was opened, loads of European youths transiting Africa in trucks used to camp on the Marina Club beach. McGeorge liked the ambiance, the told-you-so of falling fortunes. Nothing ever got fixed. The manager made additions instead: constructed meaningless walls, relied on unrelated plastic decorations for effect. People had moved in, most likely the manager's family. Each time Antonia and McGeorge showed up their numbers had grown. There was an atmosphere of village now—kids played while women dressed each other's hair. Antonia prayed that soon the Ministry would close down the place and she would be spared these trips.

Clothes and sheets were spread on stones around the parking lot while behind the dining room a long clothesline dropped between two poles fraying on the ground like a shedding snake. The kitchen seemed to have moved outside to accommodate charcoal braziers. Inside, a huge grease-covered stove had been abandoned; empty gas canisters, beached and rusting around it, were bashed in as though someone had tried to pound the last vapors out of them. Since their previous visit, outhouses had been constructed to replace broken toilets whose bowls and handles and floaters were thrown around nearby.

"P'raps they'll prepare us some tea," McGeorge said. "Shall we give it a go?" shouting "*CHAI! CHAI!* "like some old bwana, bubbling and carousing into an ogling crowd of women and kids while Antonia stood back like a trespasser. Not waiting for a response, he swooped toward the sea and she rushed after. "But what say, Tony?" he hollered. "Shall I take up this aqualung business and do a book on reefs?" Down there, in the warm, seaweed-clogged fringes of the water, her ankles, stroked and grabbed by the stuff, were the first to know that some things can endure.

Their tea came in nicked and stained cups. The sugar was crude and full of hairs. The milk was watery: small pearls of butterfat (a gift from Sweden) floated on the surface. She watched a march of tiny ants making their way across the table. Antonia rubbed her finger on their path and made them scatter in confusion, searching for a trail. She and McGeorge were the only guests that night. A waiter brought them a menu and a light bulb, climbing a chair near them and fixing the bulb in the socket overhead. All the choices had been scratched from the menu leaving only vegetable soup, beef stew and rice, carrots and cabbage, fruit and coffee. But the waiter told them there was no meat or rice and the fruit was finished. They could have *ugali,* he said. "Africans' food." He found the idea amusing.

Their coffee was served to them on the patio in the old style. The waiter had to bring the same bulb to them, standing on their table and clipping it into a socket behind them. The light opened a patch in the darkness, fell on neglected plants and cracked pots. The man's feet left sand on the table that he brushed aside with his elbow. He warned them to stay off the beach after dark because of thieves. McGeorge declared it rubbish: he couldn't imagine thieves sitting out there on a deserted beach waiting endlessly in the dark for someone to chance by. But Antonia declined an after-dinner stroll. Yes, she could imagine thieves out there she said, waiting and waiting with all the time in the world.

TWO
◁ ◇ ▷

A strange dog came into the village from the beach. Its head was low and its mouth boiling like soup. People ran away leaving it to drag there. They called it *shetani,* a devil spirit. Everyone saw that it was going to the pump where schoolgirls in uniforms drew water for their mothers' kitchen pots. A man shouted and the girls ran screaming, leaving their pails in the mud. A sick dog. Fire burned from its eyes. The two skinny brothers from Bogoro led the men slowly out behind it now, filling the path, following at a careful distance, watching. Boys climbed trees and laughed down at it, shouting, "*Hey-Dog! You-Dog! Hey Jiwa!*" But the dog couldn't look up. It was breaking. Small, black, and cracking like twigs behind it, its legs were snapping. Then everyone came running. Everyone but the Moslems. From a distance they hurled rocks at the demon's head.

Esther Moro, bangle bracelets rhythmic as rattles on her moving arms, turned from the spectacle and told her friend Hadija, "This dog has died of germs, not devils," which meant little to her and less to her friend. They had ideas but no education. Two friends, close as sisters. They put pictures cut from European magazines on their walls—beautiful models, black like them, showing how their bodies could flow and even look wet, showing bones like sweet soft branches, showing the small high breasts of schoolgirls under shining dresses made of gold. One of them wore a dress of feathers. Another had tall white boots that the girls dreamed about.

Hadija wagged her bottom. Her hair was braided into

many ropes: beads clicked there like seeds in a dried pod. She was wearing her purple jumpsuit and dark glasses, carrying her purse with sequins, shoes so high on platforms that she tipped through the doorway. She cried out, "*James Bond!*" and created a pose that in England you called "sexybaby." They knew about cinemas, pictures moving like real people on a white wall, shot through the air on beams of light. In the beams there could be a fast small car of the color red in which they, Esther and Hadija themselves, would ride.—"*OH, MISTAH BOND!*"—Tears of love.—"*OH, JAMES!*" Hadija came and touched her friend's neck with perfume from China, colored green. Inside Esther's nose the smell of it beat like Makonde drumming.

Things of wisdom.

Things of foolishness.

Esther was aware of two worlds, even more, side by side. And of the workings (wise and not). Inside a clock, for example, were pieces of wire pressed somehow into curls like hair and tiny disks of gold that locked and clicked together making a sound that tracked the hours of the day. Otherwise, one simply had to look at the sun to know. Such things were grim puzzles to Africans who could be, she thought, fools in the search of wisdom. She knew men who piled iron wheels and rusting parts in small dark sheds and tried to turn them into cars but never could. Similarly, Mr. Ntiro once tried to make a broken refrigerator become cold with an engine taken from a motorcycle. He had drawn a picture on a paper to show everyone while his wife boasted about stones of ice that would make their Coca-Cola cool.

Arm in arm, in their tight pants and high shoes, laughing and gusting puffs of the Orient, jiggling beads and bangles, the girls came forth. A crowd around the terrible dog clucked like chickens. Mr. Ntiro ordered the men to pull it away using ropes. He called this "self-help," being a socialist. The Makondes lit up cigarettes and walked away. Mr. Ntiro suggested they could also dig a deep hole right there and push the dead dog into it, but the women said their children might dig in the soft dirt and die of contamination. Flora Kahama waved a small white cloth and said the dog already stank. Esther and Hadija passed them all by, noses in the air, tripping in the pits and ruts of the village paths.

Later, on the bus to town, they were like two butterflies fluttering, locked in the thick cloud of their green perfume. Boys who had no manners teased them and the old women scolded them for wearing pants—against the law. Outside buildings began to grow like thickening forest. Cars ran like frightened herds of cattle, bellowing and kicking up the dust. It was early and the girls had time to dawdle when they left the bus. Up and down the avenue, Hadija's swaying bottom thumped on Esther's hip, her braid-ropes brushed and tickled Esther's cheek. Over the rooftops of the bazaar, evening kites of Asian schoolboys had begun to fly. Only the people who knew that the kites were made of paper and held in the wind on long strings would not be frightened by the sight of the huge wings roaring in the sky. "Those are the dreams of the Hindis," a man called Mwema once told Esther. "They write them with messages and their gods can read them as they fly."

Meanwhile, Moslem men, praying in their mosques, had left shoes piled on the steps outside. Their women, wearing black capes and forbidden to enter, waited, like the shoes, outside on benches looking like crows. Their children played with toy cars on the curbing or tied strings to the legs of beetles that buzzed in circles around their heads like airplanes.

On a corner where an old man was selling pencils and bananas, they entered a juice kiosk and smoked cigarettes in the dark back room while sitting on cardboard boxes marked with Chinese writing. Hindi boys blew sweet breaths of cinnamon and clove in their faces and felt their breasts. The boys were chewing *pan*—certain seeds and oils wrapped in leaves that turned their lips red. Hadija loved one of them, Sharad, who had a motorbike and took her to the beach so fast that her hair, when not in braided ropes, blew out like passion and Esther (the next morning) had to spike it with combs as the Masai did battle with spears. Sharad, Hadija confided, wore green condoms and his long thin penis was as beautiful as a stem.

Esther herself had known such feeling only once in her life, for a boy named Francis, whose leg was crippled and carried in a brace. Love and pity had been one to her then: his painful limping as hypnotic as far-off singing. Drawn, she

took him and discovered his body with her own. When they
had to separate forever, he wanted to give her his small radio
that ate batteries. In those days she washed laundry in a
Frenchman's house and Francis's father was the gardener. It
seemed so long ago. Embarrassed by the trouble with
Francis's leg, Esther made up a story to tell Hadija and
claimed her young lover had been whole and very beautiful
with the black-black skin of a Sukuma man. Each time she
told it the details of the story changed, a confusion of images
from sleep, from waking, and from what had been real (the
face, the skin) until Hadija suspected and asked for the truth.
But Esther had forgotten.

From the kiosk they went to the port. They were
literate in the matter of flags and knew that a ship had
arrived from Greece—the blue, crossed lines, the field of
white. The Greek sailors, they also knew, would be hairy and
rowdy as children. They would smell of onions and the
smoke of fierce black cigarettes. Some would be ugly and
some, of course, would be beautiful. Esther understood such
balances in life and was prepared while Hadija expected
only the best. Esther had fixed thoughts about beauty but no
clear picture: she knew it when she saw it. Zobetta, their
teacher, who knew all about men, said it was happiness that
made beauty because a bitter heart ate from its owner.

They all had worries when it came to white men since it
was hard to tell which ones were either beautiful or happy.
There were the physical things—hair, for example, on their
chests and sometimes down their arms, like monkeys, which
could be frightening, if harmless. They were often, if British
or American, bothered by terrible skin, a condition that was
not, Zobetta told them, contagious though sometimes the
girls worried. In their favor, they could have eyes the color of
the sky and hair the color of tea, which everyone thought
attractive. They had long straight noses, which indicated
their cleverness. The trouble with them was the things they
wanted to do. Zobetta warned the girls, who lived in a room
at her house, but they didn't believe her until something
happened and then her words would fall in place like lessons
on the chalkboards of school children. "The University of
Whores", Hadija called it. These were the threads of chance
they picked up and as they walked hand in hand, as eyes on

the streets wove stories around them, as buses blew dark smoke in their faces, as the road sloped down to the bars near the docks, it was easy to be fearful with the thoughts of beatings they might sustain or the vile things they might be forced to do.

The bar they entered was already full of sailors and girls; a melting of sight and sound that characterized tense moments like these. Esther flushed with heat even though the place was cold inside from air conditioning. The two friends, clinging to each other, stood near a table, shy but on display. Others sat in similar poses around the edges of the room or danced in pairs to attract attention. But it was too early: the men were only interested in drinking and growling, though some were singing their Greek songs that sounded sad. Zobetta was there, waving her two girls along. She was wearing a new wig of black curls. Her wondrous breasts were gathered somehow and held forth brewing like a storm. She was almost drunk and would be drunker, they knew, would still be drunk when morning came—the wig would be gone and her own hair stiff with suffocation, her breasts slack under her cloth wrapper—offering tea and warnings: "If you invite devils in your house, you must feed them." This was something girls like Esther and Hadija knew to be true, Esther especially, as she thought herself a little wiser, knew death and the power of dreams and kept deep secrets in her heart. She was also (she suspected) more beautiful to men, which made it easier on nights like this when housemaids and secretaries came out to sell their sex to sailors for "extra-bonus" so that sometimes the regular whores went home with nothing to buy sugar the next day. Esther was one who never had to sway her bottom or hold out her breasts or press against a man with her hand as a signal. She simply looked into the crowd and picked the one that she wanted.

That night she saw a sailor who was all alone in a corner. His quiet drew her to him. The other Greek men were speaking in rude signs to the shy girls and trying out their English. Some knew a few words that became a way of joking. "This is table. This is you pussy. I eat you pussy. Okay, baby. I love you." Her sailor was unusual among them, not only his quiet but his hair, which was red, and his eyes, which were pale like the water over the corals. Even so, his eyebrows were heavy and black and he had a black mustache. Esther tried to understand the signs of good and evil in these odd looks but failed. She searched his face for marks that she might recognize; then, failing, sat at his table. Since they had no language with each other, they couldn't speak except to make gestures and nod. He offered her beer by holding his glass her way and pointing first to it and then to her. She simply sat there thinking but of nothing she was able to hold pinned in her mind. He touched her bracelets then picked up her arm and shook it like a toy, happy with the sound and smiling. So did she. She noticed that his hands were beautiful, smooth and small, which made her feel easy and so she told him, "Okay beer," two words known in every language.

They didn't dance but waited watching the others, his hand on her wrist, a way he used to claim her. Again and again he took her arm and shook it to remind her of the contract, to measure the time until they would be alone. She saw his eyes grow heavy with his drinking. "Okay beer," he said and they both laughed.

The room he took her to presented the bare symbols of her livelihood like picture stories children drew with sticks in the sand. This was, for her, a comfort and made it her room—Room 17: the bed, the nightstand, the chair. She had stood here before many times and so believed in the safety of familiar things. But even as the room made sense of who she was and what she had to do there, she read that neat arrangement of furniture like someone perceiving deeper marks of the unknown, like letters in writing that came together magically and formed the words she longed to read. She knew, no matter what, the chair, the table, those objects that gave her ease now would be no help to her if there was trouble. No, she was not a fool and knew this every time she entered rooms like this, touching surfaces as she passed through.

Opening the window, she showed the sailor a secret she knew about Room 17—an alley full of moonlit cats, crouched shapes with shadow legs so that they seemed to have six or eight or even more. He leaned his head into the night and hissed the cats to hiding. They both laughed.

Then he took a bottle of spirits from his pocket, clear spirits that she thought might have been gin but that she didn't recognize when he made her taste. She made a face to show him her dislike; it was something vile that made her think of urine. He drank from it in gulps despite its strength, a manner she found hungry in the wrong way, and she remembered that dog of the afternoon raging toward the water that would only madden it, only poison its saliva. The association disturbed her because she knew how warnings could be given. It made her stir, sway around the room as a girl in her position might do, not wanting to wait, not wanting to linger through the night with this one.

She tried to figure out what he wanted her to do—to get undressed, to let him undress her, to do something she might never have done before or even imagined—but all he did was pace and drink speaking his Greek language as though she could understand. They all did it: talking and talking when they couldn't be understood, something that bored the other girls who always complained. But Esther linked the sounds to human qualities and hoped he might evolve from the abstractions of those words to someone she could trust. She was attracted, almost lulled, by the quirks and cadences of his speech and recorded them—the lisping *s*, the wide *o*—to make Hadija laugh tomorrow when they brewed their morning tea and Zobetta's little daughters came around dancing, asking to try on their bangles and high shoes.

He went on talking so long that Esther grew tired, almost lonesome. Once there was a flicker when he looked at her as though she were involved, and she responded, not absently, but with hope, in a mixture of impatience and concern that she tried to think was courage. She didn't like to feel ignored this way, alone and abandoned to his voice, and yet still watched, still held captive by him—an ominous contradiction made clear in that small room, in the dark, against the thick humming of the air conditioner and his increasing distance. Because each time he passed her, he seemed farther away, as if the miles he walked had carried him in a straight line. She tried to answer him in her language, speaking of the cats they had seen in the alley, a joke they shared, and she made the hissing sound and showed with her hands how the cats had scattered. Like a fool. Because he didn't understand.

Soon the sailor calmed. He put a hand out toward her which she took, and rising from the chair followed the motion of his pull—his fingers plucking at her body like someone grabbing chickens at the market—to stand in front of his breath, a mouth fallen away then pressed into her neck with muffled laughter and his wet tongue. Of all the sounds that came up from the bar below them—through the window or through the floor—battling with the air conditioner, laughter was the strongest and Esther received it now, imprinted with her faith, her craving trust. She was already drifting away from her flesh and the parts of her he would use. She barely felt his touch, his probings.

The bed was limp as old cloth: her back sagged into it. She was thinking, oh, at last, soon he will let me go but he stood up suddenly and was gone again, walking around, confusing her. She wanted to make the room responsible—a deception; the chair was still against the wall but everything had changed. He was somewhere hidden, perhaps in a corner, behind her, behind the light. Not even a shadow appeared on the floor. She prayed that he had left knowing certainly that he was someone who might hurt her. She had seen in the opening of his shirt a chest where black hair threatened, each one rising from a pock of skin, so close, as close as that, when he pulled her holding her shoulders back to get at her neck that way.

She had an impulse to run until he appeared, first a shadow marked against the wall, a man with head and arms and shoulders. Then he was real, coming toward her holding money in his hand, spreading the notes apart like a fan for her to choose. She shook her head to tell him no—no no no—she would not, had her hands curled into her chest and clenched there until they hurt. No. No. No. He came closer and raised a finger. One. She must take one. The hand insisted. It waved. It pleaded. She went on saying no.

"Okay," he said and opened up both palms in her face letting the money fall into her lap. She laughed gathering the notes and offered them back to him as if offering flowers, but instead he grabbed her breasts and eased her down, gently, to where a pillow met her head. He knelt over her, his mouth as drawn in as his shoulders were hunched, arched, leaning over her, placing his elbows on either side and looking down, a face dropped forward, hanging like an old man's and wrinkled so she couldn't find the expression. Instinct folded up her knees and brought them against her stomach which made him fumble there, and then, bending his arms, he pressed down on her curled form. For a moment they were tucked together; too complicated, too mistaken. She knew that not just his body was involved in their meeting. The worst thing, Zobetta often warned: he didn't seem to want her for her sex.

At once he collapsed and threw himself next to her with one arm left across her chest. She didn't take a breath but listened to his, wanting to be certain of his sleep. He was made of tricks and sudden changes. The arm that held her was tense, too stiff, so that he couldn't hide the truth with his closed eyes and heavy breath. No, he was awake. But she thought, I have only to wait. So drunk. So close to sleep. Without moving, head propped against the pillow, she tried to look down, to find clues as she could, to puzzle out what he was doing and how she could get away. She had a view of his dark trousers and a white belt, a shirt that was rolled up around his waist. Her thoughts, restless and instinctive, searched for answers there along the ridges of his form. She closed her eyes against a dryness in her throat and waited, hanging on to the sounds of laughter from below, more like rhythm now, a way to measure time and her chances. Her only dread was that it would cease and there would be quiet and everyone would be gone.

To slip away, to slide out from under that watchful arm. To run, fast, fixing her clothes, smoothing things, adjusting her step, swaying a little and then the bangles softly announcing it all. To get away. She took the chance, moved the arm but just a little and then watched it, watched where it angled, where his hip rose and one leg fell away crossing the other beneath it. She felt nothing, no quiver: the arm made no attempt to press her down or hold her there. She tried again, this time lifting the arm and shifting her body under it, rolling to her side as one asleep might heave. It seemed heavy to her, but loose in the joint. After a deep exhale, his lips made a kissing sound against themselves, a wetness that convinced her. She moved again, enough to throw her legs over the bed. She was able to bend her knees and reach one foot to the floor. Close to exhilaration, her desire to escape assumed its own proportion, was all there was. She mimicked his exhale, his sputtering breath, hoping to obscure herself in the pulse of his sound, hidden away.

The arm rode on her shoulder and a hand with dangling fingers reached her collarbone. He was asleep, she was certain. The hand measured her progress, slipping as she moved, along that rim, that arch of bone, raking finally at the sleeve of her blouse. She heard it thud behind her on the bed as she shook free, both feet hard beneath her, hands on the iron bed rails. Carefully, she checked his legs, which hadn't moved, and his breathing, which continued as it had. So she stood, took one step and then another, sensing all the while that she was hiding from the truth of what was happening behind her, but too afraid to turn and look, so pressed on, the steps faster, more deliberate, until the sound of the bedsprings told her what she didn't want to know, what she had known all along, and his voice, in three strange Greek words, was shouting. She knew she had to stop.

Turning toward him, she spoke English: "I have see. You sleep," and tried to show him her meaning in gestures, pointing to her eyes and to him and sleep—her head drooped, her eyes closed. After that her hands fell flat against her sides and her breath stopped as though her own arms had cut it off and were holding it in. His hand came prying at her elbow to pull an arm up, away from her side like a handle, using her wrist to guide it. The bangles made the only sound and pressed like ropes. He pulled at her arm, as if she were a thief at a door and she was resisting this time, even as the pain, even as the fear—oh, no, no, I beg—even as the arm, back behind her, was forcing her to bend, to cry out—no, no—until he let her go. She was weeping, rubbing her arm and trying not to shout at him though she couldn't stop.

He smashed the empty bottle on the night table and rushed at her with broken glass. She sank to the floor, rolling up to protect her head, her neck, her stomach. Somewhere inside the coil, she heard her heart. There was no shape to its message, no picture drawn for her in the dark press of her closed eyes. Against all her strength, he opened her tight seal and began to cut. He pushed her head and went on until she passed out of her terror and pain and didn't care and wasn't afraid to open her eyes. He will kill me. I am dead. His arms were moving. His lips moving. Her last sight of him was of his teeth, and his head shaking like a man in a climax.

There had been warnings. Esther Moro could see the pieces of this new trouble fit the outlines of a dream from which the meaning could only be gathered now, much too late. Once long ago she had seen two white boys as they climbed down from a bus and stood close, very close to her. It was the first time she had been that near—enough to examine, to see the strange skin and hair and eyes. She thought their eyes were beautiful, the color of sky, like glass beads, and their hair seemed unreal, made of ripe grasses or other growing things. The dream came later. In it one of the boys came to her offering her sweet things to eat. He had a knife that could open and close and he was showing it to her as though it were a children's toy but when he opened it, it was his thing grown hard and red like his skin. As he forced her legs apart, it became a knife again. She hadn't understood the meaning of the dream until now.

She was waking slowly, not knowing where she was or why she was in pain. She saw the dream riding on a terrible memory, for a while so blurred she couldn't tell if the sailor had been real or something else. She could smell the hospital, a signal to her senses. She remembered what had happened and kept still, afraid to move, afraid she might be pouring away, bleeding away to nothing. When she turned her head, she saw a bottle hanging near her bed, and traced a plastic pipe that passed from it to her arm, where it was fixed under a white patch of cotton. She trembled as she moved her arm, but the patch was firm and she felt a sharp pain as if something had stuck there like a leech.

She knew what it was. Had heard how, in hospitals, there was a way of putting blood into your body; or even the horrible reverse, of taking it out. Villages told stories of relatives who had been drained of blood—yes, she was wide awake now—something, they said, the government did to feed soldiers when they wanted them to fight fearlessly. There were also stories of poisoning and witchcraft, people who changed, ran mad, possessed by devils that had entered them. And so she pulled the wire out and lay there, breathing, hoping it was not too late. Her father, who once worked for a German doctor, had learned about sickness and medicine, but he never liked this business of changing blood. He had seen it done in the war. Instinct alone had told him it was dangerous. She watched it drip on the floor.

From that German doctor, her father, Musumbi, had taken tools: thermometers, a stethoscope, a small cone for looking inside ears or down throats. He had a tiny hammer and could test the way a knee worked, which made his patients laugh. He even had a book containing pictures of transparent bodies showing you everything inside. Though others laughed, Esther knew the book was no joke. "After people die," Musumbi told her, "white doctors cut them up and look inside and then make pictures." Which sounded like abomination, too horrible to be true, but she believed it, witnessed pages of bones and organs and had traced out the same in the goats and cows they killed to eat.

After her mother died, she would go with Musumbi to villages where he treated the sick. He was called "Daktari," like a white man, and he wore spectacles. Her father knew how to mend bones and, like an African doctor, he understood the use of leaves and bark and flowers that grew in the forests, the medicines of the poor. She had a daughter's pride: knew he was better, more clever than anyone else. He was the one who gave her inklings about germs and told her how they got inside you, taken into your breath from a sick person's coughing as in the case of tuberculosis (everybody knew it), taken in the air (so small they could not be seen without a special glass) and down into your lungs where they ate you until you died. You heard people coughing with it. You saw the spots of blood they spit out on the ground—tiny invisible germs, airborne and out of control. No one was safe against such things as breathing; there was no magic that could protect you. These were his terrible ideas and in time people began to say that Musumbi was a devil spirit himself.

He had been a tall man who had no fat, but at an early

age Esther became aware of a difference between his poverty of flesh and something heavy that could not be seen, though sometimes he appeared large because of it and frightened those around him. It sounded in a deep voice that came from within him. Sitting in huts with village men at night, he would talk, his voice would roll and crash like flash rivers in the rains. Listening to him those nights until morning, Esther feared it was his restless talking that was taking from his flesh. At other times, his silences, long periods of them, seemed to be the cause of his emaciation. Sometimes she couldn't rouse him from the bed or stool on which he sat, and the deep sockets of his eyes would remind her of skulls pictured in his book. His bones seemed hung on threads beneath his head, strung like beads. He clattered when she shook him.

Villages. Huts and grain stores and animal pens settling into a valley or along a ridge; a gathering of chickens, livestock—all these familiar things had been threats in those days. Entering as she and Musumbi did, as outsiders, there was trouble with the doctors who practiced as *waganga,* who her father insisted were killing more people than they saved. He had a vision, a way in which he picked out African things and called them bad, dark, and foolish. He referred to what he learned from white men in his youth as good and wise. White men who did not believe in charms or curses of talking snakes. She took her father's side, knew the *waganga* who forced people to drink dog urine and other outrages to be harsh and spectacular. But there were times when the logic of the villages seemed to defy her father's messages. Too many things remained unexplained except in the African terms that he denied. Too many things that he, himself, didn't understand using his foreign ideas: she heard them rumble in his talking, even in his growing silences, the weight, the heaviness he carried on his thin frame. Her image of him was complicated and too hard to fit with what she knew to be true, things she had seen with her own eyes.

Once a village man had killed an owl and hung it from its feet in a tree. It was a large white owl, a kind only a few of the very old ones had seen before, which the man said had been sent to him by a powerful witch. The village crept beyond understanding like unwanted dogs, frightened by the voices of the *waganga* who said the bird was a djinn not dead at all. One that could come back again and again in other forms to drive people mad or inflict deadly illness. Each day the man came out, smaller and smaller the people said, to pick and eat from the rotting flesh. He stuck feathers and bones in his hair. You could peer at him from behind a wall, amazed by images that rose like dreams. His eyes bulged out, rolling, his head turning on his neck. Sometimes he clawed the tree.

After he died the village came out from hiding, pressed around the kiosks or in their doorways, wondering what to do. By then there was nothing left of the owl but its feet tied in the tree, too serious to be ignored. They gathered. Esther was tiny with her head on her father's hip. He was trying to tell them it was simply from the poison of the rotting meat and nothing more, a matter of the germs, what you could smell in rot. They must, he told them, bury the poor man. But the *waganga* said they had to burn his house while he was inside. They said no one could go near the place—the ashes contained the power of the djinn. This, Musumbi argued, was the foolishness of Africans and to prove it, he went into the ashes of the house, taking her with him by the hand. They stood a moment there as he bent and filtered the terrible dust through his fingers. A few villagers looked on in horror. When he came away, he told them, "See that we are safe. There is no djinn." But Esther had seen something, though she kept it secret—the white owl rising from the dust and the man with it, grown wings and flying, telling her why the man had killed and eaten that bird.

Her father's presence endured, even after his death. He was the one who sent her warnings of danger in her dreams. He was the one from whom she learned the ways of rebellion. Wasn't it from him, now, this message, this impression of that strange blood, not red but black as it appeared in the bottle there, entering the channels of her veins, thicker, heavier, poisoning her own, pounding in her heart? Bursting there. She would not have it. Conflicting notions of her life met, but she knew what to do and had done it. She had pulled the needle out and watched it drip on the floor. She lay there with no strength left, lost to her ordeal, drifting into sleep, waking again among the nurses who were discovering what she had done.

She didn't want to hear what they were saying and floated beyond the voices by keeping her eyes shut, her vision focused on an inside blackness dense with safety. But the words intensified, came through. She pretended not to hear them, not to understand what they would do, knowing she had made her mind up to pull the tube out again. She heard a voice—"Esther, you have lost a lot of your own blood." She was like a vessel emptying, a gourd, filling again with that strange liquid in a bottle, not real blood. She opened her eyes. She saw, surprisingly, a white woman in a doctor's coat standing by her. She heard the woman say that they would have to tie her wrists and her arms and her legs, felt the tight bands. She didn't struggle then; the voice had made it seem important and was giving her still another idea.

She felt the needle stinging into her. Her eyes were still open looking nowhere but at the light—"Esther, can you hear me?"—to let them know, to let them understand the meaning of her fear even if she, herself, did not.

When there was silence around her and she knew they were gone, she had studied, with misgiving, the blood that fed into her arm. She wanted to believe that it wasn't poisonous or filled with disease. She wanted to know the white doctor and the things the white doctor knew, a kind of sharing, moving arm in arm, so close that secrets passed outside of language through the rubbing of skin and the contact of their hair. She felt a sudden closeness to her father, Musumbi. The doctor, being white with German-colored hair, aroused her instinct for the coexistent, of dream and reality, of past and present, and she took this to be a sign. She imagined her father and his German doctor side by side or holding hands the way African men did when they were friends, even though she suspected that Musumbi had really been the white man's servant, ironing shirts and polishing shoes.

"They keep it in a refrigerator, this blood," she had once been told. Like their milk? Like the way they keep their meat? She had stored the information away. Now she felt it cool in her veins like death. People who worshiped the power of extreme cold that turned water into rocks.

Her life was, for a moment, centered on that bottle and the woman who hung it there, overlooking the fear, sorting out what she had heard, had seen, what she could figure out, wishing she could express the gathering thoughts that words failed to stop and make clear, that fell around her in the damp air that smelled of sick.

Whose blood was it? Someone in that room with her? Someone whose disease might pass into her, an invasion, like the ants that came and drove men from their houses? A sound of dripping water in the corner revealed itself, a noise she was able to identify easily and relate to a thousand simple things that gave her the sensation of safety when there was none, none at all. She could feel herself slipping away from what had been those hours of fear in that room—a view of cats, the moon, the silent chair, the breaking glass—and listened to the water, letting the sound grow in her mind against the forming image of danger, wild with tiny serpents swimming into her blood.

She had waited there, surrounded by the sick, awed, a strange feeling which reached, in her, a core of passion and philosophy. Her idea was that trouble came with forces that had been created in the world: in the weather and the sky. *Viumbu.* Not just this matter of germs as her father thought: she knew the moon-caused evils (epilepsy, madness, miscarriage), the dangers of blindness hidden in certain winds, the fevers that came with storms or lay in pockets of mist and waited. Thunderborn measles and lightning that struck in the hearts of old men. Not random, but deliberate, built into the scheme of things. To remind her, there had been a terrible, constant moaning, like a howl, like the sound of an animal, somewhere in the room with her; from another bed, far enough away to make it seem beyond, as though coming through a filter of trees or across the night. Around her people complained or laughed, poses that showed they, too, knew they could be victims. Perhaps, as Musumbi said, she was wiser than she should have been, a gift or curse, wiser than he was whom she came to pamper and watch over, whom she tried to keep from harm.

When the white doctor came back much later, after the

bottle of lethal blood was gone, "Esther," she said, "are you awake? How do you feel?"

Esther didn't answer but stared up at nothing, wondering if her yearning would be clear. Shadowy forms reflected on the ceiling, movements in the ward: this was her concentration and her prayer. The doctor asked more questions that she didn't answer, could not, not even to move her head yes or no or blink her eyes. Her attitude was fixed, not even to see the doctor's face once again as she spoke—"only to help you . . ."—or even flinch when something rustled the sheets below where she had been hurt and she felt soft fingers on the skin of her thighs. This time Esther accepted the privacy of treatment and the covenant those fingers came to sign at last on her wrist, to count the beatings there—the pulse. Musumbi had showed her how to find it, echo, he told her, of the heart.

Early that morning the nurse had told Antonia that the girl was awake and had pulled her IV tubes out. The staff hadn't noticed it until much later, wandering the ward, they saw the patient disconnected and the floor around her covered with the mess. The matron had sent the youngest, shyest one of them all to tell the doctor. Standing in the door to Antonia's office, she stammered out what was happening. Antonia charged in, finding the matron there, staring at the figure in the bed. The ward was silent, relieved with daybreak. A dying man who had wailed all night long was still.

"She doesn't want the blood of another person," the matron explained.

"I see," the doctor said. "But she must have it. You'll have to tie her down."

"But she doesn't want it," the matron argued, a young woman, new to the job. She seemed to shrug, to relax away from the need to move, shifted her weight and turned her head toward the wall. It was a gesture hard to read, either defiance or chagrin.

"Didn't I tell you to watch her?" Antonia said. She saw the chin deflect. "Do you know what that means?"

The chin was firmer now. Defiance. A hand on the

patient's sheet was moving with mock efficiency. They hadn't cleared the blood-soaked rags from the floor or moved aside the bed that had been jostled by the night's events and blocked the way into the ward. A faucet in the corner sink trickled water extravagantly against the time when the whole city, even the hospital, would be rationed, weeks on end without a drop. Everything gathering there to be given back to chaos. The filth and disarray. She saw a broken chair balanced against the wall and piled with clean linens but left untouched for days now, a detail that made the terms of her tenure clear. There was nothing she could do about any of it: she had to accept it or get out.

She spoke to the girl by name: "Esther,"—trying to convince her—"you lost a lot of your own blood. We want to give it back to you."

No use of course. An emotion seemed to shield the girl, almost palpable—fear or disdain—and no response, no sign of life beyond the shallow breath.

"We don't like to. . . . We will have to tie you. . . . We don't want to." Wasted words, the face was as unmoved as a sculpture.

She saw a type of ideal beauty in the features, like the ebony carvings Makonde tribesmen made and sold to tourists. They understood the sensuous look of their race, the softened planes, the liquid texture of the skin, dense as buffed wood. She didn't flinch, this girl, except to open her eyes and stare at nothing even as the matron came to tie her wrists and pierce the vein.

Antonia saw the patient Esther Moro several times before they dismissed her from the hospital, a thin, frightened girl, like so many who should never have left the villages. The story hung in the air a while, impersonalized to a political event. The sailor was white, the girl African, he had simply gone back to his ship with nothing to pay, the angry journalists had written. But Antonia could still hear the high shrieks of women amplified like sirens in the empty corridors. She could pick out the word, *haribika*, ruined.

"They wanted to kill her!" the women were screaming, all of them prostitutes, makeshift parodies of magazine models and film stars in plastic beads and illegal miniskirts and pants. There were flurries of detail, the way they found the victim, the sailor who attacked her, all too fast, too jabbering to follow. She shooed them off and found a blood-drenched form there on a stretcher. A face with skin as fine as unglazed ceramic. A woman was grabbing at her and sobbing, "with a bottle! with a broken bottle!"

She remembered cleaning through that chaos of tissue, nurses pressed around her, panicky and racing, because she was the kind of doctor who liked to practice medicine this way. Emergency and deft repair. To her it was basic, the real satisfaction she took in what she did. After it was over, washing up in her darkened office, she reclaimed her hands under suds, an oily texture giving way to the delicate roughness of clean skin. She smelled carbolic in the soap. Her fingers flexed as she shook them dry. Outside she could see the huddled shapes of waiting patients camped in the hospital grounds. A few children, still awake, were running carrying things, perhaps tin cans. The light, when she turned it on, drew her image on the glass, superimposed. And made her seem to be a part of them apart: a ghost who was immune, not only physically to whatever was being suffered out there, but in her heart. Just as she had touched the surface of that girl's trouble, hands sheathed in rubber gloves, a beauty she found in such disturbing things.

THREE

◁ ◇ ▷

At home Antonia found Charles, aproned and gesticulating, waving a dishrag in front of her purple door.

"What is it?" She was running, out of breath.

"Wasps," he told her.

There was a season each year when they came down. From the trees? From the sky? They would get into the house, flying low, sometimes at eye level, displaying their pinched middles: bright yellow stripes on black abdomens, red legs dangling like streamers tipped with orange feet. Lethal wasps canvassing the place. Charles would not go in when the wasps were there; chattering and fearful, he would tell her about the time he had been stung on the back of the neck, how he had swollen up and gone blind for ten days. She had to go inside alone with her fly swatter after the humming beasts, whacking, missing, then standing very still until one roared again. "Open the damn windows so they can get out!"

"Better to kill them, memsaab," Charles begged. He had braved it inside now, near her, under a blanket, lifting window latches and running. One came swooping by her as if to tease, then it beat out of the way to the ceiling. She took a chair to reach it. But it tore away. She saw another sheltering in a corner where a swatter couldn't possibly do its work. She chased it, then slammed it as it flew. It spun on the floor, abdomen curled in pain, stinger out and vibrating, causing an uproar. Charles, braving it, awed, stared down a while, then stepped.

She came around the chair and strolled looking at the

tops of walls. One was near a picture. Quietly she stalked her prey, swatter ready, and had it on the first swing.

Charles, growing even braver now, was tracking the place armed with a rolled-up newspaper. "Here," he called.

She came and found one under a windowsill so she had to brush at it, dislodge it, risk its fury. When it settled again, on the rim of her bookcase, she took the hem of her skirt and pressed the thing, felt its juices explode (black, when she looked at the muck, tinged with red, still quivering). Then suddenly she was aware that her skirt was up around her thighs and Charles, embarrassed, had turned away.

Basking in the quiet that follows the killing of wasps, she drank refrigerated water into which Charles had squeezed a lime. Then she surveyed the room, deciding where to sit. She didn't have a customary—*her*—chair. Not a creature of domestic pleasure or routines of any kind, each time she stepped through that violet door might have been the first. She decided on a bath instead, but in the bathroom discovered that the taps were dry. Her loud "Goddamnit!" sounded against the sputter of air in the pipes. She recalled a notice days ago saying water rationing was about to begin again. So she went and stretched out on her bed instead.

The room she looked at, tipped sideways to her vision, was a mess. She had a habit of strewing stuff around, which rendered poor Charles helpless—papers, books, shoes, newspapers, odd bits of jewelry, letters, stray hairpins, emery boards. He never knew how to pick up after her. Never knew where anything went. She often caught the man sweeping and dusting around everything like an archaeologist on a dig, careful not to disturb. She must have slept, and deeply, too, because she woke up not knowing where she was, too miserably groggy to move. She tried for a second to capture a fading dream—Paul Luenga in his old green sweater, and her mother, Olivia, somehow linked: a sitting room full of furniture, curtains in the wind. They were all there holding onto a piece of cloth, having an argument about it as if there was some sort of normalcy among them. In reality they had only met once, the three of them, in circumstances engineered by forces that pursued people like Olivia Redmond. It made her daughter laugh. Rolling her face to the ceiling, she wiped sweat from her cheek, then dozed again, translated into the end of the day. She was the gray-violet light at her window in which the dream had taken place.

Poor Olivia. She thought when independence came to Tanganyika her husband would finally leave, would not want to live under a black government. But even after his farm was nationalized and they were forced to move to the coast, Bill Redmond stayed, invited to be an agricultural adviser to the new president. Antonia got the news in Boston. She was a student by then at Radcliffe. She knew her father's decision to stay was as inevitable as hers had been to return and she understood that he simply, physically, could not leave.

As a student, she had returned to Africa whenever she could. Linked by air, the distance back was no more than two nights in a plane, her circuit marked by transit stops in European airports where she saw the color of the travelers change. Standing in lines with tickets and boarding passes, she enjoyed picking out skin tones and facial features, trying to guess where people came from. Sometimes dress gave it away: Nigerians (who traveled most) in expensive robes, talking about how dull life was in East Africa. You reached the equator at dawn to land in daylight, sun cracking the black sky just before the mountain, a wonderful coincidence that the pilots veered to see, the snows there, the tropical ice. Black sky with a purple strip, not brightness yet, only a change in color, a deepening in the dark, a kind of richness that grew to red. It came as an arc, slowly turning orange, which you saw from above, widening with the passage of the plane and sweeping off to narrow bands. Soon there were clouds and then a special clarity, light her father had once compared to champagne. And then the peaks of ice.

The Redmonds' house on the coast was a wandering pink stucco affair in the diplomatic enclave of Oyster Bay, built by an Italian. In cups of courtyards and patios, it seemed to hold the sun in the same way African women put out pots and basins to collect water from the rain. The garden was pink to match, bougainvillea, hibiscus, frangipani, low and redolent. There was something trusting in the way the house spread its fingers of patio toward the coral cliffs there—grass giving way to cactus, flat green dishes angled to the blue. During unpredictable seasons, provoked by surges of rainfall in the April monsoon, the cactus opened hundreds of yellow flowers which Antonia always hoped for, drowsing on those midnight flights, and felt something tangibly like regret whenever it happened that she had just missed them, found them finished and drooping their sticky blooms from lumpy pods.

Olivia lived totally indoors there in two air-conditioned rooms, dwindling and dwindling until all of her could be contained in airmail envelopes, an acid voice lamenting on thin sheets of paper to a daughter far away. Seven years after they lost the farm, she wrote to Antonia in Boston, "Your father has had a heart attack and died. There is no need for you to make the trip here as I am returning immediately to America." Antonia was in medical school then at Harvard, her final year.

She and her mother met at a motel. "Thirty wasted years," Olivia was saying. "No one will ever know." Antonia delivered an embrace that hulked, felt like a giant crushing the bony frame, touched shoulder blades as thin as tissue. A little cut-out mother. Her idea had been to reclaim America but she was daunted by the place, the speeding freeways, the confusion of machines. She went searching for her family and found there was nothing left. Antonia remembered an uncle on that side who had been killed in one of the wars and another who drank himself to death or maybe the two of them had been the same uncle after all. There was her grandmother, her mother's mother, who had gone to live with a relative, an aunt or cousin, and when she died, they actually forgot to tell poor Olivia in Africa until more than six months had passed.

Olivia decided on a flat in Philadelphia with no reason for the choice except the fact that Bill Redmond kept a bank account there and once called it home. Beyond that there was no reference to the man at all, no pictures, nothing, not any clue that the old woman had just come over from Africa. All that was lost to her or thrown away, her time there decanted, her life shrunk down by thirty years.

Antonia helped to empty boxes of bric-a-brac, the china cups, the Spanish porcelains, the German ceramics. "And *his* things?" she asked. But her mother had given them away—"those ugly trophies"—to a hotel they were building. The tusks, she said, she had sold to an Indian. Which was illegal.

"But everything is illegal now. You'll see. They'll make a criminal of you, too."

It was funny how Olivia in Philadelphia was no different, no less out of place. Even the new objects she had to buy to set up housekeeping, the mundane things like brooms and mops, even those were uncomfortable around her, a sort of irritation. She took nothing from her surroundings, no form or color, and gave nothing back. It occurred to her daughter that she had no gene at all for protective coloration or whatever it was that made creatures able to adapt. She was always the same, a wisp of smoke, the unchanged essence of the burning thing.

Antonia was relieved that day to return to Boston, the flight less than breathing time, the plane sighing over the gray water and oil-black mud flats, landing it seemed on the sea itself. A swirl of dark birds (grackles or starlings, something that didn't bother to fly south for winter) rose as she got off the plane. The seascape, the landscape was all black and white there, a scene from a Bergman film that drew on dread when she had felt so buoyant getting on the damn thing. Set free.

Inside, voices on the loudspeaker, announcing arrivals and departures, were nasal and undistinguished as bare tin.

"A relief to get out of there," she was saying later, at home, stretched out and drinking wine. "But we're not far enough away. Anytime she wants, she can come here."

She was living with Paul Luenga. Ironic: on their bed his black leg across the sheet seemed suddenly dangerous, a secret made into an issue now that Olivia was around. Made it seem as if she'd been trying to hide. Made a guilty edge. He only laughed because for him there was a certain justice in it all, the real fruits of the colonies. He recited an African proverb that translated loosely into something about chickens coming home to roost.

After Christmas a letter came announcing Olivia's plans to visit her daughter in Boston. Because she didn't want to hear about it, didn't want to listen to it, Antonia told Luenga, couldn't he move out for the weekend? Almost a

jest, she was laughing as she said it. He smirked but thought
he might. "We'll jam your stuff into a closet." But it must
have been that neither one of them wanted to postpone the
inevitable, because nothing was done and then it was too
late. He never got around to clearing away his socks or razor
blades the way anyone might in a comedy like this. Forgot to
go out for a hamburger and walked in on the two women. It
was funny really, how the expression on Olivia's face did
have a hint of satisfaction, a feeling they all shared that
moment. It was a climax predictable and clear enough that
each of them was glad that it had happened though Antonia
had a creepy feeling that their reactions had been just a little
too cultivated, too tended, and looking into Paul's face she
sensed doom. He was just a little too smug going to the stove
that way to make his tea, his affected American manner, so
casual, the tossed-off "Hi!"—the victor and his spoils.

"Just like your father," Olivia told her in the lobby of the
Eliot Hotel when it was clear that her visit had aborted,
repeating like the Raven, "never mind" and "you'll see," with
sentences falling in between marked by her themes of
self-negation and spite. The dark races. The evil side of
man. Ham. All those things. Antonia, she said, was aligning
her fate with these people, black on the outside and black on
the inside. She'd see.

As a freshman at Radcliffe, she had met Paul Luenga at
a party, something at Christmas for those who couldn't go
home. The empty dormitory reminded her of war movies
and evacuations: she expected sirens and bombs and felt a
residual excitement in the emptiness there. She liked it,
being alone in the space. The bathrooms were vast and her
showers emanated like mists in the void. The corridors
became surreal with ghosts of messages still pinned on the
doors. She read them as she pottered with nothing much to
do: *Cheryl came looking for you. Steve is here!!!!* Next to it:
Mary-Beth got the new coat. They seemed like whole novels.

One of the professors had arranged a series of events: a
carol sing, a night on the Boston Commons to look at
reindeer, a party Christmas Eve for what he kept calling
"exchange students." There were nervous Christmas
decorations, all handmade, Santa Clauses, elves made of
walnut shells and cotton wool, a knitted holly wreath, a circle

of figures shaped in dough. Like a detached entity, his wife's
voice made introductions, reading the tags each guest had
found waiting near the door. Antonia hadn't caught the
African's name; the hostesses's voice had slipped over it too
quickly trying to avoid mispronunciation and his jacket lapel
covered it immediately when he put his hands into his
pockets. But she caught the accent, slightly British, lilting,
trying to contain a desire to soften the final consonants with
the vowel *i*. She knew it well.

From a distance, Antonia studied his face and tried to
tell what tribe he was—her airport occupation, a sign
perhaps of boredom rather than interest—and thought she
saw something in the eyes but later discovered it was his
mouth that gave the thing away. They had a brief chance to
speak in line at the buffet, only long enough to make
identifications: his name was Paul Luenga and he knew of
her father. "The coffee baron." He smiled. At the table an
Iranian called Abdi got very drunk and made raucous fun of
the season by crushing walnut elves to get the nuts. He
leaned, breathing garlic from an earlier meal, a gesticulating
hand grazed her breast too often to be an accident, spoke
of peaches in "E-ron" that men wrote epic poems about, that
men would kill for. He made her laugh despite it all: the
garlic, the spongy hands, the diamond cufflinks. An
economist, he made loud predictions about the world based
on the location of oil.

A thin Sudanese engineer and his wife remained
embarrassed the entire evening as though it were all
personal and an affront. His dark suit was shining with wear
and the seams pulled open on the yellow stitching of a hasty
repair. His wife had elaborate hair, a series of braided arches
that swept over her head and around her face in heavy
curves. Not hard to imagine it undone, exploding. She was
the one the professor's wife attended to distraction because
she was, it came out later, an artist. She begged the favor of a
portrait, but the engineer refused. "Her religion doesn't
allow it," he said, which made Antonia wonder if they
followed different faiths.

After the coffee, they drank more punch and the
Iranian jabbered, whispering lavish asides about Antonia's
red gold hair—"In my country, you would cover it or it

would drive men wild, to poetry or murder"—still making her laugh. She shared a few odd glances with Paul and saw when he smiled he had the space between his front teeth that would drive the women of his country to song or murder—a tiny window that promised all would be revealed. The guests who stayed late went out into a light snow.

"Ah!" the Iranian said and tipped his face to it.

Falling in love with Paul. They both had tried for it, made it happen, a combination of will and desire. He was married, to a woman left behind in a village, nothing either one thought of as real. He was older. He had children. But even so. It had to be Paul. Winter so cold that chunks of ice heaved against Massachusetts. They both had been astonished by the frigid air, had both felt wonder. Her hidden genes awakened, energized, while he complained it was sheer hell. In defense he filled a window with lush plants and said this wasn't anyplace that God intended human beings to live. They were finding proof now, he pointed out, in a place called Olduvai, that the first men had walked on the earth in the highlands of East Africa. He maintained that the Northern Hemisphere was the price which had to be paid for being white.

Until then, they had both been innocent of the solstice; days too short to wake in, an amaze of ice and snow, of cold and dark. Neither one had memories of spring—she went with friends up to Vermont and saw blood-red stems against melting snow, yellow earth and frail sugary greens, fiddlehead ferns and willows like dream trees. There were streams bursting in woods eerie with trees that had pure white bark, stark black branches budding against a white sky. African trees lost leaves according to a subterranean time, obeying things they understood down in their root systems, death and rebirth going on at once, a continuous fall and replacement hidden in the secrets of the rain and earth. Never bare. Never cold. Never given up to air.

Even the summer was too cold for Paul. He waited, a dark shape on the sand, self-conscious in a bathing suit worn only once, fed her a towel, dried her hair. They didn't make love until the fall. November, the month the jacarandas would have been blooming on the high plateaus at home, covering the dusty towns with carpets of purple flowers. On the hills of North America, trees blazed. They came together like a twist of autumn leaves—her gold and his deep burnt red.

Paul said the fate of Africa would take its shape from broken pieces like the shards of ancient pottery. "We'll be the archaeologists of our own destinies, forming the vessels after the facts, rediscovering the old energies, the true foundations." His sadness had dazzled then like hope. When Antonia met him he had started writing a long narrative poem about a man searching from village to village for the god of water. Everywhere the man went, he found only the shattered signs of the god's passing—cracked pots, dried streams, emptied wells. At the end of the poem, the man finds the god in an old forgotten spring close to a village even though the women there have been walking miles and miles each day to get their water. The man becomes a tree and puts down roots. Antonia thought the metamorphosis at the end was strained, unnatural, something only he wanted to be true. Too much like desperation. She had preferred the middle sections about the villages, remembered Paul's radiant melancholy each time she saw the pear shape of a water jug, a gourd form pressed into the small of a woman's back, or heavy on a head, on the impossible strength of neck. He never finished the poem but revised it endlessly. Originally he called it "Odyssey" but she said "Ooh, no, I hate African writers who make pretentious claims on Greece . . ." and then he called it "Adam" to which she might have said the same except it struck a chord, given Olduvai, and a story Moslems told about how Adam, expelled from Paradise, had gone searching the earth for water until the Angel Gabriel led him to a spring that bubbled like a miracle from some black rocks in the desert, in a place they came to call Mecca.

He had gone back to Africa before her, to give her time to think it over and to give him time to adjust:—"In case I—What is it you guys say?—in case I *revert?*" The idea being he would write to her if his perspective changed on seeing home again. It had been almost ten years with no summer flights, no stops in Europe, no heavenscapes and mornings over tropical snows. But he wrote, a flowery, Victorian letter, begging her to come back. The country needed her. He needed her. Their first job was at a rural clinic in the south. What they both had dreamed of—the mythical service, like Schweitzer—rain beating on the tin roofs, a mist of netting in the wards. She thrived on the anachronism, the kerosene lanterns, the tents, weeks they climbed through ridges along the lake through a succession of villages like doctors dropped in from another century. It was how she got her taste for medicine practiced on the run.

Two years later he was in the capital, starting a medical school at the university, running the government hospital, a bureaucrat. It shattered his will; honesty given over to duty. He was, they all said, the only one qualified, which, in the end is the tyranny of Africa. So he sent for her, too, and put her up in a house on Oyster Bay. She didn't like it and thought of leaving the country then but simply couldn't despite McGeorge's bleak forecasts and all the friends who left, despite the nagging from her mother on thin airmail forms. All of it only triggered her defiance. She believed there had to be a point to Bill Redmond's emigration. There was no substance except her place here, the only place she knew. Even though Olivia's letters never stopped, kept coming until they became one continuous letter—"Just remember if you stay, these are the kind of people who throw stones, who are afraid of dogs. You'll see."

For a while, she had no idea that things were any more than difficult, no sense of what Luenga began to call "the real trouble," whatever it was: something gone drastically wrong beyond the droughts and bad decisions and bad advice, what they thought at first were growing pains. What was it? Looking for an answer, possibly for the blame, he turned into the wanderer of his own poem—lost in the middle sections where there was no hidden spring, no miracle, no place to root, only broken pots, village after village in ruins. Easy for him to see, from that point of view, the distortions and nothing else. He darkened and drew away from her, politicized.

In love, it never was important for them to see "eye-to-eye," as he put it. She was never sure whether they did or didn't; at least in most things she thought they did.

Which may have been her female longing. He attributed her point of view to deep sources that would never change, while she found her ideas could shift and flow, a surface phenomenon. So she never understood the rift, only noticed a time when they began to bicker like old married types.

"Still, after all these years, Tony, you're no more than a visitor, a tourist." A colonist. He developed a curious habit of turning everything into a political event. Even their sex life. She worried about getting on top for fear he'd see some parallel to the colonial situation in it—or what was it called? The North-South Dialogue.

"Who decided to arrange the model of the world so that the so-called North is on top? There's no such up and down, no over and under in space. That's how far your damned sense of superiority, your arrogance has taken you, and that's the legacy of inferiority we've inherited from your so-called science."

The so-called North? How did it happen, she wondered, that he, of all people, had managed to brainwash himself? His real subject was identity. A catechist: Who am I? What am I? (He wasn't his black wife's husband, nor a son of England. No Harvard grad really.) Where am I? (If the world is not North and South.) Where have I come from? Where am I going? Africa was the world's last question. Old answers proved wrong, new ones never discovered. Here perhaps they would at last reveal, in a yellow cradle of earth, man's origins. The Garden of Eden in Olduvai. When you went there you saw footsteps, more than ancient, Pleistocene, frozen in volcanic ash, an adult and a child in step, whispers of a past beyond imagination. And her own lost present.

It would have made sense for her to leave then, would have been easier to fix her exit to the end of a love affair. But they hadn't separated suddenly so that she could have, brushing her palms, said, well, that's done, and bought a ticket. Not even suddenly in retrospect the way change sometimes appears afterward. She retained an image of his face behind a book. He had taken to reading Marx and Lenin; those heavy volumes piling up one by one on the bedside table, instead of Shakespeare and William Faulkner. And he started talking about the West and about the North in tones that made the globe seem hostile, itself a plot. In time their arguments would end at an emotional impasse like people fixed into religious models, desperate to believe that theirs was the only truth, the true truth. This was not her style; he bored her. She didn't have the energy to revise the history of the world by trying to figure out what would have happened if Europe hadn't ruined Africa.

What he claimed to have uncovered in her so-called efforts on his country's behalf was a wayward form of ego, which in turn, he said, revealed her racial feelings, and these were the cause of the guilt which made her go on. A vicious cycle, he said. A different form, but still the arrogance of Bill Redmond. Meaning, of course, the West and not Bill Redmond solo. Each man, however, had to face these convolutions of blame for any kind of collective crime; just as, he said, young Germans right now felt guilt for what their fathers had done.

"Oh, for God's sake, Luenga, let it be," was her refrain. Perhaps she was supposed to confess like a Chinese landlord to a bunch of glowering peasants in dark padded jackets. More often she had absolutely nothing to say to him and noticed she was happier when he wasn't there.

She finally said no to the fancy house knowing it was just as much for him. He hid behind the privilege he accorded her and that haunted them both. That was his way all along, to make it seem because of her and then, in turn, to make it possible for him to hate her for it once the language of revolution had separated his mind from the bizarre things that were going on around them. Everything beside the point became political: where you lived, what you ate, what you wore. The worst of their serious rows came when she insisted that he arrange other accommodation for her. Because she was willing, she told him, to put on a show of self-sacrifice or any of the other shows put on in places like this, if he would tell her which hypocrisy was most appropriate. That was when he sent her off to the midlevel government housing in Kinondoni. And she agreed.

The move bothered Charles more that anyone else. "To go down," to live that way, with people who were less. He had even tried to convince her to leave, to go away to America:

"You leave this place, madam. No good, no good." By then it was clear that she would stop living with Paul.

Not surprisingly, without him, her society changed color from black to white. For a while he wanted her to go, as he wanted everything to go, and she thought, at times, he worked behind her back to make it impossible for her to stay. As a result she was watched, her company noted, her activities followed. It never bothered her; there was nothing she could hide, and even as the country pulled away from her, as she felt herself more and more alien, the reverse process of what her father had known, she found herself staying on without really knowing why.

Antonia still went to the pink stucco house on Oyster Bay, but now as the guest of strangers. The last time it was Italians, a young couple with the embassy who made jokes about a project they were supporting: Napolitano "experts" attempting to establish vineyards in a horrible place. They served up some of the acrid wine and then switched to a Barolo. Now it was occupied by Cubans who had come to give advice on sugarcane.

Sprawling gardens and billowing porches, once dreams now delusions; all the houses on Oyster Bay were touched by the sadness of fantasy. Dinner parties here blurred together. Candles in paper bags around a circular drive. Luminaria. Sounds of voices pitched to some standard, an aggregate laughter accompanied by the clinking of glasses. It was part of her blasphemy to walk those sweeping driveways on foot through the heavy incense of wet frangipani. Shadows were moving on a distant lawn closed off by high croton hedges of striated leaves, lights strung around a patio and guitar music from speakers deep within the house. She stood waiting there admiring the camouflage of a walking stick, insanely complete with thorns, catching at first only the faintest movement of its antennae in the low branches of a hibiscus. Car lights behind her stunned it to stillness: no one would ever know it was alive.

There was no breeze and the surf sounded as if it were barely reaching the shore. The occasion was official: someone visiting from Washington. An invitation had mentioned his name, Dr. So and So, in connection with one of those American public-health projects. Antonia was never certain at these affairs what her point of view ought to be—American or African. Holding her gin and tonic, she was often pushed into talking politics, usually in the same setting, a bright fall of bougainvillea to her left, a pale face to her right behind its own glass, so eager to hear what she had to say. Visiting public-health types had only one thing in mind—population control.

Did the faces behind the drinks look surprised or tired? She could never tell the difference between shock and weariness in these things. It was almost comical at times.

"I suppose these affairs bore you to tears?" He was a youngish man she had met several times before at "these affairs." A year perhaps, or maybe only six months ago, there had been a wife. Now he was single or seemed to be. She sometimes suspected they were being paired up. His name, Ted Armstrong, was paraded in front of her, hints of his story: a nice guy who got a rough deal, a wife not really up to things. She knew the expatriate urge to engineer the crowd, to balance and matchmake and include: a same-boat instinct that gloated at the littered wayside but opened arms to reformed returnees like the funny doctor.

"On the contrary," she told the man. "I enjoy the eats. I couldn't possibly tell you how much. And then I'm really lucky because I'm not expected to have anyone back."

"You know, I came across some of your father's work the other day," he said. "I hadn't actually connected you with the other Dr. Redmond. People go around calling you Dr. Antonia. You've almost lost your last name."

"Maybe I should complain. It makes me sound old-maidish, doomed to sainthood, already legendary."

"Tell me what that's like," he asked her, "to be a saint. I've always been curious about what people have to do to prove their love for their fellow man."

She saw he had had too much to drink. "Oh? A cynic? Old before your time?"

"Is that what you call someone who doesn't like the business he's in?"

"What business is that?"

"Helping Africans."

At dinner, outside on card tables splashed across the patio, she found his name card next to hers. He did try to avoid the black hand clutching a bottle of wine that appeared floating in thin air beyond a white cuff, by waving his hand tentatively over the glass, but the glass was empty and had gone begging and would be filled in any case. His talk was loud, not relaxed by the wine but rather strained by it, wanting to silence all other sounds as though he were shouting himself down or madly trying to put a stop to some nagging voice in his head. She suspected that men who got strident when they drank too much had nothing to hide. Which may have been the thing that troubled them.

While the conversation sputtered with questions like a car that wouldn't start, the doctor remained silent concentrating on her cold soup—consommé: croutons bristling with Parmesan cheese. The black hands floated at the table taking and bringing bowls. They were the hands of old men, the reliable ones, the well-trained ones, but they still moved with that air of confusion, always hesitant, always scared of getting it wrong even after so long. Like Charles, though she had never ever criticized his work; instead lived through his ups and downs (his interest in his job waxed and waned with the moon, she sometimes said). She did it with a martyred silence for which she disliked herself.

"The Halsteads have the best cook in town," one of the four at the table remarked.

"But Emily has a terrible time with him. He drinks."

She knew when Armstrong offered her a ride home that night he'd say, "Have a drink at my place. It's still early. It's on the way," or words to that effect. She knew in advance that she'd agree.

Theirs was the only car on the road, headlights lifting shapes from the dark, mostly palm and papaya spun aloft and hurling as they sped. Driving too fast but she liked it. The wind was warm through the open window and her long hair, once pinned up, had come undone and blew around her face. In her mouth it tasted bitter of shampoo and salt. She could either spit it out or chew it as little girls did. He was telling her about his house, which was too big for him alone. "Don't apologize," she shouted. Hair sliced at her lips. Then his lights caught the place and held it up for them, a stack of porches and balconies, something awful architecturally.

"My wife hated it," he said. Inside, as it came to life with a click of lamps igniting, she got the feeling that he had been robbed, as though the drawers had been emptied and left hanging open, the pictures stripped from the walls, white patches left where they had been. "Sure is a mess," he said, "but up there," he pointed, "is a porch. My salvation."

He was waving a bottle of brandy at her and she was nodding. She could see that he was someone who didn't keep a servant. Upstairs his laundry strung rooms together across a wide hall. It made her wonder about his life here. And about her own. Standing by as he fiddled with the latch on French doors, she held his drink in one hand, hers in the other. His hunched back, the inebriate's concentration, a small event like this one repeated without tense, back and forth in time, fixed her in this place. He could have been any of her lovers, save a physical detail or two of skin or language. Turning the key was a gesture tipping to the future as much as to the past, like something geological, her "I am," riveted to this land. Like a rock, like this building's marriage with the sky.

He was right. She, too, would have lived up here on the high porch. It was almost cool. She looked down on a grassy patch to where the land fell away over coral cliffs to the sea: living walls raised inch by inch over millennia by tiny soft echinoderms, skeletons, bones, raising huge structures that buttressed the land. She had a professor at Radcliffe who said the coral structures far exceeded those of men. Higher. Grander. But no more permanent. The cliffs were dead rocks now and the sea was washing them away. She knew that during the monsoons the waves had enough power to send their spray over the iron railing where she pressed her toes.

"You've probably noticed that I'm not used to being a bachelor," he was saying. "My wife, Jenny, got sick of the overseas life—moving every two years. She went home, found all her friends had careers, were renovating houses, collecting antiques. So was it feelings or ideas? I mean did she change her feelings about me, or did she change her ideas? About everything? Maybe if there had been kids. She'll probably have kids now, in a clean hospital. No offense. A shopping cart in the Grand Union, pulling stuff off shelves . . ." He was awkward, trying to push the conversation to some personal level. The pasts. The secrets. Perhaps they had to become that sort of couple: perhaps he expected her to tell her story, too.

He had a lean face, tired, and with thick hair, dark brown. The windy drive had loosened it, cowlicks and erratic layers. His eyes were the same dark brown. Disappointment was his theme: the demand for mediocrity in all things, the apotheosis of the superficial. Moving in two-year cycles, things, even emotions got pared down, he said, but no closer to the bone. Instead there was irrelevance and imbalance. But—now he was kidding—the real cost had been in terms of a model railroad he left behind so Jenny could bring her sewing machine, her loom, her piano, her Cuisinart. At least he was seeing the humor of it all; soon he would go nuts. After fumbling and shifting, the breeze established itself at last. They were quiet then listening as it rode in harmony with the tide.

She woke throughout the night thinking of him, of his plundered house, the toy trains left behind. His cynicism seemed too much like humility turned inside out, gone sour in its own defense. Or was it innocence, an American trait. Anyway, she liked him—the brown hair and matching eyes attracted her, touched some ideal of coordination given away in the gene for color, an attempt, at least, at perfection. You had to trust a thing so carefully attuned. Fingers in the rich dark hair, the bitter eyes. She wondered about Jenny, remembering a lithe blonde, a deep tan, and the way love dies, the wedge of changing feelings and ideas. And closed her eyes, held by her own dead love—the throes of it, still wanting to know what happened. There in the legend he had contrived, searching for water, the thirst, the dessicated pride, she found an image, a scrap of his poem that sometimes surfaced. Not an explanation so much as an epitaph: "Only dry thunder," he had written, "Shadows of the vulture in the rhythms of the sky. / She comes—the woman—with her empty gourd / To tell him / Sir, there is no water."

FOUR

Esther Moro sat stiffly in a chair facing the doctor. She was dressed simply in a cotton frock with awkward ruffles attached at the shoulders. Her eyes began to search the floor. She pulled a cheap ring from her finger and dropped it into her palm, allowing her hand to close over it, a flash of yellow metal and pink glass. She backed into her subject the way Africans did, the way people eased into cold water for a swim, taking it an inch at a time against the backs of their legs, always ready to run into the shallows.

"I am walking in the night," she said. She dropped the gaudy ring into her other hand and rolled it against a ridge of curling fingers, then back again into the cup of her closing fist. As a result, she said, she couldn't sleep. "*Siwezi kulala.*" Which made her tired. And so, she couldn't work and therefore she had no money. And nothing to eat. Piling up the problems until she finally said what was wrong. It was pain, she said, a swelling pain in her stomach. She continued to gaze at the floor. Restless, the ring tumbled in her hands.

She looked at the doctor quite suddenly and asked, "How does a mosquito bring malaria from one person to another?"

Rhetorical: you had a feeling that if she knew the question, she knew the answer, but she cocked her head to listen as Antonia explained and then repeated, just to make sure she had it dead right: "From the blood of one into the blood of another sucked in the tube of its mouth." This was a deep point. And then she said, moving still deeper into her own thought so that Antonia was the one left swimming, "I have seen frogs come from inside of a woman, many of them, falling to the ground."

"You have seen this?"

"Yes."

"And you think this is the cause of your pains too? Frogs inside of you?"

"Yes." She slipped the ring back onto her finger, twirling it there, eyes straining ahead of her as if to see a detail in the distance from which she could pull a conclusion. "From the blood you put inside me. It was no good."

Like blood, the doctor understood, carried by mosquitoes in the night. "Did someone tell you this? A *mganga?*"

"No. I don't like *waganga*. They don't help people and they're thieves."

Examining the girl, the doctor found nothing gross. No fever. No lumps. The organs were all the right size. The breasts normal too. She was not, she said, pregnant. Antonia believed that scar tissue had grown around the lacerations causing the girl pain. She offered an X-ray and prescribed analgesics. At times like this, she envied the *waganga* their clever blend of psychology and herbs and magic. A *mganga* could have treated Esther for what she thought was wrong, the frogs in her stomach.

"You know, Esther," she said, "I don't believe that frogs can go inside people."

"Yes. I know."

"Then why do you think I can help you?"

"Because you put them there."

Not just this bizarre self-diagnosis, but the girl herself was a surprise. Usually patients were silent behind their symptoms, making her guess it all, hoping for an injection or a bottle of pills, something simple to let the trouble vanish though she knew they kept their secret thoughts of witchcraft and poisoning and listened to their own doctors at the same time, eating powders made of leaves, carrying pouches of tiny bones. She found things all the time—beads strung along the bedstead, a bird's claw, red parrot feathers. There was an edge of panic even in the slightest ailments, a sense of dread, the knowledge that everything could collapse. What she had to do was to make it better right away or they would run for other treatment. Right away, when the only miracles she had on hand were penicillin and sometimes a scalpel.

When Esther Moro came back to her, carrying the X-rays in a folder, her expression was amused, closed around private perceptions as though she were sure the evidence she carried would be in her favor, that Antonia would now see the reptiles living inside her. She was wearing the same awkward dress, the same gaudy ring. Her ruined hair was wrapped in a magenta scarf which brushed her skin—deep brown, matte finished—with reddish tones. One of those narrow girls, built to be wary. Antonia thought of lanky nomads in beaded crowns watching their fathers' cattle, watching dust storms rising on the plains. She sat on the edge of the chair with her feet pressed close together. She slid the ring back and forth over the knuckle, turning it, fidgeting with it until the gesture became a screen between her and the foreign doctor. She complained again about her pain, then sidetracked, took a medical book and opened it, a finger tracing patterns over the diagram of the circulatory system.

"Here," she told Antonia. "The way the blood goes."

"Can you read?" the doctor asked her.

"No. But I know this." She pointed. "This is a man. This is his heart. The blood goes here."

"Well, what do you think, can anything as big as a frog fit in there?"

She shrugged. "They can." And laughed, not, Antonia thought, because the idea was absurd, but because she knew the doctor thought so. She could see herself from both sides, an African talent. The X-ray, when she saw it, astonished the girl who gasped as the light came on behind it—soft pulpy forms cupped in a pelvis like shadowy offerings in frail hands, a spine piled behind in spectral links.

"What is it?"

"That is inside of you."

She seemed to recognize the area, placed her hands palms down against her abdomen and asked, "Here? Inside?"

"Yes. And there are no frogs."

"And this?"

"Your backbone. And this is your pain."

Scar tissue, a web of it, and adhesions. "Like strings tied

inside you." She rarely talked to patients this way. There wasn't time. Even when she tried to explain things they would disappear behind faces wiped clean of any emotions at all, eyes suddenly blank.

"You mean here?" She was pressing, trying to feel, looking at the film and then at herself. "No," she said. "What can this picture tell you? What can it say? What of the things you can't see?" She stood for a moment, holding her hands against her body, then asked the doctor how scars could grow from nothing. She wanted to know what it was that made a wound heal or not heal. She knew, she said, that sometimes a wound would grow and swell and burst. She knew sometimes a wound could inject poison into the blood and kill a person. She spoke as if she had rehearsed, was talking around questions she had been asking for a long time, drifting away from her own problem on this tangent, the mystery and drama of infection. Antonia was amazed, then moved, an emotion she couldn't name. She sat there listening, answering the questions as she could.

But there was nothing that could comfort Esther or make her laugh. In her bed, hidden by her netting, unable to move, her pain was more a sadness in her. The house was only half finished, a lace of mangrove poles like arms and legs daubed with mud, scrap pieces of tin on the roof and cardboard walls made from open cartons, all picked from the trash and sold by traders who carried them to Mikorosheni in the backs of taxis. Her window was only a frame stuck in the wall and covered with a plastic sheet because there was no money to buy glass. Zobetta had built the house. She was a capitalist and rented rooms—against the law, though she said this was her pension. "Because men," she explained, "throw women away like the skins of bananas. In the same way they spit the pulp of sugarcane."

Esther and Hadija kept their room swept and dusted clean. They had a taste for crocheted and embroidered cloths that everyone made and if you didn't buy them, they gave them to you. These cloths, unlimited as wishes, ran through the house, patterns of flowers and butterflies gathering on beds and tables and chairs. Esther kept flowers in a jar as she had seen French and Hindi people do, for the sake of beauty, but sometimes she thought instead of shrines and offerings, the mystery of people giving place to things. They had a large picture of Jesus tending a flock of sheep and surrounded by children. Birds flew near his head, flowers tumbled to the edges of a golden frame. There were the pictures from the magazines that gave them their ideas of fashion, equally shining and new.

Esther couldn't talk. No words would come to her lips even though Zobetta tried to shake them out, telling her not to cry. She was staring then, at the square of light her window made, blurred chalky light under plastic sheets. She was thinking of Musumbi, her father, and his great rattling silences. She was as thin as he had been, an arm no bigger than the bone underneath it.

Everyone had gone to see another demonstration of Mr. Ntiro's new cooker that could boil water by burning sunlight instead of charcoal and kerosene. Yesterday, Hadija ran to her shouting, "*Kumbe! He has done it!*" and gave her a cup of sun-brewed tea, which by then was cold. The Makonde, Hadija told her, had teased, trying to light their cigarettes by holding them to the sun, jumping up and down, standing on high things and reaching far and laughing as they watched Ntiro at his stove. But they couldn't argue when they saw it happen, gathering steam and then the first small bubbles of it rising. There was a lot of talk, a shining disk that turned the sunlight into a flameless fire. Esther listened, knowing all the while that Ntiro's wife, Malindi, had been frying her *mandazi* on Zobetta's fire.

Esther was in trouble. A warning had been given to her twice. Once in the dream and once again as that sailor hurt her. A dull throb made her fear the deep cause. Pollution. What she had told the lady doctor about the frogs in her belly was a way of seeing it, whether the frogs were there or not. Strings, the doctor had said, proving this with an X-ray picture like a distant view of mountains through the rain. She could not be absolutely sure those were her bones there, the sack of her own stomach. Not sure of anything at all. She did know something was there. Sometimes she could feel it moving, swelling, or making her dizzy, even feverish. And though the doctor (no, she was not German) had said, "Frogs cannot go inside a person; you know it," Esther, with her own eyes, had seen such a thing in the Pareh Mountains, in the village of her husband, Josephat, when a certain woman, Mrs. Manda, had opened up and poured them—tiny jumping frogs—on the ground.

Very quickly, anyone who came to that village learned about Mrs. Manda. She was from another country. She had married one of the village men who had a shop, selling tea and eggs, sometimes potatoes. She was very black like the people from the lake and she told everyone she was, in fact, Baganda tribe, and her father had been king. Even her lips were black. Even the palms of her hands. When her husband died, she stayed on and ran the shop, being more clever and making more and more money. She had a farm where chickens lived in houses like men. She had a car. That she had no children was questioned, something seriously wrong, together with this matter of her husband's mysterious death. She grew fat, being rich, and people told stories about her. They noticed she was getting fatter and fatter, swelling and so dizzy in her head that she was having trouble walking. Josephat's other wives told Esther that Mrs. Manda had been made pregnant by seven men and she was about to give birth like a great puffed-up fish. Five of the men, they said, were Makonde who were so short they had to stand on ladders to reach her hole.

Sitting in front of their houses, women watched their children and talked about these things while they braided each other's hair. Esther hesitated in her doorway in the shadows, a stranger among these people who lived in grass houses, who had no furniture, who let their livestock inside. People who washed their clothes and cooked in the same pot. Who painted their bodies when they danced. Who circumcised their girls and shaved their heads. Her life was divided. Left alone in her hut, she might feel herself safe. She could hear the other women outside talking. Their language was easy, occasionally stupid. Inside, the darkness and the lingering smoke from her cookfire seemed like pity. She would lie there on her mat curled up until she heard her name. There were times when she would be called by Josephat and she would have to go to his hut when all she understood was that she belonged to him. Then there was the time she spent with other women in the circle of huts, an area she entered carefully but with hope, stepping slowly, trusting the sun, the soft assuring grasses of the wall tickling her arm.

Sitting there with the other women on stools, taking beans from their pod and spreading them on flat baskets to dry, Esther saw the fattened Mrs. Manda burst forth. She ran in circles making loud noises like an eagle catching fish. She tore off her clothes as though they were on fire. "She is drunk!" someone cried. They all began to laugh at her fatness. Her skin was piled like fruits at the market and her breasts were jumping and waving like arms. When the piles of her black skin opened, you could see another color under it, like tea, like the skin of a Hindi, slick with oil. Her nipples were huge and people said they saw flames shooting from them as she ran. Esther said she saw the flames, too, but she didn't. What she did see was Mrs. Manda, completely naked and shining like someone covered with water, squatting—everyone was watching, gasping—like someone about to give birth or move her bowels, straining and turning green. She screamed out and suddenly the frogs fell out of her to the ground, so many of them, jumping away from where she was. Everyone ran. Later, it was said that she had killed her husband and that the frogs were her unborn children changed by spite and witchcraft so that his seed could take revenge. The *waganga* made her leave the village. They burned her house, her shop, her chicken sheds.

Esther recognized in this event and any like it the balances of guilt and cleansing, actions that could be understood in the simple act of washing hands—you achieved a freshness by water, by soap—a knowledge deep as demand, an axis to the turning voices of conscience. Much more than magic—oh, she knew the instructions of *waganga*: purifications by fire, by water, by sacrifice—but more than those things, she was wondering now about medicine, the equation of sick and guilty as an explanation. Musumbi told her, no, no there are only germs which you can see under a special glass that makes them appear bigger, a kind of eye. No one, he said, had ever seen the things the witches talked about, curses carried in smoke, in the moon-cries of bats. All that was trickery. *Ulongo*. He was able to point to pictures in his book to show the truth.

Things happen that have no names. In time, memory and event were collected and she came to understand. Rain and rivers, for example. There in her mother's village was the dry bed, children playing among the rocks or digging in the sand. Next day there would be a river flowing in the same place. No one told her how. She only came to know that when she heard the rain at night, the river would be there in the morning. Esther had known, in the same way, that her favorite cousin, Kazi, would become sick though she had no way to talk about these things or even give them words in secret to herself. But when her mother told her a few days later that Kazi had a fever and could not be with her to play, a circle closed, like the rain and river, around these invisible things.

A *mganga* came: Esther watched him enter Kazi's house, a small withered man with a hump on his back. The hump, the adults said, was where he kept his power to heal the sick. She waited. Then one day they told her they were going to take Kazi to another village, to a more powerful *mganga*. Esther wanted to go, but her mother made her stay in the house. Looking out, she saw them carry Kazi from the village. The women were crying. They were all going in a line. She sneaked out and followed behind them ducking behind trees, listening and watching. They put Kazi in a deep hole and covered it with earth, a way, she thought, to cure him, the prescription of the *mganga*. They left him there and went back to the village. Her idea was that when he became well again, he would push the dirt away and return. And so each day she went to sit and wait for him.

It was the memory of Kazi, like a warning, when she saw her aunt Zidora bending near the fire preparing dishes for their evening meal. Esther went close to her. She took the spoon, pretending to stir, leaning closer and closer, wanted to reach out and sweep the vision away, leaning until she fell, catching her hand on the side of a boiling pot. Her mother grabbed and swept her away, beating her and shouting. In the smoky half-light she searched for the burn and licked at her hand until she felt the sting of her tongue. She was crying, wiping at her running nose, weeping until she screamed, going into the sound as if into hiding—from the thing she knew.

Later, growing up, she began to associate these warnings with what she learned about contamination, not only in the skin (which changed to gray and grew dry in sickness) but in other marks—even in her own pollution, the sadness of it, the swell and pain for what had been done to her. Her thoughts had a furious quality when it came to these perceptions, a feverish confusion in the face of unseen things. She desired instead, as Musumbi did, the security of knowing, like the knowledge she had of river and rain, the clear connection. Even if it could mean a flood. Even if. But the X- ray the doctor made had not gone far enough and it remained unknown between them what was wrong, would take more than the story of Mrs. Manda to convince—"Perhaps, Esther, you saw something else . . ."

Just before he died, Musumbi told her that he would go to work for another doctor, that he didn't know enough. The idea had been very real and exciting to Esther: she asked for details from him and drew pictures in her imagination of a face, of hands, even apparatus, as Musumbi had described them. Then, somehow, she forgot, in all the trouble after he died: her forced marriage, her flight. Now she felt the accumulation of signs.

After Musumbi died, Esther's uncle took a bride price from a man called Josephat in the Pareh Mountains. They went there, first in a bus to a town called Sameh and then climbed up to the village. Esther carried her own box of clothes on her head, an aspect of maturity as important as her new shoes. The hills embraced her. Views down into the valley flooded her heart with the energy of a mingling dare—notions of what she was supposed to be and of the protection she needed as against the wild urging of her own will. If she could risk standing there in the ashes of abomination, not afraid of the white owl, hand in Musumbi's hand. He was the one who had been able to say, "I will do it, go, even as a stranger, to the capital city, to the ocean, to where I knew Herr Grass . . . I will find another teacher there." But she let her uncle lead her into the hills.

Entering the village where Josephat lived, she looked deliberately ahead, eyes pulling faces from the circles of shadow as she passed, dark floating shapes, objects out of focus. She was dizzy, the box grown heavy on her head, the shoes rubbed into her feet. The people here lived in low round houses made of grass with crooked broken lintels over their squat doorways. There were no strong edges, no deep contrasts, even the obscure tumbling words of their language, and the filtering faces, moved like muffled sounds around her. She saw a parade of girls her own age who had shaved heads and white triangles painted on their brows.

She was too young to understand the meaning of marriage. Looking down at her shoes, she invented a cloth to dust them, a small tin of polish from the kiosk that could be opened with a coin or the side of a knife. Black. A strap across each foot. The buckle metal shone like money. She listened to her uncle and this fat man who he said was her husband. She did not like the way it felt inside a grass house, the rasping dust and shedding seeds which chickens ranged for around the edges, picking, sifting. The furniture was low, stools and mats. There were no tables. No beds. Her uncle and her husband were arguing in the Pareh language. Their arguing grew; she heard them talking about money and hoped when they stopped her uncle would take her by the hand to lead her away from this place.

Josephat's other wives were two; they stood on each side of her clucking and humming to the conversation. One of them was tall: she moved closer to Esther, so close their arms were touching. Esther leaned toward the warmth. When the men finished talking the tall wife took Esther's box and led her to a small grass house. They bent to enter. A chicken ran by, its wings thudding on Esther's leg. There was a sleeping mat on the ground, a webbing of dust against the grass roof, eyes of light peering down. Esther wondered what would happen to her in the rain, in the pouring house, and wept, rolled up on the mat until the tall wife came to her carrying a cup of steaming tea. "My name is Sara. Yours is Esta."

Too young to know the meaning of marriage, only to suspect—to have heard the jeering of women, to fear the intimacies and beatings—part of her body where a baby will grow, where a baby will come out, where women bleed. She imagined shame, the parts of a woman that turn inward, that in a man grow out like threats. Her breasts were very small, the nipples had begun to stand out and under them were hard lumps like stones that were loose, moving under her skin if she pushed them. She feared this husband would ruin her breasts because he stared and played with them. He made her sit on his lap and with his finger and thumb, he squeezed to make her cry out. She had discovered that each time she cried out, he stopped as if the cry was a pleasure to him. He stopped squeezing then and held her there moving the little stones from side to side and laughing. When he squeezed, she quickly cried out to end his game. He talked to her in a language she didn't understand, but she heard in his voice the sounds made when talking to small children. One day he made her stand and took off all her clothes. He put her on his knee and parted her legs, looking carefully and then rubbing his finger there until he found where he could press it up inside her and he smiled and held her close to his cheek . . .

Whenever he called her to his house, this is what he did. She wanted to pull her small breasts from her body. To cut them off so he couldn't hurt her any longer. She went from his house to the river where she dipped and washed, dipped and washed. The water, cold and drenching, clung to her knees. Floating sticks that reeled in the current moving steadily away gave her ideas of escape in a boat. She lingered there playing, watching twigs and thinking, while girl voices grew up behind her, rose over the bank, and fell close, resting finally like a caress. She heard her name, "Esta!" turned, saw their shaved heads, their white blazes. They wore white aprons, their breasts were bare, and their bodies had been oiled. An old woman was watching over them.

So many words were similar that learning the Pareh language was fast, easy for Esther. She learned from Sara. They worked together in Josephat's fields. In the river they washed his clothes. The children were playing. The women were singing. First one would start a song, another joining until the voices, as high and unmatched as birds, filled the forest. Esther liked to walk in front with the wet clothes bundled on her head, then to duck off the path and hide. She came out darting, like a bird herself, from behind a tree. They all laughed as she jumped, even as she tripped and the clean clothes fell to the mud. Everyone came around the mess clucking "Esta! Esta!" and she ran again, chirruping, following the wind.

At night they drowsed outside on low benches shucking beans. Old women yawned and smoked pipes. Sara said, "Come Esta, my back is aching, my neck, my shoulders." She wanted Esther to rub her there. "I worked hard today. My body aches all over . . . here and here, yes . . . " only telling Esther what she felt, thick and warm, where the pain was, rubbing it away. "Come, Esta, my back is aching . . . " the way her mother used to say it, and then would, sighing, fall asleep. Just as Sara did.

Sometimes she went with Sara to gather wild spinach in the woods, then sold it in the market in Sameh to buy sugar and tins of milk for their tea. Near the riverbank kneeling in the sun, they were arms and hands combing through the weeds. They tied the spinach in bunches, two for a shilling, with long threads of grass. Their palms were stained, their fingernails, too. A basket of leaves was light on her head. She could carry it and swing her arms, feel long in her legs and free watching her feet step out, her bare toes. She cut up steeply toward the village, took the basket from her head and crept, hearing voices. There was a long house there, a kind of shed, closed on all sides. When the girls were inside, the door was filled with mats and branches, rocks were placed in a pattern to warn intruders.

The old woman—the circumciser—who guarded them, carried a cobra in a covered basket. She could see their washed white aprons spread on branches to dry. She could hear them singing songs. These were the girls who had bled. When they came from the house, they would be "real women," circumcised, ready to be wives and have their babies.

"What will be done to them in there?"

"They will be cut—here." A hand passed lightly showing where.

"Are you cut, Sara?"

"Yes." she laughed. "I have to be."

Esther had a dream about the house. In it she was an initiate, her head shaved and painted, her body oiled. She wore the white apron. She had learned the circumcision songs and was laughing at the old woman who told marriage stories and made jokes about the penises of men, some beautiful (a lover's) and some not (a husband's). There were benches along the walls where the girls lay. She walked between them as though she were invisible. She saw their legs open and between their legs they were made like flowers. On her own bench, spreading her own legs, she looked down and saw that her flower had petals of blood. The circumciser passed the long row of girls with her knife: they moaned softly but they were brave and did not cry out. Esther felt the pain of all of them. When the circumciser cut her, the flower dropped into the old woman's hand. She screamed, calling Esther a witch.

Sara said many girls dream of their circumcisions, but she would not show Esther where she must be cut. She would not show Esther on her own body or on the body of her baby daughter. Esther feared it was because the pain had been so great and her fear too great to speak of—a kind of ruin, an abomination. She looked carefully at the pieces of her own body and tried to imagine, felt the flesh with her fingers. The skin was thick and full of water and when she touched she could feel the sensation rise in her stomach even to her head.

She knew that girls had died in the shed. She had heard talk of terrible fevers and bleeding that would not stop, of swellings that turned green. She feared her own menstruation. She asked Sara, "Is there a way to stop it from coming?" Going down to Sameh to sell wild leaves at the market, she constructed escapes, journeys she made with Musumbi, links of walking and waiting, down to the flat land where, he said, there was a long road that went to the sea. Because of him she was familiar with the process of buses and fares, of passing unknown, of being no one. When she told Sara, "I will keep the money from this spinach. I will run away," her co-wife laughed, saying "Ha! Esta! You!" and bought little plastic clips like bows to fix into her hair while Esther rolled her coins and tied them in the corner of her *kanga* cloth.

She waited, watching for signs. Sara said a woman's blood will come with the full moon. The other women nodded. Mama Izak, the first wife, pregnant to the brim, told her that soon her small breasts will grow, her hips will widen, she will be circumcised, and Josephat will put his dirty fingers into someone who has not been cut. They all laughed. Even Esther. She endured the time she spent with him, sealing herself off, pretending not to know or feel. He showed her his fat body and his penis, hard, which he rested in her hand. He would forget her for weeks, and she could forget him, sitting in the circle with the women, hands that peeled cassava root, that winnowed rice, that wove sisal strings into baskets. She liked to clean the rice, to toss away the chaff, to pick the small stones, to pour the clean white grains into Sara's clay pots.

This was her secret: she had seen her menstrual blood, black and thick on her leg. Not like blood at all, there was no flow. On her finger, it looked muddy, slick, signaling hope and dread. She understood, watching the women who surrounded her, how that blood would become a shield—the importance of cloths washed in the river and spread to dry on rocks. No one else could touch them or go near. A guarantee of freedom, a claim on the privileges of isolation and rest. Not now. Not today. A lonely woman sitting near the river, a curving shape, beauty in the falling light. What made it happen? The marvel of cycles was a dim shadow in her imagination—again and again as they watched the moon and counted the days.

She knew how to make herself sick by drinking a certain powder made from leaves. Lying in her bed, she moaned, swollen and full of pain and vomit.

"My stomach is aching . . . my head . . ." Sara brought her tea. When Josephat called her, Mama Izak told him, "No, not today. Esta is very sick. Curled on her mat."

Yes, she knew the use of leaves. The memory roused her. She kept some of the leaves still, in a small box under her bed together with a picture of Musumbi and the German both wearing hats. This and the broken watch he carried like charms to ward off evil, only these she held against the unknown future that she faced. Five leaves. Brittle and gray. In an envelope. She looked at them carefully and put them back. They had to be pounded and then mixed with water. Closing the box, she felt choked by the thought of that drink. She had no idea what she would say to the white doctor if she should drink them. What could come of it but anger and risk? Still, all her life seemed waiting for this chance, something that remained without a name standing inside her like a seed waiting for her cloudy thoughts to pull away and give it sun.

She heard the others coming home. Zobetta's voice, being shrill, arrived first and then her daughters were calling, "Esta! Esta!" She could hear Zobetta tell them, "Esta is sick, resting," but they came running anyway with more news of Mr. Ntiro's magic stove. Hadija was there soon with a cup of stew he had produced—all of them standing, she said, watching as the onions glistened, fried in oil. Zobetta said such stoves meant no one could cook at night, which was when everyone ate.

FIVE

◁ ◇ ▷

The doctor saw a patch of purple satin. More than aggression, the color was memory. As she turned down the port road and caught the sharp blue rectangle of the sea between white walls, saw fishermen like a migration of white butterflies returning on the tide in dhows, as the green lawns of the presidential offices cut into the brown swing of the hospital path, there it was again . . . the purple satin. She turned and faced it as it moved along behind her a little wobbly on extraordinary shoes, like a great flightless bird. Soon, the doctor thought, the hospital would fill with broken ankles as girls like this one came tumbling. She seemed to deflate as the doctor came toward her.

"Are you following me?" Antonia asked.

"Please, memsaab, sorry to disturbing you." Her head bowed, displayed a neat pattern of corn rows over a long skull and then fell forward. Clinking beads like chimes hung on the end of hundreds of ridiculously tiny braids, a style, ironically, made popular by a white woman in a movie about—was it?—Tarzan or something else?

"Yes, what is it?" Antonia felt the tension, the supplicant posturing there, apologizing before she spoke.

"Sorry," the girl repeated. "Sorry." Her eyes closed. Somehow she had got her hands on a set of false eyelashes, which were resting on her cheeks untrimmed. She reeked of cheap perfume. "My friend is Esther Moro," she said.

Antonia nodded.

"Is she sick?"

"Very sick. She stays in her bed. She is crying, vomiting.

She wants you to help her."

"If Esther's sick she'll have to come to the hospital."

"She won't come. She says the hospital is no good. She says you didn't fix her. She still has pain. How can she get food if she can't work?"

"Perhaps she can go home to her village."

"Who will pay?"

A breeze, hot devil, carrying dead leaves and dust, spun around their ankles and up toward their eyes. The girl's great lashes battered against her face.

"Where is Esther now?"

"She's in Mikorosheni." There was a sign; the purple suit inflated. She knew somehow she had won.

"And what's the matter with her?"

"She drank leaves to send the frogs out."

"Leaves? From a *mganga*?" Antonia asked.

"No. Not from a *mganga*. She knows these things."

The two women walked toward a dirt path, a lacing of ruts, once mud, where bicycle tires had left crenellations. At the end of it, where it joined the port road, people were shifting a load of bananas from the back of a disabled car to the roof of a taxi. A production: hefting, engineering, all those fingers of bright green.

There at the bus stop, giving in to their fate, Antonia hailed a cab for the two of them. The driver took them a long way round, stopping to retrieve a parcel from a house along the way. He sang to an old cassette that Antonia vaguely recognized as Jimmy Cliff and drove like crazy at erratic speeds. He turned furiously angry when he saw where they wanted him to take them and left them on the ratty edges of the squatter village, a maze of mud houses tossed at random under umbrellas of mango and cashew trees, flung over winding tracks around water taps and pit latrines and garbage dumps. There were small plots of maize and cassava, broad dark leaves, red veins and black stems etched into the spreading shade. It smelled of cookfires, of charcoal and kerosene and the rancid coconut oil in which everything was fried. Children fluttered at the sight of a white woman coming toward them, gathered behind her, scattered if they drew too close. They came with her into the house as if they belonged to it, holding hands in little clumps, blowing to the edges of the walls like torn papers in the wind. A wide central hall, mud floors, faded cloths in doorways; she looked into an empty room where water boiled on a charcoal brazier, glimpsed long slung chairs rubbed with age, a wooden table, red canister of tea leaves, a green tetra-pack of milk. Three tarnished plastic cups.

Esther's room had the swept and holy look of a monk's cell, but without the austerity. Antonia saw the picture of Jesus, the doilies, magazine images like icons. Even the patient, enshrined, saintly behind a thin gauze of mosquito netting.

"Esther?"

Lifting the net, the girl rolled to her side. She had the same story: frogs from the blood transfusion were inside her, causing her terrible pain. Her stomach was so full that her throat had stopped letting her put anything down. She appeared to have lost more weight but her abdomen was large, so distended with gas and fluids that it had become painful to the touch.

"When did you drink the medicine from those leaves?"

Barely audible, a tiny bubble of a voice from somewhere near the top of her throat, said, "Three days past."

"What happened when you drank it?"

"I vomited."

"Where did you get them?"

"I picked them."

"And who told you about them?"

"My father. He knew about medicines." She had moved away from a band of spent sunlight that fought through her window, that cat face, almost yellow now, jaundiced, but her eyes wide with energy.

"Your father was a *mganga*?"

"A doctor. Like you," she answered. "He knew how sickness can go inside a person. He could fix bones."

"Where are these leaves, Esther?"

"They are here." An envelope by her bed had three left, an inch or so long and hard as bay or a decorative shrub. Antonia held a leaf, curiously exciting to someone who handled pills and capsules. Fingered it like a playing card. It was oily where her thumb had rubbed against the thin ridges of vein, and aromatic, a slightly medicinal smell. Yes, like bay or eucalyptus.

"I don't want you to be angry with me." Esther said.

"I am angry. Are you still vomiting?"

"I'm sick in my stomach. There is a terrible pain and I can't keep food. I vomit. Or I have diarrhea. You will have to help me not to die." She pulled a cloth up over her breast and spoke in English, "I have no money," as though the plea would stand a better chance in the doctor's own language.

So that was it. Antonia didn't want to give the girl money, though it was clear now that everything had been leading up to this moment since she hailed that taxi and agreed to come out here. In retrospect, she had known what she would find, what she would be made to do. These things followed such predictable patterns, so irritating, like hair shirts, like penance for some remote original trespass even though she tried to fight against being held up like this at gunpoint, the obligation, against always playing it out—the same scene, giving alms, recording it with a sense that everyone concerned was acting in a drama of failure. What would this bit of money really mean? An admission that she was actually involved in this farce with the frogs? And what would it lead to? That she would never see the end of Esther Moro?

About to say, "No, if I give you money, I will have to give money to all my patients," reasoning from reluctance more than experience because no one had ever made such a bizarre claim as this before, something made it hard to deny Esther Moro, a difference in the girl that thwarted Antonia's routines. As a medic, she was trained to deal with bones and bowels and blood, with invading bacteria and viruses—germs, as Esther said. Yes, a mechanic. And as a white woman in Africa, she should have been one of those people who said you could never figure out what an African like Esther Moro might be thinking. But had she really expected the girl to survive what she had with that sailor with no more problems than just some scar tissue? As though there were no psyche behind that black face? No dreams, no nightmares? She sat a minute or two on the other bed and tried to think of what to say and failed. Tried to think of how to hand the girl some cash without the desperate overtones.

And failed at that too. She could only laugh as she rolled the notes into a cylinder and reached across the bed. Esther took them with a shrug like someone victorious and yet resigned. Both saw the joke and lapsed into a mood. But the silence didn't pall. It drew them close. There were sounds of other people about the house. The children who followed the doctor in were still inside, intruders who had conquered; they now ran in the hall with cups of tea. A small boy leaned into Esther's door. Another joined him, staring. Soon there were five.

Leaving the village, trying to retrace her steps—there were no landmarks where squatters lived—she went instinctively as one walked away from natural things like the sea or a mountain, direction not defined by compass point, following an impression toward a drifting edge, this periphery of rust and dead grasses, of empty milk cartons. Always the pathetic dogs, the smell of kerosene and shit.

This time Antonia shared a taxi with a Makonde carver, a seat full of ebony statues, and a strong smell of marijuana. He wanted her to buy one of his pieces, leaned over the seat and pulled them forth one by one, like Dante, to show her. Wild images, devil spirits, his *shetani*, named for jealousy, slander, abortion, he intoned. All the deadly sins. He was laughing. His teeth were filed to points and a filigree of scars decorated his face. She was the one who left the taxi first, hard as it was to get away from his pitch without buying anything. He held her last chance—"*Hiyo mwisho*"—out the window, a chameleon *shetani* with red glass eyes, tongue out and stalking. She watched the car go, wishing she had bought something from him after all.

Days passed, or was it weeks? Each morning Charles brought her coffee, stopping a moment to tap the doorjamb twice to give her a chance to tell him, "No, wait a minute, Charles." She saw him through gauzy screens—her own mosquito net and the net she kept there in the door, a shadowy form carrying a tray. If she said nothing, he came into the room, bare feet like leathery slippers scuffing the floor. Often she heard him bring a stray sandal from the opposite side of the room to the edge of her bed, to arrange the two together so everything would be ready for her. Pretending to be asleep. Waiting for his ministrations to end, she sometimes wished that he would leave her to wake up alone, make her own coffee, pour her own juice, and wander naked in the house. But she noticed when he went on leave, she always felt odd, pressured, a barometric change.

She sat on her bed and drank—a funny luxury for someone whose fridge was breaking down, who had no car, who often had no water or electricity—fresh coffee, beans roasted each night and cooled on a chipped Spode dish near the sink, then ground in the morning, brewed and carried to her bedside laced with sugar and a touch of cardamon the way she liked it. Her life was pitched on discords like these. And time that she marked out by events instead of minutes or hours or days.

She remembered the crises at the hospital, not the patients; sounds of nurses gathering or a siren bearing toward them. Then she should know she was going to face something that had to be completed by her hand or not, in terms as simple as that because there was no one else. One night brought ten Indians to her—four alive, six dead—all from one car that had crashed into the back of an abandoned army truck left in the middle of the road, on the one stretch of tarmac in the whole country, like a drag strip where people could speed for old time's sake. Full tilt into the back of the truck.

The doctor worked—like a seamstress, she thought— and managed to save two of the four. There was an awful moment when the nurse came to say there wouldn't be enough blood, that they would have to choose whoever had the best chance for survival. The dead that night had strangely animated features, fixed in their last expressions as though a camera had caught them relaxed and enjoying this fast ride, as though the collision came before they knew a thing. Like the pictures of them that appeared in the paper a day or two later to announce the deaths. *Om Shanti shanti shanti.*

It was a story she told McGeorge, who said, "Ten in one car!" and added, "Well, I always said they breed in cars." He was in town for supplies. Had borrowed a car—"Bruce's car"—although she recognized the old red Renault. "The old boy had a nasty time getting it away from his harem. They've taken to calling him Sugar Daddy, the latest concept they've picked up from the developed countries."

He came leaning on his horn to drag Antonia off to dinner. His hair was long now and bleached in streaks from the sun; the way he liked it, curling on his collar and full of dust. He hadn't shaved. He looked much younger than he was, his real self emerging even against his age. Antonia wondered how he managed now to live in London in those three boxy little rooms filled with clutter, no more than closet space. It was, he said, his "larval" stage, the worm slinking in the silk suit, the hair slicked down, the eyes slightly popping from the head. Like a butterfly, he understood the cocoon and the escape and how to metamorphose. No matter how long he'd been away or where he'd been. His was a special context, in which England wasn't allowed to change.

"There are people down there who still use lip plugs," he told her. "A small tribe. Bantu. The women strip in protest when they get fed up—take everything off, go round to the in-laws, and just sort of stand there. You can imagine how embarrassing that is for everyone." The city they drove into gave them a sense of lost time, of old photographs that could still be relied on to the last detail, a feeling you had that you were not stepping back in time at all but to the edges of it, with the broken windows and eroding walls all whispering behind you. On the sidewalk, a young Swahili woman in a black cape that opened and rippled in the wind, closed it tightly as the car approached, turned her head away from their eyes, then swung around and followed the car with her stare.

McGeorge said, "Peppermill has heard about some very unusual sex deviation down there—got to do with bestiality. Story about a man and a chicken."

"It's cheap, McGeorge." But she was laughing. "It makes us all look like fools."

"Come on, we're all junior anthropologists when it comes to that. The only way we can understand anyone different is by latching on to what's most bizarre about them. You spend far too much time looking at kidneys. A kidney is a kidney. You lose touch that way."

As they had turned a corner, three Indian women in saris, moving as one, stopped short on the curbing to let the car pass, but instead McGeorge obliged, calling out in Gujerati, and they drifted by like statues on a float. Behind the car adolescent boys were tapping the fender with schoolbooks. They went to a restaurant called the Shish Majal, a place with plywood cutouts of Mogul arches, cheap Formica, and the smell of disinfectant. Her lawyer, Mr. Laxmanbhai, was there and joined them. And the American girlfriend, the writer, talking about a book she had just completed, a novel set in Kenya, called *Game Park*.

"I wanted to do a book that really took you someplace, told you the inside of an operation, like Arthur Hailey does. Like *Airport*. Like *Hotel*. The kind of book people *want* to read." Her name was Cynthia Dale.

"I wonder what provokes these one-word titles?" Antonia asked. "Is it the rush to get it over with, to go on to the next one, like checks on a list? Like these throbbings of yours, McGeorge?"

"Tony's a doctor," he said. "Don't listen to her." They were laughing, breaking into hot crisp pappadum. Laxmanbhai held up a chip and left it on his plate, saying it was too greasy.

"I asked myself," Cynthia went on, "what is something everyone wants to know about. The answer was extinction. You know what I'm saying? As in species. As in we're all headed for it. So I sold my house in Malibu and checked into Africa. I haven't looked back, believe me." She was tall, with curling dark hair, a slender woman with remarkable fingernails, long, painted blue.

Laxmanbhai did not trust the food when it came. He examined everything by digging his fork into it, holding pieces to the light. It was clear that he wouldn't be able to eat any of it.

"I gave myself two years and that's exactly how long it took. I sold *Game Park* within three weeks. My agent was ecstatic. That was seven months ago. Now they're fucking me around. It's too long, they say. They want me to take out all the natural history, all the stuff about the animals. All the good stuff. Like about dung beetles and hornbills. I used animal point of view a lot. My concession to sex was a couple of baboons making it. It takes place in seven days. These are not obscure symbols that no one will get." She wasn't having trouble with the food, an unpleasant curry. Nor was McGeorge. There were slices of green mango tossed with salt and this was what Antonia chose to eat.

"So how were you coming from Kenya across the border?" Laxmanbhai wanted to know. A legal note.

"We flew to Rwanda. I came overland, hidden in a truck."

"These people are counting elephants in Selous," Antonia told him.

"Not merely counting," McGeorge corrected. "Observing. Very little is known. There are serious questions to be answered. Why, they've only recently discovered that when a male gets ready to mate, he gets a green dick—very drippy, very smelly. Peppermill thought it was some horrific strain of elephant V.D.: you could smell it for miles. Well, no, it's a condition called 'must.' As in 'I must.'" They were all laughing, all but Laxmanbhai, who only laughed at religious jokes.

Cynthia said, "For me, this is all-consuming. This is our one last chance for tenderness, the way we relate to endangered species."

There was dessert, a usual feature, halwa: carrots boiled in sugary milk, which Laxmanbhai was willing to try. A little on a spoon, placed on the tip of his tongue. "Is it well cooked?" he asked the waiter.

They talked more; mostly about Cynthia, her life in the tent in Kenya. She had walked every inch of the game park with the rangers. To her this was Africa—wide, splendid views, the promise of seeing leopard, a pride of lions, giraffes marked out in silhouette against fiery sunsets. Land Rovers. Dust. These were the things. She had had malaria and all the standard dysenteries and skin problems. All of it a very cheap price to pay: survival, in fact, she said, was part of the reward.

Her book, she said, would appear under the name of Daphne Scanlon, a pure pseudonym of no significance. In California she had written advertising copy under the name of Lynn Almquist, but the sign on her mailbox said Dalton, her ex-husband's name. She considered these names as marks of her transitions from one stage to another,

something like incarnations. She swore she didn't have a
multiple personality or anything like that. It was more a
form of camouflage. Or—she laughed—manifestations,
like some Hindi idea about all-being, the many in one. This
time Laxmanbhai was chuckling too.

The waiter brought them a plate of seeds, dill and
fennel and sesame, to aid digestion and freshen breath. "For
better defecation," he told them.

After the meal, Mr. Laxmanbhai drove Antonia home
through streets so empty you would have thought there was
a curfew.

"Where is everyone?" she said. One man alone was
hunched around himself and hurrying, turning now and
then as if he heard someone behind.

"We are living in fear," her lawyer said.

When she met them again, they were shopping,
running around with lists at Patel's. The sign over the door,
DEPARTMENTAL STORE, was barely legible. Old Indian
movie magazines were displayed in the window, stars with
lush lips and liquid eyes, architectural patterns of the Hindi
script. Under burlap awnings small boys sold eggs one at a
time or in paper bags made from government reports. A tiny
girl in rags jumped from a perch among them to meet
Antonia. She held up a hand with no fingers. The other was
cupped to receive coins.

Inside there was a smell of mothballs and coiled rope.
Cynthia Dale was standing in front of a shelf with tinned
goods from China, like gherkins in ginger syrup, stuff even
starving Africans wouldn't eat.

"Have you tried these?" Cynthia asked. She put five tins
in her cart. "You have to rinse them." She looked thwarted
but courageous. "The ginger offers a mild surprise. I think
of myself as a Dada cook."

A blond kid next to her was examining a jar of
something thick and black. The label, printed in Chinese
characters, gave no clue to what was in it. There was a
picture of a bridge and a dhow. "I know," he said, "it's dhow
paste." He had a German accent.

"Great on toast," Cynthia told him.

"There have been rumors of strawberries. Possibly butter," Antonia said.

"Patel doesn't know anything about it," Cynthia told her. "Another hallucination. We're all becoming food fetishists. I heard they were going to get some cheese, see. Danish. Under the counter. Whoever was smuggling got scared and threw it in the bay. I almost went out and rented a scuba tank." She was tossing dark, syrupy balls of half-processed sugarcane in the cart. A sack of coffee beans. McGeorge had gone among the plastic basins, one suddenly on his head. He stood there swaying, talking to Patel.

"So you are counting elephants with McGeorge?" Antonia said. She had her hand on a bar of raw blue-colored soap, unwrapped, a new product, most likely from Mrs. Patel's kitchen, her endless enterprises.

Cynthia said, "Peppermill believes that old myth about the elephant burial place. A deep cave somewhere full of tusks. He doesn't want to find it: he only wants to believe." It fascinated her, too; she stood leaning on the cart. "When one of them dies," she said, "the others pick up the tusks like they know how valuable they are. They carry them away. I've seen it myself. You never find them." She picked up a small piece of rock salt, licked it, started filling a bag with them.

"Yes, I've seen it too," Antonia told her. The blue soap had a spicy smell at first and then a harsh undercurrent of lye.

"Listen," Cynthia said, "McGeorge says you're a doctor. You work here. Maybe you know. There's a clinic down there. I heard they just ran out of insulin and can't get any more of it. Can that be true?"

"It can be true."

"But the cook at our camp, his daughter's got diabetes. Every week Peppermill flew over and got the stuff. So what's going to happen to her now? She isn't going to die without this insulin, is she?"

She leaned over her shopping cart not understanding how such things could happen. Insulin? Gone? Like saying the sun wouldn't rise the next day as far as she was concerned.

As it turned out they couldn't leave that day. They had

been stopped on the road just out of town, McGeorge explained, and the Land Rover searched. They had to get more permits to prove they weren't spies, carrying so many cameras, so they pitched up at Antonia's for the night.

"Travel in Africa," McGeorge said, "is something you achieve. You don't simply do it." The story: a soldier with buck teeth like a bloody Somali stirring at the sight of all that gear, black boxes and lenses, everything in leather cases. Suspicion excited him, made him high, made him more suspicious. More soldiers came out of the shadows making it impossible for McGeorge to offer a bribe. Roused to interest, they had surrounded the car. They all had guns.

"These are people who do absolutely *nada* except smoke grass," Cynthia said. Her dark hair was limp: there were streaks of dirt around her neck. One of the soldiers had jammed his arm in through the window to show her a chameleon that clung to it. She had screamed.

But around Antonia's table that night, it didn't really seem to matter. They might be a day late getting back but there would be the story they could tell. And the casual arrogance that, even now, it was still risky to go out in Africa, that if you survived, it still meant something. These were such familiar rhythms to the conversation: images of close calls in the bush, strange men who loomed to block the way. Sometimes everything out there seemed as uncontained as it had been when Livingstone went up the Zambezi, and there was a certain wild romance to that, which added to men like McGeorge. In remote parts where countries ended, or along the corridors of abandoned road that once linked settled areas, armies came to raid, often foreigners from across closed borders, as absolved as they were wild. The uniforms and guns only meant that they would have their way. This was what they thought of that night, talking late.

Her guests spread sleeping bags out on the floor. It pleased Antonia to see the night shaping that way toward faces rising around her in the dawn. Even Charles, who stayed very late, fussing with the pillowcases and extra coffee, liked the company and the scent of safari in the damp canvas and the leather gear. Cynthia followed him around the house learning the language—"How do you say this?" "What is the name of that?" Stepping into someone as you opened the bathroom door, smelling of toothpaste, the perfume of wet soap, a strange towel on the rack: these were sentimental things for someone who lived alone. And finally, in the stillness, it was the sound of breathing in another room or the toilet flushing after you had turned out the light and rolled to face the wall. Voices outside stirred as Charles ended his day, and far away, down in the squatter's village that had sprung up behind Kinondoni, Antonia heard Makonde drumming like a faint pulse coming through a stethoscope.

SIX

◄◇►

Esther Moro was holding the Bic pen and forming letters from her name, E-S-M-T-R, just as her sweetheart Francis had shown her, which was a wonderful thing to see and do. Together the letters created messages, identified things, became unequivocal. She felt that if she knew their workings, confusion could be limited, narrowed to the process of controlling more and more words this way, a source of wisdom. Musumbi had told her, "I must learn to read," explaining that once he did, his book would become more than pictures hinting at the truth. There would be names.

Esther, roused from the sickness she had induced by swallowing those leaves, had been once again to the hospital. When the nurse gave her the admission cards, she said, "Can you write your signature?" To which Esther had nodded yes, and then had retreated to shame in the face of the pen she was handed. "Oh, no, I can't write," she almost wept. Because her letters, she knew, were too big and sprawling to fit there on that small line. So the nurse had written it for her, the name, in characters that flowed together. Esther had waited tending the card with the *E*'s and *R*'s. What would she say to her doctor then, except, I am still not well? A feeling, not a place that hurt. Pain in the heart.

But when her turn finally came, she was taken to an African doctor, a man not *her* doctor at all. Not the one she wanted to see. "Where is the other doctor, the memsaab doctor?" she asked him.

He only laughed, saying, "You like her, that white one?" She refused to tell him what was wrong. He held the X-ray to

83

the window, he read from papers the nurse had given him. When he touched her his hands were hard, pressing under her ears. He looked in her throat. She was embarrassed, kept her face away from him. It made him angry. He told her she was wasting their time, and scolded, saying she should return to her village.

"Yes, yes," she said. She counted her bracelets without using numbers and told him *yes*.

"But where is the white memsaab doctor?" she asked the matron, who was busy carrying little jars. She tried to peer inside the other rooms. The other patients crowded.

"She is busy in surgery." A voice over a shoulder. She was pushed against the wall looking at a man in a chair with wheels: his feet were wrapped in rags.

Zobetta was watching Esther write. She herself had a writing book with pictures of animals and the letters *p-a-k-a*, which was cat.

Esther wasn't interested, found the letters of her own name more satisfying. Zobetta showed her the letter *Z*, which started, she said, the name Zobetta, an *O* that fell inside it. They lingered, thinking, until close by, they heard the sound of Sharad's motorbike and Zobetta's daughters shouting, "Sharad! Sharad!" telling everyone what was known.

He brought them rice—against the law—in a twelve-kilo bag, from the hiding places of the Hindis.

"Do you love Hadija?" the little girls asked him. Chiku pulled on his arm. He was standing, making *namaste* by way of greeting, pressing his hands together and touching his fingertips to his forehead. His lips were red from chewing *pan*. His breath was savory, filling the room. The little ones were climbing against his legs as Hadija slid along the hall wrapped in a cloth he had given her: only her face showed and a blue color she had painted on her eyes, a little red dot on her head like a Hindi girl so they were all laughing. She knew words in his language: "*aaaacha*," she said "*teeeeek*." Sharad's belly made a little ridge over his belt. His hair was shining. He had beautiful eyes with long lashes.

"Gold Feeenger!" Hadija shouted, popping out of the cloth to dance in her mini. And then they were gone.

"He is a Hindi," Zobetta was saying. "His mummy and

daddy will make him marry a Hindi. Tssssss," she complained, "those who break stones with other people's teeth, don't know how much pain there can be."

Esther kept her concentration for letters that day—"I will learn it," she told Zobetta, "how the letters go along and along to make my name." Zobetta leaned close to the paper as if she could smell it.

"If one can learn . . . " she sighed.

"Then I will find a place, for example as a nurse, helper to the memsaab doctor." Zobetta had to admit it was a good idea, even possible. She rocked, holding a baby in the pillow of her chest. Everyone had been astonished that day when the white memsaab walked straight through Mikorosheni and into Zobetta's house. Following Hadija. Everyone had stared (if they had windows to look out). Mr. Ntiro had spoken a greeting and been answered. He had been wearing his necktie that day and stepped right out, as if by chance, into her path.

"To see *my* Esta!" Zobetta boasted.

So disappointing after that to wait at the hospital and face a different doctor in the end. She had seen the sick ones all around her, pulled to them by love and horror. When she saw this suffering, she understood more about Musumbi, what he had known. It was as though he, himself, had shaken her and said, "Look, Esta, see them, see what it is . . . " Perhaps she had been too young before, too close to him hanging to his hand. But she felt it now, those poor ones, waiting, waiting in that corridor and under the trees. A woman said, "My baby . . . " and opened her *kanga* cloth. "He is passing blood." Esther had seen nothing but a cinder there, a dark ash. And she ran from them. It was a moment that troubled her, a strange sensation that lingered in her heart and hands long after she left the sight of that child—to hold him, to stroke him, to burn away with him. If she were a witch?

She was the one who had seen the trouble spread out everywhere like the frogs from Mrs. Manda jumping into the forest, transformed into poison mist. She had watched it roll along the side of the hills morning after morning though it never brought rain to clean the evil away. People noticed that the animals were getting sick. Chickens began to die. Every night there were dry storms and lightning that started fires streaming from the trees. *Shetani* fires that flew out like balls. There were fevers all around. Mama Izak's baby was born dead. She lay on her mat staring at nothing, moaning and weeping. And Esther saw, once again, the tarnish of blood on her leg, then a little more, redder this time like real blood, like something wishing to be released. That was when Musumbi sent a sign—a bright dream, the great white owl standing on her mat. As if flying were possible. In the morning she wondered if she had been awake when she saw it.

She told Sara, "I will take Mama Izak's eggs down to Sameh and sell them in the market." Twenty-five eggs cushioned in grass like a nest riding on her head. She tied a thickness of cloth between her legs, the way you did on a baby. And she wore her shoes. All the way down she felt herself seeping into the dry cloth, afraid she would be revealed. Her walk was hindered by the small steps, legs that rubbed; her feet got sore. She saw the market below her hidden in the dust like wishing and an echo of it pounding in her ears.

Kneeling close to a woman who had tomatoes and gave her tea, Esther sold the eggs, one shilling each. Together with her savings it made her rich. In the afternoon she bought a small plastic purse and walked, carrying it, to show she was not afraid.

Events arose. Their meaning offered signs to her. Boys, for example, poking the belly of a dead dog with sharp sticks until it exploded and the flies that covered it swarmed about her head. She batted them from her eyes and ran. There was an old Kwavi woman who held her wrist and shouted though Esther couldn't understand a word. Still more Kwavi came to surround her, peering, listening, their faces hovering over chokers made of beads, the hoops and dangles of their earrings. Laughing. Then the crowd broke away, and the old Kwavi woman, ranting, scattered the crows. Esther saw a circle of people and in the middle a man and a sick baby who was vomiting worms. She pressed closer to see them, wanting to help, to use plants as her father had done, but she didn't know how. And who would believe her, who would let her try, a small girl all alone? But she felt how it would be to soothe, to ease, to care for the child. All these things were flags that authorized her escape, to run from pollution and capture, from the madness of the Pareh. To travel as Musumbi had done, to look for her place in the shadowy marks on the horizon, clusters of village roofs spread over a distant hill, the rising smoke of cookfires in a valley, or herds drifting on the plains. Always over there. Always far away. Something better than what you had. She knew that if the Pareh had circumcised her, she would have been captured like a bird in a cage. If they had cut her, she would have become one of them and would never be able to leave.

At night when it became dark, the empty market was her refuge. She hid from soldiers and policemen, who might beat her or ask questions, under a stall behind bags of potatoes that smelled like dry leaves. After everyone had gone and the gate was locked, she could see policemen walking around, passing at an interval, drinking beer. Mice and rats came from their hiding places. She had to stay very still even as they ran across her body. Their sharp feet pricked at her and their long tails felt wet as though they were leaving their urine on her. She rolled herself into a tight ball against contamination; afraid if rats made water on her face, she would go blind. She withdrew tightly into herself, a striving collapse. More than her being was in retreat—her hair was crushed against her knees, her menstrual blood was a warm thickness held inside—until the changing light came softly like clouds. Then there was the sound of unlocking gates. Voices collecting, grown louder in the dust. She took the change and stood up brushing off, carrying the purse. She walked outside and saw the bus, paid her fare, and slept there in a seat not knowing where she would go.

The city appeared as Musumbi had described. —"First you will see clouds like mountains themselves. These will tell you you are reaching the sea." The roads began to break apart until there were many, like branches of trees. Esther saw cardboard houses set in deep ravines, the rusting roofs of tin and then the same shapes echoing, grown bigger, the permanence of stone and cement. Whatever little she had understood about geometry took dramatic form in these big buildings. At once she became aware of architecture, the power and heaviness of manmade shelters, of messages conveyed by materials—brick, stone, cement, patterns made of blocks. There was a wealth of windows. She noticed stairs. Thick timbers and beams instead of slender poles. Instead of feathery dry grasses, she saw the pressing weight of tiles on roofs. She was surprised by paint. By colors meant for flowers and cloths fixed densely to the rising walls.

Climbing down from the bus, she was caught in the continued rush of angles. An array of doorways. Men stacking crates on platforms. Everything gave way to something else, spreading out or gathering. Cars met here, trucks came together like voices shouting. And their horns! Esther felt the numb pleasure of someone who is trusting fate, the surrender of expectation. Her existence as she ventured out was an invitation, a desire for everything. Images registered, but there was no recall: she let them come, things she had never seen before or seen just briefly outside of understanding. Indian women: always seated in their cars or behind the counters of their shops. (Did they have legs under their bunching clothes?) Now close as breath to them, strange details were the only marks of distance: a glittering thread of gold woven through a sari, a sparkling red stone against a nostril, bright wet lips, smudged eyes, an arm of bangles to the elbow. There was brown skin folding in a midriff. A long black braid. And who were the African women in the black capes and hoods? Who were the men in the long white robes and small caps? Esther was too interested to be worried or afraid.

Right away she realized there would always be someone to follow even if she should happen to reverse and go the other way, a riddle that she took to be an advantage. Because there were so many people, strangers, all moving. And she was anonymous enough to turn and wander aimlessly, making the headway she needed against her doubt. Without knowing, she walked in circles (not one doorway, not one kiosk seemed the same) until a group of Kwavi women selling medicines became her sudden anchor—oh, I have been here, past these ones before—and she lingered near them, reaching for a bottle of black oil.

The woman pulled it away, hunkering there, swirling collars of beads, her coiled armband, her metal anklets. Esther could go on without direction now, working her way back to them until she could take her place among them up against the wall, her plastic purse tucked under her arm. She ate her supper with them, a cob of roasted maize and paper cones of groundnuts. The Kwavi, noticing her, offered tea in a tin can, a piece of cardboard for a bed. She was not prepared for the streetlights or the dying of the town, as though it simply blew away, fading like mist drawn off by the moon, the great buildings massing in the dark.

Morning framed her dilemma in the rumbling sounds of shutters thrown open on shops and the anxious faces of the Kwavi who had no houses. They were around her talking, jabbering like chickens. She understood they wondered who she was, but they had no real way to speak to her. She told them, "No mummy, no baba," shaking her head, opening her arms, hoping they would understand as they pecked around her, laughing, in their blue capes.

Her purpose had a rigid form that day, unlike the calm surrender of the day before. Instinct and the thrust of traffic, cars and buses and people moving under headloads, drew her into a sprawling marketplace where she walked through open aisles among stacks of carrots, curling pumpkin leaves, heaps of cassava root. She passed the pyramids of beans, the small green Hindi dals, dried yellow peas, the broad flat red *maharagwe*; bins of loose black tea leaves, of crushed tobacco. These were familiar textures that encouraged her, inching toward a gleaming bank of limes and standing for a moment to listen carefully to something caught in midair, a woman's voice, calling to her children, speaking in Esther's own language like a rush of assurance, like a hand placed around hers.

She stayed close and listened until she located the source, a woman bent arranging cassava root, four-four pieces to sell, a shilling a pile. There were two children. The mother's hands were busy breaking bananas into theirs. And then another tiny face appeared tucked behind a falling stack of potatoes and the mother, swooping down, gathered it up, attached it to her breast. Esther reached the end of the aisle but turned back, speaking to the little girls, first a greeting and then a story about a rabbit and his wife and a trick the rascals played on an elephant. They were huddled there like two small friends, when the other one, running to join them, knocked into the cassava and Esther, leaning to help reassemble the piles, found a way to speak to the mother in the language they both shared. That she was an orphan. That she ran away from the terrible things that could happen among Pareh people. The woman was laughing—"They are not people," she said. "And their witches—very strong."

Her name was Cheupe. She had no husband but was like a man herself. She astonished Esther, being able to fight against men whom she often chased from her house with sticks. Her color would turn red then and shining like the skin of onions, her hair bursting. She made wonderful sounds like horns. Esther calmed her with soft words and cups of tea or sweet fried cakes, totally absorbed in her but wary of her rages (a woman who could beat a man!). Full of admiration, Esther practiced walking, talking, acting like Cheupe. She sprinkled hot pepper on her food. She drank beer. She smoked cigarettes.

Cheupe had many boyfriends. One of them called Mwema had a car that knocked and clanged three floors below them in the parking spaces, doors held on by wires and no window glass on the sides. In the rain they covered it with plastic bags. He gave Cheupe small tins of margarine that no one else knew how to get. Sometimes they would all go in Mwema's car (huddled together against the wind) to sit outside at night along a fence and watch moving pictures in the sky. Here they saw white men and women kissing or Chinese men smashing at windows with their fists, leaping onto trains and out of buildings. They saw men riding horses and shooting guns. These were cowboys who lived in America. They saw the man known as James Bond. To watch those images, the moving figures, the moving mouths, to see inside their buildings by way of cameras (Mwema said)—"That was an elevator rising through a great building on a wire." (He took Esther downtown one day and showed her the same thing.) To think of all the wonders and the world. To taste the sweetness of chewing gum and Coca-Cola.

It was a time for happiness. Esther slept and woke each morning in a room dense with children. She was the one who got up first. Standing on the cement floor, she felt a coolness on her feet like cleansing. She moved among the sleeping

forms in quietness and felt, once more, her love grow.
Mornings gave her the clarity of usefulness, a way to
salvation. Outside, on the landing, among the other tenants,
she would light the kerosene stove to boil tea. She would slice
the bread and look for jam or scrape the last bit of
margarine. A small girl, Bemba, from upstairs was always
there nearby ready to take the empty tins. Her hands and
feet were covered with spreading warts: she moved in
limping painful steps. Smells of stale medicine reached out.

Esther would give her the empty tin and then run
downstairs—views of streets and rooftops flickered and fell
into the town—to where a man sold milk in the parking lot,
from the basket of his bicycle, an illegal thing to do.
Sometimes he would be arrested and the police would drag
him off to jail, leaving the bicycle for the tenants to keep in
safety so he could start his business again when he returned.
And up again, stairs building a rising pattern of iron back
and forth against themselves. Past Bemba, who had water in
her tin by now, who moved aside, a silent jump into the
shadows turned to isolation—"If you touch her, you will get
this." People burned the things the small girl touched.

Everyone was awake. Folding up their beds, setting out
their tables. Things were collected behind the curtained
doorways. Esther heard the sounds of glasses and spoons.
But the milk was bad, curdling now into the pots of tea. They
were all out on the landings complaining—"This milk!"
Esther tested it and saw a bluish trickle, something watery go
in her cup. "All bad," the voices shout. *Yote. Yote.* They began
to hurl the cartons, streams of ruined tea slapping against
the ground. She almost thought the building would topple
as they leaned. They raged, running down the stairs after
the one who rushed off on his bicycle. "And the price!" they
called, "*Too high!*" If they could catch him, only catch him
and his bicycle. Already cats had come to lick at the sour
milky sludge that filled a ditch down there and at the broken
cartons everywhere.

If they suspected rain, the tenants set out basins in rows
among the parking spaces and afterward ran down to wash
their babies or their clothes. Esther took Cheupe's children
and made great sudsing lathers, dangling them by their arms
until they kicked out and cried joy. One day she took the

little Bemba and bathed her, too. The other women watched
this, standing back as if a devil had arrived. The little girl was
so dirty and covered with dark pastes from the *waganga*. "It
can catch you this—" the women said. Esther felt the disease
before she touched the child's skin, a rough pricking at her
palms. But the water soothed the space between them, made
it easy and cool. The poor skin seemed to drink, to suck it
from her palm. Afterward, drying her with a cloth, Esther
was drawn strangely to the flesh, to each toe, each finger, to
the sore palms and wrists where the warts began to grow up
the thin arm. What was it? A memory of ash and the white
owl, and suddenly an image of the child's pure smooth skin
restored. The others were staring and then began to call out
their fears, afraid of the basin, of the vile water. Esther told
them, "You are all fools." Which only made her want it more,
to take the child by the hand and walk away with her. See, I
am safe. There is no djinn. The rain went on and on and
then no one could get the clothes dry. There was laundry
hanging in the landings up and down, across the rooms in
pieces so that she felt the world was tearing, shredding apart.
When the sun finally came out, they all ran to drape the wet
clothes out windows or on the fences that surrounded them.
Children began to march along the edge of the ravine with
tin-can drums. One of them brought a baby dog and walked
it on a string like an Englishman. Men with shovels arrived
and dug sand from the marsh to heap into the back of trucks.

The third floor gave Esther opportunities to look at
everything, to gain a sense of timing and where everyone
was. She leaned there on her elbows waiting. Cheupe would
soon finish loading her vegetables in Mwema's car and
would drive it herself to the market. There was a radio
playing somewhere near. Esther had made a decision, more
like a plan, because she had noticed that the trouble on
Bemba's hands and feet was smaller, drier, the result of the
bath and Esther's hands.

Hiding in Cheupe's room she stood the child once again
in the basin—"The *waganga* and their dirt!"—She looked at
the water chopping as she cupped hands full of it against the
child. As if wind or current had stirred it. Esther's breath
was steady, her heart quick in case someone might come. But
as she felt the water cooling everything, her eyes shut and

her heart calmed. There was still the radio and the wash of music as soothing as a rain. Esther was drifting on it as if she imagined the outer world had gone. In the child's body which she held firmly there was something different now, a shape held against the quivering lids of her closed eyes, a pulsing that her hands explored. A realization.

Cheupe had Masai blood, which Mwema said explained her habit of wandering and her love of beer. It could be seen in her red skin tones, in the long face, the teeth spaced apart. Esther watched her at night put on dresses that had short skirts and shoes that had high heels, knowing she made changes inside herself as quick and deliberate as different clothes. She sometimes looked for anger when there was none and broke things for no reason despite the warnings of bad luck and broken glass. "These are *my* things to break," she said. When she got drunk and stayed away for days, Esther and the children waited and touched the edges of hunger. Mwema would come with a bag of maize meal when he heard that Cheupe was caught by the police and put in jail. When they let her out, she came raging up the stairway ready to break more glass and beat her way through Esther to her children until, at last, she would cry, weeping in her room among the piles of worn-down dresses and plastic flowers for her hair. These were the times Esther went to her with sweet tea and soft words, times she had seen the bruised mouth and blackened eyes, signs of the police. Acting this way made Esther alert, a demonstration of her fidelity. Anger like Cheupe's and contagion merged in her mind. She believed that Cheupe had a sickness. Her love developed, deepened by alarm, and her watchfulness, too. It was like the fearful premonition of loss she had come to feel with Musumbi, a kind of jealous intensity against his talking, talking, talking and the sudden awful silences that were taking him away from her. A need to take his hand and bring him things, to ask him, "What will become of you? And then of me?"

The room was full of boxes all packed and stored with extra things to use for guests—blue teacups, four of them with saucers emerging from crumples of newspaper. There were such a lot of small bowls and spoons. And the broken things Cheupe bought because she thought there would be ways to repair them—an electric iron and electric kettle, a tiny box that made a flame for lighting cigarettes if you put something like kerosene inside it. If you could find it in a shop. They would sit, the two of them, looking through the boxes. When Mwema came, he brought them sweets from the Hindi restaurant where he worked, or jars of curdmilk or chapatti breads. Esther walked outside after eating such good food and tramped the landings checking on the safety of the children. Or ran down if she heard them calling "Esta! Esta!" when they wanted to go along the road to look at trains or the men digging sand. Sometimes she just sat in the parking spaces where there were seats taken from abandoned cars to make a meeting place and women gathered to embroider tablecloths and bed covers until it was dark. Threads flickered there over gardens of stitched flowers and wild birds. The women gossiped, agreed or disagreed, with their sucking, clicking tongues. Once a month white nuns from a Roman church came and bought the finished embroideries and sent them to a place called Belgium. These were the rhythms of her days. But watching Bemba, clear of her disease now, she felt the shadows of premonition.

It was Cheupe's Masai grandfather, Mwema said, that made her like to wander. Once she was gone for ten days and on the eleventh Mwema came and said the police had made a case and were going to send her and her babies away, back to her own village. Out on the old car seats everyone told Esther it was what they called "revolution" (Musumbi had explained it once as a kind of freedom), but it seemed to have more to do with policemen and soldiers who came in trucks. People were willing to agree to revolution, still wondering what it was. A confusion of words and ideas. You could really only learn about it in school, they said. Once university students came and gathered at the same car seats in order to explain, telling everyone how to place the blame. It meant there were foreigners who were rich, which made the Africans poor. An evil situation. There was the business of government that knew how to give everyone shoes and medicine although it would take time. The students gave out papers with drawings because no one could read. But the drawings made no sense either—once there were cows and arrows pointing at hands that floated with no bodies attached. A picture of a flag with a cross over it. A smiling face. Farm tools hanging in the air.

The meaning, Mwema told her, "is that if the police find you, Esta, they will return you to your husband's village." She cried for them for days and nights on a cot in Mwema's room behind the hotel. How they had been scooped up, all the things in boxes strapped on an army truck, men who held Cheupe's wrists, the wailing babies. She couldn't eat. She was no more than a rag Mwema dragged, holding it in the direction of a white face, a door of shining wood, a house someplace with banks of windows and many roofs. A man, Ignatius, Mwema's friend, was talking to a French memsaab saying Esther was his sister who needed work, could certainly be the one to do the laundry. He said their mother had died in the village and that he was left to care for this poor one here. Esther was positioned, told to stand outside the door and appear sad. She looked at her feet (in the bright black shoes now too tight) while Ignatius talked to the woman, a shadow behind a screen. Her shoulders were bare, and her legs. All in English, which Esther didn't understand, voices that were pushing up against each other, more the woman's than the black man's. She seemed ready to turn away, to leave them, but Ignatius opened the screen: he made her look. There was paleness of skin, a covering on her head, long nails and rings. Esther could tell from the way he spoke that he knew how to hold onto the woman. He seemed to beg her. The voices climbed as if a tree, she heard the steady rising of words making an arrangement. Then he was smiling, nodding, saying "Thank you, thank you, memsaab."

"If you will do it perfectly," he told her later. He showed her how to put the dark clothes in one pile and the light ones in another. In a tub in perfumed soap, she stamped them with her feet to make them clean, then rinsed the suds and hung them to dry. Before the end of each day she ironed them with an electric iron like the one Cheupe had, using heat that came up through the wires.

Washing clothes for the French people, Esther went on

learning. In addition to their elaborate ways, they themselves were hard to predict. You never knew what made them angry or how they got their pleasure, emotions that revolved around their food.

"The French eat terrible things," Ignatius told her. He was their cook. "And late at night, too, like Moslems during Ramadan. This," he said, "is the reason they remain skinny and speak through their noses." Esther, herself, had witnessed the preparation of frog legs and snails. And they had a way of saving wine in bottles for many years until it became precious and a source of great happiness (if it was still good) or anger (if it had spoiled). They kept it in air-conditioned rooms with coats made of animal fur.

Esther tried to understand them from the things they threw away and from the clothes she washed each day, which they wore in layers like insect wings: clothes worn at night to sleep in, clothes worn for going in the sea and for dancing and for playing the game called tennis. She suspected they were somehow favored by God because they lived lives that were sturdier, ordered, out of danger, in houses that couldn't fall down or burn, in rooms that were full of chairs and tables.

At first Esther didn't want to do it, pad softly through that big house each morning to the basket of clothes. There was a confusion of rooms that all had cold air blown into them. Sometimes the sight of the French memsaab gazing at a book and holding a cup of coffee would stiffen Esther's bones. They would share their eyes, words of greetings. Esther was always aware of the woman's legs, her feet, her painted toenails. She wore clothes that floated around her or otherwise were tight to her body, pants pulled across her hips, swimming clothes that covered her two breasts and her crotch and nothing more, as she stretched out in the sun to make her skin color change. These wild activities supplied an element of humor. Sometimes at night there would be shouting and a series of lights flickering through rooms. Objects crashed: once something came hurling through a window from above. A jar of flowers. Then silence. These things flew because, Ignatius guessed, the memsaab had played the bwana's phonograph records and put them in the wrong cases. That particular day a record had been left on a windowsill and had melted in the sun.

Music from the phonograph came outside to reach them. Solomon, the gardener, put old chairs behind the carport where they could go to sit and listen. The sounds of it were swollen, not like music at all but something more, like their food or clothes, a complication. It surrounded you like water or like sleep. They couldn't sing or dance to it. Its purpose was a puzzle, deeper than anything the Frenchmen themselves could reveal in the way they lived. Esther had seen one of the records and touched it, music pressed into a flat black disk, an easy thing to break. She had found it in the trash and taken it to show the others. Ignatius told how the music was stored by electricity as words would be printed on paper with ink. The machine put its own electricity out and found the music with a pin. The thing looked smooth, but when you touched it you felt the tiny scratches that contained the miracle of sound.

"Too many things—" Solomon said. He thought the story Ignatius told was a joke and held the disk to the light. Worse was the radio Ignatius had that played music from a little box that slipped in and out. "With no pin? Explain that." Solomon asked. But there was no explanation. It was something: there was a button to push. The answer didn't matter.

Solomon's son Francis liked the French music. It was possible to sit with him and listen, in the chairs behind the carport. Esther and Francis became sweethearts there, among the hidden details of the night—shadows moving behind the lattice, a vine of white flowers opening to the moon. Behind a hedge that closed the quarters out of sight, beyond the cookfire of Ignatius's wife, there were the dwindling noises of the house and its servants, the last cups of tea, the last glasses being washed, lights dimming in the kitchen, a smell of insect spray, and the Frenchman's music coming from within, from a room filled with books and padded chairs. Someone, the night guard, passed very near against the lovers' hush, against a hand on her hand like a leaf that had fallen.

Esther had seen Francis on the very first day as she stood by the kitchen door looking at her shoes. A student, he had been reading a book and this impressed her. He was sitting on a low stool.

"Do you go to school?" she asked him. He only nodded.

She leaned against a tree eating a mango Mwema had given her when he said good-bye. Ignatius walked near them with a bowl of food left over from the French to take to his wife. A warm smell of onion passed between them. She made a face. "Do you eat that French food?" she asked the boy.

"Sometimes," he said. "You have to put a lot of salt." He seemed to be fixed to the spot. Later she brought him a piece of cake Ignatius made using old bananas, a delicious thing of sweetness that she wanted to share. If she could make him be her friend! He took it, but they didn't talk. When they finished eating she went to her room to rest there on a bed. She could just see him as he stood. He pulled his leg from under the table like a heavy stick and rose to balance on it, tipping to hold the chair. Then he arranged himself so he could walk, a sequence that stilled her—her breath sucked in—she saw him turn, looking toward her room. She closed her eyes, a thud beat against her heart until she knew he was gone.

After that she made up a game and would wait, here or there, until he was in place, and only then would she appear, so he would never feel the shame and she would never have to watch: she felt such pain. But sometimes angled toward a high window, suds curling and puffing at her ankles, she watched him. What was wrong?

She tried to find out everything there was to know. "I had a fever," he told her. "A sickness called polio. You can die." But he didn't tell her where it came from or why. With him she discovered that the ugly ways of Josephat could be transformed, purified. Sara's prophecy, the songs of women about their lovers, a kind of love that conquers you. Esther couldn't believe them when they told her—no, the bruising painful things, the horrible dangling pieces of her husband. Couldn't believe them until with all her skin against the young boy's, she marveled.

Cruel or gentle, the hands that touched her always found their balance in her heart. She understood then the sadness that had split Cheupe and that rolled inside her father. "We are only men," Musumbi had said, while she suddenly knew that he had wanted to be more. And when Francis touched her, she might wince remembering the fat old man until she felt the difference there that was love.

Esther went again to the hospital, this time walking by the sea through the smell of rocks exposed to sun and turned to land, substance where there had been none, a daily process that unlocked pictures in her mind to think of everything like those rocks covered by water or streams of light or even darkness, dreams that could be revealed in the way their long weeds hung like ropes. She was suspicious of the small dread creatures that walked about when the sea rolled back. At the same time, entranced, she had touched dark slimy pods or bright red stars that had their eyes and mouths underneath, even as Hadija screamed and ran. If she could do that, could stand exposed this way and make her doctor see she wanted to be taught—no more than that, an act of love. She wore a cloth from Zobetta with great flowers the color of limes and cashew nuts set in circles of dark green, hoping this would make it clear, as bees were drawn to things of brightness. She could have stood in the door where patients waited but instead she went to a nearby hill, under a flame tree, so that she could look down into the yard. She reached over her head and picked a long dark pod of seeds holding it to her lips, a shape that, like the sick ones stalled below her, could inspire fear, a world where nothing could be trusted.

The sight of the doctor would convince her that there were no witches and no magic, that everything was sea rock waiting to be known, as if Musumbi were alive and talking to her. She saw her then, a white dress and a pale face looking up. For a moment they were one. Esther started from her perch feeling the air lift into her cloth, the edge of it dragging as she pulled it over her, her head tipped down, to raise her arm in greeting and look up, heart beating, to see her prayer unanswered and the one she loved, gone. Now there was just a bright shape moving too fast, her red-colored hair, a struck match, and then nothing but dust that could have been smoke. She was left wondering how she could make the doctor know.

SEVEN

◁ ◇ ▷

It was an American Negro who held Esther's hand. He led her down a hallway that smelled like boiled potatoes and perfumes. In his small room there were photograph pictures on a cabinet, even more on a table. Smiling everywhere. He gave her, as they had agreed, a pair of blue jeans and, because they had smoked *bhangi* and were thirsty, a Coca-Cola taken from a box of ice. Downstairs in the party, there had been a disco and shining lights. They drank beer from tins while pictures of Bob Marley and Jimmy Cliff flashed on the wall. Hadija, shouting "Wild man!" sliced through the boys as she danced. Later she stood up on a table wearing something different, a big white shirt with words printed. The lights chopped her in small pieces, a vision that disturbed Esther, made her feel sick.

Trying to smile, Esther had known from the start she didn't want to be here, to play sex again, for money or for anything. She breathed the anticipation of shame; under the new hair that had grown back over the missing parts and the pain, was the sign of her ruin, scars over her legs. Even those inside, growing under her skin. A bus had sped the two girls to town as if traveling all the streets they had ever seen before. The clouds over the sea reminded her of mountains like the Pareh. Even as she and Hadija waited for the Americans at a hotel that smelled of Hindi food, she kept saying, "No-no, I don't want to."

"They are only Americans," Hadija assured her. Because they were like little boys. Marines, a type of soldier that guarded doors in embassies. They ran along in the

100

mornings: their chests, their legs, the white ones turning red, and the Negroes, very tall, turning black like Africans. Hadija said it was this running that kept them polite, being noisy in public but so quiet when they were alone. After sex they mostly wanted to make sure a girl was happy.—"Did you like that? Was that good?"—Still, Esther was afraid though it was more like shame. Hadija was angry, called her a fool, asked her where she would get money for her tea.

His name was Gregory. He wore short pants for swimming so Esther saw his legs shaped like bottles and as hard and shining as glass. His shoulders were wide but his walk, that came from his toes, told her he would be light in sex. His eyes were slanted: his skin brown like a Hindi's. He had a white man's nose. Esther wanted to believe that his fingers, barely touching hers, were signals of a gentleness within. In his room, the disco was a distant humming; the executing flashing lights were a blur left behind her eyes, almost forgotten. They were sitting on the edge of his bed looking at their knees. Somehow the pictures reassured her: she saw a baby, an old woman in a chair. He noticed she was looking at them and stood to pull them down to show her.

"My mother," he was laughing: "and this, my brother, Sid. His baby," trying some Swahili, "*mtoto wa ndugu yangu. Did I say that right? Sawa-sawa?*"

She said, "*Mzuri,*" knowing he would understand.

"This is me—uh, *mimi*—uh, *katika shule,* you know, at school. You know basketball? *Mpira?*" He ran around the room. A kind of dance, playing with a ball that wasn't there, showing how to throw it.

"Yes, yes, *mpira,*" she said and then she was crying, pouring and couldn't stop. Because she saw his goodness and the burning of her own shame.

"Say what?" He was coming to her. "Hey . . . you afraid? *Unaogopa?* Shit, don't be afraid. Hey, come on now," stroking her head then. "Hey now, hey, shit, come on now," he was saying.

Trying to tell him, she spoke Swahili, slowly, hoping he would understand. The detached words that he himself had used floated in the air like chances to reach him. He listened. She held the blue jeans back to him, but he pushed them back, shaking his head, "You okay now? *Mzuri?* You *sawa-sawa?*" He pressed the blue jeans into her arms. He held her hand.

At home, Zobetta brought her tea. "So the fire you kindled," she said, "burned your own hand."

Esther sobbed, "Where can we go for safety? Myself, I wish I was born a Kwavi or a Masai so I could wander. That is freedom. If I could make my own house and put my children in it, I would take off these fool clothes and wear African's clothes." Because the new blue jeans thrown on her floor made it seem that she was either lost or trapped. They were the cause of it or the blame, making it seem that she was nothing at all. She had no way to live. No one did. Not even Zobetta, who knew it most of all. They were all gathered in Mikorosheni, she thought, around catastrophe, living in danger, against the law, with broken, foreign things.

Just that week a house had caught fire, someone, a child, had knocked over an oil lamp. Everyone had rushed in to save them but it was too late: the house was sticks and cardboard and had already burned. People screamed, calling for water, but nothing could stop the fire. The woman who lived there had five babies inside and they all burned. Mr. Ntiro ran to find a taxi. At the hospital two of the babies died. They saw the woman still sitting by the ashes crying everyday. "Because we don't have electricity," Esther told Zobetta. "Because our houses aren't made of stones and cement. I wish there were no lamps. The Masai have no lamps. They don't have kerosene. They don't have cars which only kill people. They are the ones who are safer than we are."

Hadija did not agree. She wanted, she said, "To get down and boogie." She was putting on the blue jeans, as stiff as they were, easing the zipper with her groaning, her beaded hair like fire sparks. The man that lived next to them had almost killed his wife in a beating the night before. Her son, a big boy, had to jump between them to save his mother. She was swollen from the blows. Hadija said that soon the boy who saved his mother would start beating his own wife. For this reason, she was strutting, wagging her solid bottom: she had finished with Africans completely.

Sometimes Esther wished it would all wash away—a great flooding, an angry God and an old man with a boat. Animals saved in pairs, mothers and fathers, a story Francis read to her from his Bible. She concluded that God was still angry at Africans who were a flood against themselves: soldiers in trucks, police with clubs, ministers who stole. Going with Musumbi across the Kwavis' country, they had seen fires like small glass beads in the sun, a beautiful sight along the ridge, a necklace to the hills. But later, seeing what had happened, it was different. People were crying and holding their windows so they could build new houses someplace else as the soldiers ordered them, forcing them by burning down their villages. Divine wrath was the only explanation, a way to punish, a way to cleanse.

She believed in God. Especially Jesus. Images: she saw the pictures of Him on the cross, killed because He showed His goodness to the world by touching the sick people and making them well. He was pure love that poured, she imagined, from His hands and His heart. She had seen a picture of that heart shining like the sun. Pictures of Him touching lepers, the lame (like Francis), the blind. Who would want to kill such a man? The question raged. Francis had no answer, and neither did any of his teachers when he asked, except to say it had been written, which meant, Francis said, it simply had to be, an offering, a purification of evil, though this reason contained, for her, an obscure message, a story that hadn't finished yet, one that seemed to return to itself in hope as well as despair. Because evil was not gone. The sacrifice was empty. The glory still a promise.

She could have learned so much from Francis. They stuck for hours to his books. He taught her letters. Explained the diagrams and pictures. Explained the numbers. How did it happen that the French were suddenly forced to leave the country? Ignatius said that presidents were fighting like women in the market fight over chickens. —"The drumming of small boys," he said, "never stops." So she sat with Francis in the carport and watched men who came and packed things: each glass, each bowl wrapped in paper. Ignatius counted seventy-four cartons. After it was over, the French memsaab looked smaller, skinnier, in the empty house. In her short pants, her legs were sticks. She and her French husband were like pale insects when the night came, flashing against their walls, shadows and wings, pinched wasps. They had no music now. Their wine was gone. Their house was filled with scraps of paper and dust.

The memsaab put her old things in a box and brought it out to everyone in the quarters—money in envelopes, saying, *"merci."* Shyly, Esther picked out what she wanted, a dress with butterflies and flowers, buttons in a plastic bag, a nightgown of torn lace. She took a chipped teacup, a small kitchen knife. Later, crying tears, Francis wanted to give her his radio. On the rocks near the sea, it had seemed there could be no changes like this, but now, without curtains in the windows, the Frenchman's house blared the end of their love.

Friends came to visit the French, filling the spaces with echoes. The servants put their things in cartons, too, (Ignatius counted three of his own)—a way of measuring the difference that became a joke. Their black faces hung in the shadowy doors of their small rooms as they watched the white ones floating in the empty rooms, in the glare of uncovered bulbs, passing like their French words through the air.

Mwema was her bridge over the changes in her life. He stood against a counter where Hindi cookings were piled up and the afternoon was smoking oil: a kitchen where Africans carried food on trays. Esther heard the sound of knives chopping, smelled the little seeds these brown men ground up and ate. A fat face belonged to Mr. Waliji, behind a mustache and a glass of yellow juice. People who knew ways of taking juice from everything, who ate things that she never dreamed of.

Mwema was saying, "She is my sister . . ."

"You have how many of these sisters?" Mr. Waliji was laughing. He scratched his belly.

"You know," Mwema smiled, "we can say sister . . ."

"Yes-yes," the Hindi waved because there was a stack of samosas coming out. Waliji gave one to Esther. "Take it. Take it," saying, "What kind of work do you do?"

She answered, "Washing clothes."

Mwema added, "She knows *everything.*"

"Everything?" Waliji said. He stopped to shout over his

shoulder at the men behind him, his hand reached into a bowl of cut-up limes. "Go on, child . . . put some . . ." he told Esther. "Do you know cleaning houses?"

"Yes," she answered.

"French people, was it?" He was laughing, suspecting a lie, holding out his belt. But Esther had a certificate, written on paper and folded into an envelope, which proved it all. Which said she didn't steal things.

Before she went to work at Waliji's house, Mwema had warned, "The Hindis will beat you." But they didn't. The worst was an old grandmother who made screeching sounds at her as she worked in the kitchen chopping up their vegetables. They never touched meat, so each day she cleaned and chopped, cleaned and chopped, things she thought would kill a person. Mr. Waliji and his wife, Mrs. Nargis, carried the old grandmother to the kitchen to call out the instructions and to watch and make sure everything was done right and see that she never put one tiny little piece of their Hindi food in her mouth. If they gave her something, they were generous, "Take! Take!" Mrs. Nargis passed out sweet cakes in the afternoons. But if they thought she had stolen—they even made her leave the onion peelings on the table as a check, the tops of tomatoes—they would be yelling, taking money from her wages. It made Esther throw a bunch of carrots to the floor, raging, shouting back against the accusation, "Africans do not eat food that has not been cooked!" And the old one started to cry tears, saying, "Wash them! Wash them!" in her own language—"*safkaro, safkaro*"—like a poor hen, until Esther felt so sorry, kneeling there in the carrots because there were so many people to feed each day, so many different things, and the men with their terrible bellies and burpings. All day cutting and grinding, boiling and frying, sauces in little bowls, in the heat from their stoves, in the burning air of onions and peppers that hurt her eyes, all to be eaten so quickly she wondered why. And all that was left was Mr. Waliji and his brothers barefoot in their wide Hindi pants burping and smoking. And in the morning she had the toothpicks to sweep. And the ashes.

At their nighttime meal they were voices in another place like fighting birds in distant trees. Esther rolled and baked chapattis on an iron plate, outside because of the heat, running in with them, sometimes twenty or thirty in a single night. "Take! Take!" Mrs. Nargis told her when it was over, holding leftover food on a dish, perhaps eggplant, which Esther hated. Later, she would seek the silence of the night, out in the empty streets of the town, under a light, as the Hindi houses closed their shutters and the other African housegirls clattered their last dishes, put the next day's beans to soak. At night all the Africans who worked for Hindis came out and sat in doorways, talking, smoking cigarettes. Cooks and watchmen and their friends.

"Esta is so quiet and she is working so hard . . ." Mrs. Nargis sometimes gave her extra money in secret, ("Take! Take!") because Waliji would not agree to increase her pay. Even the old grandmother: "Esta, Esta, come. Come." A coin or two pressed into her palm because she was the one who braided the old one's long white hair and massaged her swollen feet. Stiff, folded in a white sari, she was all white except the dark circles under her eyes. She said that Esther's rubbing made her pain go away, chattering about it when the women gathered to cook. Esther could feel it when she touched her, even in the space around her, the stiff joints of her hands. Once when Esther looked she had seen a child sitting there, which frightened her. She ran away even though the old woman was calling.

There was always the heat she could draw off where the pain was. The old one stopped shouting at her. There was no anger left in her. "My husband . . . my husband," she tried to explain her trouble and sorrow. A mummy she left in India. These things made Esther sad; she held the old woman's hand as she wept. She put a few more coins into Esther's palm. In her bed, a corner of the storeroom behind the bags of rice and flour, Esther wanted to die from the sadness in her own life. She had to shield herself against loving or trusting them by smiles and obedience. Or else she made her hands busy; she focused her eyes on objects that were close or far away, so they could never know her. Because there was a suspicion that the differences she saw in their skins, in their faces and language and ways and food, were all clues to deep unseen differences, dangerous as *shetani* tricks that made you believe, like people who have been possessed—as a man might think, "I will eat an owl: I will be able to fly." A suspicion Esther had that being Hindi, or French, or even German was a kind of demon possession itself, a madness: she once had a horrible dream that Musumbi had eaten from the German's flesh for the same reasons, believing this would open for him a way to knowledge when there was no other. But instead it opened him to madness like poison in the blood.

Words could protect her—lies, making excuses. If she pretended to be happy—laughing and joking—no one would ever guess her thoughts or her desires. In this way she kept secrets, even from herself sometimes, because of what she didn't understand yet. Ideas evaporated in the distance like men spread out on the horizon, or gathered close to scare her with painted faces, with headdresses of lions' manes and buffalo horn. For Esther, acts of kindness were her only safety—pulling pain from the old woman and listening to her sobs, she could feel it all on her own hands, a sensation that made her want to wash, with salt, to scrub away what had clung like sweat to her fingertips, like the smell of perfumed oil. How was it so? She was afraid of treachery, the failure to find true answers. Like the great silences of Musumbi. Those frogs she had seen falling from Mrs. Manda were enough to warn her. Cheupe's raging changes. The ruined leg of Francis. She feared the trick—like pictures in Musumbi's book that made it seem, heart, bones, and blood, that people could be free from the world to love as Jesus had tried to do. Oh no. The desire to touch, to help, to clear away contamination; these were dangerous temptations like the flight of birds, forbidden to men.

Troubled by these thoughts, Esther brooded, pretending when it happened not to have already seen that Waliji's daughter, Almaz, would become very sick. The child's fever had come for Esther with the slap of certainty, a sinking feeling complicated by doubt, by questions of responsibility and doom. Was she the only one to have seen it? Did she make it happen? Was it, after all, witchcraft?

Entranced, she lingered at her job long after the dishes were washed, dropping dal beans one by one into a jar, picking stones from the grains of rice. Voices in the other room were pitched toward a shaded yellow bulb in a corner, a smell of something they had boiled to rub on the child who couldn't wake up. All day she had been there on the cot, sleeping, a faint light herself, luminous under her sheet. Thin arms and legs drew out her form in lines. Sweat shone on her forehead in a glowing mass of black hair.

"Not malaria," Mrs. Nargis had whispered, holding Esther's hands. "The medicine cannot work. She cannot wake. This fever, making me to fear." Soon the woman fell asleep herself, a sari piled around her in a corner of the couch, her feet dangling there, bare, sandals fallen to the floor.

It was the same as looking hard into the darkness until she could see forms emerge, straining, to understand. Or like pressing against her eyes and letting go, a dizziness of color. The only explanation was that she had become part of the sick child, felt it in her breath, which was hot, took it in her lungs and then diffused it. Her arms were full of it, her hands heavy. She wanted to put them on the child in a washing motion, remembering Bemba. Only her hands, tingling. More than once she shook them as though she had to throw away the fever, residue clinging to her shining from her own hands now.

"Is it you, Esther?" Mrs. Nargis asked. "Who is it?"

"She is waking," Esther said. Soft pleasure fell around her and Almaz, still breathing as one, looking at the mother, a surge of silk cloth. Then, as they separated, smiling away from each other, it was like falling: the bliss faded, the child whined, beads of water along her hair, holding out her hand.

"I'm so hungry, Mummy."

Her hair was soaked. "See, she has broken it, she is sweating," Mrs. Nargis called in a high voice and all the others came to the room.

Resting on her bed afterward, more than Esther's hands were aroused by what she couldn't ignore any longer. Released emotions brought all the pictures into place, all the messages she had tried to deny—the shadows of her cousin's death, her Aunt Zidora, the truth she hid about Bemba covered with warts, everything she knew about pain. She faced all of it with fascination, knowing something had been called up, a power that she brought to the sick child or a power they were able to make together—whatever it was that conquered the fever. So much was unknown and had to be kept in secret—her pleasure and her fear—because of jealousy and witchcraft and the pressure of these remote ideas, no more than shadows themselves. Seeking safety against such dreams, she had to seal herself off. In that way she could sleep even though she seemed to be awake; performing tasks, speaking words, whatever she had to do to keep alive.

Too soon Musumbi came to warn her in a dream. They were crossing farmlands and came to a dry ravine. A tree was clinging to its edge. She wanted to cross the ravine but Musumbi told her no. He told her he had heard a flood roaring. She laughed at him. She was both a child and a woman and knew she could disobey. But as she stepped into the ravine, a river came. It rushed and pulled the weakling tree away. She grabbed at the tree and, clinging there, was swept down the river. As she woke, she understood the meaning of the dream. The tree was a sick person and the river a disease. She was not strong enough to save it or to be saved by it—only to cling there.

No one knew. At times Esther hoped they would guess, would ask her to explain. Only Almaz, who came now and leaned against her legs or sneaked out in the evening while boys flew kites to stand with Esther there, holding her hands or climbing to her shoulders where she pressed her tiny fingers into Esther's hair or clung, a soft cheek on a neck, until her mother came calling. Once she followed Esther through the rain when streets were planted with umbrellas and dark shapes under newspaper hats, the sheltered doorways full of them as though they had been blown up against the sides of things. Dripping wet and all alone; a funny sight, this little Hindi girl calling "Esta!" and everyone laughing up and down as she turned and saw her, rivers of hair and small brown arms.

During those same rains, Waliji said he needed help and took Esther to his restaurant to chop cabbages and carrots in a big kitchen instead of a small one. They told her that Mwema had gone back to his village and she missed him, like one who has been deserted, the way a person can be lost or found, the way a person lived who moved from place to

place. This was chance: she understood it traveling with
Musumbi. How you escaped. How you were delivered. No
one knew where Mwema had gone. —"He sold his car," the
one who washed dishes said. "He was rich and bought a
kiosk. Far away." Around Waliji's restaurant the rain had
swelled big yellow flowers on the trees and dropped them
over the blue plastic chairs and tables on a porch there.
Frogs were jumping in the pots of plants. "Clean it! Clean it!"
Waliji was shouting. The black boys shook the plastic table
covers, stacked the plastic chairs, swept, and complained
about their lives.

Waliji's brother, Sanjay, had asthma from the falling
flowers, yellow dust and thick white centers stuck
everywhere. He wanted to cut down the trees. He went on
sneezing and his eyes watered. The skin under his eyes
turned very dark. He was a small, pale man with skin like
porridge and rough black moles on his neck and hands. He
tied his trousers up with string and wore sandals made of
rubber tires like African men. With Waliji nearby he
appeared even smaller, very quiet. At home when he sat next
to his brother, they all made fun, Waliji being so fat and
growing all the time. But at the hotel, when Waliji was away,
he talked without stopping, with loud sounds. Because he
was a friend of Africans. He came into the kitchen and
talked, picking up a broom and sweeping or taking a knife
and chopping, telling everyone to stop work and have tea.
Talking and talking, mostly about the terrible things that
went on in places where black men and Indians together
were treated, he said, like animals by white men who had
guns and put them in jails.

"Make no mistake," he told Esther, "I am black, same as
you. One day you will see the truth of it." The others
laughed when he left the kitchen. Outside, he talked to
customers, sitting at tables with them, about how in India
they had thrown the white men out but only after three
hundred years. This was the struggle of all dark men, he
said. Everything was clear. *Wazi.* His speaking of Swahili was
perfect and as he spoke it, gestures opened him and his
voice. Listening from inside, it sounded like a big man
talking out there. When the customers were gone, he leaned
on the counter to wait for more, eating small, powdery

sweets that turned to sugar in your mouth and had no taste. In between he sucked on limes, sitting at a desk thinking and writing.

No one listened to him. Except a few university students who came to eat there and never paid. They sat at corner tables writing down what Sanjay would say as he ran back and forth making orders on the kitchen—more *bhajias*, more soups. The activity made him very pale. He sneezed even more. His moles got blacker. There were girl students—Esther watched them, fascinated—who knew how to write, pencils poised over sheets of paper. They knew how to argue with the men or with each other, reading words out loud from their books. She would peer around the steaming cases of fried cakes to see them.

Sanjay smelled of cloves, which he kept under his tongue. In the kitchen he told them all to strike against his brother by refusing to work until they could get more wages. He took the chopping knife from Esther's hands and put it flat on the table, then dropped an onion next to it and stopped there with his arms folded on his chest to show her how. His trousers pulled far into his waist. There was silence. Then there was laughter. Dishes rattled faraway in the restaurant.

"Don't you understand?" He breathed spice on her and sniffed. His shirt seemed to fluff up around a skinny chest. She thought of puffing birds. She was the reason why, he said, not her alone, but all the ones like her who didn't understand. "When you and you and you (he was pointing and hopping on his little feet) ask the questions," he told them, "then they will be forced to give answers."

It was the smell of cloves that became a memory. He made her put one in her mouth, too. "The center of a flower," he told her, "growing on Zanzibar and other islands where these bad Arabs . . ." and so on, a long story, the same one about right and wrong. She bit into the clove by mistake so that it burned her mouth with bitterness and the perfume was lost. It made her wince.

"No, not biting." He laughed. "Just keep it there." She liked it then as her tongue lost feeling, as she closed her eyes around the taste, as the fragrance grew inside her. He moved so quickly, fluttering over her: she was aware of small falling bones, his knees against her own. But it was the spice that overpowered her, in her breath and his, a way to endure. When she dared to look at him one day, sitting on the edge of the bed, she saw his back was alive with the black moles, too. He gave her money. More each time. To buy her silence. She saved it in a box.

At home, when she carried chapattis to their evening meal—voices gathering at the table: Almaz calling, "I want my Esta!"—Sanjay never said a word or looked her way. His hair had grown, reaching below his shoulders now. She understood—the dark circles of his eyes, the feather hair, the jutting nose—even more about shame. Was it his or hers? She could smell the cloves as she handed him his bread.

She met Hadija at Waliji's restaurant, a face that appeared each day over the steaming piles of *bhajia* and *koftee*, bringing news. "*Kumbe* Esta! You can drive this car with the roof taken down and fast, too, like flying. Fwaaaaaaaah! Come, I can show you . . ." She dragged Esther outside to see. The rain had stopped. The yellow flowers had left long dark pods hanging in the trees. The blue chairs were arranged in the shade. There were cats.

"FWAAAAAAAAAAAAH!" There on the corner across the street, a very red car, so small that only two could fit inside and low to the ground so that Hadija bent her knees to pretend she sat in it. Her whole body shook. She held an invisible wheel. Her eyes popped. They saw two Sikh boys in black turbans and tight shining pants. Hadija waved to them holding out her breasts. "Following bees," she whispered to Esther, "one finds honey." She stood against a tree and watched them. The car was starting: a radio shouted Hindi music. Hadija swung out an arm as they drove past, calling out "Fwaaaaah!" then toppled back to fall into a chair. She slumped. "If I had such a car as this," and sighed.

She had no mother, and her father beat her, so she met boys here and there at restaurants and clubs. Splashes of perfume and English talk: she was hot pants and wet-look, super funk, reggae go-go, cool-out, miliki sound. She was Week-end-out-of-town Resort Bar Your Baby, sock-it-to-me

disco time, sex-me-over lover boy. Count down
5-4-3-2-1–ZERO. Esther knew her new friend lived
somewhere down in the *majengo* shacks near the market, but
Hadija told Sanjay, "I live on Oy-si-tah Bay, my deah!"
knowing how to show it with her hands. That day she had
her hair woven like a tall basket with blue yarns and red
beads. They were laughing, even Sanjay, a peeping sound.
The two girls tipped toward each other until their shoulders
met it was so funny, until the tears came. "*Oy-Si-Tah-Bay.*"
Hadija wagged her bottom. She got in the blue chair—her
car—and started the motor: "Brrummmm, Brrrrrrum."
She was pushing the gears. "Safari Rally. Clutch me down,
baby! Blast me out!" Poor Sanjay's eyes blinked. You had to
laugh. His hair was pushed back: his ears looked like wings,
his nose like a beak.

Advice was natural to Hadija who always gave it, telling
Esther, when Sanjay was inside, to make sure and quit
chopping up the food of Hindis and playing sex with Sanjay,
even for profit, as pathetic as he was. The only chance for
happiness, she said, was in being modern, which meant
learning fashion and the things that made beauty possible.
Pictures of models unfolded from her purse. Esther saw
serenity there, the poses and the smiles, together with the
drama of painted faces and fancy hair (Masai and Kwavi
knew it). Then there were shoes. And blue jeans.

That night, under the sky of falling kites, Esther saw her
friend shining down the street, through the haze of smoke
from the braziers roasting corn for the Africans to eat.
Hadija, taking small-small steps, her bright pants too tight,
her shoes too high, the basket of her hair exploding red and
blue. Her shirt was a picture of a dancer swirling in long
skirts, stitched on with something sparkling.

"Hey, soul sistah!" she was calling.

The two went strolling arm in arm. Esther bounced in
the promise of those short quick steps. Out of Hadija flowed
her daring, contagious, a way to forget, like perfume, like the
taste of clove. So much opportunity was offered in that
stride, so much locked together making you think you could,
after all, survive the world. Hadija edged closer, swaying her
bottom, singing something. She called it groovy-funk, until
a high building loomed, the big hotel for tourists from

Europe, blue light hovering over the swimming place like a dream lake held in the ground by shining tiles and surrounded. People were standing on boards and jumping into it.

Hadija began to bounce, trying to see everything, then pulled Esther, running and teetering calling, *"Hey man!"* It was the low red car almost hidden in a crowd. "Fu-waaaaah!" All the hotel lights made a wonderful brightness. An old man who was guarding the car pushed people who came too close, thumping boys and small children. But Hadija, because of her strong heart—she held her hand to it and breathed through her nose—was ready to find trouble and win. To win. *Kushinda.* What was called freedom. She ran right to it and climbed in through the roof. The old man pulled at her and scolded until the two Sikhs came running, which made Hadija laugh even more; and Esther was proud of the strong heart of her friend who stepped out bowing, holding the young Sikh's hand, her chin up and everyone cheering.

"Give me driving lessons!" she shouted at their turbans vanishing along the curving drive to the hotel. It felt as though the light faded after that. A taxi came to carry white tourists with burned-up skin. Then there were the Ugandans in an old blue Peugeot, friends of Hadija who called out, "Come on, hang out with us, chicks," and opened their doors.

Hadija told them, "Right on, baby."

After that, after she left Waliji's house, in the safety of the mornings, behind their own window (hers and Hadija's) while Zobetta's babies curled sleeping in her bed, Esther would learn to take the nights, carried away on Hadija's expectation, grooving. Even now, Hadija, trying halter tops with the new blue jeans from America, was spraying everyone with perfumes and talking about a ship full of Italians that had landed. *Kitoto,* she called them, tiny little boys. She rolled around Esther, combing at her hair, fluffing at her dress, whispering, *"Va bene. Va bene,"* in the Italian language.

EIGHT

◄ ◇ ►

The bright morning light in the doctor's window was a medium of silhouette, sharp shoulders on a tapering back. Antonia noticed that Paul's neck was starting to thicken. He had turned from her as if to look out the window into the sea of waiting patients. More likely, he had turned to avoid having to face her as she came in. She never felt as embarrassed as he did by their past together and he knew this, bore it like a burden. The result was that in their contact now there was a certain feeling of insecurity and aggression. She never knew if it was regret or simply nerves.

"Good morning, Paul," she said.

"Yes, Tony . . ." He stayed that way with his back toward her, turning only his head as she spoke so she was looking at his profile thinking how she still found it charming that someone with such Bantu features as Paul could look so chiseled and lean from the side as if face-to he might have been another man. "It seems one of your patients," he said, "a whore. . . ." He was smiling now, couldn't help but look at her then, "has been picked up by the police." The gap between his front teeth that drove African girls wild still disarmed her.

"The police?"

"They made one of their swoops and gathered up all the girls. Seems there was an Italian ship."

"To send them back to their villages?"

He folded his fingers into each other and pressed them to his nose, a gesture she knew. It meant he felt brotherly, kind. "One of them says she is under a doctor's care and

115

can't leave town. She says her doctor—a white memsaab—
has told her she has strings inside her tying her up and she
needs to have treatments to untie them"

"Oh dear." She laughed. "Adhesions."

"So they want you at the station to make a statement. I
suggest you tell them to send her back where she comes from."

"She won't say where she comes from. She's too smart."

"She's not your business."

"Well, she thinks she is. She sends her friends to fetch
me on house calls. She hides out up there watching me. She
sics the police on me. She thinks I'm obligated because she's
bewitched. Poison blood from a transfusion. I did it."

"If she has gyn problems, she ought to see Mutasingwa."

"She's been to Mutasingwa."

"Don't waste your time on her."

A nurse had come to look for him. She stood on the
threshold, mute, even after he had asked her twice, "What is
it?" like someone standing on the banks of Lethe, an empty
cup in her hand, all thoughts fading away, as if forgetfulness
might dissolve her obligation. He asked her again, "What is
it?" She muttered finally, but without volume, the head
tipped, the mouth pouted. *What is it?* he bellowed but the
girl had turned and fled.

She couldn't be in the same room with Paul Luenga and
not feel his terrible impatience, the paranoic edge to his
voice, the petulance. She began to identify the same sound
on the BBC in voices of the young colonels forging their
weekly coups all over Africa, shouting out from captured
radio stations, closing the airport, shrieking about
redemption, about exterminating the corrupt, the lazy, the
foreign. She almost forgot what qualities had attracted her
to him in the first place, his passion and irony. As a student,
he never lost his boyish pleasure in learning, his devilish
insights into himself. If anything, it cost him later with the
other men here who had been educated abroad, who knew
how to scheme and how to get an edge from their advantage.
He had an easy charm that passed for innocence. Even now,
his smile, opened as if it saw all joy in life. It didn't: it hid the
deep narcissism of rebellion.

Each time she went to the police station, she had to ask where it was, and it was always a block away on another street, back from the port, up in a pinched corner, across from a treeless park. It couldn't have been uglier or more derelict, like a prison itself. Just inside the entrance a crowd had gathered around an old Greek character from whom Antonia had long ago removed a gall bladder. He was shouting at a young officer while everyone else laughed. Two other officers walked back and forth in front of him as if to taunt him, enrage him more, like picadors at a bullfight.

"Drunk," one of the cops told her.

"I want to see someone about a girl who was brought in here this morning," she said.

He didn't respond, simply led her down a hall: shining dark green paint and black doors and fumes from the long unwashed latrines. The whores were lined up on benches in a room reserved for traffic hearings. Not many, hardly enough to call it a swoop. She saw Esther in a corner. Her head had been shaved. She looked cast in bronze.

"Are you the doctor from the hospital?" A tiny man looked up. His uniform had been crudely altered to fit him. He led her to a windowless room where there was a smell of mold and wax and suddenly his cologne, which she knew had come into the country as contraband. "We have arrested one female, Esther Moro, on charges of prostitution. She says she is a sick person."

"That is correct. She is my patient."

"Well, what is her sickness if she is working as a prostitute? This is against the law."

"She was assaulted by a sailor," Antonia told him. "I had to repair the damage. Now there are scars, like that one on your wrist. Inside her."

"Do you always repair such people who have broken the law?"

"I treat anyone who comes to the hospital," she said. Somewhere beyond she could hear the Greek laughing. Perhaps he had won his argument. It was just as likely that he hadn't.

"Are you aware that she told lies about herself?" he asked. "Do you know she is married?"

"She didn't say she was married."

"Her husband is a village man. She will have to be returned to him as she has run away. Women who profit from their sex make no contributions to society."

She listened nodding piously until in the end, he returned the patient to her, as though he were granting custody, making Antonia responsible and he a witness to it. On top of that he made it seem like a favor he would expect the doctor to return though she could see he hadn't figured out yet what he might ask for, listened to his nagging references to how he was bending rules to please the doctor, how he hoped she would remember. It was almost dusk, a red, dry season when the sun seemed to shrink away from the city rather than set over it, sucking the dust up in channels, great columns of it, pillar on pillar, an avenue to the sea. The doctor wondered if she would get an explanation from the girl who was so thin, moving like a marionette, all angles, beside her.

"Give me money," Esther Moro said.

"No," Antonia told her as if she were speaking to a beggar even though the girl's tone was more like a thief's.

"Fix me then," she demanded. "I can't live. I will have to die."

So they went to the hospital. The outpatient wing was quiet despite the courtyard full of campers and their relatives preparing for the night. Inside, there was just enough light in the office so that when they talked, their voices were disembodied and carried no threat.

"What is this news that you have a husband?" Antonia asked.

"I ran away from him," Esther said. She was looking into the doctor's eyes the way Luenga used to before the globe shifted under them making him move east and her west, or north and south, so that they couldn't face each other. She wore what looked like a borrowed dress, a community affair, ill fitted and too heavy for the climate, a dark green double knit. The original sleeves had been removed and replaced by orange cotton ruffles, the buttons changed to red plastic.

"How old were you?"

But Africans never knew in years: "When my father died," she answered. "I had no breasts, no menstruation." She was a seated statue burnished in the dim lights, red plastic buttons like inlaid gems. "My husband was playing sex with me in the way of an old man before his wife has grown. This is an abomination and so I took fevers from him. They are not my people. They live in grass houses and their girls must be cut before they are women. I knew if I stayed among them, they would do it to me. So I hid my first blood from them and ran away. His name was Josephat, but how can he have a Christian's name when he is no Christian?" She seemed to be excited to explain all this.

"Dreams will tell you things," she said oddly in seductive tones. "In a dream my body is painted and oiled like a Pareh girl, I wear an apron and I am singing their songs. In the shed I see them on benches and between their legs they are made like flowers. My own flower is blood and the petals are flowing and dripping. The circumciser listens to her snake. She passes along the row of girls with her carving knife. They will moan in their pain but they will not cry out because they are brave. When she cuts me, the flower falls into her hands. She screams out to them that I am a witch." Esther's eyes said she expected Antonia must have understood this all along, had held the dreadful flower in her own hand that night, had wielded her own carving knife.

"A dream can tell you what you fear," the doctor advised.

"I am not safe," the girl answered back.

"But you escaped? Isn't it so?"

"He came again as that Greek sailor." For her it was the context as much as the act, and it was clear she thought there was still danger.

"Do you still feel pain? Is that it?" Antonia asked.

Her answer came as a complicated verb form, *iliniumizwa*. It has been caused to me that I am hurt, with the agent left unnamed, a way the language had of dealing on the outskirts of events.

They were both silent then. Outside in the empty corridor they could hear the *thwack-thwack* of a mop as it hit the wall from side to side. No soap, the doctor was thinking, no disinfectant in the wash, only the slosh of water and dull streaks of mud on the once shining red tile floor. They sat listening for a time.

Esther's face remained long after she had gone, projected in the dark. Antonia thought of the bronze heads of Ife, those perfect ovals, almond eyes in a high dome, a nose deeply bridged with gently flaring nostrils. She began to see Esther often as a patient, but each time they lingered as they had the first afternoon at the end of the day. Teacups, a collection of them going back through other afternoons, made it look as though a party had just ended, and the two women left behind to clear up had put off the chore.

Like an artist or a puzzle maker, Esther scattered images and clues around her secrets and her shame. There was a Greek flavor to it, flight and submission. She had run from her circumcision, a fate that caught up with her in an anonymous room, a broken bottle and finally there on the operating table. Antonia guessed that Esther wanted something from her but she couldn't have said what. And offered something to her.

There in the circumcision shed Esther might have died. No worse than becoming one of them, hung in a tree like a dead bird while the old man, Josephat, picked away at her bones. Someone always did die and was hidden from the villagers. The old circumciser and her snake told stories about magic transformations, girls who were turned to fish and swam away, while the little girls held each other's hand, listened, dreamed of their time. Who dies in there? Why? Why this one and not the other? Why not all of them? Or none? A decision made by a snake.

Even when Antonia tried to explain to Esther about resistance and immunity, the girl's intelligence refused the explanation and sought answers in causes that existed beyond. There was no end to it—witchcraft, jealousy, guilt, a thing like hubris and the balancing that takes place when humans tried to go beyond and did forbidden things. It was all tied up with this father of hers, his pretensions and his failures—"If he didn't make them better," Esther said, "then we had to run "—and with her search for a place. Like Antonia's own search through the villages outlined along a horizon or in a maze of city streets, down the twisted lanes of a squatters' settlement.

They were both attracted to something in the raveling themes of sickness and healing, of destiny and the nature of men, like wobbling reflections in a sideshow mirror—this black village girl and the white doctor. Esther was absorbed in the mystery of disease, things that weren't allowed to be mysterious to a doctor, something beyond the sleuthing work of diagnosis, the dispassionate listing of symptoms, staining of microbes on a slide, growing a culture on a petri dish. Blood caught in a centrifuge. The X-rays of darkening lungs. It seemed that Esther would have liked to latch onto something as cold as that. She would have preferred the labs and clinic. Asking, "How do you read the messages in a person's blood? In their urine? In the pieces of them you take and put in tubes?" Antonia could tell her those things, let her look into her microscope or at her books for fun, but it was the questions that she couldn't answer that bothered her. Antonia did not want to admit that we were, after all, just like ancient man howling at the sky, seeking a reason. Only here the voice was soft, whispering, contained against pale evening light in rows of windows and a tropic courtyard full of leprosy.

"Why does sickness come to some and not to others? If you do no bad things, if you are good, then how can there be trouble? Why is there pain? Why do we suffer? A young woman dies and an old one lives on in pain. Tell me why? We Africans say it is in the hands of devils and witches; this is our stupidity. But what makes a sickness go away? What makes medicine work? This can only be magic. And it frightens me because I will feel it rising inside a person and I will want to pull it away, as Jesus did, to throw it off."

What was it Esther talked about? Lost in the twist of the girl's ideas, Antonia wondered if there was a single stem to which the tendrils of her vision clung, something she was growing toward—a confirmation or a desire. They were almost visible, these buds of her truth. What Antonia sensed was a secret Esther still kept, so that she came out of these sessions with the girl even more uncertain. Even more intrigued.

Antonia wished there was a way to keep Esther from facing unknown men in dark rooms. But there weren't many options as far as Esther was concerned. "I don't want to be a maid for white people or for Hindis. I want to be a doctor. Find me a job in this hospital so I can follow you and learn a doctor's work." This was said as if it were humorous. Esther laughed, but meant it, wanting there to be a chance. "I will learn to read and write." She was looking out the window, there under old trees where the sick had camped, slumped together like beached seals. "Or a nurse. If I can be a nurse, I will help those people. I will learn what to do. They have such bad sicknesses in their bodies, in their lungs, and all the places. They have fever and coughs. Sometimes at night in Mikorosheni I hear them all crying in their sickness."

A taxi driver, taking Antonia to another party in Oyster Bay, looked at the empty port and talked about a cruel *shetani,* disguised as a prostitute who preyed on sailors. This was known all over the world, the reason so few ships came anymore, he said. She heard the taunting in his voice, daring her to believe it or not as if she'd be a fool either way. An old man with clouded eyes who knew all he needed to know about beautiful women. Of course, this *shetani* made herself to be the most beautiful of all, he told her and she nodded, smiling, thinking of her patient and the twist his story gave to hers.

The house to which he took her appeared to have been awaiting her arrival; the tall French doors of the patio opened suddenly at her approach. Silence and then her name, called from out back where everyone stood admiring a parrot the hostess had displayed in a wooden cage. There were tiger orchids blooming violently in a nearby tree.

Ted Armstrong spoke to her against a trail of pink bougainvillea, clutching the inevitable gin and tonic.

"I thought I lost you," he said. "You don't have a phone." He'd been traveling anyway. There were rumors, he said, that the corn America had been sending for famine relief was being sold across the border by whichever corrupt official could get his hands on it.

A man introduced to her as John Cory said he had heard local people complaining that American corn, being yellow and more starchy, was causing impotence: the newspaper had stories about shrinking penises and withering breasts. If this were true, he joked, they could kill two birds with one stone. Feed the hungry and control the population. He wore a copper bracelet.

"For arthritis?" Armstrong asked.

Cory held it up, then rubbed his elbow, flexed it and grinned. He had the kind of self-confidence it was necessary to display: a cigar, a paunch, some Navajo jewelry, a copper bangle. Antonia didn't like him.

"Does it work, this bracelet?" she asked.

"Of course," he said.

A woman with a severe Boston accent, whom Cory acknowledged as his "old lady," circulated near them. Her voice was nasal and carried, talking about how yoga had changed her life. A young anthropologist, just in from the bush, rolled ice around in his drink. "I've been in the field almost five years now and I haven't got beyond the initial observations," he was saying. Antonia wasn't certain if he were being humble or proud. He went on discussing the classic case of Africans caught between traditional ways and modern society. Her attention faded. Ice in their glasses, wind chimes on the patio, a tinny dinner bell, and the high voice of the hostess calling them to her buffet, all tinkling.

Armstrong was hesitant but hovered near her all evening, possibly waiting for her advance, possibly plotting his own. It was a little sardonic, the whole thing: he must have seen it, too, as though they had been written into a clumsy bedroom drama by the gang on Oyster Bay. Neil Simon but with an overseas logic to it, a commentary on resignation and limited resources, because their choices had no consequence, the real expatriate problem. You couldn't plan too far ahead. And that was how he would have defined her life right at that moment. McGeorge called it boredom and said she was headed for despair.

It worked out, anyway, that she went home with him again, as she was meant to do. Turning on the light he told her, "Jenny was obsessed with painting everything white," as if he suddenly recalled this, for no reason, except the blank white walls of his rooms. The house seemed even less furnished than she remembered, or pushed back to its edges, as though things were waiting to escape the place.

"Walls. Furniture," he went on. "Everything had to be white. She could never get her own way because we never lived in our own house. We always had to have this government-issue furniture, things Jenny hated, with floral prints, or worse, Early American. And they'd always paint the houses for us before we arrived. You know, so it'd be ready. I can hear her now: '*Off white! Off white!*'" He was laughing, moving through toward the kitchen where he kept the booze spread out on the counters. "I can't take it, she'd tell me. We have no control over the simplest things in our lives. *Off white!* But she wrote me last week, in fact, and said she was using colors now, on the woodwork. She called them 'tones', a different *tone* in each room."

"So now you're without a wife overseas. Like half a function, isn't it? Why is it so unusual for people like you to be alone in these posts? People seem to do it in pairs."

"Who knows why? But it's a rotten setting for a marriage. You can't drag your wife to places like this and expect her to like it."

"Still, being single . . . these big houses, those dreadful parties. Somehow it seems as though being single might be worse than being married."

"You're single."

"Ah, but I was born here."

He had the ice out, his back to her, cursing a stubborn tray. "Embassy people look on their tours in the Third World as the price they pay for Paris or Geneva. But guys like me only get the Third World option. No compensation. Ol' Jenny started to notice how some of the older wives had allergies, nervous tics. Thin hair. She was too vain to risk it. You can stiff-upper-lip it in India or Thailand where there's stuff to buy. Here there's nothing to buy but poached ivory, and you can't take that into the States."

"That may all change. Someone's out there counting the elephants right now."

"Maybe it'll be good news, eh? Elephants up the gazoo and an ivory boom, like oil in Nigeria."

He'd been a Peace Corps volunteer. While she was learning about America in Boston, he was learning about Africa in Nigeria. There were a lot like him, who thought a life of real service was possible, based on those three or four high years, but instead they found out about bureaucracy, became people who faced failure with the excuse that they couldn't interfere in anything, were prevented on all sides in all ways from doing what they thought to be right.

Development. "You do know the latest thing we've done here, don't you? Built dams in the desert. To hold back the water when it rains. Only someone forgot that rivers change their beds in arid places. Ever see a dam in the desert?"

He went directly from the euphoria of village life to a desk job in Pakistan. Once he had been a semi-deity, a white kid who could miraculously speak Ibo. He had thought of it as a friendship but it wasn't; only curiosity, on both sides, though he learned this in painful retrospect, "a Peace Corps disease, like recurring malaria: you keep seeing how dumb you were. It brings on the chills." In Pakistan he lost his youthful idealism and learned how to be accountable. Not by choice. He was forced into it by the reams of paper and assholes he worked for. Jenny never understood how averting the experience had been, why he was perpetually pissed off.

To go. To use what you knew about growing things, about supply and demand, about controlling water. Simple things like building dams. How could it go so wrong? When his marriage fell apart he thought of quitting rather than being godforsaken on his own. Take up carpentry, a skill introduced to him by those wonderful Ibo villagers. Of course he couldn't. He couldn't *believe* — even after ten years—that something as profound as this idea of going with a gift of technology was going to fail. With no strings attached, not as a person who wanted to push an ideology or make commercial ventures or conquer, only to bring an easier way of dealing with the planet to people who had it rough. Vanity turned out to be the other side of his naïveté. Oh, he had seen the light and knew what had to be done in places like this. He knew about the dangers of discrepancy. He winced at poverty. He was positive about giving everyone the same chance and he could not believe that it didn't work. But it didn't.

Didn't she know?

Wasn't it the story of her life, too?

Now he was forced to stand outside his own values. The only way to do business. It was distortion, not bitterness or cynicism, he insisted. He wondered out loud what he was going to be like as an old man.

"Jenny never understood," he went on. "She didn't have

the Peace Corps thing. She wanted the trip but it turned out that dark people bothered her. And that was hard to admit. I could see it."

"Her obsession with white?"

He laughed. "Well. Maybe."

"I'm sorry," she told him, an odd thing to say in English. There was a word for it in Swahili, *pole*, which didn't translate. *Pole* was a word used by people who were able to accept more about the human condition than Armstrong could do.

Later she discovered that he had the type of body she appreciated in a man. The chest hairless. The legs and buttocks firm, a cleft (two neat dimples) in the pit of his back. His arms were long and still alive with muscle and his torso maintained a youthful flatness without the banded tension of someone who was working hard at it. She could see sharp pits of bone at the edge of his shoulders. The hands, deep with veins, his fists punched into the mattress on either side of her as he arched. Looking up at his jaw, the slits of his eyes, she might have been watching someone in great pain. He came too fast and couldn't stay with her afterward the way some men could. Dripping with sweat and apologizing. He had not unclenched. She stroked his back; took one hand and opened it, surprised by the dryness of his palm, turned to find he had downy blond hair over his knuckles, small tapering fingers. There was a breeze through his window suddenly cool. He sat up to it as if it were music calling him to dance.

"Will it rain?" he asked her. It was the wrong season for rain but they could smell it over the sea.

An aberrant rain, sending signals out of time. Flowers budded and red wasps came down to lay their eggs in the mud. If it stopped suddenly the buds would die and wasp larvae would be left hatched and squirming, desperate in the sun. Antonia watched them on her way home from work, tiny burrowing wasps, wondering what would come of their work in this rain that couldn't last.

That day the streets were evacuated, she wanted to say siphoned, they had emptied so quickly at the approach of dark. Charles warned her of ruthless thieves who prowled at that time of day, the kind of men who stole the shoes of those who went inside the mosques to pray.

She worked her way slowly up to Kinondoni like a climax of a story, just the other side of a long hill, the mirror image of a sister community that had never got beyond the cement-slab stage, one slab on each carefully marked plot. There were bright doors like flowers, true, but not once, not so much as once had she stood looking over that steel gray (clay soil and unrelieved cement block) and thought, yes, there is a touch of beauty here when the light favors us and our funny doors. Not once. Good God, who were the architects that designed and built the place? Their cold efficiencies were not for anyone in Kinondoni. The refuse centers set up for easy collection went unused in favor of the streets and empty plots because no one ever came to collect. There was a constant smoke of trash fires.

Paul Luenga's car was parked near the doctor's purple door like a threat or an invitation. These days he seemed to get the two confused. Not drunk, but nearly so, she saw, as soon as she was close enough—the way his left eye got lazy. It used to take exactly five bottles of beer for his eye to go haywire. Now it was more and now it was whiskey (whenever he could get it) or a local cane drink that he mixed in milk and called "punch." Lips tasting moist of milk and rum had been the death knell of their last months together. He had never been able to put his failures at lovemaking down to booze or age. It left him bewildered, worrying about what was wrong.

The ground, baked clay, could not absorb the freakish rain. Precious, it sat on top in depressions like sinks of water. There were as many women washing clothes in it as there were children playing. Already the shallow pans were filling with frogs: kids caught them, dangling the miserable creatures from outstretched hands.

Not very good in situations like this, she looked for overtures to reconciliation. From that point on, everything would have been predictable enough. They'd tried so many times. If she invited him in, Charles would be there at the sink peeling potatoes to witness the event, rigid with disapproval. He hated Luenga. Antonia never had any doubt that word went back to Paul's wife from the things Charles said in the tea stalls or the bars. Last time they tried to patch things up again, they had performed for each other, trying to reclaim their familiarity by repeating old gestures, old caresses, as if any change in those routines would have been false, an embarrassment. But their old routines had been finished by then, the kind of tyranny that plagued the end of marriages, she thought. What was it Armstrong had said about his attempt at "getting back" with Jenny: "It was okay except in bed. She tried getting new approaches from books. We did stuff. Kinky stuff. It wasn't honest, wasn't us. No chance for any of it to come up to what she had expected."

But no, Luenga had come to warn her. "Your patient, Esther Moro. Why is she coming to see you afternoons?"

His voice sounded different, older. In a country where the average life span is forty-five, he was fifty, ancient.

"We're talking," she said. "Rather she's talking to me."

"You're having games with her."

"Maybe we're just playing games together. Do you care?" Racketing frogs made it impossible to be serious. Where did they all come from so suddenly, filling the puddles of water? From the insides of bedeviled women?

"People are saying things about you again. There are people who don't want you at the hospital. I have a constant fight to keep you there. There's all this about your mother and father; questions concerning the money your family has taken out of the country. What is your interest in that girl? What are you trying to learn from her? I'm not the one asking these questions; others are. Why do you continue to stay here when all your countrymen are leaving? Am I being clear?"

"Not this again, Paul." She was biting her nails. "If you want to know, I think the girl wants to be a doctor. This is why she's latched on to me. And as for Olivia's money, I'm out of her will. You know it. I've got absolutely nothing that belongs to anyone else."

"You're not a psychiatrist."

"No, and I'm not doing psychiatry."

"It's absurd. Impossible."

"Say what you want." They could go on bickering like

this, as predictable a routine as their lovemaking had become, until the conversation (as the love had done) turned into a row, ending as he walked away from her, slammed his car door, and drove too fast like the Western men he despised. Instead, this time she was the one who walked away.

Paul in his father's house. Formal. Showered. A cloth tied at his waist. His chest bare. This was her memory. They were all smiling to see him that way, a tender sort of irony. She could see they were worried about having him back after all those years; the pride they felt because he had so obviously changed.—"He has forgotten *everything!*"—It made them happy, proof of his success and their sacrifice. Because they had faith in him and were noble.—"You see, everything. Even how to tie his *kitambi*."—They were ready to excuse everything. Even this white woman he brought there to visit them. Paul's friend (*"rafiki wa Paulos"*) though they held up pictures of his wife (*"mke wa Paulos"*) and children, away at her father's house, because, as everyone knew, when people go away, they come back changed. They were so cautious, edging slowly around the returned hero, touching, smiling, full of wonder.

Village elders had come to see him, old men who sat against the walls around a front room on hard chairs and listened to a radio broadcasting in a corner. Now and then they exchanged words. The youngest daughter carried warm beer to them on an enameled tray from China: new, the stenciled peony was shocking pink. Glasses in their hands were opaque with wear. Darker inside than it was cool, their house was the largest in the village, a sprawl of rooms, a tin roof with a deep overhang. Standing in the center hall she was aware of people busy on the peripheries, in and out of rooms, their muted sounds. The shapes of women carrying things, running children.

Behind the house all the women were cooking for Paulos on braziers. His mother, his grandmother, the wives of his brothers, his sisters. Their voices dropped one by one when they saw Antonia—*rafiki wa Paulos*—until there was a total silence. To emphasize for her the seriousness of their traditional ways, motions replaced words, elaborate, moving in front of her and then away. She could only see their backs. Whatever she did there in America where Paul had lived, whatever she knew that they didn't know . . . like language their bodies had an easy repartee. No kitchen politics, only low fires and deep pots and long wooden spoons. She saw wide spinach leaves, washed, green, and waiting on a tray. A pile of clean white peeled cassava root.

Paul's mother spoke first, "This is our cooking."

"It's very good," she answered stupidly. "I like it very much."

"We can cook this spinach in sour milk," one of the sisters said. "You fry onion. You put salt."

"Mmmmmm." They began to fuss around her because they saw she'd let them, to show her everything they had, to indicate that she should join them, must join, as they have expected her to. Because of Paulos. The grandmother tied a *kanga* around Antonia's hips and took her hand. They all giggled, pulling at her arms. She held a long spoon, laughing, being pushed, positioned in front of a pot and made to stir. A little girl had a jam jar full of salt: raspberries on a worn-down label. A silver spoon with initials. She thought she could be happy stooped there by that fire, taken in by all of it as if she couldn't get enough, the close bodies, the laughter, the smoke and steaming leaves, a longing that drew her again and again to scenes like this even though she could only stand outside, duped, part of a satire. See how funny she looks, a white woman with a wooden spoon. What did it say about her, about anyone whose ambition it is to be close to those her own kind have turned their backs on? A little like standing near a fence; if she could get close enough, at least for a moment, looking over the top, how easy it might be to forget the barrier.

"It's your vanity," her mother had said. "Vanity and greed." Even when Antonia was a child and would go to the village. "Going among them, making them be nice to you. Sharing their food. Well how else *can* they be? How else would they *dare* be?" Begging anyone she could, "Take me home with you . . ." On the edges of a crowd, watching children poke sticks at things or run with wheels, she'd be there in the scatter, rushing into the darkness of a mud house or under an overhang of thatch until Sayid, her father's man, came calling her. To sling her legs over his damp shoulders, hands digging for surprises in his springy hair; knives and talismans there. Until she was too big. Until he called her "memsaab."

A room had been prepared for her, taken from someone else; swept too clean, arranged, bare. The iron bed and wooden stool. The water jar. Easy to remember places like this where you have slept, the particular bed and room, events that mark a night. Days have a way of being blurred by tasks or the grind of travel, but nights remain. The iron bed was painted yellow. Chipped, it revealed itself formerly blue. There was a smell of carbolic soap and a once pink towel made in China that had a character in the corner, a square of interlocking combs. She remembered how long it took for the house to settle and finally sleep. The men stayed behind, talking late in whispers. Every now and then, she heard Paul's voice. She woke, not knowing the time, to find the silence total. Passing through the house on her way to the latrine, she looked into rooms where beds were full of sleepers, and she wondered how many she had displaced.

The fact of color was never so troubling to her as it was during those visits with his family. She guessed they were even more conscious of her race than she was because she stood, after all, behind her skin and didn't see it. All she saw was their black faces, understanding that when they looked, hers was the only white one among them, as though it were a flaw.

They weren't poor. The house was painted. There was glass in the windows. She had no sense that food was scarce because they talked about other things—politics and village affairs. Tea appeared each time with filled bowls of sugar and biscuits on a plastic dish. Once they brought out chocolate mints, but only for Antonia and Paul. No one else touched them. In the storeroom there was a box of beer, another of Coca-Cola. Bags of corn and rice. Paul's father was a politician and a preacher. He owned a small, busy truck, and sheds near the market where men built simple furniture. He even knew how to repair radios, an entrepreneur in a socialist setting with small enterprises everywhere; nothing obvious, nothing to call attention.

It was a big village, with houses made of cement and sun-dried brick. They had a soccer field, even bleachers, and behind it a small cluster of shops and kiosks. A small church to the north and next to it the single-story school buildings.

"My father donated the desks and chairs in the school," Paul said. "The pews in the church. Mahogany benches and mud floors, you'll appreciate the irony there." They walked through empty classrooms, blackboards left to the mischief of the last one in there, a stick figure of a man pissing. They looked from the windows across to a shed where a young man hefted sacks of charcoal from a truck and another measured it out in piles, three Swiss baby-food tins for a shilling.

There had been no school here when Paul was a kid. He was sent to Uganda. She had seen a picture of him in a uniform: short pants and a blazer with emblem. A white shirt. Taken at the wrong exposure so the black face was solid, without feature except the eyes.—"He didn't grow big until he was eighteen," his mother said. "He was always smallest. Now look!"—The schoolmasters were British in those days: they rode motorcycles. Drank Pimms' at sundown. Perhaps they all seemed to be the same because they were feared. They were posing, making the most of it. If a boy was bright they responded to him, made him a favorite, an example. This was their excitement. They took it as proof of something evolutionary they had discovered.—"Now look here, we've got Luenga, a whiz at maths"—which made them even grander.

Unlike his mates, he didn't go on to England. Instead he went to America, to Harvard, to Elizabethan plays and parasitology labs, keeping the company of dead writers and microbes, hiding, what a boy does when he's shy and a dreamer. He developed a taste for jazz and, surprisingly, Robert Frost. She couldn't see it: all that snow and frozen ground, the heaving winter nights. He liked it anyway, intoning lines, "A leaping tongue of bloom the scythe had spared / Beside a reedy brook the scythe had bared." His own poem used the rhythms and sometimes the language he found here. But he kept it private, no one knew much about him. He never postured, save for the khaki trousers, the tweed jackets. What he claimed to have learned about color when he was the only black face in a roomful of white ones was that he could only be seen as long as he appeared to be the same as a white man in every other way. An African, yes. The accent, the distress with cold weather. But other than that, a person, "just like us," was the phrase. Westernized. That was his identity; without it, he said, he was curiously invisible. To those who didn't know he was "just like us" he went unseen. A condition you have to experience to understand, he said. —"Ask any of us. You simply don't see us. Unless, of course, we're just like you." He could have been right. Invisibility was a dark man's theme. You read it every time you picked up a book written by an African—or black men anywhere. The unseen men.

The beginning of anger like his was a kind of self-hate, because he had been Westernized. That made the wedge that his family widened. Behind the tolerance and the good-natured banter (laughing as he tried to skin a goat) they were only waiting. Even though they acknowledged Antonia enough to let her share her bed with a few extra children (never with Paul: they were Christians and he was still married to Helen). Even though they let her help cook and serve the food, taught her how to prepare the tea their way . . . all the time they were holding interviews with Helen's father without saying a word to either of them. That sweet old grandmother who fussed so over the white woman, who got out all the family pictures from an ancient toffee box, back to things that looked like daguerreotypes printed on thick paper, telling Antonia how Paul first walked, his first words, his ability to read like a miracle, calling Antonia, "my child" . . . all the time wielding as much power as she could to get him back for them. The toothless crone. And the elders talking late into the night against that sputtering radio. You never knew what they were up to. All of them, until it was presented as a fait accompli. Paul one day announced that his marriage to Helen had been reinstated. Antonia laughed, which was about all that a second wife could do. He tried to make excuses about his obligations; he owed them everything, they had waited so long. But Antonia believed his decision to comply went deeper than that. Her visits there ended. For a while she became the woman he lived with in town. Ironically, Helen was the one who couldn't bear the polygamous arrangement.

She came at her rival with a knife. Dressed in blue, patterns of a cotton print. Antonia thought, she's the mother of a child that has just died in my care. A tumor on the baby's kidney and a doomed surgery. Funny, she wasn't scared, thinking, Oh dear, some *mganga*'s told her I did it. I killed her boy. And it's true. In a way. With my knife. Now I face hers. Sometimes she told the bereaved what would have happened anyway. But they didn't have to believe it. The language of diagnosis meant nothing, not when someone wants to know why. It went through her mind: What will I tell this woman with the knife? That her baby would have died anyway? The rest was a reflex. She felt the blade touch her collarbone, but she was the stronger. She took the knife. The nurses ran toward them. Then Luenga.

NINE

◁ ◇ ▷

Esther lacked strength, Zobetta said. Too thin, too full of silly ideas. She brought tea. This was because Esther did not eat. The bones on her chest rose under her skin. Her arms were sticks.

"You may feel the shame," she said, "but who is truly the whore? The one who takes the money or the one who pays?" There was a soapy flavor to the tea and Esther couldn't drink it. The milk was bad. Opening packets, people were never sure: they sniffed first, they dipped their fingers. They asked questions about it: What have they put inside the milk now? What animal did they take it from? Some said it was taken from dogs. Others, men who worked at the factory, talked about white powders that came from Australia.

"I have lost my hunger," Esther said. She had no money to buy food and had to eat what others gave. She had lost her desire, even for the porridge Hadija prepared, once her favorite, sprinkled with the cinnamon she got from Sharad and brought to her in Hadija's best cup, with a flower and the word LOVE.

Handing her the porridge, Hadija explained the alternative of "Sugar Daddies," so a woman didn't have to go from one man to another like a chicken picking in the dust. "They are almost like real husbands," she said, "but with cars and *duty free*." Her eyes opened. She held a small stick like a cigarette and puffed and flicked an ash. She sipped from a glass that wasn't there. "Johnnie Walk-hair Red!" she said. And told how you went out fishing for Sugar Daddies among Nigerians. You wore red pants.

But Esther couldn't listen. Other thoughts battled in her brain. Too much to be pitied and understood. Feelings that had become events. There was a boy called Richard from Tabora who was crippled and in a wheelchair. His mother pushed him, ignoring what everyone thought. Esther watched him as she stood with Zobetta at one of Ntiro's meetings. A Dutch boy and Dutch girl had arrived on a motorcycle and wanted, Ntiro said, to teach everyone about cabbages. How to grow them and cook them in special ways so children would agree to eat them. Africans, he said, didn't know the value of vegetables. Esther eased up gently into the crowd, pressed between the two skinny brothers from Bogoro with their hollow eyes. Ntiro had called out, his voice like a woman's, that the Dutch ones could only help if the villagers worked together with them in cooperation. In this way, they would learn science, also lacking in Africa, which told you about fertilizer and insect poison. He began to talk, as he always did, about the Chinese, in a different voice, one that was deep, showing his admiration. How the Chinese had risen out of poverty and ignorance by revolution and then, in their kindness, had come to build a railroad for their African brothers. Zobetta was behind Esther complaining that even though there were thousands of Chinese all over the place, not one had ever spent his money on a whore: their peculiar eyes signified impotence and their language, too, which sounded exactly like the cries of tiny lambs as farmers bit off their balls.

Esther felt the whole world as the villagers wove around her, their faces and their arms. Their whispering sounds seemed gathered against the silence of the emptied houses and kiosks. So close, she thought, if I could dare to touch them all . . . a welling, fearful sensation. Emotion and the crowd made her dizzy. She could vanish; it had happened last year to a Makonde woman who vanished as Hadija stood there watching. Dreams rose though her eyes were closed, all the sick ones lifting from the crowd, their coughs and broken skins, like ghosts. The boy called Richard from Tabora stood and ran even though he remained in front of her fixed in his chair with wheels, still crippled. She moved close to him, brushing the chair with her arm, seeking substance. Only a dream. Nothing real. When she drew back, a Makonde, Musa, who sold kittens for a shilling, touched her shoulder. "*Malaya*," he said. Whore.

For days, the boy Richard loomed, and Musa's word struck at the vision like thunder. Any place she went it was the same, a road leading to a single destination. She felt the way she did in the forest at night with Musumbi, the lights of village fires getting closer and closer. You were always frightened of what you might find there. Esther wondered what would happen if she asked the white doctor why she saw these things, moments when she wanted to say, "Is this thing possible? What happened when I touched Almaz? The child Bemba?" All these things like madness or possession. She knew how white people became angry at Africans suddenly, for no reason, as unexplainable as rain. Remembered the French memsaab shouting, "*Feddup! Feddup!*" at Ignatius, pointing her finger. You had to go carefully with them, like entering a village at night, gathering detail upon detail from the shadows, hoping to sneak beyond the danger of hidden things. She wanted to believe what the white doctor told her about sickness and nothing else. Things had been written in books. Pictures that could not be denied: germs seen under a glass that gave them life. "Science," which was a way of living and more, a kind of hope. —"I will go to the city. I will find a teacher." To escape the fools.

The doctor was beautiful, Esther saw, but hidden. Esther wondered if it was knowledge, thickened by details because the eyes of white people were often pale, never giving away a thought. Beautiful, but with a tired face for all of it. Musumbi told her once it was because they came from places where they grew in ice, walking through it in special shoes.

Sometimes Esther and Antonia would sit together across a desktop and their tea that was never boiled long enough to give a taste, with no words between them. Sometimes, they explored: "Water is dangerous," Esther said. "Rivers come in floods. Or they are dry and have no water." She waited for an explanation and felt like a child because the doctor looked at her that way. "When there are bad things, people throw them in the river. Even sickness.

Your people understand this, that's why they boil the water before they drink."

"Yes-yes, we do." It made the doctor laugh, who said, "but because of *bacteria,* the germs your father told you about," and showed pictures from a book. Then she let Esther look at everything through a special glass, like the X- ray, that penetrated to reveal what eyes couldn't see. Even a drop of water opened to a world of shapes that moved, flowerlike, with worms that swarmed. Esther's eye pressed against a tube; she covered the other, as she was told, with her hand. The moment was too full and made her recoil; then she returned to look again. Surprised, her thoughts began to swell and bud with no sense of what they would grow to be. She looked at blood and skin, everything confirming what she believed, that all things could be shown if you only knew the way to see them. Her breath was thick; she felt the doctor's pleasure close behind her like whispering.

"What kind of evil things are thrown in the river, Esther?" she asked later. Her hair was loose and feathery and she twisted pieces of it like a rope, then let them go.

"At night sometimes I would hear talking about things that made people jealous or sick. If you could throw them in the river they would be gone. The *waganga* always knew the way."

"What things?"

"Charms." Esther knew it was a risk to talk like this in a room full of books, but the doctor already knew everything and folded her arms in front of her as if to hold it all. They could be friends this way, Esther thought, except for something that was around them: jealousy, or a feeling like it that had no name. Hers, and the doctor's, and the Africans' who stared perhaps with evil eyes.

"I will save money. I will become a clothes designer . . . " Hadija was saying. She and Esther were walking to the beach to get a fish. She wore her red pants, even though it was not the kind of fishing you did in red pants. "I will fly to Parisfrance in a plane . . . fwaaaah!" Her arms were wings. She wagged her bottom at Mbele, who sold charcoal. There were no Sugar Daddies in Mikorosheni but she didn't care. She practiced. She put out bait. She sang, "Oooooo, oh, oh, oh, oh, oh, oooooh, sugar sugar. Oh, oh, oh, oh, oh, ooooooh, honey, honey," as they went.

In the early morning, young men stretched in doorways and tied up shoes. Old men came out and sat on benches with babies. Women sent their boys up trees to pick the ripe papaya. There was an empty plot before they reached the beach; three women and the Dutch boy were digging. Mr. Ntiro with a Thermos and a cup of tea was there at a table writing things. He had posted a picture of Europeans' food floating in a circle with arrows pointing at cheese, which was terrible and could make you gag, and meat, which was too expensive for Africans. There was this business of their vegetables: cabbage, for example, and lettuce that was no more than watery leaves.

Esther told Hadija how the French cut cabbages into small-small pieces, put salt on them, then a cloth and then a rock, pressing it every day until it sank to the bottom and cooked in the salt by turning sour. You had to keep it outside the house because it smelled like shit. Finally you cooked it in a pot with pig meat and wine.

"But truly, is it food?" Hadija opened her mouth and made a fool face. Because the cooking of Europeans never ends. And so, they went along, singing all the songs they ever knew:"Baaa-by love, baaaa-by love, won ju be ma baaaby love."

And on days like this, because there were such possibilities, Esther told Hadija, "I will learn to read. And then I will learn to be a doctor." She could see chances from the crest of the beach, out against the sky where the Swahili men had put their nets to wait for the tide. Quickly as the sea reached them and as it rose, they pulled their nets against it toward the shore, calling out to each other, water at their chests, arms held high. Esther was still amazed at the rise and fall of the tide like the very first time when, one morning, she had come alone and found the bay was gone and a long flat stretch of empty sand was in its place. She had stood there, breathless, waiting to see what terrible thing would happen next like standing on the edge of the world. Until she saw men walking below her, carrying nets, as though nothing at all had happened. Later, she saw reflected in its cycle the rhythm of the moon.

She and Hadija, leaning on each other, sat and watched. The skinny brothers from Bogoro came—it made them giggle—and a skinny dog, as though they were three the same. And after them Flora Kahama, carrying a pumpkin, who stopped and said, "I have a job." She sat with them. Hadija put the pumpkin on her stomach and waddled like someone pregnant.

"At the university," Flora said. "Picking up the fallen papers and washing floors." Because the son of her mother's brother was the new manager; the only way to find work. There were so many cleaners there, she laughed, because the new manager had to hire all his own people but couldn't sack the others, that soon there would be only one paper for each of them to pick up and throw away. By now Hadija had given birth and was nursing the pumpkin.

Flora said she would get Esther a job there, too, and she did. They went to her cousin's office in the back where men were still building the university. They sat on trucks full of lumber and bags of cement. Or stood holding windows. She and Flora walked in past piles of bricks and stacks of broken furniture. Under a fan, Esther stood near Flora with her hands drawn together. She was looking down at them and at her feet. The cousin was busy in his office like a rooster.

Flora told him, "My friend Esta has no mother and no father. A thief has stolen all her clothes and her watch," she said. "Her brother is a soldier . . . " This last story was no more a surprise than Ignatius telling the French memsaab she was his sister, because Flora was clever and knew how you got jobs. Her cousin was nodding, looking in his desk drawers. He called out the window to the men in the trucks.

"You were saying, Flora?" he said. "Your friend? Her brother?" Papers were collapsing on his desk or jumping under the fan. He wrote on one of them. "A simple note," he explained, "so I don't forget."

"Aren't we all comrades?" Flora asked. "Are we not all cousins? And her brother, fighting in Uganda. Maybe killed. Who can help her?" Making it all seem connected to all the things Mr. Ntiro wanted them to learn: the revolution, the liberation, the names of places far away. People who were friends. People who were enemies.

"Yes, I know a lot of cleaning work," Esther told him. She unfolded her letters from the French and from Mr. Waliji. Finally the cousin, fluffing through a book with pale green pages, wrote her name, Esther Moro, and said she could have a job. That day, waiting for the doctor at the hospital, she was happy. The hard starched cotton of her working uniform, the bad color of it didn't matter. She accepted the promise of change, an accumulation of signs.

They were twenty-five who had to wash the floors, but only twelve mops, so they went along two-two, one carrying a bucket and one a mop, going like snails. She heard the bells that broke the stillness between buildings, and watched as students poured from them, carrying their books and all the things they knew. It made the air thin; the sky seemed farther away as if their thinking made a difference. She lingered outside the buildings or classrooms where professors stood in front of blackboards giving instructions. It could have been magic: she saw chalk writings, characters, letters and numbers and more. Ideas held together by circles and lines. She hated to wipe it away and thought if only she could eat the dust in the way that Moslems washed the ink from their writings and drank the wisdom of God.

Sometimes, after the students had left him, one of the teachers stared at her. An African, a foreigner, his name was Nkosi: it was all she knew. His beard impressed her, his painful walk. He had a space between his teeth. He was small in height but wide and very black. He had a strong way of speaking that came through the closed door. It was English: she understood it as music. When she asked him what they studied in his room—a blackboard rich in lines that crossed in boxes and fell—he said, "Money and how the white men use their tricks to get it all." Certain days he would wait for her, watching as she and Flora worked. He seemed to know her mind. He had traveled far like Musumbi, even farther, to places where no black men had ever been seen before, where there was ice and coldness everywhere and children who peered into his window just to see. That was his joke, but she saw sadness instead, like a wound. Parts of him, he told her, had turned to ice there. His wisdom and his weakness were like two arms that held her. If she was sad for him, it only contained the seeds of love.

Hadija said, "Is he Nigerian?" because he was so black. "A Sugar Daddy?" She had seen him driving a car. And one day when he came to Zobetta's, Hadija went circling, dancing, making him laugh. She asked him for a cassette radio and a driving lesson. Esther told them he was a teacher. "He teaches money." An idea that Zobetta liked because she wanted to put some in a bank and carry a small book that said so.

There were many foreign teachers at the university, black ones from other African countries and white ones from Europe. The Europeans swam back and forth every day in a big pool and made their children swim back and forth shouting at them to win. Women with voices of cats, with pale hair and skin that grew brown dots as though it didn't know what color to be. One of them had eyes the color of Coca-Cola bottles because, Flora had heard, she put little pieces of green colored glass in them like spectacles. To look like a terrible *shetani* rising from a drainpipe.

Esther told her doctor all these things as they drank tea and listened to the hospital cleaners with their mops, a rhythm in the halls beyond. It made them both laugh, but Esther preferred the times when they were serious to make the doctor understand that shame such as her own meant there would be payment.

Orphaned and sold. Always sold until she was ruined. Even now. "It's the same as if I stayed in Pareh," she said more than many times but never could explain why. It was her fear of the things she saw, her vision of this child Richard walking, how she wanted to cover him somehow and then, as one pulling away a cloth, strip his trouble from his body. She wanted answers that would come to her as if these were lessons that she attended in the same way the students at the university watched as teachers wrote things for them.

"You are lucky," was what Esther told Antonia. "Your power comes from books and teachers and it cannot betray you."

Sickle of coral cliffs cutting the Indian Ocean. Oyster

Bay. Not a breath of air: the houses hung like lanterns in the trees behind huge lawns or floated like lighted boats on a dark sea. Antonia walked to the event in a gentle rain, cousin of mist, a mango rain, they called it. An unusual season. Headlights behind her picked out her shimmering reflection on the wet road.

"Why, Dr. Redmond! Are you on your way to the Clayburns'?"

She took the ride, shaking her umbrella and pulling it into the car, shivered with the first blast of air conditioning. "One of these days," she told them, "they'll fix my car."

"Well, just tell us what part you need and Harold will send for it for you. In the pouch. We're not supposed to." The woman's perfume reminded her of someone; she couldn't think who. Reminded her even more that she smelled of hospital, which came out in damp weather like dormant mildew. Not antiseptic, not clean, but a trace of old corridors and yellow soap.

Luminaria lined the circle of driveway. She saw the hostess, Scotty Clayburn, wearing something diaphanous and telling a handful of guests that it was a nightgown. "The *only* place you can find anything cool enough for this climate is in lingerie." Scotty was sure, she said, that no one would ever know.

"Of course, now we *all* know." It was Ted Armstrong. Antonia was glad.

Festive napkins, hearts and doilies and cupids dangled from the awnings. "For goodness sake," she said. "Valentine's Day!"

"Be mine," he said. He had been drinking.

"Scotty Clayburn," a peripheral voice, whispering, "is walking around in a *nightgown!*"

He kidnapped her after the coffee, before the brandy, pleading that the doctor had a headache and needed a ride home.

"You're not staying?" Scotty Clayburn asked. "We're just about to roll up the carpet. An aspirin maybe?"

No, no aspirin. The eyes that followed their exit under an arch of bougainvillea seemed to approve, either of the scandal or the pair. It was St. Valentine's, after all.

He didn't want to go right home and drove toward

town. She leaned, tipping toward him to fight the long sweep of the bay, as still now as a lake, mirror to the black sky. A carnival ride.

"They've got a Cuban act at the Simba Club," he shouted. She shouted back and shook her head to loosen the strangling hair, saw his face in the rearview mirror, eyes gone haywire like Luenga's when he'd had too much. And smiled. Because the Simba Club was such a lark, and she hadn't been for years. Some time ago it had lost its Third World swank and air conditioning, and most of its famous red velvet interior had been done in by fire. She remembered the victims; a combusting nightclub and its toll.

The Cuban act, however, turned out to be Angolans, a troupe of acrobats and fire eaters. Announced by a drummer and a tinny record player. An enormous Angolan was balanced on a unicycle and riding across a bridge of tables. With the light of a flaming torch, he examined his genitals, smiling into a balloon of striped clown pants. His mouth and his eyebrows had been painted red. Antonia and Armstrong were pushed into a corner near the bar, bombarded by flesh there, pillows of breasts pressed into her back, soft buttocks resting on her hips, an elbow in her ribs.

The Angolan's cycle was growing in stabs of changing light until the big black man soared over the contraption on two tiny wheels that he pedaled from stilts. He showered sweat into the crowd, shaking it from his temples like the god of rain. Now, a small man, high on stilts as well, wearing white lipstick, a blond wig, and artificial breasts, blew a cloud of flame into the audience and the one on the unicycle moaned in English. "She no love me. Booooooo hooooooo." He made a sweep on his contraption and grabbed a breast. Which popped. On the ground, a man as thin as wires was doing the limbo under a burning bar braced on Coke bottles.

The big performer began another act, jumped over the limbo act and said they would now contact their ancestors on a toy phone he was brandishing. A bell rang. The patter was fast; English too broken to understand. Only those close enough to the dance floor laughed; the rest were craning to see, or had given up and were dancing with arms in the air to disco music that came from overhead. An acrobat burst in wearing a frightening mask. He called out curses on the crowd and spun a bicycle wheel on his head. The troupe stole another table and made a tower, on top of that a human pyramid with the phone and the masked dancer on top. He screamed into the receiver. The limbo dancer in a leopard-print nightgown breathed fire and ran around the others as if to torment them.

Ted Armstrong moaned. A whip cracked and a juggler appeared. The little man, his false breasts gone, but still wearing the blond wig, compressed himself into an asana and the big one tossed him in the air like a ball until he popped open and landed on his feet. It was the finale: the master of ceremonies in a frayed tuxedo passed a hat while a residue of German tourists clamored for more.

No longer swank. Antonia noticed, not having taken a sip yet, that she didn't get a glass with her beer. And, of course, it wasn't cold. Then in the crowd that moved on the dance floor, she saw Esther's friend Hadija in red pants and Esther, too, wearing Hadija's purple jumpsuit. She was with a man. Antonia didn't like him. Found him instantly not right. He was old. Already gray. His face was wide, with square, full features and his eyes were small. He had a huge beard, too much like aggression. He was short, but broad and muscular with a narrow waist, a long torso, and small legs, and he walked awkwardly, with a pronounced limp.

"There, in that purple outfit," she told Armstrong. "My bewitched patient, Esther Moro."

Later on his balcony with the brandy they had foregone earlier, she confessed. "It must be latent maternal instincts. I'd rather not have seen Esther there, that way, with that particular type."

It was late enough for them to think they'd rather stay awake the rest of the night and watch the sun come up. "One of the advantages of living where I do," he said. He brought a Thermos of hot coffee up there and some mangoes to mark the dawn. He didn't move toward her but waited, cautiously, like an actor in the wings, for her to give the cue. For what reason? Because he was embarrassed by the last time they were together?

He had leaned his chair back against a bit of wrought-iron railing to face her, teetered rocking there a second or two. Grinned. Which made her feel silly. Red filaments on the horizon hinted of dawn, so far behind him it seemed they had to be in India.

"I'll never get used to seeing the sun rise over the sea," he said. Californian. He had swung around and changed his seat to be near her on the wicker couch. It had been enough of an opening to bring him near, to trace the outlines of her face, to risk her mouth, and she his.

Charles never liked it when she returned home early enough in the morning to make her arrival reek of the night before, in some car or other, blaring her sin to all of Kinondoni. It probably wouldn't have mattered had they lived more privately and in better circumstances. Once she caught herself asking to be left off at the bus stop, to save the old man from a weeklong mope, but then thought no, better to keep things straight with him about the way I live my life. So she faced his great self-righteous sulks. Bad enough that she had taken him from her father's house, "a proper house," he called it, though his own in the village was made of mud and twigs and practically falling down. He never thought of that. He couldn't really adjust to the switch in station like a disillusioned, bitter wife. He would tell her, in English, "It is hurt my heart. I who see you born . . ." placing his hands so far apart to show how big she had been then. He must have had such dreams for her, ones he never dared for his own slew of children. She had no idea how many there were. But that morning he kept his back quite firmly toward her, an apron tied aggressively at his waist, black hand immobilized on a pile of green peppers to show his ire.

"Hello, Charles, I'm back . . . "

"I am see," he answered. No use trying to bring him around with flimsy excuses. She heard the deliberate hard ticking of knife on chopping block—the Charles machine, her food processor, turned on to drown out all talk.

"Is there coffee, Charles?" she begged. In fact, she had smelled it. She would have preferred juice, something tart and citric but she asked for the coffee. Juice might not have been ready, might have taken time, put him on the spot. Bad enough to come home like this, delivered on the doorstep like the morning news.

The man's name was Nkosi. On Monday, Esther told Antonia who he was. A South African, she said, driven from his country by the white men there. She was dressed in cheap market clothes that day, awkwardly cut and crudely stitched, a cross between a penitent and a prisoner. In contrast, there was a wrist full of gaudy bangles. Nkosi had lived in Sweden, Esther said, where he had a Swedish wife and Swedish children.

"Are you angry that he's my friend?" Deliberately she shook the bracelets, a village sound like dried seeds in a music gourd.

Already Antonia could feel the sway he had over her. "Do you sleep with him?"

"Yes."

"And he pays you?"

"Yes. He gives me money."

"Then nothing has changed."

"I think you are angry."

No, not angry. Not even surprised. His limp was the clue when she considered Esther's obsessions with the miserable. That boy, Francis, she had loved on Oyster Bay. Her father. The sounds she heard of the world coughing. Esther's fixation after all was with the halt, the lame. The face across from her mimicked the colors of the afternoon, cast in a reddish light. On the desk, the Dar es Salaam *Daily News* promised POVERTY WILL BE ERADICATED! in headlines so big the page was filled, crowning the litter there like a castle made of alphabet blocks.

"Perhaps you like him because he reminds you of Francis, because of his leg."

"The sickness that eats muscles."

"It was polio?"

"That comes with the rain . . . " She remembered a village someplace, and a sick boy who had died. There had been a famous *mganga*: he had long pale hair like a white man's, tufts of it on his shoulders. He tried to draw the sickness from the boy's ankles using sharpened sticks. Each time she saw how the sticks would flame and char. Her father had said it was a trick; the sticks were the tools of madmen. But she had watched carefully, had seen the sticks smolder on their own and flare. Like the boy's body, she told Antonia. "But the sickness," she said, "was in his throat."

Uncanny, since that's where it would have been, Antonia thought. But what was the point really? she asked herself now. Operating like this on the boundaries of Esther's hallucinations? There was simply no way to tell her, "But you didn't see those frogs. You didn't see those combusting sticks." Not when she was convinced that Esther had seen them, even though they didn't exist, which was what seduced her in the end when it came to Esther because there she was.

Did she think she could really offer Esther help, something normally dispensed in pills, or injections? —"What do you want from her anyway?" Armstrong had asked. "You don't expect anything from her or any of the rest of them, do you? You don't expect to be able to *influence* them? Only bureaucrats still have that kind of arrogance." He laughed. "Even the missionaries have given up." To which she answered, "What I really want is to see her go to her home." And he: "They all need to go home. To start over again, but this time without us. Too bad that isn't going to happen." —Did it mean she ought to give up and shrug things off, when she had just begun to feel her way in this territory. Expecting what? Something she had never reached before. Standing in a high patch of sun to warm her back, each year when she climbed Kilimanjaro, the horizon a low flat arc, the dissolving edge of the world below. Never like the others who wanted to reach the top, despite the fun of mittens and parkas and boots as though that icy peak had played a great funny trick on the earth's Equator. No, she had always wanted to go down, to the riverbeds and plains where there was life.

"Ummmm, well, I think if you really like Nkosi . . ." Antonia hesitated. It was girl talk, not her thing.

"*Anakaa tu,*" Esther said. The bangles were a soft percussion against an even softer voice. "He's just there." In Swahili it didn't mean place but rather a surrender to the terms of existence, as though he had become part of the atmosphere, part of how she would live, beyond choice. "He's good," she insisted. "He knows kindness." She settled in the chair then, lost in her concerns, her hands folded in her lap, the restless bracelets stilled. She wanted to know the things that could make a person crippled. Not just a disease like polio but other things. Her questions skirted witchcraft, a favorite subject, searching for any evidence to deny it. Explanations. Proofs. So she could finally believe there was no magic.

It was always hard to follow her: thoughts born out of conflicting perceptions, what she physically saw and what she intuited, the ways she imagined a disease came and went. Not the imagery a doctor was used to—war, the invading bacteria, the enemy cells, the battle of antibodies. Esther spoke in other terms, of drawing off and rebalancing, convinced that sickness was bound to the world beyond. She spoke of charms hung on doors, of amulets around a child's neck, forces alive in the air. Ideas she must have taken from her father or the *waganga*.

There was a boy in Mikorosheni, she finally admitted. His mother pushed him in a chair with wheels. Her attention had come to him and she kept seeing him, always in her path. She linked him with Francis and Nkosi and saw a progression there or a demand. To her, parallels were significant: she determined cause and effect by aligning similar things. Pregnant women who ate joined fruits would deliver twins. A broken gourd predicts a drought.

"His legs are closed," she told Antonia. "They say his mother carried a covered pot before his birth."

Antonia looked away. Perhaps both of them had the same image then, a blackened clay form and the crippled child sealed inside. "He should come to the hospital," she told Esther.

Clouds had made a ceiling outside. It changed the color but not the luminosity. If anything the light was even brighter under pressure, whites intensified before a storm. When the two women stepped out, it was into layers of sky. They separated, Esther saying, "*Haya . . .*" not good-bye, meaning, yes, okay, a little hesitant as though there had been no conclusion, until she heard Antonia say, "*Tutaonana*," and knew she could come back, that it was still good with them.

Her gestures became formal when they parted, or when they met, greeting the white woman with a nervous smile, waiting until Antonia held out her hand first. Her nod was almost a bow with the eyes lifted in question. It was a trained response, lost to insincerity: Antonia was never sure what Esther Moro thought let alone what she might do next. Chances were Esther felt the same about her. That bow, those peering eyes. She thought of Luenga's grandmother and all her solicitude. She had held Antonia's hand, had laughed as she braided the long straight hair while her daughters giggled and combed and ran about with strands of it shouting, "I have one!" That old black hand on her shoulder, only to get closer and closer each time and examine and pick out everything that was unworthy.

The weight of the clouds pressed the islands off shore, changing the perspective. They dwindled in an unreal distance as though they had sprung loose and a storm had dragged them out to sea. Now all the light was contained in the water, swelling up and breaking in sharp crests of waves. The last dhows raced for shore.

Esther knew where the crippled boy's house was. It could be approached through the village or come upon from the beach, from behind the sand dunes where there was thick brush and heavy vines. Unseen that way, she watched the houses where the people from Tabora lived. A path lined with flowers in tins led the way to wooden steps, to a porch under a grass roof. The plots of maize and cassava were green and full, holding the light themselves and shining as if in welcome. Esther learned that each day the boy's mother swept the porch and steps. Chickens gathered; the mother gave them food. Then she brought her son outside in his chair with wheels.

Going through Mikorosheni, she felt the village around her and the way people lived: houses blown by wind (sometimes at night you heard the noise and in the morning found another one had appeared on weak poles; sometimes walls were banana leaves and nothing more). Poor houses tilting toward each other or leaning into the paths as if to gather strength. If they were small and close together, the doorways were like doubts that kept repeating, holding darkness inside. She heard in passing the sound of a baby crying or the echo of a story that had been told around some new trouble. Rooms. Esther's thoughts were eyes peering into windows; disturbed, as if the village had thrown itself down to fall on its knees and beg for life.

Someone had said that the boy, Richard, from Tabora, was closing and twisting.

He was a shape in the shadow. There could have been walls around him, thick vines that reached the roof and fell like green water over the house. Full of white sticky flowers streaked with red. The black opening that marked the doorway had more substance than his curled form. Esther wanted him to remain that way, distant, untouchable. Going there to see him was her reassurance that they were being held apart, a way of testing, because she was afraid that she would be brought to him the way she had been brought to Almaz by a power not her own. Her presence so close to him but hidden, was kept a distinct, a separate thing.

One day a man appeared and took the boy upon his back. They came out together in the sun, a monstrous image with two heads. A dog followed, barking, jumping toward the dangling legs. But the boy was laughing and that time Esther couldn't look away. The man spoke a greeting to her, "*Jambo*," and the boy, "*Jambo*," his voice riding behind the man like an echo and finally her own voice, "*Jambo*," connecting them all. She saw his thin legs, his bent spine. She felt a sudden tightening in her chest, something that gathered and finally broke out of her toward him. She looked down expecting to see an appearance, something terrible extruding there because there was a shape to it, a size: she felt she could touch it. Real. Like the frogs that came from Mrs. Manda. But there was nothing. She rubbed her hand over her chest without thinking. She began to follow them automatically as though, there on the back of that man, she, too, was carried, weak in her own legs. Trees and houses beat a rhythm against the answering sky. She had glimpses of the white sand and sea between each pulse and a vision, again and again of the boy, grown up this time and walking. A young man in detail: he wore a silver watch.

Then Hadija came running, calling her name. From the corner of her eye, Esther could see her friend's face gaining against the terrible thing that was happening to her. She lifted an arm to shield her eyes from the sun and called back, "HADI!" as loud as she could. Like crying for help. Hadija's arm was firm and warm, like touching earth, heat rose between them taking water from their flesh and mingling it there between them where they met, arms folded, and the two of them staggered like drunks. Esther smelled wine on her friend's breath.

Cashew flowers were blooming: the village was perfumed. Hadija moaned that Sharad was going to marry. A girl of great beauty whom he had never seen. She would come veiled and pure. He would slip a mirror under her veil and see her eyes which would capture his heart, and her long beautiful Hindi hair, like no other hair. Then he would take her and break her virginity. He would have happiness and Hadija would have misery. A heavy sadness was settling over her life. Sharad and his wonderful penis sheathed in green.

Esther knew her only safety was to stay away from Richard, but coming back from her work at the university, she turned, taking a path that brought her near his house, going closer than she should. Her purpose was bravery, to see if it would happen again—the strange tightening in her chest. She went close enough to see his face, a tiny oval with the lips and eyes of a pretty girl. She had reached the steps. Shadows in the porch gave way to objects, a wooden mortar, clay pots. A stool with three legs.

"Do you hurt?" she asked him. His mother walked out toward their voices from her sleep; her eyes were heavy. Esther told her, "I am learning to be a nurse." Small figures of other children appeared and ran around him, playing, bringing things.

"God will help him," his mother said. She told Esther that the hospital had not helped her son. They gave him medicines that only made him sick. They said there was nothing more. "You can go. You can wait there every day.

Waiting and waiting. What is the benefit?" She yawned lifting her arms, which were fat and strong. She moved close to him and closed around him, lifting him, whispering to him. "The *waganga* ate up our money with their powders and their oils. We are Christians," she said, "Jesus will help us."

Esther asked if she could take him sometimes, in his chair, to this place or that one around the village. Because of becoming a nurse, she said. In order to understand these things.

"We are Christians," his mother repeated. "He is a gift from God." The other children swarmed, pulled an explosion of white flowers from the vine, put them around his neck.

The next Saturday Esther took him to Zobetta's, where they drank tea. They passed the field where the Dutch ones had planted cabbages; she explained to him the strange pictures of food circling in the sky with arrows and smiling faces, as if she knew. After that she took him to the beach where they watched the fishermen. There she recited a story from the Bible that Francis had told her, about the many-colored coat. She carried him to the water where other children were playing. He was light, straddled on her back. She swung him around and down in front of her. He called out his joy. The children turned and raised their arms, holding their small boats made of scraps. First his feet touched and he began to kick them. Then she lowered him gently so his poor legs were floating there.

"This is swimming," he said. His legs drifted like broken sticks. The water was rising. Fishermen were echoing shouts, heads and arms, approaching from the sea. "Just like a fish," he went on. The children had come by then, singing his name, "Li-chard, Li-chard," bringing shells and seaweed and cans of water. If the waves would only take his sickness to the shore and then wash it out, an act of cleansing offered by the turning earth. She stirred the water, running her fingers over his ruined body. Was the light changing as she scrubbed, growing brighter, forming sharp hard blades like knives? Was there any truth in the things she saw? At last the water frightened him. He grabbed harder at Esther's neck. "I want to go back," he said.

She had asked the white doctor, "What do they do in America to help someone like that?" And was told that there were many things called therapy, in English. When the doctor said that sometimes they used water, it startled Esther, as if to confirm it, to tell her she was doing the right thing. "In the water?" Because it was somehow a truth, a knowledge that was always there.

So she urged him again and again into the sea. He was always waiting for her, calling "Esta! Esta, *mimi niko!*" behind the thickening vine, all leaves now, the flowers gone, dense as rock. His mother liked to stand in the doorway knitting white bed covers, a motion of elbows, a face that gazed. "You are such a good one," she told Esther.

"This is nursing," Esther told her. "And in English called *therapy* that tells you by water, or by pulling and bending, this is how to gather strength." The idea pleased Esther, an explanation she could make as they all listened. Her voice was weighty, but the words came easily and clearly, a tone Musumbi used to convey. "These are things which come slowly. The muscles will have to grow new. Inside and strings." Richard's mother looked carefully trying to understand, a kind of devotion. She said she thought his legs were truly straightening. Her sisters agreed and said that he was gaining flesh as well, that his legs had more the shape of legs instead of twigs or other broken things. When Hadija pressed on his foot one day, he pressed back. "*Kumbe!*" she cried. "He has his strength." She gave him a pair of dark glasses with shining rims for the sun.

Esther urged him into the sea and made a seat there for him from the bottom of a broken boat.

"How does the water come and go?"

"Because of day and night and the turning of the earth." It satisfied him to know and her to tell him. Even as she said it, she could feel the movement, could see it in the rising water, a pull against what was stationary (the sky, their two figures) urging the sea. In that tension she found a harmony between what she desired for him and what was meant to be, in that persisting vision of him, whole and well, this time a tall boy running with his brothers. And she was not the same either, was more, saw it in the mirror of the dark glasses that covered his eyes. She was a child and a woman, a tree on the shore, a bird—images, pinpoints of reflecting light. She took the water and dwelled, gently touching, washing his flesh. Her hands were directed to the back of his neck and rested there. She held her fingers against the base of his skull. The action was slow as though they were passing through a dream. Both of them knew it; both of them knew the outcome. She felt something strengthening each time she cradled him in their place in the bay. Soon she began to see the difference until a day when he told them. "I can stand." And he rose and stood there.

More than cleaning at the university, the boy Richard had become Esther's work. She told the doctor, "Now you can see how his legs are able to open and close. He can move by himself. Like this. Soon he will be able to walk."

And the doctor had said, "This is good, Esther."

"I told them this is therapy as you said. So they don't think that I am a witch." Now there was knowledge between them, they smiled at the same things. This made Esther feel secure. To Richard's mother and the others, she had said, "In America, they put the water in great tubs and push it with motors," all of them gathering on the porch to listen. "But we Africans only have the sea, which pushes by itself." That made them all laugh.

Plastic beads that popped apart and snapped back together made a circle around Esther's neck and wrist. She carefully selected the colors in a pattern of white and blue and red, the colors of the doctor's flag, to wear them when she went for tea, to what she called her "classes" at the hospital. To tell her, "He has walked, by himself," because it seemed that they had done this thing together.

Hadija appeared behind her, fighting for the mirror so she could glue on her lashes made of plastic hairs. She smelled of beer and *bhangi*. Instead she put the lashes on her lip like a mustache which made her remember Sharad. She said, "I have seen her," meaning Sharad's wife. She sighed. "Yes, I have." The mustache made Esther laugh. "She has big watery eyes." Hadija opened her own eyes and leaned into Esther's face. "She is small-small but has tooooo much gold. Her father has a big white car, an American car called

Pontiacar that you drive from a steering on the other side. An old car, you know. But big. Like a ship. And this one has tiny feet. Rings on her toes. Sharad will break her with his thing." She dropped to the bed and thrust her hips.

Then she was following Esther complaining even more, "Her hair is shining and down to here. When she pulls it from her braid it will make a blanket. Even her ears are tiny, like sweet baby's ears. And so beautiful. She has pale skin like a white girl. You'll see. I will show her to you."

Zobetta called from the stove, "Life is more bitter than chewing and swallowing a mouthful of quinine tablets."

"And Sharad saw me," Hadija said. "He even winked his eye at me. But even so, he turned away." She went moping in the hall. She wanted tea. She had the lashes on her brows now, dipped her voice to sound like a man's. "Yes," she repeated, "he turned away. Oh, my heart!"

Zobetta said, "When your eyes are full of smoke, a handful of pepper will be thrown in them."

Esther left them. The village was soft around her, rain blessed, pillows of green. People rested. Tended plants. There was maize. There were pumpkins. In the hollows there was rice. She felt giddy, revolving; that green and her memory of dust when there was drought. There was also times of flooding, sopping darkness with no sun. Not only rain, but sun, which was needed in balance. This was always something she had been coming to. Therapy was not witchcraft. The forces of the tide told of the turning earth, day and night, rain and sun. These could not be enemies. They did not struggle with you but with themselves. The moment of harmony was hard to find, easy to lose. She could see that this was what the *waganga* tried to create, what the doctors searched for in their books, in their tubes and testings. This was the object of prayer and sacrifice. And the object of magic. Ideas took shape in her mind beyond words, like rain getting closer.

But even as such thoughts arose, what she saw pulled them down. The sadness of men. Across from her on the bus: an old one counting and counting a few coins, a Makonde with a carving on his knees and holes in his pants, a woman with a sack of chickens. Their feet were in a row, bare ankles tipped over the edge of muddy shoes, a line of knotted toes, something sore and swollen. They were people who, as the Masai said, scratched on the earth for their lives.

When she was finally seated across from her doctor, the feelings she had were dim, the words for them seemed foolish. All she could say was what she knew certainly, "He has walked. Alone. With no helping."

"This boy? Your friend Richard?"

Esther nodded, She felt proud. Safe. It had happened and she was the same. No one knew. "Will he stay strong?" she asked.

"Perhaps," the doctor said. "Sometimes the heart is stronger than the body. We need hope." Hope seemed weak in the face of that secret power she knew was hers. When Richard had asked her, "What is it?" they had both looked to see.

The doctor told her, "It makes you happy, Esther, to help people. You must go on." They were two friends then around a happy event, leaning on their elbows stirring sugar in their tea.

Esther tried to ask about Jesus, as though He might offer the answer. "How did Jesus help people by touching them?"

"Those are stories from a long time ago. Two thousand years ago. People were different then."

So she showed the doctor the fun of her new beads, presents from Nkosi, a sound of sucking and popping that made them both laugh. When things made the noises of people, then everyone laughed. There was pleasure in the doctor. Esther could see it, so they walked together out on the port road crowded with buses and taxis. People stared. This was a notice that they both responded to and held each other's hand so everyone could look and wonder how it could be.

TEN

A man died in his hospital bed. No one knew what happened. He was just dead, the nurses insisted—a chart left blank. The head matron said everything had been done correctly, despite several hours in which no one could say who had been in charge of "that particular patient," as they called him. There was no remorse as far as Antonia could tell. Merely a sigh. She examined the corpse to no avail. The family had refused an autopsy. There were three wives, brought into her office so she could explain, but they had no questions and she had no answers. The youngest was no more than sixteen, her legs badly bowed from rickets. The oldest held her hand. It was the middle wife who wept, blotting tears with a crisp white handkerchief. A rich man whose sons would bicker over the automobile he had driven.

"He could have gone to London," the middle wife kept saying. The others nodded. "To London," she repeated. Behind them was the open door, behind that two nurses chatting in the corridor near a hamper of spilling linens.

Antonia railed at Paul Luenga in the hall, "Nothing is being done right." She hated her helpless tone, the way she held the old man's blank chart in the air. "They don't even clean up," she said, aware that she was overheard. Nurses disappeared as if by magic. "At least you ought to get them to clean up."

It was his frustration, too, but he hated it from her. "What are you talking about? One dead man? The end of the world?"

"Is this your bloody historical process then, this damned

stupidity? That little bow-legged widow? The other one harping on about London?"

He had taken the chart but wasn't looking at it. "Calm down, Tony," he said before turning away.

It was about standards, about the trap that technology had become. She could see how he had stood aside and watched it all happen: the hospital getting worse and worse, worse than any *mganga* clinic. They were surely worse now than any of those old men waving their ibex horns and grinding down the beaks of eagles. She began to think those who dealt with herbs and charms would take her business away. Retrogression: she could see the smug faces of those who observed Africa out of hotel windows, from behind their cameras, in their reports. Telling the world how it was sad, but true: things had been better in the colonial days. And for everyone. One of the best native hospitals in the world had been on Zanzibar: now the place was a death trap.

Luenga thought it was progress. "A seed must rot before it germinates." This was a proverb he dragged out, not so much an excuse as a taunt. Better if there were no standards. "Only when you completely ruin us will you understand how much of it is your fault and then you might leave us alone." She wasn't interested in predictions like that, retrospect in advance. It seemed too much like resignation.

Esther in her pop-bead necklace offered her respite, even humor: the red, white, and blue. As though she were on her way to a Fourth of July party. She had been elated, her step, her color. Her eyes were almost blindingly clear, wild in the serene contours of that face. It had made Antonia happy just to see her. She had listened to Esther talk about her "therapy" with this boy in Mikorosheni, and heard something transcendent in Esther's attitude although the girl said nothing but the barest, "He has walked. By himself." There was no choice but to believe her, to congratulate, even encourage her. Esther seemed to thrive with the boy, to emerge from her depressions. Her questions and Antonia's answers: the clinking cups of tea were the scaffold of a growing fondness.

"I bent his leg like this. I felt a thing right here."

"Yes, part of his bone." There were the pictures she wanted to look at, on and on until she worked her way to this bizarre idea she had about the sea, which she thought she got from Antonia. But who would have expected this amazing response? The boy walking? Antonia hoped she wouldn't drag them all, all the "poor ones" as she called them, the ones she heard moaning and coughing in the night, into the water, to some bench she rigged below the tide. Perhaps it was wrong, but there was less reason to urge her into a nurses' uniform, even if she did manage to read and write, so she could blunder around the wards in a place like this killing old men. No, it was better somehow for Esther to be where she was, doing what she was doing. It was the reason, because Antonia had caught her euphoria, that she had reached for her hand, out on the port road, two women with a secret, daring the world. To the very last touch of fingers at arms' length. An African good-bye.

At home, tacked on her door, she found a note from Charles:

> My dear good Madam, my home brother is sick and die and I am sorry for trouble to you and forgive me. Please I go home come back soon with God blessing. I pray your good fortune. You humble servant, Charles Juma.

Messages would come from his village and he would be gone. With never any warning, for a week, two weeks, something he paid a price for because she would do absolutely nothing in his absence, partly spite, partly ineptitude. There was a pattern, coming home at last to find he had returned, stranded in the living room. He would have started a hundred little jobs around the place and none would be finished before he was. Her revenge. He went off like this once or twice each year so she would have guessed he had five hundred brothers by now. There was nothing she could do. Employers had no rights in this matter, but how, even if they were not his blood brothers ("same-mother-same-father"), even if they were friends or cousins or some such, how did so many of them die? Funeral after funeral, a way of life. If she weren't a doctor, if she hadn't seen for herself, she would have thought he was making it up.

She rattled about in the little house shooing ants and flies. There was, despite the rain, no water for a bath. When Ted Armstrong arrived, she planned to have him take her to his house for a shower. She didn't change, folded something clean, hung a string of beads over the uniform. She thought about sitting up on his balcony while he brought her a drink—over the dark circle of bay, high cliffs of dead coral rising from the sea. From there, at low tide, you could even see the new outer reefs like strong arms holding the continent, rocking it to sleep.

Armstrong arrived with someone, Adam James, a correspondent from one of those newspapers, *The Washington Post, The New York Times, The Chicago Sun.* A middle-aged man who had a flask of whiskey and a round, blistered face—sun or booze. There was a tremble in the hand, a scraped knuckle that hadn't healed in a long time. As a doctor, she recognized old sores. He wanted to have a look at her house.

"Who built this? Bulgarians?" He wanted to know everything. "About your hospital? Working conditions? I don't suppose you want to discuss it."

"Today they were shitty," she cracked. "If you get sick, go home."

Armstrong asked, "Do you think anyone had a good day around here?" opening his arms to encompass them all. She could hear the sputtering of Makonde drummers starting up below, a rhythm she recognized right away as a wedding. Soon the women would be ululating, running through the streets to flush out the shy bride, making an even greater mockery of their twentieth-century themes: concern and working conditions and how did it go today and what did you get done.

James persisted, lighting cigarettes, "What about cholera? Isn't there cholera in the south? Everyone says so. Isn't anybody doing anything about it?" As he paced, looking over her books, he told them how he covered Africa. He picked at the sore knuckle when he talked. "I have a dart board with words on it—famine, corruption, genocide, drought, cholera, civil war. I throw a dart or two and then write a story. This way I don't have to travel so much." He hated airports in Africa. The stress associated with them was giving him an ulcer. "I've learned to bribe. I even write it down as a business expense."

At Armstrong's Antonia insisted on her shower and left the two men downstairs to cook once they decided that a restaurant would be silly. A meal was to come out of packets from America. Hamburger Helper. But she found the meat still frozen, rinsed to no avail, a gray lump on the countertop.

"You can't rush these things," Armstrong said. Abandoned, given over to a liquid diet, like a cliché about men in the kitchen. Antonia didn't mind: she pitched in chopping onions while Adam James hovered near her grumbling about how Americans took care of themselves. His cigarette was an extra appendage, the long ash, the slight tremor. Then he left to carry his message to Armstrong in the other room. She was still cool from the shower, which she had taken cold, wrapped in a *kanga,* tight under her arms and across her breasts, her favorite kind of native elegance. There in the kitchen with sozzled men scattered in the other room.

Mostly Adam James talked about a book he was working on. He thought of calling it *African Headlines* or *Headlines from Africa.* There was a certain insanity here. Opera buffo with sinister overtones. One couldn't take anything seriously and yet it could be deadly serious. Ask any Acholi in Uganda. Ethiopians themselves laughed when some joker translated "broad masses" literally so it came out as "fat people" when everyone was starving. He had a friend in Lagos who was still in jail for pointing his camera at something—no one said what. People who renamed their countries, their capital cities, all their streets, constantly as heroes rose and fell. Because it was all a burlesque in the first place, all getting to be old hat, almost boring; even the most bizarre things. He had met, for example, a Brit who was actually counting elephants, flying around in a Wright Brothers plane with a grid. A camp set up somewhere. Cameras and papers all over the place. Your classic lunacy in the bush. Mr. Kurtz, he not dead.

Antonia was laughing. She said to Armstrong, "Some of my best friends are lunatics in the bush." She would never be able to explain. She could only giggle, with her spoon stuck in a dessert Armstrong had whipped up; something, he bragged, made entirely of chemicals, meant to be lemon flavored with the name "dream" or "yum" used to describe it.

"Well," Adam James said, "those jokers *might* be able to hang on counting elephants. But, let's face it, the government is strictly on the side of the poachers. The fucking prime minister is financing them. An ivory fence in Hong Kong. It's well known." Before he fell asleep, he confessed it was time for him to go home. The sore on his knuckle was bleeding.

Making love with Armstrong lulled her, a state she described as relaxed-alert. Perhaps as a result of watching Adam James, she wanted a cigarette, the one she smoked every two or three years. It gave her a funny buzz, a hit, particularly at times like these in pitch-dark rooms, after everything else. Armstrong, because he didn't smoke either, had to rob the corpse on the living-room couch.

"I also undid the poor guy's belt. Took off his shoes."

They were two flaring points of ash in the dark. A taste she didn't much like coated her mouth. She thought that if she stood up she would be dizzy; as it was, she swam behind her eyes. Only their voices and the sucking drag and exhale of their occupation.

"Guys like James . . . " Armstrong chuckled.

"Hmmmmmmmm . . . ." It could have been hashish she felt so removed. Neither of them needed to say too much about guys like James. Except she said, "There's a tyranny in an overall view like his. Details take on too much significance, or none at all. You cling to some; you miss the rest. A tailor-made perspective." She was trying to say that even though he knew it all, he didn't, and that it was too bad he was the one taking the story back. And he probably would have agreed.

Their minds were drifting, unhinged by sex. Armstrong talked about a transfer. "I've been offered Nepal," he said. "And Manila." Language that made the world seem like a box of chocolates.

She might have been talking to herself when she brought up Esther in that cloud of smoke they made because she heard his breathing slow down, come thickly through his throat. "What's going on," she said, "when a person does something crazy, totally out of character? But spontaneous, so you're really left surprised at yourself?" She could see herself as a kid, hand in hand with some little friend she wasn't supposed to have from the native quarters while he drew harder on his breath, thickening now until it was a snore. Could these actions be preludes to change like flutters on a Richter scale? Or are they meant to restore innocence, the body's reflex against that loss?

Armstrong was dozing, rolling over, curling into the position for sleep. She thought she heard him say good-night against a yawn and ran a finger down his shoulder in response. She was awake and soon began to prowl. Downstairs the front door had been left wide open, and the night watchman, fearful for their safety, was propped, sleeping in a chair against the screen. Adam James had made a calculated move to the floor, his head on a cushion, his trousers and shirt flung to the side. She went to wash the dishes, going beyond, the way she did at this hour, scrubbing at the sink, the drainboards, the cabinets with a surgical intensity and speed. To leave no stain. No sludge of grease.

Such big houses, walled against the day by details of their furniture, yield their darkened spaces to the night. A breeze through louvered panes. Sway of palms. She paused climbing toward the balcony, a world opening out behind her in the textures of silence. These were the times she told herself if she were someplace else, there would not be this same feel, this value to things. This was her depth. She didn't go to bed but sat outside alone watching a late rising moon take the horizon, dense and buttery yellow. No pale blanched disk of a moon, this was the kind that gave rise to stories about cheese, melting into the black sky.

Armstrong decided to accept a new assignment. There were unlimited choices, Katmandu, Rio, Delhi. He contemplated the globe. It made her more willing to risk a little more with him, more time, more talk, knowing his departure would mark a neat sharp end to things, knowing nothing would trail on for years. A woman of contexts, she liked the background of a short interval of time, felt more attracted to him knowing he would go away, drawn to the sudden intimacy possible with a stranger. Not the pain of watching love die—an empty bed, harsh words, slammed doors. Short terms were easier on emotions: perhaps what she liked after all about being a doctor. She couldn't remember having the compulsion to heal the sick the way Esther did, never had been moved that way by the sound of the world coughing, or the sight of its blood. Technician, even in life.

With men, a short time meant that she could be foolish and go ahead and made mistakes, because she was often more embarrassed by the mistakes she didn't make than the ones she did. They threatened to expose something dour and distrustful in her nature. Had it been a lack of imagination and guts that she had never gone ahead and made the mistake of marrying Paul Luenga? They had almost done it back then in Boston to assuage their Catholic landlady. Even though Antonia knew about Helen and the two kids.

Yes, she had almost insanely agreed to become a second wife. "I won't live with Helen," he had vowed. For all purposes it would have been a divorce. No, that madness in Boston had been temporary. It wouldn't have been a valid marriage on any front—not by American law (bigamy) and not by African law or custom or whatever it was that men like Luenga and their grandmothers finally decided to accept. It would have been a gesture, a pledge made to each other, more she to him when you took it apart. She would have, after all, ended up with Helen Luenga as her co-wife.

Sometimes she wondered if that gesture would have changed them. Made them able to stay together, which was what they both really wanted, perhaps even now. But figuring in retrospect was a sign that you were about to have regrets and she had promised herself, quite firmly, that she wouldn't. She had seen what usually happened to the white wives of African men, though she could never describe it except to say that they were nervous and defensive and disappointed in ways that other wives weren't. They had an aura as obvious as their brown children, designed—perhaps as the children had been—to protect their decisions. They had a serious fallout rate.

"They say landing between the mountain peaks in Katmandu takes years off your life," Armstrong said. They were walking toward the town along the beach below his house. Rocks gave way to stones, then to greasy pebbles, then to white sand in a cradle of a tiny bay; a half-finished apartment building and a bridge like a hyphen linking land to land. She took her shoes off at a place where there were hundreds of little plastic packets riding toward them on the tide.

"What's this?" Ted Armstrong had one, was pulling a paper from the plastic, opening it. Messages. The one he had was written in Hindi, in big square letters, a child's hand. "Can you read this?"

She shook her head saying, "It's some Hindu festival. You make wishes and send them out to sea. Here! Look!" She found a wreath of flowers placed around something that had been burned and a long line of melted candles. He was still fishing around, opening packets. "Maybe this is how they send their mail to Bombay, it might get there faster." And then "Wait! Here's one in English . . . " folded into a wad, so creased, so pressed down into itself that each letter (square and fat and half-printed) was virtually in its own box.

It said: "I hope my father will get a visa for Canada and my brother Riaz will return from whichever place where he is gone. My mother is so sad and crying all the time. And I will get a new perfume and find my love."

Girls. Antonia remembered them out here over the years, hundreds of them with candles and floral wreaths solemnly ringing the bay just before sunset. Giggles and high songs. She had stopped to listen once, to look, to admire the arrays of silk and black braids swaying as they sang.

"I love this," Armstrong said, holding the wish, with no sense that he had rudely violated it. "If only I could read Hindi." He would have gone on opening the packages except that she stopped him.

"Let's go back," she said.

At his house she showered. He had hot water all the time but never any water pressure: the shower she used dribbled such a tiny stream she had to make a cup with her hands to catch and carry it wherever she wanted. Like an

Indian dancer, she didn't splash but tipped it, enchanted, in
movements that wanted exotic music.

"Say, what are you doing in there?" he called. "I've got some
drinks perspiring on the balcony. One of them is yours."

What she liked about the tropics was that one just
stepped out of the shower from one warm wet medium to
another, no need to flinch from the cold or even reach for a
towel. You were damp, opened to a damp breeze, and could
go casually like that feeling clean and naked to his high
porch and find him there. She sat near him tickling the pale
underside of his arm or the coarse line of reddish hair that
ran down from his navel. Their bare toes were arrayed in a
row on his glass table like so many witnesses. He had the
finely tuned ankles of a girl and strangely feminine feet,
more feminine than hers.

He led her by the hand to his bed. No air conditioning.
They had both agreed that refrigerated air was chilling and
his was an old house, built to take the sea breeze. Instead, the
old original ceiling fan cooled them there. Antonia turned
out to be the one who benefited from Jenny Armstrong's sex
manuals. Lesson by lesson. This time he started with his
mouth on hers and then his tongue and worked his way
along her body to her feet, never touching her with his
hands. Something Japanese. She had to promise to be very
still and she was.

Along the port, along the fringes of the industrial
area, on still mornings the old rusting crane had a kind of
sad dignity etched as it was in big geometries on the white
sky. Not so its arthritic creaking when the wind blew.
Pathetic crane.

On days like this Antonia woke up sweating in her sheets.
A bath accomplished nothing permanent. Already, walking to
work, she estimated the temperature was one hundred. She
didn't have enough energy to bitch that her car had still not
been repaired. Twenty months? Two years? Learning to do
without, "You'd be surprised at the things you don't miss," she
had told them on Oyster Bay. A rash claim: she missed that car.

This was the season in which the sun took forever to rise, stayed low in the sky and cut under trees through alleys, ripped along the sides of buildings in horizontal beams like knives slashing away at the shade. No shelter. No place to hide. Kids were out in the open, squatting, crapping, then chasing their mothers down the road.

Antonia caught sight of the hospital's red tile roof, then the dark shelters and the verandas.

"Dr. . . . Mrs. . . . " It was Esther Moro pressed against a tree trunk so that she looked like the bark itself, then like a thin figure carved in relief: Antonia thought of the nymph Daphne changing, becoming the tree in order to save herself.

"Esther, what is it? What's wrong?" She led the girl past the crowds to her office.

"There's a woman in Mikorosheni," she said. "She has something growing here on her face." She was holding back like a child who has been bad and is more afraid of what she's done than the punishment she'll get. "If I stand near her I will belong to her. I want you to give me medicine and take this away from me."

"Take what away from you?"

"This." She shook her hands, rubbing at them as though they were trapped in a mesh, a spider's web. "Because I am a witch and a madwoman."

Antonia took the hands, which were hot and trembling. "I don't understand," she said.

"You must come and fix this woman," Esther told her. The doctor stroked her, calmed her, led her to a couch. Like a child she folded herself in a corner, given up to softness, taking comfort as awkwardly as it was offered. She held her *kanga* to her chin, trying to smile. Everything from their last visit has passed, the two of them striding that way along the port road. Perhaps there was something badly wrong with her. Manic depression. Schizophrenia. Words a doctor with a practice in Africa didn't have much time for.

She slept, or seemed to, curled on the couch with the *kanga* over her head, breathing so gently not one of Antonia's patients noticed she was there, until Antonia herself looked and saw the cloth, empty, deflated and formless as though Esther Moro had been snatched away or, by magic, made to disappear. She had been examining a patient, her thumb on the raised glands of a strep throat, so red in there and the fever so astronomical there was no need to bother with the culture. Her instinct was to leave at once and follow Esther but a nurse was in front of her with cards for the next six patients; the first had an X-ray of lungs so eaten by tuberculosis there was no chance the drugs could work.

"I have a cough, a pain here, and blood," the man explained.

But Esther came to Kinondoni that afternoon.

Extreme heat had brought down masses of caterpillars from the trees. It had happened rarely, no more than five times in Antonia's memory. Masses of them, moving it seemed toward the sea like lemmings. Hallucinatory: they had electric blue heads and striped bodies, red and green with jet-black feet and yellow beading down their sides, great hairy shoulders and slick juicy skins. A carpet of them. People had come out in crowds to witness the event. Except Charles, who wouldn't leave the house, sure it was the end of the world, a plague on mankind, the wages of sin. He was certain that if anything that looked like that bit you, you would die. Hanging from the front window, twisting a rag, he shouted at her to come in at once, to watch herself, not to get bitten.

He had slammed all the doors and windows shut. The house was stifling. She horrified him by coming in and flinging everything open saying there was no danger from such things. He followed behind her closing everything again saying he would not be the one to sweep the horror away, dead or alive, until the two of them had squabbled twice around the place and Antonia found herself facing Esther at the purple door, there in a patch of slithering larvae.

"Esther!"

"I have done it!" the girl said.

She couldn't rest, she told Antonia, but lay there thinking carefully and she knew it was wrong to hide from the sick woman when she was so clearly called. A garbled story about an Asian girl with a fever, another with warts, things she felt about someone who is sick. Psychic impressions. It was the real basis of her fantasy, Jesus walking through the villages touching people. A healer.

She had gone to Nkosi, who told her she was not a witch or madwoman, explaining that African people still lived close to forces that Europeans had lost to their machines. He went with her to Mikorosheni and told the woman that Esther could help her, could take the trouble away with a power in her hands. Esther had placed her hands on the growth that covered the woman's face. A feeling like wind, she said, had swept over her. She didn't know who she was or where she was until she felt that she was lifting the growth from the woman's flesh. People watching had screamed that her hands were turning black and when she looked down, she saw them covered with something like dark oil, the substance, she concluded, that had been poisoning the woman. They could all see the growth was smaller, shrinking, until it disappeared. Esther ran to the sea. She washed herself there.

Listening, knuckles in her mouth, the doctor smelled on her fingers the sharp oil of a lime she had squeezed into her late tea at the hospital. It was ridiculous. She wanted to laugh. Not at what had happened down there in Mikorosheni but at herself for ever thinking she had any business at all with Esther Moro's psyche (if you could call it that: her old vocabularies were falling by the wayside). She stood making small, dumb humming sounds of dismay.

"You don't believe me," Esther said. "Nkosi told me. She can't believe you. No matter if you love her."

Trained for it, the doctor prevaricated: "It's not that I don't believe you. I just want you to be well, and safe, that's all."

Unnerved, her fingers there, playing about her lips. But Esther was leaving quickly, in a loping run as if her limbs were wired loosely and she might come apart. For a moment it seemed she didn't diminish even as she gained some distance; then she was a thin shape, wavering, turning up a lane.

Then she was gone.

ELEVEN

Esther marked the day she ran from the doctor by the terrible worms she found there at the door, a sign for her to turn and go, the wonder of their color and their terrible crawling to show how danger can seduce, even as she stood there determined, with her pledge, knowing who she was. It seemed the day had passed in circles finally ending there, against everything Nkosi said. Because she wanted, wanted. Answers to her questions if she could at least have found the words to ask them: how her life and her father's spun through shadowy knowledge, even the doctor (she had thought) wanted to know. Had she not held her hand? But she should have known as the doctor's eyes disappointed her, fingers touched to her lips as if to say I can't, I won't, I don't . . . *siwezi, sitaki.* These words were like walls.

There are two truths, Musumbi told her, theirs and ours. They know only one, their own. Esther knew that he had been turned away as well, given things: a hat, the tools, the spectacles, when he had once believed the German would take him far away over the water to Europe where he wanted to go, where he said he belonged, feeling that he had been born in the wrong place to the wrong people. "There was a war," he told her, "a matter between the white men and their countries. He had to break his word." But when she worked for the French she understood that he could just as easily have been a joke to the German man, kindness given behind the doors of a house like the kindness to a dog. "Men from far away with skins like albinos," he had told her

171

because she had never seen one of them. Hair as soft as cloth and pale eyes.

People came and waited for her outside Zobetta's house. Their problems dug into her thoughts and filled her with desire. When she came among them, she took impressions that came to her like commands. Her own voice had a way of surprising her—"Is there someone here who cannot eat without feeling great pain? Is it you?" A face there in the crowd, a thin form, a man. She knew even before he spoke, "Yes, yes, I am the one."

Inside the house, she had touched him. He cried out, "I feel, I feel a knife!" and vomited so much she felt his agony. The story spread that what came out of him was a sackful of biting ants, pouring out, caused by witchcraft. She heard the word, *uchawi*, whispered outside and through the village. *Uchawi*, even as the man was still lying there in his wonder. Just the way she had heard the word around Musumbi as he bent listening to a heart with a stethoscope, as he squeezed a drop of blood upon a glass to search in it for clues, even as he walked into the ashes of another man's madness to say, "There is no djinn."

"But I am not a witch!" she was crying.

Nkosi was the only one who could explain it, a teacher, and that was why, she told Zobetta, she needed him.

"Something given to Esther by her birth," he told them. "*Akili.*" Special knowledge given also to people who can play instruments or sing while others only howl like dogs. Oh, he knew how to talk and his beard that rode on his face proclaimed his right. Even his hands, which spread out to catch the air like nets. "A power in the air," he said. *Umene.* Lightning or electricity.

"If sounds can come into a radio through the air or pictures on a cinema screen, you don't need to know more than that to understand how Esther has her power," Nkosi said. He believed in no god and no devil, nothing but birth and death. And Africans, he said, were closer to these things. He called it "physics" a word in English that described the forces, the pull of being born and dying. He was increased by his thoughts and his words, so true that everyone listened and was silent when he spoke. His head grew. His hair breathed. His eyes opened. The pleasure of it was real, made him hungry, made him laugh.

Zobetta was afraid of men like Nkosi. Too clever. Using what he learned in places like Sweden and England. Like the government ministers, skilled in treachery, in things that turn to anger and sadness. "The chickens a man keeps," she warned, "don't know when he plans to slaughter them for his meals."

"What about his wife in Sweden?" she asked Esther.

"Their love was finished," she answered. But she wasn't sure. She had heard him talking in the Swedish language on the telephone, recognizing anger in his voice, the kind that came from worry and from love. Afterward he turned on Esther and shouted out in English words he knew she could never understand. Later as her lover he asked her, softly, to forgive even though Zobetta said that no man ever did. It was easy for her to believe that he was more than one, a twist of characters. At times he resembled weather that could change without notice and fill and flood or drain away, clouds vanishing when you had hoped for rain.

There were also the letters. Esther found them unopened in his trash basket. She guessed they were from Sweden and took one to show the stamp to Hadija's friend who worked in the post office. Then she began to save them, still unopened. She kept them hidden in her box of sacred things, charms or claims on him, knowing it was wrong to throw them away. She saved the letters as a shield. They lifted softly from the other papers in the basket almost by themselves, swimming into her hands, some as light as leaves and others heavy with words. She felt the messages inside, things she wanted to know and took them as her own by virtue of her love for him. She had never had a letter in her life.

His friends were revolutionaries who were preparing for a war. Even the women appeared in faded soldier clothes and fell into chairs or on the floor around Nkosi's house. They could have been branches cut and piled ready to burn. Beyond them seemed to be the cleared land ready for rain and planting in a country far away that they were slowly, Nkosi explained, making their way to. When they moved, they rustled and crackled. Sometimes they all disagreed and argued, leaving in low military cars, everything about them the same dull green to match their drier natures. At times they flamed and came to Nkosi's as if in secret, one against the other; easy enough for her to see spite in faces as thirsty as theirs.

Nkosi told her nothing, not even their names, but soon enough he came to her and said he had to leave and he wanted her to come with him. She understood right away that they would go from village to village and that she would become his purpose now as much as he was hers. When she told Zobetta and Hadija, she put it in the context of a dream, one in which her father, Musumbi, led her to the plains. Just like a memory she saw the Kwavi fires and heard their cattle. Women in blue capes surrounded her, gave her warm milk in a bowl and meat that had been roasted and rolled in salt. Then they handed her a sick baby wrapped in a blanket. Opening it she saw he was white and he held his heart in his hand, a heart with a crown and a drop or blood, a picture Francis had given her long ago of Jesus. When she looked for Musumbi, he was gone, but searching for him, it was Nkosi that she wanted.

Zobetta laughed and said it was only a dream and could make no sense of such things while Hadija was amazed and covered her breasts with a *kanga* that had airplanes, trucks, and tractors on it and was meant to predict the future. Still Zobetta thought it was a good thing for her to go. So many people came to her for healing that voices had started to accuse. Makonde women who smoked on pipes and watched from under trees, dark as crowbirds and with shrill voices, claiming their medicine was better after all.

Coming in with a big suitcase and emptying it on the bed, Hadija said, "I bought this case for you. For your journey." She had been out to Oyster Bay where Americans who were leaving were selling their old things to Africans. She dug through the pile.

"Look!" She held up white plastic boots, her dream at last. But with a broken heel. She had a lipstick: 'Orange glo,' she said in English and made a translation for Zobetta's babies, "*Ya ni machungwa-glo.*" Panties, with a stain, dangled from her hand. She put them on her head. There was a headscarf with a picture of a building, and an umbrella that folded into a tiny pocket.

To go away, to leave them and wander the way she had done as a child at her father's side. Inside her heart, wavering sadness and determination became a kind of pride. Packing her things in the case—a piece of red tape held a torn corner: a stick had jammed a broken lock—Esther felt like one returning home. In the bottom she hid the letters that came from Sweden. Her clothes were over them. And on top she put a photograph of herself with Hadija and Zobetta. They had their arms around each other, Hadija shining and bent with laughter. It had been Sharad holding his father's camera, scolding them and testing and chirping the way Hindis did, running back and forth to push them into position until he finally snapped, then cursed, then said he had broken it, tried to fix it, moaned the picture would never come out, but it had. Zobetta's chin tipped down, her legs looked bent, pulled as she was by Hadija's jumping. Only Esther looked quiet, photographed, held that way in time. She was the tallest and her eyes were anywhere, the way that pictures could make you stare. She appeared to be hung on the end of her own outstretched arm and falling away from the other two, off the corner of the frame. Now she understood this had been a sign that she would go away.

"How do you do this thing of healing?" Zobetta wanted to know. She had come in with her chair and was sitting in a corner. She talked about a girl from her village who had gone to live with Italian nuns. She wore a certain kind of hat like nuns, a long gray dress, and a white collar. Beads hung at her waist. She had learned to speak Italian. This girl could make blood stop flowing by staring at a wound with her eyes. She could remove imbedded things. It was, the nuns said, a power from God.

Esther could only tell them that she didn't know, "I feel things. I see pictures." This was all she said.

"If you can do it, fwaaaaah, just like that, you will become very rich," Hadija told her. Her face rose above a silk slip that was the color of white people's skin. Like a Moslem girl in purdah, her wide painted eyes.

"No," Esther said. She felt somber, different. She had seen the meaning of beauty in her breath that grew deeper and slower and the quiet pulse of her cooling heart, the throb she reached, a voice that had no words, streaming signs she took to be truth. There was no expression for it except her shy, "I feel something. My hands belong to it." So she could convince them all it came from someplace else, without her seeking it.

"But from where?" A baby had jumped into Zobetta's lap, was painting orange lipstick on the woman's mouth.

"From Allah!" Hadija breathed, pointing to the sky. Her bracelets crashed.

Outside, hearing that Esther would go away from Mikorosheni, people gathered quietly. Mr. Ntiro was there saying that in China the young people had gone, with no shoes, to the villages to help the poor and the sick. Like an army of goodness. Hadija ran to block the door in her purple suit and hobbling white boots, smoking cigarettes and whispering stories about Esther's mysterious powers. Esther could hear her own name coming back to her like an echo. Makonde were looking in and nodding because they had this kind of healing themselves—an old woman, well known, who could stop miscarriage by holding the woman's head in her hands.

Two truths. Theirs and ours. And they know only one. The suitcase filled and standing freely beside her bed contained her excitement and the sound of Nkosi's coming leapt to her heart. They would travel, Nkosi had decided, on the new train, the train the Chinese had built, as far away until it stopped.

Mikorosheni: "among the cashew trees." In the right season, the ripening cashew fruit were all but obscene; soft labial segments thick with juice. They had no peel. And no pits. They were wet, oozing, the colors of swollen and bruised flesh. From their succulent bodies hung the nut, suspended outside, a fetal shape in a hard gray shell. The air down near the village smelled of their strong perfume. Women who harvested the nut brewed a quick wine from the discarded flesh, a raw drink ready within hours and still bubbling. By nightfall it turned to vinegar, sour before it matured. It left a bitter taste and powdery residue.

Two old women were gathering the fruits, pressing them into plastic buckets. Makonde women, with lacings of facial scars, tufts of frizzy hair, slack breasts. When the doctor was close enough, they asked her for a cigarette. Antonia told them she didn't smoke. This was a terrific joke: they laughed. One showed her an empty pipe and laughed even harder. She had no teeth, lover of the hilarious.

"When you come back, *mzungu*," they hollered after her, "don't forget to bring tobacco."

The village closed around her as she walked. It was more like something natural grown wild than like something built or planted by men, even though everything had been put there, the cashew trees, the mangoes, the coconut, banana, papaya, cassava, maize, rice, all patched as random and tentative as the claims that held them. Even the houses had outgrown themselves: lean-tos, porches, sheds, tins, washing stalls, pit latrines.

It was as gentle in Mikorosheni in the morning as it was threatening at night. These small plantations in the sun, clustered houses of mud and thatch, families under shaded porches or on benches near their trees drinking tea as though it were profound, a sharing of pleasant things. A small boy offered her an egg, then ran away with it. A tiny girl took hold of her hand, her older sisters teased. The doctor told them she was looking for the crippled boy whom Esther had healed.

Everyone knew about Richard, although there were conflicting stories. A young mother said he had lost the use of his legs after he had fallen from a tree. Another argued that he had been ill, with a fever, for a very long time, and when he recovered, he had no strength and couldn't walk. The boy's parents, she was told, were from Tabora and they lived on the other side of the village with their own people. If Antonia went there, she would be able to see the boy for herself, how he could walk now and play like any other.

A woman who nursed a baby said, "His father is a night watchman at the bank. They have four children."

An old woman corrected, "They have three."

"They speak terrible Swahili," an old baba told her. "Dirty, and useless." *Chafu na bure.* People from Tabora. He insisted that the doctor share their tea; it was already prepared. A child was introduced to greet her in a formal, archaic way, "*Shikamu.*" I will wash your feet. The performance was approved. The baba beamed.

Antonia knew the correct response, "*Marahaba,*" which pleased the old man as well. Do it again. Seven times. These old rhythms were soothing in the shade.

They dispatched a silent adolescent girl to show her the way to the boy. She wore a polyester dress with geometric designs: too tight, her breasts made eloquent pyramids in dark blue squares. There was an awkward drama about her that reminded Antonia of Esther, an aura of the actress, of someone who knew a million things she didn't know. The hesitancy in her step made it clear she guessed that her charge might want to approach in secret, perhaps observe unmarked from a distance for a while. She wove a path to the edge of the village that rimmed a shallow bay, drained now by low tide to a vast white stretch of sand. Grounded boats were flung there in an exaggerated perspective, perfect replicas of each other, smaller and smaller and smaller until they reached the pale horizon. From the beach, the two women crept up, clinging to a fence until they were back inside Mikorosheni. Houses were better at this end. Cement blocks. One had been painted in a checkered pattern of red and white.

"He is there," her guide said. "That one. That small one." *Huyu mdogo.*

Several children were playing on a wooden construction, an inspired version of a jungle gym, made perhaps by an industrious father. There had once been a slide, collapsed now, rusting. The boy was not as small as he was delicate, with fine bones and limbs, a long neck and narrow shoulders. He gave no real indication that he had ever been as helpless as Esther claimed, confined to a chair, ruined, his legs locked and shrunken. Only traces remained; he was less robust, less agile, perhaps. He couldn't climb the wooden scaffold. He couldn't run when the other children did but toddled after them calling them to wait.

"This is his house. This is his mother."

The woman was bent from her hips, her head dropped nearly to the ground, her legs stiff, a classic African stance, cultivating her crops.

"We are Christians. We believe in Jesus," she told Antonia. Smiling, she showed a small gold cross that hung on her neck. The doctor recognized that the woman was afraid of white people. "We are Roman Catholics."

"This is your boy? The one who was so ill?"

"Jesus helped us," she insisted. "We are Christians."

"How long was he sick? Can you tell me? I am a doctor."

The woman shrugged.

"Did you ever bring him to the hospital?"

She was pretending that she didn't understand, looking for some help with the language. "Hospital?" Then she was walking away saying, "I will make some tea for you."

The tea was rich with sugar and milk.

Antonia asked where they came from.

"Tabora."

"Do you know the hospital there? Do you know Dr. Temeke? He is my friend."

"He is a good man," the woman said. "A Christian. Like us. A Catholic man."

Despite her birth and all the years she'd had to practice, Antonia was clumsy with the woman, had no skills at all in talking to her. What she had been able to do as that disobedient child, running and playing in places like this, eating the food, drinking the tea, telling stories: all gone. She had forgotten how to build a conversation of parable and innuendo, how to find answers in allusions and indirections, never telling more than you dared, never hearing less. But what was there to know beyond the fact that the boy was climbing there on a jungle gym, and there, against the wall of that trim house, she saw abandoned a small chair to which some bicycle wheels had been crudely attached.

She traced her way back. Memory was direction this time: a cluster of houses, a man frying *mandazi*, a woman selling dried fish. She hunted for the house where Esther lived and lost her way, passing a plantation of cabbages, surprisingly neat as if a European had been dropped by parachute and struggled there: elaborate ditches wove among the rows; little signs on sticks. She was looking for the charcoal shed and found it. Women were waiting in line to buy, wrapped in their *kanga*s. Straight backs and necks,

heads tipped to balance baskets there. Relaxed arms hung
limp at their sides. Theirs was a rare kind of peasant dress
that didn't turn women into broad-beamed versions of men.
An image came back to her: a field of corn just planted and
the women all standing up to rest, random or in a pattern
(you couldn't tell) like columns from a ruined civilization.

From there the path led back toward the sea. She
remembered a green-painted doorway, a man in a suit who
had greeted her. There was a row of recently built houses,
scraps and doorways arranged quickly before the police
could stop them. Someone had carried a brilliant amaryllis
in a rusting can and placed it in the sun. Turning to look
behind her, to try to get her bearings, she caught sight of the
house, framed by two trees, and recognized the aborted
room that hung there on the back. She saw the woman they
called Zobetta picking through red beans spread on a
winnowing basket, on a small stool with the basket over her
knees and hands that hovered at her task. She was lost to the
rhythm. Oblivious and curiously alone for a place like this.
Until children began calling attention, "*MZUNGU!
MZUUNGU!*" like an alarm, "*MZUNGU!*" not just to tease the
white woman but to warn everyone else. "*Mzungu-mzungu.*"
Singing as they streamed around her.

Esther's friend appeared in shining red pants. She
collected a baby from the crowd, a toddler, a boy, using him
as a shield as she came, greeting formally, "*Shikamu!
Memsaab!*" with his little penis resting on her arm and his
eyes full of terror.

"Is Esther here?" Antonia asked.

"No. She has gone to travel." The little penis hardened:
the eyes filled with tears. "Did she forget to tell you
good-bye?" Her head tipped; bright orange lips formed
regret. "Tssssssk . . . this is bad." She sucked at her tongue.

They knew, of course, why Antonia had come down to
Mikorosheni and where she had just had tea. No doubt they
already had a full transcript of the conversation. "I really
want to see Esther," Antonia said.

"But truly, she has gone." Tears poured down the baby's
cheeks. His mouth was soundless but open. The penis
spurted. This did not bother Hadija.

"Gone where?"

"Just gone. For a journey." Which seemed natural enough to Hadija. She jiggled the baby; poked at his stomach, pressed his cheeks into an opened mouth. She wanted to brag about her friend and, moving closer, whispered, "She has a power . . . if you can see how she does it, fwaaaaaaah! She is shaking a little and her eyes are like this and if you are sick, then you become well." The false eyelashes and orange lipstick added to her pride. She was looking down at Antonia, as if she knew the doctor's limits all right: the problems of someone who had to see to believe, someone spiritually hemmed in by the burdens of proof.

"I have seen the boy from Tabora. Richard," Antonia admitted.

Hadija drew in her breath as one who had scored the winning point. She lowered the baby, who rushed off screaming, and pulled a tightness of red satin from her crotch, then whispered, "They are Christians," so there would be no suspicions about witchcraft. She told the doctor that Esther "saw things." This was ability, she explained. *Akili.* She spoke like someone who knew. "Esther can see the trouble. They say she can pull it out by burning. You can see it falling on the floor. Like spiders in a sack. And then your stomach doesn't hurt. Just as you make an operation." It would have been pointless to press for some reasonable description of what had been going on. She should have known, even before she tried, that everything would be trapped inside these bizarre reports, leaving no clear lines to lead her to an answer. So she didn't even bother to ask, "Who are these people she has cured? What was the matter with them?"

By now the children were three deep. She sorted through them as a doctor might—the running noses, the yellowed eyes of jaundice, the bellies swollen with parasites, feet as crusty as old broken shoes; a professional making estimates of the time and money it would take to do the repairs while the next batch filtered in, already on the fringes, among the cashews. A boy in a woman's blouse had taken her hand and was whispering *mzungu* to the others as though he had claimed her for his own. To no avail she told Hadija, "I have taken tea. Two times," laughing, trying to make them see how bloated she was. But they were pushing her inside. Cups were being assembled, rinsed in her honor in a plastic basin. She smelled the fumes of kerosene as they pumped the stove, sat on the low, breaking chair. In silence but surrounded. One of the little girls brought a glass of Coca-Cola and a fried *mandazi* on a dish. Then she was given tea. Children crouched to watch her eat and drink, giggling as she swallowed. Hadija was prim on a low stool, hands folded in her lap.

There were no cabs to take the doctor home. She had to walk the three or four miles to Kinondoni. Past the crowded bus stop and carvers' sheds where Makonde chipped at ebony and ivory. From the road she could hear their cassettes, smell the marijuana. They held up salad sets and ivory beads as she came. Along a dusty stretch, alone suddenly, she smelled the stink of some dead animal and walked a little faster. A young Sikh was sitting with an African girl in a truck. They weren't speaking, just staring ahead, as though they were deeply involved. As Antonia drew close, he leaned from the window and said, "I have broken down." It all had the quality of a dream, his turbaned head, the voice, the message and its echoes.

What could be behind the stories of Esther's cures? Reports that were as certain as they were hysterical. And that memory of Esther, her obvious jubilation amidst the slither of the caterpillars: "I have done it!" (Barely breathing, as though she had joined a deep conflux.) What did she touch and drag forth to convince those people that she had healed them? Powers of suggestion? Spontaneous remissions? It meant only that something had happened that couldn't be explained. Something that couldn't have happened, so there would be no chance of proofs, only theories and dismissals. Not hard to think of Esther and Christ now: the brooding solitary figure, the beautiful face, always in danger, reviled and loved in one breath. In the end such healers would have to be lonely people, praying out of sight in empty gardens like Gethsemane, wandering away from attention, carrying some kind of cross and perhaps just slightly deranged.

She decided to walk through the squatters' settlement that had grown around Kinondoni, dense with life, looking at the back of the cement houses set in rows. The shacks down here fought for space, their small territories marked out by stones or rusting tin-can barriers. This way she found her house from behind, her uniforms like white banners blowing on a line.

McGeorge was there, with his gear all over her living room and Charles jollied into cooking something special for him with ingredients that he had brought up from the bush.

"I'm going back to the U.K. tonight," he said. "We were robbed." His hair was very long now. Soon he would have tied it back and joined another century. "The cameras. The film. A fucking inside job."

"When?"

"Last week. We'd been filming the poachers. Somebody didn't like the idea. Cynthia's given it all up, of course. She's gone to live on Zanzibar and write a big historical novel about the Arab coast."

"But not you? You're not done, are you?"

"Not bloody likely." His smile was a **V**, which his eyebrows (very Irish) complemented. "Why does one have insurance?" He offered her something in a flask. "Not much left," he said. "Peppermill and I spent the last few days pissed as farts. They took all our footage. Means someone paid them off."

"The president's brother?"

"In cahoots with some Indian diplomat."

It was brandy in the flask. Something very cheap and raw. She winced and declined, pointing to her liver.

"What a film!" he moaned. "We had managed an interview with this old Ruaha type bragging about how many tusks he's bagged in his life. Couldn't understand all the fuss about tusks. You know, in the old days, they used to leave them lying around like bones after a barbecue. Bloke must have been a hundred years old." McGeorge sighed.

Conversations like this soothed, convinced you both you were still at home in Africa—topics that folded around extravagant things: stashed trophies, wild people, old tribal customs. All the years they had heard the farfetched sound as ordinary as the smell of Charles frying a plantain in the other room with onions and fresh coriander or the perfume of ripe guava stewed with sugar. Stories about women who went to live with lions in Kenya, or daft explorers, a

Canadian with a swimming pool full of diamonds. One of Adolf Hitler's mistresses loved Africa, was still filming Nubians as they cut each other ritually with wrist knives. She was seventy-something. And there were the men who raced their cars over dirt tracks through the bush, past the naked Masai. There were people who counted elephants.

They ate. McGeorge with gusto, heaping praises on the cook—"Always the *very* best!"—licking fingers that were glossy yellow with curried oil, a scoop of rice and coconut in his palm. Amazing how Charles found things, stored them in the tropics with no refrigerator, hoarded them like gold. He coaxed onions and garlic and fresh spices from the sand flat on Kinondoni with the water from her bath, against the season when there would be none.

Extravagant things. She leaned across the bowl of fragrant guava (a neighbor's tree) and told him about Esther Moro: "She puts her hands on people and they get better. She *sees* things."

"Wonderful!" he said. "You know I desperately wanted to do a book on witchdoctors, call it *Waganga*. There was a chap in Barabaig who could actually call up windstorms. Gillian himself witnessed it. The old boy had pythons that came when he whistled. Gillian had a snap of him all got up with feathers and monkey skins, baboon skulls."

"Esther would object if you called her a witch doctor." She laughed.

"Honestly? You mean she's like one of those Americans who comes on the telly asking people to send in their socks and ten bucks and their bunions will vanish?"

"No, not like one of those Americans."

"Our Lady of Lourdes? Crutches strewn from here to there? Blind people seeing?"

"I don't really know."

"What's the matter, Tony? You seem sad about all this."

"These things have a way of steamrolling, of getting so unbounded they collapse. Of meaning other things."

"I'd leave it if I were you. You can't expect any kind of truth or loyalty from these bastards. So why give any?" He squeezed the bridge of his nose and belched. A bitter sound.

"It's not that," she said. "Only another absurd situation like all of Africa. Whatever happened has made people believe she cured them, so she believes it, too, I suppose. It's a naïve kind of charlatanism: I'm sure the man who egged her on will try to make something out of it. Money or politics. She must be with him now."

"Wasn't it Koestler," McGeorge asked, "who said about holy men and charlatans that you mustn't ask which is which? Only ask to what extent he is fake, to what extent he is holy. It isn't one thing or the other. That's always been your trouble, Tony."

They inevitably came to this wry point—the trouble with you or me—all relating to how you handled Africa ("your Africa, my Africa") and the mistake Antonia made in trying to fit Esther into her own image (my Africa, my Africans) like some fond memsaab out of the nineteenth century. One of the blind ones who never saw a thing. Charles brought them coffee in a pot she had gotten ages ago in Zanzibar, peaked and shining brass.

McGeorge stroked the old man's wrist. "The absolute best," he said.

The taxi that came for him was painted puce and had a light inside that wouldn't go off. It was eerie to watch him go down the road. There were no other cars at all: the people walking in the night parted slowly, shadow figures in the headlights and the glow from the cab windows in the dark, so it looked like a spaceship, hovering, floating, sweeping over the ground.

But he had trouble with his papers and called her in the morning at the hospital. He sounded thousands of miles away so that at first she thought he was in London and wondered at his speed.

"I'm a prisoner at the airport," he told her, "eating bread and water." The phone made a dismal sound. "There's been a terrible brouhaha, some wild idea that suddenly all the displaced coffee farmers, after twenty bloody years, doddering as they all are, have been putting money behind an attempt to overthrow the government, hoping to collect compensation from the junta. They think I'm one of them." It was a phone they both knew was bugged, but by Bulgarians, so it didn't really matter and didn't usually work.

"Always handy to blame the foreigners," he went on.

"I'm sure they keep us around so they can kick us out when the need arises. Did you hear anything at all about a coup?"

"Nothing," she said.

"You mean they haven't blamed the U.S. yet? They usually do. Soon they'll remember you're American, Tony, and kick you out. I'd pack up and go if I were you. They're ripe for a military go-round and you know what hell that can be. Still, knowing them, it will be pathetic. They're not even good at violence. Unlike Ugandans."

Right after work, she went out there to find him. The cabdriver, jolly and full of chatter, hinted that he made ends meet these days by smuggling. He had a handsome, Swahili face with vivid traces of his Arab blood, the long nose and curling hair, brown eyes with flecks of green. His head, tipped in the rearview mirror, eyes on her eyes, urged her to speak. Did he think she had contraband to offer, or wanted to buy? Was he trying to bait her and then catch her? She remained aloof, changed the subject to the weather. She found McGeorge wandering in an empty corridor, a rumpled airport species, doomed to waiting.

"I've been let out to do my business," he said. "Rather like a pet. There is my master. WOOF! WOOF!" he barked in the direction of someone standing in a shadow. Airport police, an officer too young to smile or wonder. Too young to know that visitors were not allowed in the transit lounge, so Antonia just walked right in. No doubt the boy still viewed the comings and goings of white men as part of God's grand design, beyond real question, as incomprehensible as rain or poisonous snakes.

"At least I'm going to be allowed to leave," he sighed. A plastic couch sighed with him as he sat. "God knows if I'll ever get back in. Do I deserve this? For all the bright little books I've done? Tree toads and giraffes? A boost to their sagging, nonexistent really, tourist trade? Well, I suppose it's over." He began to pick at his fingernails.

"The best of both worlds," she said and laughed.

"You'll never know what I went through this morning. I thought they would put me on trial right here in the bloody airport and then haul me off to prison." He was looking across a low table leaning there on his knees and propped on his elbows. He could have been a prisoner and she a visitor, the young officer standing guard over them at the exit. Or vice versa, she the prisoner and he the visitor. Closed borders made funny definitions of whose freedom, whose movement, in fact, was being curtailed. Those on the outside and those within. She wondered briefly if she would be allowed to walk out, right now, if she had a ticket, if she chose to leave with McGeorge.

"Don't say you haven't been warned what buggers they really are." He crossed his eyes at the guard.

"Oh, I've been warned."

"They're not even humane," he said. "I'm bloody-well starved." There was no food in the lounge. He held a cup of tea but the milk he had poured into it was sour and had curdled when it hit the tannic acid. He took a spoonful of sugar and ate that.

An Ethiopian woman, dressed in white, was waiting for the same plane. She also had been denied a visa.

"Even though she looks like an angel," McGeorge said. She claimed her son was in the country though he hadn't come to the airport to meet her. It was probably illegal, her coming here in the first place, if these ad-hoc laws were accepted. Certainly the woman hadn't understood, had only assumed she had a right from God to be with her child, had assumed she could go where he was, no matter what. These were natural things: she knew nothing about politics. No, they would send her back to London, an expensive way to spend a few days, in the air between two countries in which she didn't belong. Impossible for her to go home: she was a refugee, she had been trying to explain that. The question was, which regime had she fled, the point on which her destiny was hung. She didn't know: she had merely accompanied her husband, knew little of what revolution and counterrevolution meant except that she was almost finished now. And her husband was dead. At that moment her face was blank. She looked too prim, too glowingly clean to be in that shabby room of orange plastic furniture mended with black electrical tape until it had run out. Now the chairs and benches spewed out kapok stuffing, which McGeorge absently pulled at, wadded and tossed, until balls of it circled him, the punctuation of his distress.

And hers. She finally left him trying to find a way to

sleep on a pillow of rolled-up newspapers in that storm of kapok balls. She wondered how long it might be before she saw him again and what the circumstances and where. She almost thought it would have to be an accident, a collision in space, as though they were satellites drifting far off course, faint radio signals—"Bye-bye, old girl." And that little soldier at his post, not so innocent after all, asking for his bribe.

"My tea." A whisper. "How will I get my tea, my money for tea?" His hand on her wrist.

Downstairs at the departure gates the crowds jammed. It looked as though planes were coming and going on an airlift emergency, arriving empty and leaving full, usually with Indians. The obvious imbalance created a nervous atmosphere, made them want to get out of the place as quickly as possible. Made the customs officers a barricade. They were surly, emptying Indians' suitcases, strewing shirts, socks, trousers, underwear, a blaze of silk saris, an embarrassment of tampons. Hoping to find what? Ivory? Too much gold jewelry? Packets of foreign currency? Here was one arrogant young bastard shaking an old guy's shoes and finding ten or so Krugerrands. Oh no. It made Antonia laugh, as unfair, as predictable as it all was. What sounds of desperation came from that exchange of words they were having: the Indian's sputtering explanations, the African's deadpan. There was no doubt who would win, of course, unless the Indian could find his way to the right price in one of the holding rooms at the side. How many rands would it cost to get on that plane? And had it been a ploy? A rabbit garden? Was that the only shoe in there stuffed with gold?

There had been a picture in the *Daily News*. Not on the front page where headlines proclaimed, JUSTICE WILL PREVAIL! but on the back page with some news about Bulgarian farmers. A blurred photo, badly reproduced. A woman seated in a group of people, impossible to recognize as Esther Moro except for the caption: "This woman is shown in Tabora where she is said to be healing the sick." And then again a few weeks later, amid news of a cabinet reshuffle (the minister of finance was made minister of agriculture; agriculture was made education; education, water resources; external affairs, defense) and a headline quashing rumors of a coup attempt, THERE IS NO DISLOYALTY, another picture of Esther appeared. She was named this time: "Comrade Esther Moro, the woman who heals the sick." It was taken near the Ruaha and showed Esther wearing a white robe, which made her look bizarre, like a nun. She seemed to be standing in front of a large crowd. It gave Antonia an odd, angry turn, a mixture of worry and annoyance. She examined the print carefully, so eerie, staring at a newsprint image of someone she knew. Over and over. To no avail, as if she had expected the picture to reveal as much as the face when she had seen it live.

She had torn the picture out and put it in her purse like an icon. It stayed in there until she forgot about it, appearing from time to time with its expression changed as the paper crumbled and found its way to the bottom or surfaced again. Days followed that seemed out of season, held her in abeyance as though she were waiting for the picture to give way to the real thing who might appear among her patients or looming near that flame tree. Made her feel a stranger even among her own kind, like a phantom American, there on Oyster Bay on the edge of a patio like the proverbial brink.

An abyss of lawn.

Was this the fabled embassy wife who had her swimming pool filled to make a rose garden? With topsoil imported from Italy? Was that it out there, faintly marked by a tile rim, mythical in the dark? A social scientist was advancing a pet theory, that Africans have no concept of the future. He called it "futuriety."

"Time is cyclic in traditional societies," he said, "governed only by the natural year repeating endlessly. Children take the place of elders in their turn. There's no advancement in a collective sense (individually, yes) either materially or technologically. No need for it. No need to invest in the future or protect it. You simply *ensure* it by having children." He had a round boyish face; only the creases around his eyes gave away any age at all.

They were all listening, a small circle around him, perched there like dancers, arms bent in similar angles holding their drinks. Scotty Clayburn (she also had a round boyish face) nodded vigorously. Was that another nightgown she was wearing?

Funny, Antonia's hostesses had stopped seating her next to Ted Armstrong. Perhaps it meant the community had accepted them as a legitimate pair. There were people who said she had a "room" at his house. "A bathroom to be exact," she told them. "God knows I'd be filthy otherwise. We're down to two gallons a day in Kinondoni."

Someone said, "They ought to hire Bedouin advisers to teach everyone how to take a bath in a teacup of water."

"And get clean," another added.

"You mix it with sand and scrape."

John Cory was there. His baldness made her anxious and distrustful. It was the only spare thing about him: he was fatter than when she had last seen him, more opulent, wore a diamond ring and one of those embroidered shirts from the Philippines, a shirt with a name that everyone seemed to know. Balong? Barong? Made of something impossible like pineapple fibers. Such shirts looked ridiculous on fat white men. He was talking about one of the countries in southern Africa, Angola or Mozambique, about factions and turmoil. She heard it in nasal tones, a Boston accent: "We ought to let them kill each other off. Like Shiites and Sunnis. Vietnamese and Cambodians. Protestants and Catholics in Ulster. I'm Irish: I can say it."

She wondered if he thought his observation was original, or if he were just being sarcastic, parodying what he was supposed to say. The guffaw was ambiguous.

She spoke to him, "You're interested in South Africa?"

"That's right," he said.

"Well, so am I. In a man named Nkosi."

"Sam Nkosi?"

"He teaches at the university."

"Is that what he says?" He began to laugh.

"Economics."

"Well, maybe. But he's not on the staff."

She was surprised.

"He's just hanging around. Giving lectures. This is what they do with guys like Sam." His wife, the yogini, had come to stand silently nearby, staring into the center as though she could see their talk.

"They?"

"Oh, you know, the *Movement.*" He laughed again, without humor. She didn't know what she expected him to say, what kind of relief a man like Cory could have offered.

To Ted Armstrong, there on his balcony, staring into a candle—no, not a breath of air—the flame as waxen as the stem, she said, "I can't tell you how uneasy it all makes me. Cory tells me Nkosi never worked at the university; he's some kind of pathetic case, out to pasture. There was a picture in the paper, poorly reproduced, of Esther wearing white robes or some such get-up."

He was laughing at her.

"Don't laugh. They brought in a suicide today, a girl about Esther's age who drank insecticide. We couldn't save her. On the stretcher when they brought her in, I thought My God! It's Esther! and then I had such a wave of—of what?—weakness. I almost fainted. I was afraid of hallucination, the blood flower, that I'd see her cut that way again, my own hands slicing what was left of her away. Me. Thinking with my glands. I tell you I was pouring sweat."

He said, "I hope you're not asking for *my* advice."

She wasn't. The outline of his face was no more at that moment than the flow of wax down the candle, the only telltale sign that the fire at its wick was real and hot. She slapped at a mosquito after watching it land on her wrist to make its attack, knew it was anopheles, small, yellow, malarial, a compact body save the swooping curves of back legs that seemed to float behind it as it drank her blood. She felt a reassurance in that kind of danger, an excitement, even something pleasurable about the sting, the quick reflex of her slap, and her skin closing over the insect's prick, the spot swollen only slightly in its own defense.

TWELVE

Traveling with Nkosi was Esther's memory and her dream, closing the circle left open by Musumbi's death. Sometimes she replaced Nkosi with his image, his gestures, and the curve of his jaw. Nkosi was growing thin. At night he went among the men and talked the way her father had done. She heard his rolling voice telling about freedom, saying that all black men were brothers and had to fight. He knew how to use a map for travel and understood the shapes of countries, the lines that marked the edges you couldn't cross. On the map, roads were also marked by lines. Towns were black dots. "We are here. Now we will go there," taking her finger to trace the way. Esther submitted to his guidance: it marked the end of the years she had waited, wondering, trying to find a way to her true life.

The train that had taken them on their first journey sped into the countryside with no problems. It was decorated with Chinese letters, more beautiful than any of the letters Esther had once struggled to learn, the *e*'s and *r*'s of her name.

"No one but a Chinese man can do it," Nkosi told her, and said there were a thousand, a hundred thousand such letters, all different. At the stops along the way, these Chinese people stood in lines, completely still, like grave carvings. They began to sway, hats like roofs and shaded faces. Then they scattered running toward the train and calling to each other. Their wide cloth pants flapped around their legs. African travelers leaned from the windows and watched them pull and drag on pigs and sacks of rice.

Someone near the window said that if a Chinaman didn't eat pig meat and rice each day, he faded in sadness and died. The train would leave them. Speed was its message, diminishing the straining men who faded to dark spots and then nothing as if they had never been.

Nkosi was telling her that there were Africans in Ethiopia who had a great alphabet with more than two hundred letters and he wrote one, saying it was a *t*-sounding letter, the only one he knew. She was able to learn from him this way, an opening to the world and to ideas. It was important. He solved mysteries: the way the sun drew water from the earth into clouds, heavier and heavier until it rained and started again. His knowledge attracted her deeply like love.

She noticed from the window of the train that they traveled at two speeds, going faster among the brush and anthills close to the track and slower through the distant things, so if you looked out too far away the train didn't move at all. She found a correspondence to the way she felt when she was with someone sick. Time was fuller, slower, hardly moving, like the fixed distance, the houses and grain stores along the horizon and the hills becoming part of the sky. She felt that way, she had decided, because she was different and as they found their way through the villages along the Ruaha she marked herself apart by what she wore.

"I will wear a long white dress," she had told Nkosi. She put a strand of dark red beads low on her forehead and then another higher like a Kwavi crown. In a town near Tabora a woman gave her a red collar for her robe. Then she found in the market there a chain and a medallion with a green glass stone. It made it easier dressed this way to escape the questions and the need to explain. She tied her waist with a blue sash. Disappearing under the loose cloth, feeling the heaviness in her hands, she knew what it was to be compelled. People said that sometimes they saw a vapor surround her hands or felt it in the room, a stirring like wind. The ones she touched told her they could feel their bodies growing, filling them with this power she had.

In Ruaha, the river broke into fingers. Walk away from it in any direction and it appeared again, like madness. The villages were close but hard to reach because there were no roads, only fields of maize and sugar in between. An old man was their guide. He told about the medicine plants and about the red palm nuts that ripened and fell and could make elephants drunk, a dangerous time when the big animals ran through houses and crops and no one was allowed to kill them. You couldn't drive them away, he said, because when they were drunk they were not afraid. He knew the minds of elephants, he told them, as he talked his way into the villages there.

People brought her fish from the river and the sweet meat of fat rodents that had stolen grain from their fields. They looked like Makonde. Their skins were black: they cut scars to decorate their faces and they played drums like many voices calling words. Their houses were made of grass and they slept at night with their goats inside, leaving on everyone a rich smell that Esther liked.

In the morning, a woman whose daughter was very sick came and begged for help. The baby she carried on her back had green eyes like a white man's. Esther and Nkosi followed her through vines. A section of the village had houses made of tin and the women there had tied their hair in yellow cloths, all matching. Strings of heavy, dried-out leaves hung in their doorways. They crossed a small bridge made from a fallen tree and saw a big green lizard there. Esther's robe trailed the ground. The glass in her medallion was the color of the lizard's skin. Her detailing mind took in these significant things and read the language of existence there. It was how life touched you: a lizard in the sun to match your stone, the baby's eyes, the leaves, all green.

The stream had marked the edge of the village and beyond it was a forest of tall palms, their red fruits ripening like threats—"Children try to collect them when they fall, but the elephants come in the night to shake the trees and then what can we do?"—The baby gazed from its mother's back. Esther knew where they were going as soon as she saw the building. Low, with mud walls, hidden by tall cactus plants. There were no windows to reveal the secrets it held inside. Just then small girls with bundles of sticks on their heads came up from behind. She heard first their giggles and then their silence as they left the path and pushed ahead. It was a circumcision shed.

The woman told Nkosi that he could not go inside where the sick girl was. Esther pulled back touching his hand, but her pulse drew her, swept her into the darkness there. A smell of smoke. Not like the Pareh, the girls here had been made fat and their heads were not shaved but dressed in soft tufts, three along the top, and from each one, a spike of twisted hair. They were wearing beaded waistbands and necklaces. An old woman sat in the entrance boiling water and the steam filled the shed like a cloud to seal them off.

The girl who was sick was at the end of the shed on a string bed. She was naked and her hair was crushed so that what had given the others their great beauty had ruined hers. Her breasts were no more than bird's eggs. Her skin was dry from her fever and almost gone and her bones seemed to be liquid, glowing from within like X-ray pictures. Time divided: a train passing in the world and the division of Esther's self. Part that wanted to weep and say, "No, no, I have no power at all: these are only stories and tricks," so that she could be fixed to earth, stilled like all the rest of them. But part of her was speeding, had begun to flow out around the girl as though she would vanish with her into death, a kind of healing. She felt nothing as she touched the skin, nothing warm or gaining, and when she lifted her hands to say, I can't, from that stilled distance, the girl was dead.

She would have turned and fled but she was weeping, backing slowly away as the mother saw and screamed. All around her voices were crying out like weaver birds when there is a snake in the tree. Then she was outside, walking steadily not thinking at all, with Nkosi at her side pulling at the ropes of vines until she saw his hands were bleeding and his shoulders shining under his white shirt with the water that poured from him.

"I killed her," she was saying, at last coming to kneel where he had fallen with a groan of angry words in his own language and her head against his face. "Baba," she called him. Like stones the red beads in her hair ground into his flesh there, long ago carved by slashes now hidden by his beard.

All she could remember was woven with her own story until she saw herself in the ruined girl's place and this scared her more than the angry villagers who began to talk with opened mouths. They were afraid too, forming circles around her. She listened to men who stood and sat and stood again pronouncing judgments. The air was stifled with their voices which growled like ancestors in their throats. Her heart in answer beat out words, tiny, trapped in her stomach, too small for them to hear. It was Nkosi who walked among them speaking, which calmed her, though the voices remained sharpened like chipped rocks between her and the wish she had to wipe away all pain. She closed her eyes and wished for blindness so she wouldn't know, wouldn't see the things she saw. Her hands felt raw, cruel, hanging there.

A white man in a Land Rover stopped for them along the road. They had come to a city on the sea, saw on the map the place where the rivers flowed like lines on a hand through sand and low plants. White birds as thick as clouds. Nkosi pretended that he didn't know English but the man went on talking, mixing languages. He had long pale hair but his eyes were black. His skin had been darkened by the sun: it could have been an African's skin but it was burned and dry. Esther understood that he had lived in Africa a long time. He loved animals. In his country there were none, no lions, no elephants, no zebra, no giraffe. Because of this, he would never go home.

Driving at night they were no more than light. Insects fell around the car. Stars. Sometimes he left the road and drove through the bush on small tracks. "Because of the soldiers," he said, "who have closed the way." He only stopped to pour petrol into his car from the cans he had strapped to the sides.

Esther dreamed of the white doctor. She was climbing, following a path. In the distance she could see the red tile roofs of the hospital and the people waiting closed inside the circles of stones. She found a tree and stood in the shade. Looking up she saw there were no leaves, only the red flowers that gave the tree its name. A tree of flames. Her excitement told her the one she wanted to see was near—white doctor coats moving, sharp in the shadows. She stiffened. She saw the doctor's face turn toward her, eyes seeking hers, until she moved or simply disappeared. Above Esther's head the flowers of the tree burned.

She felt like a person drowning: like the fishermen who washed up after days, swollen husks. Or she was like a dry blown leaf. The doctor's voice was whispering, "Did you kill that girl in the shed?" But it was Esther's own body, stripped and on a hospital bed, blood dripping into her veins. She couldn't answer the question. The meaning of the dream was a puzzle. And the puzzle was its meaning. *Fumbikiwa.* Closed together. Was the ache to touch these sick ones only a trick? Were there djinns that ruled in a human's heart?

They went on a bus from some hot city. At the station it was pleasant to stand without identity among strangers and look at maps. The lake was a shape colored blue. Rivers were lines flowing out of it. The hills were marked by shadows. This was how men found their way though the world was round, she knew that, like the moon, not flat.

"How many days until we reach Kigora?" Voices. But the driver didn't say. He coughed into a rag and shouted out the window for a key.

"Necessary to be adding three-four days for breaking down." There was a Hindi voice behind them. And laughter because a journey was a chance.

They left in the morning for any destination, jumping through the city and then rising above it, leaving everything below in the merging clouds and sea. The land seduced her as the hills and trees gained. It made Esther tired. Dozing, she woke each time the bus stopped to let on more passengers and slept then until she felt it stop completely, waking to an exhalation and a silence. She had heard it from her sleep. No one was moving. The driver was trying with his key to make it run. Then there were loud angry words and then they were all laughing and climbing out. These were occasions for brewing tea. From their sacks, people took out stoves and formed groups around them. The driver began taking pieces off the bus and shaking them, trying to put them back on. People argued about which direction was Mecca so they could pray. A Christian told them he could pray in any direction and at any time he wished.

Kigora seemed impossible to reach for the trouble, but to Esther breakdowns were the essence of a journey—she laughed and roamed about talking, talking—the centers from which all else poured as if the travelers had floated to the surface or been sifted out like winnowed bits of grain. It was a way of life: days passed waiting for mechanics and spare parts. They lived on tea and shared food. She kept herself outside of real trouble—walking to the edge of thoughts, looking instead at a dry stream below them, children collecting white pebbles there—until it looked as though the water they had carried would soon be gone.

Fearing lions, many slept inside the bus, which rocked and heaved through the night if, inside, someone stirred to come out. It was hot in there, they said, without air, and smelling bad: so they came finally to sit near the fires. All night Esther thought, listening to what she believed was the dark sky scraping the land toward day, a sound that made her shiver, made it seem there could be no way to understand the changing of light to darkness despite what Nkosi had told her about the turning earth and the fixed sun. Temperature changes in the night were proof that more than the sun brought heat: movements far away but felt. It turned hot suddenly; you woke up covered with sweat. By morning it was cold again. It was all outside, madness and peace, sickness and healing, arrangements made by the world. In the morning there were Masai who broke loose from tall anthills as if they had been formed there, brown-red and dirty. They watched from a distance leaning on their spears, their legs bent like water birds'.

A taxi brought mechanics who were, everyone agreed, too young, who walked around and hit things with their wrenches and looked underneath. They lit cigarettes. Everyone said that only old men could fix things. Nkosi laughed at them and said they needed to bring some white men back to show them all how. He went to sleep, or pretended to, with a *kanga* over his face. The mechanics took a piece from the engine and cleaned it with water and blew on it, and then the driver, who had to be woken up, tried to make the bus run again but couldn't. The mechanics tried again, this time by lying down under the bus. Children bent trying to see, then stood looking at the legs and feet that stuck out. One of the mechanics had four toes on each foot as though he had been born that way. The Masai had moved closer now, were sitting on their heels.

The mechanics brought pieces out and lined them on the ground. People gathered, growing certain, impressed by iron covered in black oil. There was a smell of engines to convince them, the mechanics were dirtier, smoking their cigarettes. They seemed to know the meaning of the pieces and could arrange them, or tighten them with their wrenches. When they crawled back underneath, the one who had four toes remained to slip the pieces one by one into hands reaching out to take them. Legs struggled. Everyone was close, talking about the wonders of it. "If you put only one little-little piece in upside down," an old baba warned, "then it cannot go." He stood under an umbrella. There was a noise of wrenches and banging iron and then the mechanics were out again, brushing at their clothes and circling the bus as the driver climbed inside, then pressed his key. So close now. Skins brushed skins. Children jumped wanting to be lifted high. The bus was roaring. Hindis, who were so tired, were folding their cloths, building their parcels again with plastic and with string. Everyone was pushing to get in, joking, piling parcels, finding old seats. The Masai touched the sides of the bus and waved, then ran one-one, each to look in the mirror at the driver's window.

But the bus broke again; this time not far from a town, so they all had to walk in, including the mechanics, who carried pieces. Downhill. They looked into the brown crossing of streets and the black clusters of buildings. Boys ran up to carry things for a price. Trees appeared as they got closer, spiny like cactus with no leaves.

Sometimes Nkosi was more like a shadow or a question. Sometimes his language made it hard for them to share: his ideas were too far away, too linked to things (he said) that Esther would never understand. He knew too much about white men in their own countries, another story, one that didn't help, that always got between. Although at times it seemed that black men were the cause of all his trouble now that the white men were out of his way. That night in a hotel, he had crawled under the bed to ridicule the mechanics, clicking with a stick and shaking the bed while Esther laughed. He had been drinking beer. When he came back, switching on the light, she saw him flare and tip against the wall. Hard to remember where she was, she cringed, fearing he would beat her. But he couldn't: he was too gentle. His hands gave way to hers: he told her of the buses in Sweden that never broke. Later when she woke and the light was gone, she made out his form sitting in a chair, nothing but a blacker shape gathering in the dark. Her heart said that she was the one meant to care for him.

The hotel was a bar, low, made of wood, with covered windows. A blue cat was painted on a hanging sign in the front. At night, like Esther's memory, the sounds of women rolled in and out of the back courtyard where there were rooms and the toilet in a corner, until morning when it grew quiet. Under a water pump in the middle was an empty bucket; she heard it hit the ground again and again, tipped and dragged in hope. Voices were calling, "There is no water!" She stood and watched as people appeared around the yard in the doorway. Doves walked near the pump. A cook was yawning in the kitchen against the turmoil, "Where we will get tea?" But a boy was coming, bringing water in, in a bucket.

There was another bus, another driver, though all the passengers were the same, smiling greetings. The Hindis were bright, clean, had changed their clothes. The old baba folded his umbrella saying, "This is a better bus after all," which everyone believed. You had only to look at the tires, he said. He, himself, he told them, had slept in the market with his daughter and her children. His back was sore, but they were all safe. He thanked God. There were still pieces of straw in his hair.

Healings were like dreams in the villages along the lake. Esther was welcomed by stories that were told about her, the sudden lifting of a fever, of deaf ears opening. She listened, posed in the center of circles that were made around her as Nkosi explained. Villagers fed them, gave them rest, helped them with money. It was safer for her to be silent then, as though she were given her powers through a kind of sleep, a voice that was not her own calling out. It was safer that way if she failed. People always wanted to know, why has the one I loved died. They wanted a reason, they wanted to know every small thing. They gathered more and more reasons until they could fix the blame. She had to forget and give herself to the mysteries of balances glimpsed all along in everything she saw. It meant trying, something she thought about, wobbling like a person who stands on one foot. Here was stillness like distant images in the rush of movement and she reached out for it, hoping for exhilaration.

Esther would have said that some who came to her understood these things and were ready to be helped, others remained behind walls without knowing what made it so. She relied on impulse, the sudden vision of what was wrong and the comfort of her moving hands finding place against the flesh of the sick, pressed against bone, hot along the ridge of a spine. She might be thinking of anything then: the night sky, the day infusing, and this deep link as she turned between the lightness and the dark.

In Kigora a fisherman's cement house was lined with matching cups and dishes. His children wore new shoes with rubber bottoms that were thick and white. Esther went with them—they were running, straying—to follow the cliff, to see the water. Her mood was expectant in the clouded light as if something might break, a beam of sun or an idea. The lake was flat, made of colors that had no names; the water was sweet and had no salt. She told the children, "There is a place, far away, where the water is filled with salt," and watched their eyes that saw the mystery of it.

"*Chumvi?*" They were making their high noises, laughing, streaming.

"Yes."

"*No no no no,*" they shouted, "there is no *salt!*"

She chased their shouts as they ran down calling *yes yes yes* into the echoes. Along the lake she kicked at stones. The children showed her where the hippos came like fallen trees carried to the shore. When she sat on a rock the children all climbed over her, tumbling, rolling, as if they had been loosened. She felt their wholeness, their perfection, her own desire. But she had never been made pregnant; a message, this barren body said that she was not whole, not a woman, but something else, something slashed and ruined, something that has not healed. The children she held there were like magic blending together, blessed. She touched her own sadness then, the contrast she had lived by, but her confidence deepened like the rhythm of their circling forms and her own repair seemed possible, her own healing, each time she felt this kind of love. She looked for signs, a way to do it. This was her joy: it came slowly like the climb back to the village.

That night Nkosi did not return. She waited for him. Around a lantern, with the other women, she listened to a radio, voices from another country and their music. The fishermen's wives made jokes about the kind of fishing that was done at night, about the catch of radios and cooking oil, the bolts of cloth brought up in the nets of their clever husbands. They embroidered tablecloths from threads that came from Parisfrance and England. She sat among them watching them work. Later she walked out toward the cliffs against the danger of the dark. Distant villages were spots of fire thrown across the water. The city of Kigora reflected light over the water, a shining; black shapes in black light, the huge rocks were animals resting near the shore. There was no moon, no way to see if a man were climbing toward the village.

In the morning he came back. She tipped her smile to him from a bed full of snuggling children. She had worried but now was glad. There were men, he told her, from his own country, soldiers. He had met them in the town. This was all he would tell. She was infected by him, knew he wanted to go be with those men, his own people. But the picture she saw told her something different. He was alone. She knew he would fail in his desire; thin as Musumbi. She looked at his shadow on the wall, which seemed heavier, more like a body than his real one.

He went out again the next night, "to see his brothers," but returned quickly while the rice was still cooking. He didn't eat, walked in circles through the village. He had been drinking *pombe:* she could hear it in his voice as he stopped and talked to everyone, in words that echoed what they heard on the radio, stories about his own country—he pointed to show them all the direction—in which a man could be stolen in the night and made to dig the earth in mines so that the white men could become rich.

She waited in her bed listening to his rolling voice grow and fade until he was at last a sound moving in the room. As her eyes conquered the dark he looked like a djinn, his beard grown larger than the rest of him, his arms as sharp as twigs.

"Your children," she asked him because it struck her suddenly that his wife was white, "are they Africans or white men?"

"You can't understand," he said. His clothes were falling. She smelled his flesh. "They are abominations," he said.

Too close to see him she searched in blindness for his back. Her hand found the stem of his spine, the bones that jutted there. He sighed and lay next to her and fell to sleep. Her eyes could pick out shapes on the wall, quivering branches, a light that rose and fell. Someone passing with a lantern. There was just enough light to find her box, to reach without sight into the bottom and take the letters. She knew there were other things in them beside the words speaking to him from the paper there. She felt the thick answering of photograph pictures to show him their faces, to urge him home. And because she thought they all would lose him, she yearned to know. She slowly breathed on the envelope cases the way Hadija said you did to loosen the gum that sealed them. She opened them like pockets and peered inside as if for lost things. There were the letters and folded with them the pictures. It was too dark: she held them near the window hoping for the light again, but there were only shadows. The faces loomed like white marks with no features. She recognized that they were pleas, that they wanted him back. Or promises. Or signs of love.

Before the dawn she woke and dressed and creaked out from the house. More than her curiosity was aroused: she was involved. Having broken the sealed letters in darkness she had seen only faint outlines in the shining prints. She had to see more, to discover the importance of his life—to look for demons, to understand what divided him. She savored the event, invented a ritual to mark it: I will go to where I can see the lake; I will arrange rocks in a circle; I will sit in the center with the envelopes; I will wait until . . . her invention stymied, she stood on the edge of the forest, thin and cracking in the dry season, and from there saw a gathering of hippos below her near the shore, shapes forming on the day's advantage. She knew they would bolt and run into the water soon and made that her moment, told herself, when the animals are gone, then I will look at the faces of Nkosi's children. Delay gave meaning, substance to her adventure.

She watched the hippos rouse then like rocks brought suddenly to life: others were still crashing close from the tall grasses, obeying the day and nothing else, bumping and pushing. They piled on the ground. Began to roll. What was it in the light that signaled to them there was no safety for them on land? Slowly, the biggest pushed into the lake, and then the rest, rushing and black. Soon they had all disappeared and the lake closed over them. Impossible to tell where they went or how far, like fish, until, as the sun hit the water, you saw their heads, first their red ears and noses and then their eyes checking the way.

Opening the envelopes, Esther was not surprised. She had seen the children of mixed race and though Zobetta said such children were always ugly, Esther was filled by the beauty of these three. They were like angels. Their hair was soft and took the light as its own. She tipped the pictures to see their faces better—boys or girls? Round, fat faces. Their mother floated behind them with the kind of hair Zobetta said came from squeezing lemons in your tea. It was white hair and it broke over her round face. Her shoulders were curved and her body heavy. Her neck was wrapped in a scarf and her clothes were thick; she seemed to poke out from them as though they were her house. Her eyes were squinting, swollen, Esther thought, from her weeping. Caught by their beauty, by their loss of him, by the loss of him she saw for herself.

Who is the tall man that comes to us and leaves again? He wears a dark coat and shoes. He brings a box of presents, magic things, small cars that wind and drive across the floor, strings of beads, pictures of cities far away to hang on walls, fine clothes for women, shoes. This is because he travels, lives with white men. Musumbi: the women are laughing. Her mother's hair is where she hides. Mu-sum-beeeeee! Her aunt Zidora makes the name a song. They tease him. This Esta, this one, doesn't even know her own daddy. He picks her from her mother's arms. Call him Baba. Say Baba. She is stiff, afraid of him, running away, a kind of love.

She went back with her secret. The fishermen were hiding sacks inside the tank of a great stove that the villagers said could make a cold great enough to harden water into ice and turn fish into stones that couldn't rot. It was a stove, they said, that burned petrol like a car, but when she asked Nkosi how a fire could make cold, he only laughed. Perhaps he didn't know. It had never worked: you could see it there darkened with oil, pipes coiling and wires broken all around it. Japanese people came and put it there, the women said, but had become frightened when they saw the giant fish that the Germans had put in the lake. "They liked to eat it without cooking, like savage men who lived in ancient times."

Nkosi was inside looking at his map. He showed her places: Kigora and the road and the place they would go next. "Sameh," he said, which made her look carefully at the dot. She drew her finger slowly back and saw the shadow marks that described the mountains there and remembered the day she had run away from just that place, thinking of the meaning of the circle that her journey might make at last.

"Must we go?" she asked him.

"Yes," he said. "My people are there!"

THIRTEEN

◄ ◇ ►

Once Kigora had thrived, a big town on a big lake, one of the colonial capitals, a center of trade and a link with the interiors. Years ago, when she was traveling with Luenga, Antonia used to go out there every two or three months to work in the hospital. Later, she went alone, on assignments, visits that dwindled to every six months and finally, now, to once a year, as if the country were forgetting its outer borders, too far away and the roads all in ruin. She flew in a Cessna. The pilot was a burly, smiling boy with red curling hair, just new, from Ireland. Over dry highlands, hills stretched basking and naked in the sun. People were down there in the desert, hidden, uncounted, living it seemed without water. They saw the circles of thatch and squares of fenced-off pens. The crosshatch of paths. The compact wooliness of their grazing sheep. Village geometries.

The pilot followed the trails of men and animals, then skimmed a forest of leafless baobabs and rose with the country to the high desert that would fall in rust and brown steppes to the lake. There was a train of nomads leading camels, tribesmen from another country, from the southern fringes of the Sahara. Ironic, they probably thought in their wisdom that the desert was a secure place to hide, as hostile as it was open, where only men with their skills could survive. Of course, a small plane flying low could follow them. They scattered as the Cessna stalked. Antonia saw there were only a few men in the caravan, probably carrying contraband. One of them looked up: he was close enough for her to see his squint, the black amulets he had tied around his neck.

Soon came the narrow fringe of dark green that marked the lake shore. No prevailing winds made sense of patterns of the weather here: there were only zones and microsystems. Deserts embraced slashes of jungle like this one. Once walking to a village through a dry ravine down there someplace, Antonia had found a spring and then its fall. The spray was trapped in an eroded **V**. Huge ferns and vines had taken hold. It had stunned her like finding a gem. The bushes were thronged with colobus monkeys, flashes of black and white in the marvel of leaves. She had told Luenga, "I have found the water-god."

From above like this, she could see how Kigora town had grown into the contours of the land. There were two main roads, no longer paved. The high road tipped against a slope where bare hills pressed their feet into that rich edge along the shore. The low road was built up with shops and offices that followed the crescent bay. The hotel was a monster, the ruined hope of a big port.

Nurses from the hospital had come to welcome the doctor. The hotel even put on a tea, with milk and small yellow cakes dotted with red icing. Unita Anjalo poured, like a British matron. She had been trained as a nurse but she practiced medicine, probably one of the best in the country, surely one of the best surgeons. She had told Antonia her story once: "My brother had polio. The villagers knew that this was a disease that spread, that ruined the limbs. The way you treat it is to throw the child into the lake. He will then be born into a new body. But the English D.O. heard of this. In those days we were frightened of those men, you see. He came directly to my father's house himself and said the whole village, everybody, would be put in jail if we did this thing. He took my brother in his car. Now my brother is alive with only a small weakness in his leg. I also left the village then. But walking. I came a great distance to that D.O. and told him, I want to be a nurse."

She seemed suddenly older to Antonia, her skin darkened with the change: face, arms, legs, black cutouts in sharp contrast to the brilliant white of her nurse's uniform. Antonia sipped her tea.

A young nurse said, "People say one day we will be alone in the world like the Chinese."

"Yes," another said, "see how the Chinese have come to show us their way." Her name was Omoye. She was known for her strong arms that could lift a full-grown man.

A third nurse said, "They eat with sticks. I myself have seen it."

"Do their men have penises?" the fourth asked. She was called Nellie. "No one has seen this. Not even the whores. They never come to our hospitals, so how can we see if they do or if they do not."

"Because they have doctors who can cure people by the use of pins which they stick here in your feet. Or in other places." Theirs were voices that teased, as the teacups rattled elegantly in their saucers.

"Fool," Unita said. "Of course they have penises. Are we not all made in the image and likeness of God? Are we not all the same?" There seemed to be too much gray in her hair.

"Tell us, Dr. Antonia," Omoye said, "about this man who has another man's heart stitched up inside his body. It is true?"

"Another man's kidney. This is a wonderful thing." It was Nellie like an echo.

Antonia said, "Yes, yes, it's true!" They were all laughing, gasping, popping their tongues in awe.

"I heard in America there are people who exchange all their parts. A woman can get a penis stitched on. A man can get breasts. In this way they change themselves and find happiness." Omoye knew more than the rest.

"What? Do they think God has made a mistake?"

"What about brains? Can you get a new brain?"

"No. That not. That is a fixed thing."

"But I have heard there are doctors who can make surgery on brains."

"Yes. Even this." There were the cakes then, being passed around.

"Can *you* do it, Dr. Antonia? Can you? On brains?"

"No, no, I can't." She was charmed, laughing. They were all almost roaring now.

"Ah, you will go learn this. I'm afraid of it," Unita said.

She was suddenly sad. "You will go away and never come back. Isn't it so?"

"No, no . . ." against what sounded too prophetic, but the old woman was too wise to ignore.

"How can they break the bone of a skull?" Nellie asked.

"Such a wonderful thing."

They made a row together, lifting cups of hot tea to their pursed lips, dreaming of the world.

After they left her, before the dinner hour, Antonia walked out from the hotel on a circuit she and Luenga always made whenever they came here together. First along the beach to a cement landing built for fishermen. Big canoes were there, gunwales painted (a German archaeologist claimed) with certain symbols that proved Egyptian contact thousands of years back. That, and the local custom, outlawed now, of burying boys with their dead kings.

Two young fishermen were there hefting an enormous perch from their canoe. It had filled the boat. Perch of frightening proportions, brought from abroad by a foreign scheme, were eating all the other species in the lake. From two small girls, Antonia bought twenty shillings' worth of sun-dried fish. She called them minnows and relished the way Charles cooked them in a pungent salty sauce to spoon on rice.

A path went up, bending to accommodate rock outcrops. She crept, angled to the slope, using her arms and hands to steady herself and pull. From the top, a view: the lake, the canoes, the huge hotel, the dying town. She walked north. The forest hung in the sky like storm clouds. The lake had no color. Lizards with red shoulders and blue heads marked rocks along the way like staked claims. These were the only defined images. Even the large boulders strewn across the landscape had soft edges, evaporating.

She passed, at some distance, a small village of round mud houses decorated as the canoes had been with hieroglyphs of their theoretical past—perhaps, if you looked carefully, a sun disk, a lotus, a scarab, the ankh. After the village was a slight hill that, as it peaked, revealed, on the other side an open flat meadow, possibly an empty marketplace.

People had gathered there in the wide ring and in the center was a woman. She was Esther Moro dressed in a white gown decorated with beads and a cheap, gaudy medallion. Antonia sat down on her heels at the top of the hill and watched.

She wondered what decided the radii of circles like this one. More than an arm's reach, more than a jump away, an empty space and then the wheel of people. Esther was sitting on a low stool. Nkosi hunkered at her feet. From where Antonia sat, she couldn't hear more than a murmur when Nkosi began to speak, making gestures, finally opening his arms to offer an embrace. A woman wearing a blue dress fought her way to the iris that framed the healer. Once exposed, the woman drew back, then came on again as if she had been pushed from behind like a dancer on display. Esther held an open palm her way, but the woman was locked in place, rocking back and forth.

Someone brought a baby to the center, a big man, Nilotic, black and hard as obsidian, holding the infant like an offering. Nkosi urged him forward. The man hunkered at Esther's feet with the child on his lap. Others came forth: only a few, no more than fifteen. When Nkosi stood and led Esther away, the circle around her collapsed. A few followed after her. There had been no laying on of hands. No exchange of money. No loud words or invocations. As far as she could tell, nothing at all had happened. The meeting could have been for any reason. The point suddenly was that something had prevented Antonia from interfering. She had backed away from them, in fact, seeking the protection of the cresting hill. Caught unaware, she had been stopped by an emotion she didn't understand, something that made her hesitant. Do I want this? Do I need this? Like a person contemplating a purchase.

But it bothered her all night under the gauzy layers that were between her and the climate, the thin sheet over her body, the netting over her bed, the screen on the window. Pictures: the blood flower, the broken bottle, the scalpel, the way these things had been twisted in Esther's mind, like demons in her blood. There was no way to imagine how badly she had been abused as a child. She thought of clinical definitions like hysteria, manic depression, schizophrenia. In other parts of the world there would have been drugs and therapy, ways to define and understand what was going on with Esther. Here there were only the *waganga* with their pots and oils and bones, smelling of beer and somehow marked as different from other men, a freak with the hair of a white man, or an extra finger, men who dressed bizarrely.

In the morning, Unita wanted Antonia to help her with a burned child. Three years old. It was her arm. She had fallen into the cooking fire. The family had doused it with kerosene, widely used as a disinfectant. The arm was ruined to the elbow. The kerosene had colored it an angry purple and it was grossly misshapen. Her parents did not want the arm amputated. The loss would mean trouble: two arms would be needed to plant and harvest. No man would marry a woman with one arm. She would have no children to take care of her in her old age. No.

The child appeared to have blocked off the pain. She smiled at the white doctor. Her grandfather was holding her, weeping into a frayed handkerchief.

"She will die otherwise," Antonia said.

"They have a hand which is made of plastic," Unita told them. "They will attach it here. It will look like a real hand. See how the wound has ruined her. She has no fingers." In the end they agreed.

Later Antonia said to Unita, "There's a woman here in Kigora, she touches sick people and they get well. Have you heard of her?" They were going over papers, order forms, and lists of things Unita needed to run her hospital. Mostly they needed doctors. The one they had six months ago had gone back to the capital, an alcoholic who had been relegated to Kigora and who simply never came to work.

"Only foolish people believe such stories," Unita said. "We are supposed to be Christians." Which meant they ought to be beyond things that smacked of magic and superstition.

"But Jesus himself was a healer of the sick. And his apostles," Antonia said.

"Mmmmmm," the old woman answered. It was not part of her picture, whatever Jesus meant to Unita Anjalo: redeemer, teacher, the light and the resurrection.

"Her name is Esther," Antonia went on.

"Oh, yes, I have heard," Unita said. "You always hear of these things." She was annoyed, embarrassed. "Surely in your country as well. Because there is so much ignorance."

"My country?"

Unita had mastered an ironic smile. "Perhaps indeed you have stayed among us too long, is it?"

"But this Esther. What have you heard, Unita?"

"Oh, I don't listen to it. You see, she will have success and then there will be relapses. Later they will all be coming to us."

To us: to the stained and crumbling hospital. Flies had swarmed the operating theater where they amputated the small girl's arm. The nurses moved around in slow confusion. Only Unita seemed to know what to do, or pretended she did.

Omoye was the one who knew about Esther. "She can make you feel a fire. The sickness burns. It falls away like ashes."

And Nellie said, "Her face is beautiful and her eyes closed. A certain power is inside her."

"Where does she stay?"

"Up there, with the fishermen." Omoye pointed, her long fingers flashing half-moons of deep pink.

Antonia knew the place, beyond an inlet on a rock outcrop, a series of ascending cliffs and a small fishing village.

"And many people go to her?" she asked.

"Yes . . . yes." Whispering now and nodding because Unita was near and it made them nervous. They broke away, veering along the corridor where patients waited, sitting on the floor, their heads tipped up to the passing forms in white.

Antonia took her tea that afternoon alone under stilled ceiling fans (there was only electricity after dark) in a mahogany-paneled ballroom, the floor cool Italian tiles. The tables, chairs, and sideboard still remained in perfect condition from another irrelevant time. Was it sadness these passing things brought on? Or another emotion? It was an enormous space, empty now. Only three tables had been set, their cloths badly mended.

There were no cakes this time, and no milk, only the tea and sugar that came out portioned on a tiny dish. She went with her cup onto the porch and looked at the lake. The inlet was just there, and the rock cliffs.

She followed the shore then to the landing, passing four men with a catch, a perch hung from two poles, so huge it took them all to carry it, like pallbearers. Children were soaping themselves in the shallows there. A woman with a baby watched them, knitting with sharpened sticks, her baby wrapped in her handiwork, a bright yellow blanket. Over that was a towel. Nearby there was a grassy beach where hippos came at night to feed. She could see them steaming slowly toward it breaking the surface for air, wide gaping pink mouths. They would gather in the shallow water until darkness told them it was safe ashore, and then they would follow, single file, pulling the lake in waves as they came. Their routes through the bush were easy to spot, humorously dainty, narrow at the bottom to accommodate their small feet, and then a wedge, a sharp **V** in the grass for their great bellies.

Three men were washing their canoes: one stunning in a turquoise T-shirt and tight red trunks. The other two wore white shirts and frayed khaki walking shorts. The man in turquoise greeted the white woman, showing his broad chest, a silver moon and silver astronauts, black letters embossed: ONE GIANT STEP FOR MANKIND.

In the village a man with a walleye told her Esther had gone, early in the morning. But he insisted that Antonia see the house where Esther had stayed, guiding her, looking over his shoulder with his good eye. He was intense, demanding. She thought he might have been retarded.

The house was small and makeshift but made of cement. It had once been part of a Japanese scheme to help local fishermen by providing a way for them to freeze their catch for sale in distant markets. Squatters now occupied all the buildings. Laundry hung on lines stretched from the tall fence posts. The generator brought in to run the freezing plant still leaked the original oil. Covered with rust, it had never been used.

The fisherman was young, high strung, and clearly smart beyond his opportunities. Despite it all, he made money. The lake must have given him access to black markets and contraband from neighboring countries. His house displayed their goods. A radio-cassette was playing music from Zaire. A steel vacuum jug held hot tea. There was a complete set of china teacups and dishes, two big flashlights on a long table, a packet of batteries. Three children ran around in bright canvas shoes. The fisherman told her that Esther had completed her work and left the village. His sense of protocol made him show her the bed where Esther slept. He patted it, lifted the cover to show there could be no question, although now, it was clear, someone else was sleeping there.

He insisted that Antonia stay for tea. His wife washed the cups and teapot in a red plastic basin using a small pink sponge and liquid detergent that smelled of lemon. She placed the clean vessels on a low table, on a cloth embroidered with stylized flowers that might have been hibiscus. They had no stems, an array of petals and lacy stamens. Strewn shapes. Two women, one old, one young, sat on a bench across the room against a wall. The young one was working with a crochet hook, a new project, too small to tell what it would become. There would be no talking during these procedures. Antonia knew it was her presence that stopped them in their chatter. But the act of drinking tea relaxed the party. They spoke of the weather first, the price of things, the shortages, and finally of Esther.

The old woman said, "She knows about sickness. She could see a person and say, this is where the sickness is. She had a way of seeing it. Once you saw it, then you made it go away."

"People say she is a witch. But I don't believe it," the young one said. "Jealousy makes them speak that way."

The old one told them, "There was another like her when I was a girl. She was a Christian and she made you believe in Jesus, then she could heal you. Because her power came from Jesus Himself. People who believed her sewed red cross signs to their clothes and here on their chests, and they made a religion. They followed her away to another place. No one saw them again. She said there was going to be a terrible disease in our country. And she had seen the truth. It was the *mwakapindu,* the terrible cholera. So many died. My mother. My sisters. My grandfather. Many."

"Now they will save you at the hospital," the young one said, "by putting medicine in your blood through a pipe. I myself have seen this."

The doctor nodded.

"Even so," the hostess interrupted, "I saw how this Esta came to my sister whose legs were so swollen with poison, who had such pain in her wrists and ankles. I saw how she placed her hands there and held them. I was there."

"And she is well now," the old woman said.

It was almost dark by the time Antonia reached the ledge above the beach. The men were gone. She thought she would be well across the grass by the time the hippos decided to come ashore. She made a lot of noise climbing down, kicked rocks, and coughed and carried on. Close to the water, the stones made it hard to walk and the darkness came fast. There were a few lights at the hotel but none around the lake, only the hill forms, the dense matte-black land against the lacquered shine of the black sky and water.

They didn't wait. She heard them surging, sucking the water with their great bodies as they rose, heard them splash and the gentle bellows of their breath. But she couldn't see a thing. They were close. They smelled like cows. She thought if she reached out, she might touch a warm, wet shoulder or a flank. Out of the water, they moved slowly, silently like fat men in slippers, shuffling by. As they reached the grass, dried weeds broke, the only sound. The frogs grew louder, raucous. She moved sideways into the water, ankle deep and straining to see how far away they were. And when they were gone, or seemed to be, she went carefully, like a blind man, arms ahead of her, expecting the worst.

The trip back next day was long and rough. The pilot made a detour north to drop, by parachute, food supplies to some young scientists working in the hills, those red crenellations behind the shoreline cliffs. Were they the people doing research on baboons? They had called on her (as alumni) more than two years ago. Harvard graduates.

She had never seen them again. There had been a kidnapping, in Malawi was it? But that was a group from Princeton, held for ransom by rebels there. She remembered being startled by how young her callers had been and had mocked their attitude, firm as most naturalists that came this way, about the relative value of wildlife as opposed to people, making no secrets about which they preferred. Could they still be up there? Had they been allowed to stay?

Heading toward the coast they hit winds that cascaded like water from the highland plateau to the sea, currents of hot air and cold in conflict. The young Irish pilot looked grim but satisfied: this was why he had come to Africa after all. Under the silt carried on the liquid winds, land forms were muted, hiding their marks. It made it hard to find the way. He tried to use his compass but such things annoyed him. He didn't like instruments, he would rather fly naturally, he said. So he hugged the earth, searching. Sometimes he made quick turns or long slow veers, bucking his plane, his lady, against the windfalls.

"Are we lost?" she shouted.

"Not to worry." She could barely hear him. "Anyplace we want we pull 'er up. They'll all be out to have a look. Roast a goat. Man doesn't go hungry down there. Not if he brings an aircraft down where they can get their hands on it."

They weren't lost: he was too good. He found a dry riverbed and followed that to the Zambia road, the copper road, another foreign project to help the Africans get their wealth out and sold. Ah yes, it was the Americans who built that road. And the Chinese the railroad parallel to it, designed to haul the same copper.

FOURTEEN

◁ ◇ ▷

Antonia's lawyer, Mr. Laxmanbhai, had come excitedly to tell her that people had been asking questions about her residency. The reasoning went: she was not a foreign expert offered to them free. It was known that her mother had certain assets abroad. That money could only have been taken from them. What they called exploitation of the masses, Laxmanbhai explained. There would be a new policy. Perhaps she would be allowed to stay but not paid, at least until the debt was canceled. He thought someone had found out something bad about her, a thing that she had done, perhaps inadvertently, to bring disfavor. It was possible she didn't even know what this was.

"There are men who watch us," he said, "and are making reports. A person has much to wonder about and fear." He was the last of his family left behind, waiting for a visa to Canada or to the United States. A widower. His children had gone one by one.

"Only because of education," he claimed. "This is a good land, a good place, and I am happy here." Pessimism and apologetics fought in his soul.

It made Antonia laugh: someone at Immigration had given the poor man a bundle of papers for her to fill out.

"Oh, you do it, Mr. Laxmanbhai, I don't know anything about that stuff." He was so nervous though, possibly envious because she had the security of citizenship elsewhere and he had none. He had developed such dark circles around his eyes. Was it nephritis? Or lack of sleep because of this wonder and fear that he talked about.

217

She had been born among men who thought of Africa in different ways. They had never listened to what anybody said about dark continents. To them Africa was light. What characterized the written accounts of those early days were enormous brilliant skies, impossible far-flung views across gold savanna, improbable tropic mountains capped with gleaming snows. They had linked themselves to the landscape in tragic ways. Adventure was one of them, the trappings of their civilization another. Even now, so soon after they had gone, their work, their science, their culture were all fading. The coffee bushes on her father's plantation had bolted and grown to trees, all but impossible to harvest and yielding only the small, wild crops they had given to ancient man. It would never have occurred to a man like Bill Redmond that he might be denied by rubber stamps and passport controls. Perhaps it had been wrong for her to laugh. These were not formalities any longer.

She went to Luenga with the problem, standing in the parking lot near his car. His familiar gestures, idiosyncracies, once the touchstones and refrains of daily life, made her sad. They were no assurance now, only an illusion, a trick. What made her comfortable with him before made her uneasy now. She watched him remove his watch to a jacket pocket, then rub his wrist. Relieved, the hand moved in lazy circles, the fingers flexed. She stood for a short time leaning against a fender. He held the wrist a moment pressed against his mouth, almost a kiss, head bowed, an attitude of prayer or exhaustion.

"If you don't pursue it, Paul, they'll win. They'll force me to leave. All those papers and stamps. Any way they want to."

They began walking toward the beach. A small market had sheltered itself under burlap and cardboard near a bus stop there. A single vendor had coconuts. Luenga bought three, shaking them and hitting them with a penny the way women did. They were awkward to carry and there was nothing to put them in so he gave her one, which she took in two hands giving over to an urge to squeeze. Isometrics with a coconut. This one was the size of a grapefruit: the milk sloshed in its shell. An old man ran to them with a parrot fish, his finger hooked under the gills. It was bad, reeking, had opaque eyes.

"It's hard for foreigners now," he told her. "Impossible. Especially Americans. You know that."

"So you won't do anything."

"I'll try."

They lingered near the cement breakwater and faced the ocean. He dropped his coconuts and checked his watch while she tossed the fruit gently and caught it again and again. Unusually powerful waves battered the lee of two small islands that humped close to the shore. They were joined by a natural arch of black coral. She could see the currents swirling there between the islands, currents that were driving the surf because there was no wind.

"Here," Luenga said. He cracked a nut expertly in two neat parts and pried the meat out with a pocket knife. It was a perfect fruit, rich, oily, and sweet. She knew exactly what he would do with the knife, pick loose a thread from his clothes, stretch it tight with his teeth, and nick it off. As he always did.

He talked a little about his youngest son, the one Helen had named Princely. The boy had grown to be very tall, an eager student. He was sorry there were no real chances for the boy's education, but that was a temporary price they had to pay for the independence they needed so badly. He said it took all his strength not to do what others had done and find a way to send the boy abroad, because he knew that he'd never come back.

There was the lure. He smiled. She was comfortable listening to him, sucking the last sweet oil from the coconut pulp. Like the residue of desire. Like regret.

They walked out on the jetty. The tide was ebbing, exposing rock pools and mosses, tiny red starfish and bright barnacles.

"Your American friend is leaving, I hear," he said. He wiped his forehead with the back of his hand, which meant he was embarrassed.

"Yes, they are all going."

"But you. You want to stay."

"As long as I can." She bent to pick up a cowrie there, swaddled in seaweed, an egg shape, polished and shining in her palm, a black-brown surface fading to purple where its edges touched its base. "I collected insects as a kid. Other kids collected shells," she said. He knew. He had heard her one winter in Boston yowling—"Not one spider, not one ant, not one any-goddamn-thing but roaches." And then there was in spring and summer that terrible disappointment of butterflies.

"What keeps you here?" he asked. He always had to ask. Perhaps he thought that once he had been the reason, and now he faced her with this wound, this idea that he had never been, that perhaps he was only used.

"It isn't staying so much as having to go, not being able to come back, if that makes any sense." Like an emotion, the reason was hard to define but she'd heard it from diplomats and missionaries and Peace Corps types all the time, furious when they'd been evacuated or kicked out of some stinking hellhole, someplace far worse than this—war zones, Saigon, Iran, Jordan. *We wanted to stay. We would have stayed. We were forced to go.* It could only have to do with loss and will and the peculiar stubbornness that they linked with courage or freedom or even destiny. She handed him the shell, her signal that she didn't want to talk about it.

They reached the end of the breakwater and could see the shoals that ringed the twin islands where people gathered oysters and clams on low tides, and coral reefs visible only by the green glassy disks and patterns that they gave to the surface of the sea.

He said, "Remember that man of mine, this Adam—whatever his name comes to be—who goes from village to village looking for this god of water?"

"You *finished* the poem!"

"By no means." Laughing, he hunkered there and she did, too, pulling at the seaweed, dislodging stones, looking. "What does he do? What is his task?" He began to toss periwinkles. "He goes in this village and asks his question. When the answer is no, what has he finished? He has only eliminated that one place from his search."

"Isn't that the way one looks for things?"

"There is also scheming." He was smiling. The gap between his teeth was boyish, and the way he hunkered there tipped back on his heels.

"Scheming?" She laughed.

"You're laughing. Know why? Because that is such an African thing to say."

"To say that scheming and searching are the same?" she interrupted.

"To *do*, I should say. An African thing to *do*."

"I thought the water in your poem was truth, a source, some authentic bit of history you want so badly . . . all those things."

"Perhaps it is only water in fact. One schemes in that case. Water is scarce, certainly more valuable than any of those other things you mention."

"Are we talking about corruption again?" she said.

"Are we?"

"All men are corrupt. It's the nature of flesh. Ask any doctor."

"Corruption in any case." He was really laughing now, rubbing his chin on his shoulder the way he did. He would be, she thought, a gentle old man, his unhappiness and resignation taken for wisdom. She missed him in advance.

"So you've been working on it again?" she asked.

"Naaah," he answered.

It seemed strange to walk back together, precariously balancing their way along the rocks like tightrope walkers, laughing now and then or stumbling or having to be saved and not being able to put out an arm or to embrace and stagger on. It would be dark when they reached the hospital lot. Someone would be sure to see them coming in together. He must have thought about it before she did and said, "You go ahead of me." His tone had become harsh.

At home she found a note from Ramish Lal that her car was ready. She had no calendars left to tell her how many months it had been. Adjusted now to life without it, she wondered whether she ought to go fetch the damn thing after all, to have it break again, to be told there were no spares, to wait in line for petrol and pay the bribes that let you buy it. Only for those few stretches of surviving road where she could drive like hell.

Lal overflowed with maxims: "You must never be giving up on ships!" Betel nut had stained his mouth a terrifying red. His was one of the few booming businesses left in town.

The government hadn't closed him down: they wouldn't dare. She had the feeling, standing there in that fury of mechanics, that Lal alone was keeping the whole country running. His frenzied men were like gnomes in a secret cave.

He produced a bill, "Only for spare parts! I am nothing charging for the labors!"

"Go on, Ramish! Labor, too!" A conversation of exclamations and laughs.

"Thirty months! This is no business. No business, I tell you."

"But it's not your fault, Ramish. Let me pay, Ramish."

"Oh no. No no no no no no."

No matter what she said, he felt the shame, was waving his hands against her cash. She knew he'd claim the favor in another way. A night call on a sick child perhaps. And she would go.

He was smiling, patting the old fender. "Too much reliables. A very good service." She had forgotten what had been the matter with it in the first place. "Hey, now you are having wheels," pronounced it "veels." Lal said, "Everything is coming to him as he has waited."

It was a cinch then to go home. Veels. Time and space grew startlingly small, easy to conquer. Pulling up in Kinondoni she remembered the privacy a vehicle had given her in the past. Charles would have no idea what she had been up to or with whom. He was so much happier that way, like a parent who had abdicated, who didn't want to know anything at all.

A crush of kids rushed out to greet the returning car. She might have been negotiating an obstacle course bumping through that flock, shouting from her window until at last she couldn't move for the crowd and had to leave it to them, patting at it like an old pet. One child pressed a cheek to the heat of its bonnet, another picked mud from the tire treads with a stick. Charles ran out and scattered them in all directions. They scuttled along the ground out of his range, then turned and watched, intent as pigeons for a chance to come back and feast.

Later the Peugeot made it easy to get to Oyster Bay. To "swing by," which made her think of dancing. Shifting, revving, she went, she followed ruts made by other cars, surprised she knew the back way. A sort of instinct she would never have had on foot where there was time to stop and think. The wheel in her hands was an agreeable sensation. It could have been only hours ago that she last drove, not twenty, thirty months. It gave her a curious sensation, almost nostalgic, of the time she had spent on foot. There was an innocence to that, her inconvenience like a hair shirt. Down there. With them. She felt it now. I ought to be down there with them. Exposed to feel what wretches feel? An attitude of hers that might have been no more than a general sort of spite against the advantages that others took; the corrupt politicians and bureaucrats, the whole damn population of Oyster Bay. McGeorge called it *boring,* nothing more than her own brand of romance. And peculiar. She told him it was only a snide sort of yearning, no cosmic need, nothing he should worry about. Now, however, as she turned and crossed that short dash of bridge, and saw behind her the cranes and scaffolds of that abandoned construction, saw the white sand of the small cove there, and sped out onto the sickle bend of the bay shore, hot wind blowing her hair from its pins, she admitted to herself that yes, she had, in fact, missed her wheels.

On foot, she had been able to approach that ark of Armstrong's at her own speed. There had been a chance to stop and pause three houses down or so and look out at the sea, or pick a few dried pods, or even climb down the cliff and wade part of the way, coming up on his house from below. From that angle, it loomed above its hedges and fences, white boxes piled on each other like beehives. Nothing about the place was tropical or graceful. Now, the old Peugeot made her aggressive. Or was it aggressive on its own, she merely the agent of its quick advance, hurtling up his drive, playing the horn.

"Holy shit, you *do* have a car!" He hailed down to her from his balcony.

"I didn't think I'd remember how to drive," she called back, feet lifting then, released, a thump, a pressure where there had been a clutch, a brake and then there was the slide the driver had to make, thighs under the steering wheel. She jumped out, still vibrating from her ride, begging him for coffee. Not all the same as sneaking up and tapping on his door, hearing the tromp of his feet down stairs; the clicking, the fumbling locks, his "Oh, Tony, well, good!" and she then handing him a gold dried weed or a few white shells, or a bright flower from her walk.

Inside, the house was torn apart. Half packed. "They ran out of boxes. What else?" he said from the kitchen where he was filling glasses with ice. "I'm fixing gin and tonic. All there is."

Funny now that he was leaving it seemed as though he had lived there after all, would finally, in going, personalize the place. All those cardboard cartons, piles of dust and shredding paper were a form of cancellation. Upheaval like this had its own kind of energy. She felt it: the packed disheveled house was a foreshadow of the empty one. The essence of the man who lived there then was fading, a distant, diminishing thing.

How silly. It was no ghost making all that racket in the jumbled kitchen with gin and ice, wearing red running shorts (she still admired his legs, his ankles, his feet) and absolutely reeking from the efforts of his day.

"My wife used to be in charge of moving," he complained.

"Here's to Nepal!" She raised her glass.

"Have you come to take a shower with me?" he asked.

But she refused, preferring to sit on the balcony. There was a delicious coolness that particular night, legacy of a renegade monsoon that had stolen the hot air and sent it out to sea. It was one of those times that made her homesick in advance for what she had right then, knowing she was in danger of losing it. She was starting to believe that landscapes, seascapes, and skies like these were probably harder to leave behind than people, for reasons that might have to do with what endured. More than a backdrop—that graying, glowing, billowing sky seasoned with the winds from Asia—it was her context.

She told him, "I saw Esther Moro in Kigora. Nkosi too. It looked as if she were giving an audience. A crowd was around her. Maybe fifty. It was hard to tell if she were calling people to her or if they went to her on their own. Nothing seemed to happen while I watched them. Nkosi led her away. The crown disbanded. Later one of the women talked about her, about a cure, the sister of someone's husband, a deaf-and-dumb woman."

"Makes you think of the tabloids," he said, "some Indian in the Amazon basin who does surgery with brain waves. Astounded eyewitness accounts. Baffled doctors giving testimony."

"I saw something once," she said. "I was a child, less than ten. A friend was bitten by a snake. I was staying with her at her family's farm. The doctor came with antivenom, but for some reason it didn't work. Their cook, a Somali called Ahidi, took over and insisted on a *mganga*. One who specialized in snake bites. Well, the *mganga* cured her. For a long time the old man became a favorite: people said he had a cure for arthritis. And rabies. My friend made a habit of visiting him, bringing her friends around. Later, when her family left Africa, people said she hadn't been dying at all."

"And what do you think?"

"Hah, I don't know. When you're a kid, you believe in things like that. And besides the *mganga* was impressive. He was huge and wore a turban. His right hand had an extra finger. This was offered as a sign. He was an herbalist so there was no magic, no bones shaking or beads."

But an argument below had drawn his attention, something about money, school fees the night watchman had failed to pay. There were loud men's voices and a woman's, softly insisting in the pauses. The fight escalated then dropped off. Ted got up and looked down at them over the railing, but it was over by then. The night watchman was already rattling in his chair and the others were halfway down the drive. The woman lifted her *kanga*, let the wind iron it, fit it over her shoulders like skin.

"What was that all about?" he asked her.

"School fees," she said.

"School fees! For Christ's sake, I gave that old bastard three hundred shillings so he could pay his kid's school fees. I suppose he'll hit me up again."

If he wanted her to say something, to agree or disagree, or even to explain, she didn't. She changed the subject, "So who'll replace you when you go to Nepal?"

"No replacement. They're winding down the programs

here. Of course that could change when the administration does."

"Is it time for an election or something back there?" She quickly tried to divide by four. She even had to strain to remember who the last few American presidents had been. They all seemed to be nefarious pariahs according to the local view. Men who had their pictures in the paper from time to time with accusations that they were the reason apartheid in South Africa had continued.

"Next year," Ted said, "we'll get a new one. By then the mission will be down to two men. Red Jackson in Population Control and Joe Carmichael in Food Relief. A marriage of functions. You won't like Carmichael: he's too fat, possibly a reaction to all the famines he's been to. And Jackson's a walking lesson in population control—no way he can get it up."

"Boo-hoo."

"But only wait," he said. "There's going to be another colonial period. By default. I'm not sure how it will evolve, but as it gets worse and worse, people will just have to come down here and run things. Aside from all else, we can't afford to let them go on starving. They're starving in Ethiopia, in the Sudan, in the Sahel, in places that used to sell their grain to India, places like Mozambique. Can it go on forever—food they never have to pay for? Just watch," he predicted, "when the Danes and the Swedes give up hope, then just watch." It was his theme, "the grain dumper," he called himself, part of the problem, not the solution. But when it came to it, he would never quit.

"Well," he said, "are we going to promise to write to each other and then feel guilty that we don't."

"No, no letters. The mail takes too long to make it worth anything. Plus I'm sure the CID is reading mine."

"Can't we just pretend to keep in touch? Christmas cards?"

"Yes, mailed in June."

"Perhaps we can arrange to meet sometime. You name the place. But make it Barcelona. I've always wanted to meet a woman in Spain. I even went so far as to suggest that Jenny meet me there. To try another position. Her boyfriend said no."

"I prefer Madrid. The Prado and all that.

"I hear it's falling down."

"The Prado?"

"All those things. The Parthenon. The Colosseum. The foundations of our civilization. Istanbul is about to self-destruct. The Bosphorus is a sewer."

"And you complain about Africa?"

"But you'll never come. You don't fool me."

"If I leave, they won't let me back in. Nothing to do with the way I feel about you."

"I honestly wonder how you can stay here on such absurd conditions."

"It isn't easy, believe me." She laughed. "They may not renew my residency as it is. Except that they need every doctor they can get. That Jesuit in Iringa, Father Roland, he's been here forever. A friend of mine did a book about him, called *Priest!* Father Roland left a week ago. I'd have sworn they'd kick me out first."

"And when they do?"

"Then I'll leave, won't I?"

"It's inevitable. Why not get it over with?"

"I believe in crossing bridges when you get there."

It was easy to be lighthearted and fatalistic in conversations that took place on balconies outside events. One of the things she grew up with as an American of the overseas variety was the notion that she was free to go where and when she pleased. You didn't lose that idea easily. On the other hand, you might not be inclined to test it aimlessly, to put your back up against the wall just to see what would happen, what "they" would do. Certainly not here, not now, not when there was so much paranoia. "Not being able to come back," she told him, "is only half as bad as not being able to get out. I can get out. There are plenty who can't."

He said, "They ought to be down on their knees to you for staying in this shithole, putting up with them, living the way you do."

"Well, they're not." So much for human nature. Paul Luenga put it in terms of history: "There are historical processes in motion all over this continent. None of it nice. You people call it chaos and think we're doomed, but it isn't and we're not. History's new to us. We don't know the parts to play in it, how to manipulate. Who can control what happens? Could you, with all your wonderful civilization, prevent a Hitler?"

There were only perspectives. Like Luenga's. Like Armstrong's. Like hers. Even like Sam Nkosi's for that matter. And if she were a woman of contexts, she was also a woman of contraries—one of her mother's leitmotifs: "Whatever anyone wants for you, you will have the opposite. I was stupid not to keep my feelings and ideas to myself, but then you would have no direction at all. No one to spite. No one to go against and defy."

But it wasn't because they wanted her to go that she wanted to stay.

FIFTEEN

◁ ◈ ▷

In the center of a circle Esther waited. Nkosi sat near her. She had sewn bright yellow ribs on the sleeves of her dress so that its colors would draw on the mystery of a healing and the silence, a form of offering.

"A boy," she said. Eyes were shifting in the room. She saw him and his mother, an adolescent, tall. They were separating from everything else, just the two of them. He saw it, too, and came near. "What is his name?"

"Joshua," his mother said.

"He has a swelling in his throat." He was near enough for her to see it now.

"He cannot swallow," his mother said.

Inside, in the room at her hotel, she sat facing him. As if there had been a command, she pressed a thumb in the center of his chest, placed another hand against his throat. He looked up at her, a question.

"What do you feel?" she asked him.

"Something cold opening inside."

The hotel at Sameh was close by the market, doors to rooms around a courtyard closed with padlocks. During the day the doors were open and people sat in them on stools, like villagers, calling their jokes across. Chickens scratched in the trash behind an outdoor kitchen. Early morning girls were shadows that bent and carried, high voices around the charcoal stoves. Alone, before her tea, Esther walked into that market where she had been those nights, hiding her blood, the moon's old secret. Shutters there were lifting, a butcher cut a goat and hung the pieces in his stall. Children sleeping on the ground began to wake: at once they played, rolling broken wheels with sticks or yawning, urinating, squatting in the dust. Kwavi women poured milk from their gourds into the small containers of busy girls. In one of the stalls inside, Esther found small bars of soap and bought one—from India, the man said, only a few left, wrapped in green with a strange white flower that was a woman's face. It smelled like the incense they burned and the seeds they used in their cooking.

She had forgotten so much about the place, that row of two-story buildings behind the market where Hindis lived above their shops. Buildings with closed balconies. Small colored lights in the windows for their festivals, a door opening and a brown arm, the sudden swirl of shining hair. If people recognized her they turned shy and looked away to speak to her, but passing them, she was always conscious of their eyes. She walked for them, chin raised, with sweeping arms carrying her basket on her head like any woman might. It was different, seeing them in her room or being led to a house to see a person who was very sick. Then she would be lifted from the ground by their love, her long dress more than covering, a vehicle she glided in, the shiny green stone marked on her chest.

Now she was Esther buying an orange. The basket on her head was light and almost fell as she turned her head. She faced the back of the hotel, smoky with morning fires against sheet-tin walls. On one there was a painted picture of a lion jumping to kill a zebra. On the zebra's back, where it dragged its claws, were bright lines of blood. At long tables under the shelter people were awake and drinking tea. She could see Nkosi then, walking away. He had a green cloth cap pulled down. He wore a soldier's uniform.

She prepared her room, covering the bed with cloth that had lost its nature and could have been anything. Dirty red polish left around the edges of the floor gave way to bared cement in a path from the door, or flared up against the redder walls, more newly painted, and the small red bench caked with paint. Her box carefully placed on the smooth rust surfaces of old wood. She was a vapor, a swish of

iridescence in the mud red. The door was open and the light
hung there like a curtain. Through it she could see the boy,
Joshua and his mother standing, heard them whisper,
"*Hodi?*" May we come near?

Part priestess, doctor, rescuer, she knew how to convince,
how to cherish. Deliberately she glided around him.

"He is getting better," his mother said. She brought a
covered bowl of boiled goat meat with a delicious smell, and
maize porridge, yellow (she was sorry) from America.
Perhaps it was the yellow maize, she wondered, that made
him sick? Esther coaxed him, eased him, felt his pulse. Her
hands made passes near his throat. He was strong now, clear.
He could swallow, he said: there was no pain. She looked
inside his throat in the way a doctor would. Her eyes were
closed. Peace came quickly to them both with her touch as if
they were lovers. He sighed. She wanted to stay that way,
moving toward an image of tumbling flowers with one
opening to his face. It was hard to let him go: she lifted her
hands, felt him break loose from her like joy. When they left
her, she was quiet a long time, sitting in the changing light.

At night she ate the goat soup together with Nkosi and
his friend Peter who was young and small and wore soldier's
clothes. His beard was trimmed and his hair cut short. The
bones in his forehead were sharp and his eyes big. He kept a
bottle of whiskey in his pocket, which he didn't drink but
which he poured into Nkosi's glass. Despite their language,
which she didn't understand, and the secrets she couldn't
share, she felt a part of them. Nkosi's shoulder touched her
own. Her fingers were oily from eating the stew. Sweet bones
cracked in her mouth, and gave their marrow, gritty, strong.
Or meat pulled from the bone, dry and salty, gristle. Nkosi
wiped oil from his beard. His friend picked his teeth with a
stick. They were leaning on their elbows dipping moist balls
of the maize meal in the sauce, breaking the skin of yellow
fat. This Peter had hot peppers in a jar, in his magic,
stuffed-up pockets.

"Yes, you want some of this?"

Then they were tasting, laughing, burning their
mouths. The porridge finished, she longed for bread or
water to stop the fire, fanning, tipping her head from side
to side.

She could have gone on living that way in Sameh in her private cell, preparing for her patients or going out among them. The boy, Joshua, became the story that drew others to her. Service gave a texture to her days, and Nkosi, folded at the edge of the bed writing, with the paper held on his knees. Pages and pages. He never told her what he wrote except to say that there were black men in prison who were being killed. Nkosi and Peter made their notes in that small red room. One on the bed, the other on the bench, switching places, the glass between them and the whiskey. She didn't really care what they were doing; there wasn't time. Except to share their tea, thick and sweet with Russian milk. She arranged the empty tins around the edges of the room, a way of measuring. The pictures on the labels repeated: the cows, the babies, the blue skies, the tiny hills. Peter wanted to go to Russia, his heart's home, he said. He put snuff under his lip. Like a Masai, he carried it in a hollow bone. He kept his hair long in clumps like knots that were heavy, dusty, made him look mad.

One day she was taken to the Catholic mission. The cross of Jesus at the gate was like a greeting that she returned, bowing the way the Catholics did to acknowledge the power of His signs. The old white priest held her hands and called her "my child," in English, words she understood. Because, he said, he only knew English and the Pareh languages and that was all. They moved toward a bed in a darkened room. He also wore a gown, but his was black with beads that hung over a belt and swayed, a weight of them so it seemed he had even more beads underneath it chinking in the folds of cloth. She had seen these men and the nuns that resembled them: the white man's *waganga*, Musumbi told her, who knew how to drive out devils, holding the crosses, the smoke of their incense, the deep circles of their beads.

It was the cook's wife, Mary, who was sick. The priest chattered, making cross signs in the air over the woman's head, so black on the white linens. Her hair was wet as river weeds and streaming. Esther saw a child's face, smaller than the white hands that hovered over the frightened eyes—"my child." The old man smelled of tobacco and lemons. He floated with no feet and rocked away from them.

Esther knew how she had to place her hands: one on the woman's stomach, the other on her knees, holding them gently there, waiting. It came suddenly from outside as if the room had filled with it, not from Esther, but from deep within the sick one herself as though it had flown out and shaken her as the rest of them calmed. Esther had to press the woman's shoulders back to hold her there until she stiffened, filled with it, and then drained, exhausted, but it was over, shining on her pillow, her small face. People said something purged from her, like vomit, something filled with insects in a dark fluid, on the ground, but when they looked it had disappeared.

Waiting for Nkosi, the story of what had happened at the mission seemed enough like truth to scare her. What was her power? Insects in a dark fluid as though she had joined with the contagion through the barriers of what was real. No djinn? She woke from the story as if it were a dream. To have it disappear the way that awful wash across the dark room's floor had disappeared, had been too real. The priest's fat thumb marked crosses on his own forehead, lips, and chest.

"Do you want me to bless you, my child?"

She nodded. She would have whispered her own question to him, "Is there a devil? Is he here with us?" except her head was bowed, her eyes closed, as he gave her his sign.

From the time she had bathed the erupting skin of that small girl, when the only witness had been the sky, she feared what she saw and what she was against. The echoes of witches and possession, against everything she had tried to learn from her white doctor. Her own way had suddenly become more certain. Now she longed to go back to Antonia and say, "None of this can be true if what my father said is true, if what you say is true." Back to the safety of the doctor tools, the needles and knives and bottle of blood.

She was going to tell Nkosi, "Let's go back," but he was not there. Not until very late when she heard his voice in the yard loud among the men who drank from gourds of millet beer and the women who came and went. Men could be stolen, he was telling them, carried into slavery—innocent men, who stood around like this with pots of beer. He laughed. He knew a place where the houses of black people could be crushed by white soldiers, the women raped. Voices dimmed. She heard the drone of talking and then a funny story. Laughter rose. She could imagine them shifting, moving, gathering to take their beer. Nkosi went on, that because of this cruelty, there were no fathers for the children. People were moved or killed in jails. These people were heroes. Soft words converged. She heard his words growing distant as if he were leaving. He was sad, crashing, looking for their room. An old man's voice called out the way, called him "fool." Another bragged that he had owned a car that had been stolen.

"Moving black men out of their own country into deserts." —Nkosi's voice again. He was close to the door now, rattling it as he went on talking. "Out of their houses with all their things, only trash. All we have is trash."

Someone must have come near him, a whisper, drawing Nkosi away. She heard the voice say, "Brother." A woman called. A thud, as if a person had fallen and laughter and a cassette tape starting, broken music like an old car. The woman began to sing.

Esther heard her name and Nkosi pushing at the door again. She opened it, shielding behind it. Sounds formed outside. Light from another room streamed across the place where the men hunkered near their gourds of beer. Nkosi was inside trying to walk, trying to see, bumping the walls. He was moving with a purpose, not talking, feeling his way to the bench where he had left his books and papers. When she lit the candle for him, she saw that he had slipped down the wall, like something melted, washed away. He looked up at her as if she had surprised him, as if she were huge and dangerous and had appeared in the light as a djinn. He made a weak sound deep in his throat. His head rolled forward, intent, the beard flat against his chest. She could only understand part of what he said then; too many languages fought for his tongue, sounds she had never heard before. His own people were liars. Jealous, he told her. Stupid. They had tricked him. Now there was nothing for him to believe. He began to rip the papers and throw them in anger. It was his anger and his broken form on the floor, the moving arms, the dropped head that reminded her of Musumbi, sitting on the ground throwing the precious pieces from his doctor case. His heart will burst, she thought, and it did.

Soon Nkosi calmed. He got up with effort and moved toward the bed. His shoes dropped. She was silent, thinking with her back against the cool wall. A hand reached, taking hers. He placed it on his head and said, "Make me well." But the fires in his mind were as confusing as the places he had been, the languages he knew. England. Sweden. America. France. His own country, ruled by white men, was somewhere in Africa. He had showed her on a map, or with his finger pointing. In the air between the sun and moon. He had been in airplanes. On big ships. For her these were images as chopped up as the pieces of paper he had strewn around the room. The only real thing were the pictures of his children that she kept hidden. She wished she were able to extract a message, real or invented, like a clever *mganga,* staring into a pot of dark fragrant oils and finding an answer, saying, "This is what I know: this is what you have to do." She believed that those small photographs were what he had to see and so she put them out on the table, soft smiles in the candlelight. He could have spoken to them across the sky. Faces like his face were, after all, things that could not be overlooked. Their urgency and her responsibility were the design, almost complete in itself, because she didn't know what he would do.

She cracked the door open in the first light and left it that way, just wide enough so they could see: daytime, the filtering dust and the array of pictures on the painted bench, faces that seemed to wake up with them to witness. Outside the morning started with someone's familiar complaining that there was no water and the laughter from the kitchen. And Nkosi, as usual, was suddenly awake and sitting the way someone did who had only pretended to sleep. He didn't stretch or yawn or rub his eyes, was simply up as though he had never rested at all, as though the night had never been.

Esther could not be sure when he saw the pictures. His back was to her so nothing could be given away. He bent to find his shoes. He took a comb from under the bed and pricked his hair, lifting it, again and again. She tried to read these simple actions: he was gaining time, thinking. His calm, and the opposite it threatened, prepared her for his rage, but there was none. Or for his tears, but nothing strained or shook when he asked her, without turning to look at her,

"Where did you get these?" placing his hand over the accusation that stared up at him from those shining prints. She said, "They are not abominations as you said." The letters were there, too, in her hand stretching toward him. Edges of the paper touched his back. He turned then and took them from her and the pictures. Nothing had changed on his face but she felt the difference. "You must tell them where you are." Because she knew how sick he was from the yellow palms of his hands, yellow moons of his fingernails, the yellow in his eyes, what she felt when she came near him, what she could see, all broken.

"In most places," he said, "they put people in jail for stealing letters and opening them. But what does someone like you know about that?" He called her "little sister" in English and laughed and asked her to forgive him. "I made a mistake," he said. He was packing things in his case. His worn-out clothes and shoes. His books and papers.

She was helpless, aware of her feelings in retreat. And he was like weather, striking and unpredictable. He might gather like a mist and be gone, or like the magic cycle of the water, accumulate, clouds pressed by air until he poured. It made her wonder, this idea of hidden, unfinished things, as though these had caused his limp, his breaking, his exhaustion. He was a passion in that flaring room, red paint and morning light. Then he was gone.

Wandering Sameh alone. The mountains were heavy shadows behind her that pushed down like gravity. As she turned, they rose in front of her like storms. Sometimes she ran down: there were no real secrets in Sameh, only spaces that filled and emptied, car tracks leading the way or ditches made by rain and shifting footpaths. She could also climb up, toward the villages she knew, thinking she saw familiar grass rooftops, smoke from fires. Even the Pareh language in her ears returning. She was looking for Nkosi and this running was all she could do. She was like someone who had pulled on a broken rope, like a fisherman, who pulled and pulled and brought up nothing. Wandering in circles that dwindled until she was there looking in the market again.

Nothing soothed her. A length of fence was jammed

with waiting crows who watched her without moving. Children dug where women had sold rice and corn the day before, dropping grains one-one into small tins. She saw their mothers bend over something, like vultures, picking. Small dogs ran at their heels. Except for one stall, the market was closed and almost empty. It was where she had bought the soap, all gone now. A few boxes of tea and Chinese firecrackers were arranged in the glass case. She could hear men's voices somewhere near, in a storeroom behind the open shop. An old woman smiled at Esther and pointed to her goods. Then someone called from inside and boys ran toward her, pushing at each other to gain the way. Esther watched them turning at the sound and saw Nkosi's friend Peter. His hands were full of gestures and his knotted hair was shaking as he laughed. He was talking to the shopkeeper, paying him money. The boys came out behind him, carrying heavy gunnysacks. She knew it was food and thought, If I could follow them, I would find Nkosi, but Peter had seen her, was nodding, smiling, coming her way.

She told him, "I have lost my friend."

He had no answer, only words about the secrets they were forced to keep. She heard a few of these words; the rest were lost to his way of speaking, swallowed, passed over too quickly, no more than sounds as she was straining, telling him, "I don't understand."

It was the shopkeeper who told her after Peter was gone, "They are soldiers from another country. Planes have landed. Trucks have come. This is all their business of hiding. Now they have gone up the mountain to Lusutu. When they leave Sameh completely, this will be good."

SIXTEEN

◂ ◇ ▷

It was his going-away party. Women in fluttering caftans and men in white shirts came from the dark into lighted rooms. Black servants passed quietly among them. It was a pastel housescape, wash of cloud-blue carpets, pale floral couches, yellow-greens caught from the springs of temperate climates. Without those black men, the rooms would contain no trace of Africa: the Johnsons had been in the Far East.

She could see him now near the door, the guest of honor, greeting colleagues as they came to say good-bye. He was uncomfortable: his movements had become stiff. He seemed strangled and addled when he had to smile. She thought about how soon he would be gone and she would be relieved in her own fashion because their growing friendship had threatened something. She liked the idea that she was able to remain aloof, with no regrets.

"I may meet you after all," she told him once the party had formed and he was inside coming toward her with a drink. "Make it Portugal. Laxmanbhai says they're after me. Not that it hasn't happened before."

"Good," he said. He wasn't interested, but was morose, an emotion centered on the self. Katmandu was a reality now: there were tickets, details to deal with. "I've just heard that the director in Nepal is a maniac," he said simply. When she asked for particulars, he answered, "A *maniac*. Isn't that enough?"

People bunched around Ted and slowly broke away, merging with other groups, movements that seemed full of purpose. Emily Halstead once said these parties were really shopping expeditions, a type of stock exchange: —"Mustard is up to three jars of strawberry jam, stuff like that . . ." She heard more laughter than words as she walked to find another drink; someone in the corner talked about a case of tomato paste.

Antonia saw how few they had become now, lost in the big pearly room. A stray European or two had been invited to swell the party: Danes, men who worked with Ted, who stood against the wall. A German couple circulated like visitors at an art gallery, kept their own counsel in front of Mrs. Johnson's inlaid screens and picture scrolls— mountains piled in the mist, owls, tiny Oriental men at waterfalls disemboweling deer. Later, she heard the German say in a disembodied accent, "But don't you think this is the climate? People are not making solutions here now because no solutions are necessary. How do you live six months of the year under ice and snow? This is really it."

Emily Halstead embarrassed everyone by getting drunk and telling a story they had all heard before, about the time Wendall had gone into a shop on Independence Avenue and left her in the car.

"A naked man," she said, "completely naked and on the loose and no one stopping him. No one making the slightest effort. No one bothering. He was tearing up newspapers and throwing them in car windows. For no reason. Making noises like an insect."

Wendall interrupted, "Emmy, hon, everyone has heard about this."

"Yes, yes, but no one can tell me the *reason.* I want to know the *reason.* That's all I'm asking. He threw his papers in at me. *Why?*"

"Because he was nuts," Scotty Clayburn said.

Emily sighed, "They don't lock them up here, I know. I know I ought to understand. The newspapers were one thing, but his parts—"

"Emmy!"

"Wendall just hates it when I bring it up about that man's privates. . . . He was, well—" Her hand hovered over the table trying to zero in on a drink. She tipped her head to see it better and grabbed. "Sooooo thin and sooooo well endowed," she said, "and buzzing like a gigantic fly."

Antonia felt a little drunk herself. She was laughing, reaching for a stuffed olive with her tongue. There was more salt than flavor but the texture of the flesh was right and the soft sweet burst of pimiento. After that she ate a small round of rye bread spread with liver. Later, she met Emily Halstead alone in the entrance balancing herself against a large brass Buddha.

"Plated," she whispered. "Peee-lated," meaning the brass. "But have *you* ever seen one of them naked?" she asked Antonia.

That night when they made love, they saw they both had had too much to drink and played around too much, jostled themselves into different positions for which he had names from the Kama Sutra.

"Here, put your leg like this, now your arm goes here, my leg under like this. Yes, okay, now see if you can reach my nipple and get it between your teeth and I'm going to do the same. Now hold it!"

Who could be serious? She was laughing, almost hysterical. In the end when they really tried to make love, he couldn't and she couldn't either.

"Kama-fucking-Sutra," he complained once they decided to go to sleep, but soon she felt his finger working its way between her thighs.

"Come on," he whispered. "Look, look at this." He put a light on to show her how terribly hard he was, how it would be dangerous to leave him like that, how impossible life had become. He went for ice and more drinks and came back with a tea towel hung over his erection. She said, "No, no, let me sleep," but he was hopping around shouting, "How can I sleep with a hard-on?"

She was on top of him then, laughing, her arms down holding his sides. It made her feel aggressive: she began to move quickly up and down, to pound on his body with hers. It felt like anger, like revenge. He made a moaning sound but his face was tense with his effort. "I've go to . . ." he was saying. She could feel his body stiffen, thrust; she could feel him trying, failing. She gave over to the strain and just rocked there, riding, riding. She began to relax out of any sexual need, even out of feeling, but she stayed with him pumping, pumping that way. It was a new sensation; she could feel her own body, grown thick and amorphous, flow over his. She was hunched now, holding him, breathing slowly, softly over his shoulder as she went on rocking, swaying, easing, pulling with her body over his. She felt more than just his penis inside her, she felt a depth of flesh forms almost as though they were her own. The sensation was primordial, back in the dark of her reptile brain. She believed she could go on forever, tireless, wide awake, sucking at him.

He made a small noise, discomfort or dismay, whispered, "Hey, hey what?" He lifted her from his shoulders. "What are you trying to do to me?"

It was like being woken from a shallow dream. She said, "Ah."

In the morning he brought her coffee in bed and slices of pineapple. Then, all serious, face like a gymnastics coach, he arranged her, laughing, and straddled her on a chair.

The night Armstrong was to leave, Charles finally spoke about him, "This American bwana who has a little kind of car."

"Yes, he's leaving tonight," she answered even before he asked, knowing he had heard it, knew everything anyway.

"To go to America?"

His voice inflected in a strange way as though he suspected the same thing she did—that soon everyone American would have to go back there.

"No, he will go to Nepal."

He sighed, "I think maybe there are too many Hindis in that place."

He laughed. So did she, to think of a continent full of them, untempered, carrying on.

"There are mountains there," she told him. "Very high and covered with snow."

Snow. The word was like a signal. He responded from his wonder. "So it is making wintertime. Even there?" His secondhand knowledge of a white man's real life—her mother with the frost scraped from the fridge into a bowl trying to tell him that everything and everywhere was covered like this, so beautiful, piled high, and so white.

"Yes, wintertime," she said.

"Like where your mother's people live."

"Massachusetts." Laughter. The impossible word, the ridiculous sounds.

"Massas-chooo," he tried. He laughed.

"Go on, try it. Mass-a-choo . . ." This was an old routine with them, like a couple of vaudeville comics on stage for the millionth time doing their gags about the northern climate.

He had come to her once, when she was a girl, to check a story he had just heard from her father and didn't quite believe, or understand in any case. Not about ice and snow, but about how the days shrank down each year until there were only a few hours of daylight, the nights getting longer and longer. Until one day, the days would start getting long, which meant the nights were small—almost as bad. "How do people sleep," he wanted to know, "when there is not enough nighttimes?"

"It's why we tell time in a different way," she told him, "not from sunrise the way you do. For us sunrise is always at a different time."

For him the sun rose at the same time every day: equatorial, firm. There was no nonsense about the sun doing anything else.

She had once or twice done the bit with a grapefruit and a flashlight in a dark room. He was the earth and revolved around her, holding the grapefruit at the specified angle. Then he would be the sun and she would go around him. They were both so serious about it, trying to imagine. Then he would cut the grapefruit and she would eat it and he would make a joke about eating the earth. Once she had said. "Here, Charles, you take this half," and slid the plate to him across the table. She had intended that he sit there with her, but he couldn't: he thanked her and took his piece of fruit to the kitchen. She saw him carefully transfer it from the china dish to his tin plate and carry it to his room. And realized that she had never seen the man with food in his mouth.

She told him once about the poles and the equator. But he knew it all: she had given him books, with pictures and diagrams. He just wanted to hear about it and talk about it, to reaffirm his position at least.

"I wouldn't like this. I would die in such a place."

When her mother left the country, he had been frightened that she would order him to move with her, so he ran away. Her mother never understood why he left all his things behind, his severance pay, all her "gifts" she called them, the bundles of old clothes, the pots and pans. So she doled those out elsewhere. Charles had simply gone. He must have heard from someone when Antonia returned. He came to see her, confident by then that the gift of independence was no dream, that no one at all could force him to do anything he didn't want to do. He came to collect the severance pay, and to explain, "A man like me . . . those terrible long nights, that terrible cold."

Now it was a question of Antonia's leaving that gave the little dialogue some new inflections. Her irony: yes, I'll get mine after all, justice, having to leave like all the rest of them. His worry: "But not you. You born here. Not like the other American people in the cold and small daytimes and long nights." He stood holding the laundry bundled in a sheet. She saw some flowers in a vase, and knew there must be water.

"The bwana's plane?"

"Tonight," she repeated.

"You eating home?"

"Yes, I'll eat here, Charles, but late."

He nodded and left her with a wedge of papaya and a Thermos. She could hear him, in the bathroom, in her tub, starting to splash and tramp in the clothes, back and forth. He would have his trouser legs rolled up. Suds would be bubbling around his thin black ankles. Soon she would see his wet footprints on the floor, wide, but elegantly arched, splayed toes and a thin, curved rim to the thickened heel.

Empty houses were at either end of Ted Armstrong's journey. He called the period "limbo." His ex, Jenny, he said, called it "purgatory." Subsequently she revised that because purgatory implied heaven came afterward. You wait for your stuff to arrive, you can't do anything until it does so you bore yourself drinking coffee and other stronger liquids. Then when it comes time to leave, it's the same thing in reverse. It made Jenny bitter. Jenny couldn't hack it. Jenny turned into a bitch.

Sounds were exaggerated in spaces like these. Armstrong thundered upstairs, opening and closing closet doors in search of things left behind.

"It's a habit," he shouted down at her, "one picks up with frequent moves. There's always something left that's going to embarrass or incriminate you, like Jenny's vibrator. She left it in an efficiency in D.C." His voice made a hollow echo, and then his urine; she heard it cascading overhead, a sudden waterfall. There were the bulging suitcases, the scattered jackets, the stained, strewn cups and newspapers on the floor. She saw a heavy overcoat, gloves, a woolen scarf, and remembered it was winter there. Those fabrics were as odd as she found the season of ice and snow they marked. Dramas of the temperate zone: brilliant leaves of fall, short darkening days, buried in your house, in your thick itching clothes.

She shouted up that if he didn't hurry she would finish off the scotch, and wondered if she should be sad or lonesome in advance. Or neither. She had a comic picture of him up there, peering into crannies, medicine cabinets, searching for embarrassing secrets. Would he, like other men and friends she had known, be nothing more than a torn-out image in a collage?

The automatic flight board at the airport no longer worked. Instead, arrivals and departures were scrawled in chalk on a wall that had been painted black. Poorly erased, the wall had a dusty, surreal look—Lonoroma, Bomankfurt—layers of place names as though the world had been suddenly altered, shaken together and respelled to harrow tourists. Ted Armstrong's flight to London was marked on time, though sometimes, if there were sudden fuel shortages, the planes would simply not land and everyone would be stranded, hoping for another chance to get out.

There were whole families of Sikhs, some leaving, some saying good-bye. Women wept uncontrollably and clung to each other while their fat children played. A few West Africans in embroidered robes shared loud anecdotes. A handful of Germans, mostly young with beards and backpacks, examined their purchases, baskets held up, admired, compared.

Ted Armstrong was holding her hand and letting it go and holding it again as though he were trying to relay a message in moist dots and dashes. They heard a plane land. Theirs. It was the only one scheduled in or out that night. Then came the announcement, impossible to understand. She thought, all the world is leaving.

Passengers were moving toward the final checks. One of the crew had appeared, an Englishman, perturbed and hot, too hot; stains of sweat were blooming on his shirt, down his back, under his arms. All he had was a microphone against the chaos.

"Don't come forth until you hear your name called. I repeat: do not come forth until your name is called."

But the Sikhs were swarming around the man, waving their tickets, a boil of turbans in the steam of their voices. Rising. The crewman began his roll, "Abubakar, Steven. Is there a Steven Abubakar?" A Nigerian lifted his bag, parried into the crowd. The Sikhs were jamming, dammed at the exit, hurling, hoping to shout their way through. Then one of them dropped. They saw it happen: an old man collapsing. The woman near him started to scream, bare arms lifted from her sari, her head exposed.

The voice in the microphone was calling, "Is there a doctor here? We need a doctor up here."

That was how she left Armstrong. He kissed her quickly and said, "Thank you."

She left him to push her way into that crowd, sweet with perfume and the crush of silks, saying, "Please let me pass. I'm the doctor." Heard his name being called. "Armstrong, T. S., Mr. Armstrong?" as she bent to take a pulse. The man was dead, his wife stunned. She had stopped shrieking and was holding out her ticket, looking for an answer. A friend was bracing her, swaying with her, urging her to go, to get on the plane.

"She is having her children in the U.K.," a man told Antonia. "She must go. We will take care of him." But the old woman simply couldn't move, as though she had forgotten how to walk. Struck deaf, struck dumb, she just stood there and stared as they pushed her, urging her to go, to go. "She really must go." The man grabbed Antonia's arm. "Please, you tell her."

But she was going then, lifted off her feet and carried. A hand guided hers to hold out the passport and the ticket, to keep the head steadied, looking forward. No no no no no, she was shaking her head, her eyes closed, but she couldn't turn back now that the stamp had fallen. She was propped, moving toward the gate, a life-size puppet, luminous in the dark crowd, her white hair, her white skin, her pale silks. She would go, Antonia saw, into the waiting plane to make a journey she must have been raised to fear—crossing the black water.

From the waving bay, Antonia watched the plane leave. A few bright Indian children cupped their ears and imitated the sound. One of the older ones flew by on a skateboard, then came again, breathless, crashing into the far rail. The plane paused, then roared, then climbed the runway and seemed to lift, the only way a giant could, slowly, dragging its heavy body as it swung up and curved and then was gone. She stayed a while as the others left, until the silence like a weather front had changed the feeling of the air. Leaving, she saw four solemn men lifting their dead friend into a car. The man who had spoken to her so urgently came toward her.

"We will take care of everything," he assured her.

"I'm terribly sorry," she said. "His poor wife."

He waved sadly, directing her as she backed her car and as she turned, even as she drove away, though there weren't any other cars around, just the dark pavement and the crude hand-painted signs advertising the hotels in town.

Immediately after Armstrong left, someone started reading Antonia's mail, what little there was—an airgram from McGeorge, who was on his way to Pakistan to photograph that country's fabled passes: the Khyber, the Malakand, the Karakoram, routes of opium and silk. He had a funny affinity for cargoes; here it had been ivory and rhino horn. It was hard to realize that he could have gone as far as Pakistan already, was crawling toward China now on the perilous turns and angles of the Himalayas.

The censors made no attempt to camouflage the ravaged envelopes, clamped shut now with messy seals of cheap, Chinese cellotape. Funny, this invasion of her privacy, which made her public, only underscored her isolation. Singled out. Mr. Laxmanbhai said they were looking for *evidence,* so that they could revoke her visa and send her away. He used an erudite tone when he said it, a philosopher trying to pin down an abstract idea.

"Sooner or later, they will find something," he told her. His cousin-in-law, for example, was in jail right now, charged with smuggling ivory. No one understood how such a thing had happened since he was innocent in the matter of ivory. "Mind you," he said, "none of our people can be totally innocent, only a little innocent. This is our big problem. This is also survival," he said. "But ivory? No, no, this is too too risky."

As far as he was concerned, Antonia was as secure as she could be while not being very secure. She had papers to stay and papers to go out. All she was lacking was papers to come back in. He, on the other hand, had no papers for getting out, which compromised his security far more. He was terrified that some evidence might be found that could send him to jail like his cousin-in-law.

A funny man, Arvinda Laxmanbhai. Antonia's father had sponsored his education in Bombay. He wore safari suits the color of weak gravy that matched the cast of his skin. There was an air of attrition about him. When she first had known him, he had been a portly young man with blue-black hair, jet eyes, and full red cheeks. Now he was thin and monochromatic, weathered beyond distinction. He had been fond of gold in those days and wore as much jewelry as a man could, to the brink of ostentation: chains, rings, stickpins, belt buckles, bangles, watch. Gold teeth. Slowly it had all disappeared except the teeth, taken from the country piece by piece with each of his children, but not enough at any one time to arouse suspicion, to be taken as evidence. Nothing was ever replaced. Once out, the children never returned. His wife died. Everything had slowly trickled away until there was nothing left but Laxmanbhai.

He had never shown Antonia anything but the most circumspect behavior. Nothing of the untoward. Perhaps he wondered what she thought of his gradual erosion. McGeorge had told her Laxmanbhai once asked him to carry out a very tiny package and deliver it to his son in London.

"Not unless you tell me what it is," McGeorge had said. Laxmanbhai told him it was a diamond. McGeorge carried it, stuffed in the toe of a dirty sock. In London, the son, who was spoiled and oily, took it without a word.

"Supposing you tell them, 'Stop reading my mail,'" Mr. Laxmanbhai said. "Even this they will say is evidence. My advice is, let them read."

They had reached a point where they shared a certain placid paranoia. It was all you could do, save making excuses for yourself and for your kind, or even for Africa. Other misanthropic types—travel writers, researchers, reporters, advisers, developers—found it entertaining to watch their dire predictions of ruin come true. Offering the evidence. Yes, there was that king, Bokassa, one of those inland countries where they spoke French. A story of a flamboyant coronation costing millions while his subjects starved. After the coup, his enemies found human babies in his deep freeze, trussed up as roasts. There were massacres in Burundi, in Guinea-Bissau. Dead children in the streets of Addis Ababa. There was Idi Amin.

She lived for a while in a gloomy zone as though she had been flung into a fog where dim impressions had to be the guide. She didn't know what she was feeling, would never have admitted that she could be this low. Walking toward her house (children darting, calling, begging for cookies) was often a surprise, a mild shock.

There?

That?

My house?

Broadside, the length of gray cement wasn't even close to plumb, the mortar already crumbling. Windows out of kilter. No garden, not even a patch of straggling corn like the other houses had; not even a spindling papaya tree. Her father's house had been huge with fireplaces and patios with views of Kilimanjaro. Yes, this mild feeling of shock, the surprise she experienced outside lingered somehow as she made her way indoors. She took quiet stock of things, walking through her few rooms, opening drawers and cupboards. There was nothing in them that she wanted to take with her, were she suddenly to pick up and go.

Charles had an ancient cookbook opened to banana bread. Just for show: he must have known the recipe by heart. Before he went ahead and mixed the batter, he would put everything out, measured, ready to go. The four overripe bananas, two eggs, an array of little bowls with sugar, flour, shortening, the baking powder. Antonia guessed by the way things were stymied on the countertop that he was lacking some ingredient. A lemon? For the teaspoon of juice? No, a lemon was there. Milk, he had, all poured into his measuring cup. He came in and found her there bent over the gloppy page making the tally and must have guessed why.

"No fire," he complained. He was biting his lower lip in irritation and shaking the empty gas canister. It meant there were no refills. They had a standby kerosene stove with two burners that they used in times like these. But no oven. It depressed the old man. He loved to cook. She saw him carefully replace this two cups of sugar in the can and noticed how gray he had gone, it secmed overnight. Another decision would have to be made regarding the bananas. Antonia wasn't about to eat them, nor was he. Ripe bananas, he grumbled, made him constipated.

It was like that. Things left on counters, empty canisters, rotting fruits, and Charles's hair turning white, all woven sadly together. She'd seen it: the old memsaab in the ratty sweater led out to her chair in the sun by the ancient servant, both doddering, coupled, like a satire on a hundred themes. But it wasn't that. And it wasn't the censors snipping at her mail. Or the asses in Immigration asking ridiculous questions. None of those things were what was making it impossible for her to stay. Her work had a new appearance, too much like confusion, so blended with the chaos in those holding grounds outside the wards and examination rooms where she practiced, that she hardly knew, as patients came and went, which ones had been—here, she lost the word. What was it? Cured? Repaired? Helped? Seen? Yes, that was it. Seen. Looked at. Words that mocked a doctor's function. Esther, offering miracles, was her conscience, marking how she herself had lost touch. Yes, lost touch. While *she* looked at patients, Esther touched them. Quite literally, challenging the universe, changing the way things were. A disease materialized, falling away to the floor.

At the hospital a nurse put a starving baby in her hands. The mother thought he was about two months old, wizened, awful. His bones stabbed her palms. There was a redness about the small mouth that made him look angry, though his eyes were blank. And the mother, a child herself, appeared to be starving. She had been abandoned along a road somewhere. A truck had picked her up. She knew her father's name and her mother's name and the name of the man who was her husband. But that was all. She didn't know where she came from or where she was. She had *kwashiorkor*. Her hair was thin and reddish.. The nurses fed her. They treated her for lice.

Red tile roof. The shelter of porches, filmy awnings of cloth. Makeshift verandas, crowded with patients like that abandoned child. They smelled of waiting, moist and sour, and of the long walks they made to get to the hospital. Stirring at the sight of her white uniform, they began to organize themselves into the lines they would wait in all day. During the night a woman lying on a bench near the door had hemorrhaged. The ground around her was stained and flies had come to feed. An old man with elephantiasis scratched at an enormous foot with a stick.

One of her patients was a woman from Sameh whose uterus had grown over with fibroid tissue. Sometimes she bled so much she thought she would die. She had a nervous disorder, a painful tic that flickered up and down her face.

"You'll have to have surgery," Antonia told her.

The woman began to weep, shaking her head, refusing. Her eye flinched. She rubbed her pain-struck cheek. "No,

no," she said. "Surgery is the way people die." She told
Antonia she would go instead to a healer in Sameh. As a
Christian, she didn't believe in such things, but she had
heard of a child of her neighbor who had been touched by
this powerful woman and he was made well. She would go
back, she said, to find this one and be helped. Her fists were
closed, packed into her chest.

"Last week," the woman said, "there in the market,
everyone was gathered around her waiting to see how she
might call the sick ones forth. Then she helps them, or she
will tell them to come to her. I was there selling corn. She
passed close to my friend. My friend said, 'There she is,
there she is.'"

It was Esther. In Sameh. Antonia formed an image of
the journey she could take to see her. A long day's drive,
hills leading away from the sea, then falling off to dry
corrugated plains, shadows of low gray mountains in the
east, blue stretches of abandoned sisal, riverbeds climbing
like vines into a yellow sky, dusty towns. She knew the place
well. All of it farther than it had ever seemed before. She
wanted to go, to revert, if she could revert. It was Luenga's
term after all, yet surely she had some claims as a native.
She thought of his poem, everything suggesting that the
gods were gone; hers, in any case, and his, hidden as he
would have it, in forgotten places.

There was no context for her Western training now.
Ironically, she had been Luenga's lover and now the
fulfillment of his prediction: "Nothing you leave behind will
make sense to us once you are gone and your people have lost
interest, which they will do."

The hospital existed to drive her mad, the flies and filth
and idiotic nurses straggling in the halls unable to pick up
the dirty sheets. They saw no point. But the point was sharp.
In an old book she had read an anthropologist's attempts to
describe native medicine. He used a detached documentary
tone reserved by those determined not to patronize or
prejudice. He just let the ridiculous methods of the healer
stand for themselves: a patient, strange malady affecting his
bones, hypnotized and lying on the ground, speaking in

tongues. Unidentified objects are taken from a red cloth. A potsherd is placed near the door of a hut. A piece of incense is burned in the fire. The healer trembles, trancelike, covered head to foot by a white cloth. A disembodied voice fills the room telling them all what to do. A ritual: remove all shoes, face the north. There is an anointing. A libation. There are magic stones the healer puts into a pan of water and the water boils. In the steam another voice moans. The healer says these are evil spirits escaping in the air. He says it means the patient will be well. There are more visits. Finally the patient dies. Bone cancer is the anthropologist's guess.

Antonia almost laughed thinking what might have been written in his report had the anthropologist followed her around as she treated someone with a strange malady of the bones, using his uninflected prose to describe the rituals of technology, the intrusive tests, the painful medications, the diagnostic stabs in the dark, the death at last, at her hands, mired in another kind of myth, another kind of blindness.

These thoughts were framed by the relentless breakage, the noise life made as the everyday got chipped away to the most essential things. Her own stove was now covered with a board; the smell of kerosene filled the kitchen. Soon they would have to use charcoal and then, when the trees were gone, they would stop cooking their food.

How strange it seemed to go from days like these to evenings out on Oyster Bay, turning into circular driveways. Here was a house in the Spanish style, a finca of white stucco with heavy carved doors and black trim. The windows were arches filled with the gold light of a dinner party. Just near the door, a forked tree held a fall of yellow and black orchids.

"So you noticed the orchids," Emily Halstead greeted her in a batiked swoop of chartreuse cloth, her head wrapped in a matching turban.

Inside, Antonia learned that the hostess had cooked a turkey, an event that was generating excitement. Could it have been Thanksgiving? Americans had such a desperate need to keep their holidays overseas. She had been surprised more than once by Halloween—the favorite—jack-o'-lanterns lining a driveway, Ben and Scotty Clayburn dressed as Mickey and Minnie Mouse. Her own mother had tried with a vengeance to keep the calendar alive: Valentines, loud horns and paper hats at New Year, dyed Easter eggs, all saved in yellow boxes from season to season. She had called them "traditions."

No, it was not Thanksgiving. The turkey was an unexpected boon, an anachronism. A plane carrying them, Swift Butterballs bound for the Gulf, had put down with a burned-out engine.

"The birds would have thawed and rotted on the runway if Everready Stan Bennet hadn't run over and bought the lot, duty free, twenty of them, which works out to two per family and four for Mr. Ambassador," Emily Halstead said.

Twenty of them, Antonia thought. And four for the ambassador. Which meant there were only eight families left.

A woman Antonia had met only once before told her that Scotty Clayburn was sick with a mysterious fever and had to be evacuated to Frankfurt to the Army hospital there. "You know," the woman said, "you get a fever, they give you something, tell you what to do, you get better. Scotty wasn't better."

"It's this *new* malaria," Emily Halstead said, "or even some *newer* malaria."

"Isn't malaria malaria?"

"Not anymore."

"There's falciparum and cerebral. And blackwater. Poof, you're dead. Right, Doc? With blackwater?"

"It isn't malaria," Wendall Halstead told them. "The lab never found any malaria."

"Meningitis then?"

They all turned to Antonia as if she should know. She made a face. Emily Halstead sighed, almost a moan.

"They'll find it in Frankfurt," Wendall assured them.

"Have *you* ever been to Frankfurt?" Emily said. "Listen," she announced to the others, "I told Wendall, next time they try to send me to Frankfurt, just fly me home. Just pay the fare and fly me home, please."

"What do you think, Doctor? Is there meningitis here?"

Her answer was facetious, about how, as she saw it, they were all flown here and there, to places where doctors never saw malaria. It made no sense. They stared at her. Emily Halstead toasted with an empty glass.

She heard John Cory holding forth to a man she didn't know. It must have been his routine, like a standup comic. She recognized the pitch and then the words: "We ought to let 'em kill each other off. Like Arabs and Jews. Vietnamese and Cambodians. Protestants and Cath'lics in Ulster. And I'm Irish, so I can say it."

His wife stood by, her pose familiar, her cocktail-party asana, face achieving, eyes focusing on a distant nothing, lips forming a silent mantra, sipping gin.

"Isn't it wonderful," she asked Antonia, "about those turkeys?"

The doctor was more alone among them than she had ever remembered. She wondered whether Armstrong was meant to be the last. She had expected more from his good-bye kiss than that faint tenderness that seemed to reassure them both of their cool maturity in matters like this. He said, "Thank you," like a kid who had just been asked for a dance. She felt as stymied as Charles had been in his efforts to make banana bread. No fire. With all the ingredients there. Laid out and measured, and nothing to do with the ripening fruits.

Driving home she tried to see the faces in the cars that passed as her headlights pulled her toward them in the dark. The streets were deserted save for a lonely old man on foot, hurrying from streetlight to streetlight. His presence was eerie, a supernatural event that needed to be explained. She rose behind another Peugeot on the port road. It drove with no lights. Hers caught the rusting fenders, a bumper tied with string, a bashed-up trunk. And then the driver's head, large, bearded, a short man slunk behind the wheel. She felt a throb and thought it was Nkosi, pulled racing past him but saw a white collar strapped to his throat, the flash of a profile too black against the night to tell for sure until she caught him in her rearview mirror, round faced and beaming. No, another man. A clergyman.

A pair of soldiers were walking in Kinondoni that night. To stop thieves, though her neighbors said the police themselves were thieves. Hard boots clacked echoes down the moon-bleached rutted streets. She dodged potholes, meeting them head on. One jumped from her way, laughing, the other waved a fist. Their flashlights tore streaks through the pitch. No lights were on but hers, catching the rectangle of her purple door.

Charles was waiting, knitting—a newly acquired skill. As late as it was, he needed her advice in the matter of setting sleeves. Her mother would have been able to help. Antonia only smiled and said, "Charles, you *know* I can't do anything like that." He said he knew and smiled as well.

When he brought her some warm milk and tiny biscuits tasting of chicken fat, she said, so impromptu that it surprised her as much as it did him, "Charles, what would you do if I went to live in America and never came back?"

"I am going to my home," he said, so simply, so surely that she wondered what all these years of tending folks like her had meant at all. Perhaps it was his way to break her heart.

At some point between that moment and the time she left for the hospital in the morning, she must have made a subconscious decision to go in search of Esther Moro as though Esther were unfinished business, the only thing she had to tidy up before she broke away. Not a resolution, the idea came without clarity. Images, faces, movements collected from day scenes, stilled frames in time that led her thought, welled into need—that midnight priest, black, statuesque at the wheel of his car; another man she had seen with a limp; a young woman near a tree, leaning into a sun shaft, lithe, fresh; a slash of cheap pink rings and gaudy baubles; flare of purple cloth; a teetering walk of someone on ridiculously high shoes. A thin girl, a child, covered in white. These images. What she kept seeing.

She told them at the hospital that she need a rest and would take some leave. Paul sat in her office twirling a ballpoint pen that left blue nicks in his pink palm. Talking business. He had seen reports of a cholera outbreak in the southwest. Moslems had brought it back with them from the *hadj*. There had been a wedding; stricken guests. Now the Moslem villages were full of it. Because their religion insisted that they wash their dead, it was spreading fast. When it got bad enough the ministry would call in the World Health Organization. This irritated him, always needing help from outside. But there was nothing they could do on their own except close off the roads, seal off the area, quarantine them, hope it would run its course. He wanted to do this: he wanted to let what had to happen happen. He was tired. The pen was still. He stared at it.

At night, going through the papers on her desk— shuffling record cards like a gambler or a bureaucrat, charting progress or decline, recommending, prescribing, guessing—she tried for order. The small lamp made clear her isolation. A neurotic's safety, that patch of light. The boundaries of the room were distant and her estrangement from everything here complete. Almost subconsciously, yes, she was preparing, like a prisoner, or like a refugee, under the cover of night, to cross into another country.

SEVENTEEN

She carried extra petrol in cans so that her Peugeot reeked, and Charles, frantic with worry, had railed about explosions. Morning faded quickly as she climbed away from the sea. As the slope crested, she turned to look back. The city was a rusty collection of red tile rooftops. Only the wide main streets were visible from here, that long inverted Y etched in a thin endless strip of coast. All the rest was sky.

Clouds billowed, massed, they soared, rolled, did all the things clouds were supposed to do. Were towers. Temples. Airy mountains. Thick. Rich. Brilliant. Here was no drift of inland cirrus, weak whispers of rain. No grim slashed thunderheads threatening the sky. This was the real thing. Joy.

She could almost hear her father's voice: "Look, Tony! Where do you see clouds like this?"

At Kaveta she found a ration of fuel and an Indian kiosk that served tea, fried pastries, and warm Coca-Cola. So dark inside. Indians, she thought, must fear something in the sun, and love dust, the ripening smells of their spices, incense, cheap scented soaps. Three small tables tilted there, crudely hammered. There had been attempts to paint, to hang curtains, but the clutter had run riot. It was a jumble of emptiness: every container was empty, every shelf, tin and box and jar. Yet the Indians were lush, well-oiled, skilled in survival. Luenga vowed they could live on nothing but air and grow fat. A gaudy halograph of Ganesh, the merchant god, hung on the back wall, stupid and grinning, an elephant's head on a fat Buddha's body.

Another Indian family had stopped there. The man complained to Antonia about the conditions of the road. They were taking his daughter, he said, to the capital.

"She is going to the States," he said. "To University of Michigans to be studying veterinary science on scholarship." The girl said nothing. Antonia wondered if the story were true. A vet? That delicate, beautiful girl? "Do you know this place, Michigans?" he asked.

"I only know it's terribly cold."

"In this case, she will buy fur coat!" He was excited.

The mother, a wide expanse of pink silk and brown flesh, had a red mark on her head and a bright stone mounted in her nostril. Her face was tragic: this was either the first or the last of her children that she would never see again. The girl's hair was loose like a shawl and spread over her shoulders. A ray of sun had slipped through a crack in the door and fallen on the green cap sleeve of her chola and the upper portion of her arm. Offended, she seemed to contract, a thin fluttering of green, almost imperceptible, soft cloth drifting like magic over the exposed flesh. Her perfume was visible.

As Antonia paid for the tea, the owner told her, "I am naving condense milk." He motioned to a back room, a door locked and guarded by his wife, who sat placidly in front of it, hands folded in her lap, dampening her lips again and again with a wayward tongue.

"How much?" Antonia asked.

"Expensive," he said. "Hundred. I am sorry, please." For all of it he looked sincere. The price was outrageous but she asked for three tins. His wife found keys in the deep recesses of her folded sari. The tins of milk were small, the Russian product, already sweetened. She paid the man for the booty. The wife stood there, her tongue darting like a pulsing nerve in her mouth. Antonia wondered what else was hidden in that back room.

From Kaveta the road turned sharply east. Dim shadows of the Pareh Mountains appeared. On the dry plains that once belonged to the nomadic Kwavi, white men had planted sisal. Antonia had first seen the plantations with her father. She had been no more than five or six and had just learned to read. The trip with him had been her reward.

Approaching from the north had given them a different view. They saw a valley from that direction, not as endless as it seemed coming on it this way, but bounded neatly by the ripples of black mountains washing on its shores. The sisal rolled in blue-green velvet waves. It might have been the sea, save for the rigid patterns of field and road.

Once in the valley, they discovered the plants were grayish, taller than a man, and sharply spiked, not velvety as in that first view. She was warned about edges that were keen as knives. The white men told her not to venture among the plants, not even to follow them along the paths marked out in the fields, because a spike could take out her eye or pierce her to her heart. They themselves went in and disappeared like mice in grass. She watched them from the car. Black men with machetes hacked at the plants, which oozed a thick white sap, making stacks and rows.

Kwavi children came and looked in the windows of their Land Rover. Antonia stuck out her tongue and made an ugly face. They imitated making uglier ones. She laughed. They laughed. She barked like a dog. They made the sounds of cows. She did a cat. They did chickens and goats. She handed out her candies.

Mothers came. They stood in line behind the children with babies sucking from their breasts. Their heads were shaved. Their ears, full of beaded hoops, necks ringed with beaded collars. They had brass and copper circles up their arms and wore blue cotton capes. Gradually, they approached the car. Opening the doors, Antonia invited them all in. They stank of smoke and sour milk. All of them piled in, laughing, pulling knobs and sliding the windows back and forth. They bounced up and down; her father came from the sisal, in a rage.

Sisal. Now the agave spikes had finished flowering. They were as tall as bare trees. The original rows of the plantation remained like an army of advancing spears. No one had harvested sisal for years, the story of nationalized business. Corrupt managers and dwindling production. But the change had not defeated the plants. Nothing would. They were denser now, impenetrable. And the displaced

Kwavi still had to hug the roads and low swampy places of their country that had not been used by other men.

Turning westward for a few miles and then north, the road became a washboard, rills left from lapping floods that swept off the hills. She drove, the only car, through a deserted plantation. She could see herself progressing into the heart of things, into the interiors people always talked about in Africa. She heard a voice, her own, talking to herself, rehearsing what she would say to Esther, even to Nkosi, an apology of sorts, perhaps a plea.

The sound of her engine was magnified, transformed into a type of silence that matched the spaces beyond the capsule of her shaking car. Hours of this washboard and hands cramp and itch, let go and the thing moved along as if on its own. What was it that the Kwavi had said when they first saw cars? An animal of metal that can walk. They were more curious than surprised or scared; they thought of cars as beasts that ate men and then disgorged them from their iron bellies in distaste.

She saw herself, her face and hands, even her voice, as things apart, encased in that dusty metal being. Rolling. Pale, almost spectral in the fading light, behind the tinted windscreen. Her hair was slipping from the scarf in wisps. Her blouse was limp, stuck to her breasts, a rill of sweat down her belly. It was weird the way the sky seemed to cling to her machine as she drove.

In the end she saw herself disgorged, untangling her long skirt, releasing the grip of her blouse, fanning at flies and the strands of hair caught in her mouth. She could have been a tourist stepping from the back of a bus, stretching, looking around. The sun was dropping, bursting like a wineskin, spreading colored liquors over the horizon.

At Sameh, the first low hills of the Pareh Mountains met the flat earth. A bus stop and a market. Always windy, always dusty. Strewn with unguarded parcels, tied and waiting. It was a town that lived on cycles of crowds and isolation, common in places that men came to on foot. On market days the people blew in, built ragged shelters, spread their goods on straw mats, and fraying crowds rolled into place like stones in a flood. Where did they all come from? There were no houses near, and the roads in and out of Sameh were always empty.

The government built a cement market hall and tried to license stalls inside, tried to tax vendors and enforce hygiene. It had never worked. A few old women peddled tomatoes or crude furniture and baskets in there. There was a butcher and a man from the coast who sold cotton by the yard to Kwavi: blue to the women, red to the men. Otherwise, the structure went unused.

Two trees marked the place where people really did business. Kwavi warriors hunkered near their goats, hair in plaits draped across their bare backs, long and elaborate. Lovers of the color red, they wore chokers of red beads, headdresses, arm bands, bracelets. Two were standing against the wind, red capes filled like spinnakers on a reach. Another leaning on a spear was wearing argyle socks. In a blue plastic cup, a toothless woman measured husked corn. Pyramids of pale green limes. White-throated crows fighting near a water pump. A child, wary as a shopper, examined an empty tin, found it wanting, tossed it in a heap of trash. An ancient women in plastic sunglasses.

There was a smell of livestock. Of urine and dung.

People in the town knew all about Esther. They directed Antonia to a man selling meat in one of the government stalls. His child, they said, had been healed. That day the butcher had no meat at all but stood arranging dried fish on a concrete counter—terrible, shrunken, fetid things. His license was encased in plastic, faded and illegible. He remembered Esther, of course. Because of what she had done for his child, when she came to him for help, he had given it. Money, he said, and warm clothes. A new red sweater. He showed Antonia one like it that he had for sale. He believed she was going up the mountain because she had been seen getting on the bus. She was a good person, he said, very good, and had saved his son.

Antonia walked among the stalls. The light was held outside, pushed to the edges. Inside, shadows had been absorbed into the patches of gray, of brown, of simple things. Burlap sacks of potatoes reminded her that this was the place where Esther had spent those nights alone and ashamed, under one of those stalls, in a corner, trying to deny her blood.

There were small gray leaves for sale here. Thin sticks and dried stems with deep red cores. Waxy liquids and black powders. Medicines. She took some on her fingertip to her tongue, a bitter taste filling her mouth, looked to make sure the finger was clean. The Kwavi hawker didn't flinch or even seem to see what she had done.

"What is this?" she asked.

The woman grinned. "Two shillings," she answered, holding up four fingers.

Trying to deny her blood. Held at bay with torn cloths and wads of paper. Looking again and again hoping that it wasn't so, Antonia had known even then those stains were signaling a change for her, an end in her relationship with her father, making her more like her mother, a crisis of needs and paraphernalia, of tablets to ease the pain.

It was not the first time she had bled. The first time was at school, a faint wash of red down her leg after a bath. She poked around in there with cotton and face cloths but found nothing more. Still, she had known. This was the second time. They had gone to Ethiopia to hunt oryx. Her first ride in a small plane. She watched the land build tier on tier to dark green-black plateaus. She saw how the rift narrowed until it almost closed. The yellow savanna along the Awash River seemed like a gift in a land of high cliffs and broken rock.

There was a lot of game they weren't hunting. Zebra, warthog, gazelle. They saw crocs and hippos and baboons with red chest plates. The oryx herds were rare, confined to a small area, sometimes so elusive that hunters went home with nothing. They went out from camp on foot with guides, but Antonia was the one to see the oryx first.

"There!" she called. A silvery gray bull in profile, horns so straight and balanced it seemed he had only one, a unicorn. He heard the hunters, swung his torso, and ran. She was happy, squinting at his great speed. He had been safe in any case: her father never shot the first animal he saw. Even as a girl she saw the paradox, that the only way he could save the very thing he wanted to take as his own was to let it go free, and she wondered if the escaping oryx meant the same to him as it did to her. She asked him why he didn't fire, because she knew that other hunters took trophies whenever they could. He told her. "This is how I humble myself." She had been old enough to understand what that meant, but still too young to know that he had no humility at all.

What a strange rite of passage hers had been. On a hunt with men. She had been given her own gun that past birthday and taught to shoot. Now there was a whole herd of oryx, like huge white birds, almost flying, dense on the horizon. She felt the tremor and knew it was antelope, a slash like a sickle cutting the thick grass.

She oozed. Used leaves. Her socks. At night they walked to a nearby camp. The river bent for a few hundred yards and they lost sight of the fires and the lantern lights that were leading them. It was an unrelenting black, thick as fog. They were nothing but earthbound voices in it. She stayed closed to the men, brushing against her father's leg with her fist.

"What's the matter, Tony?" he teased. "She's usually leaps ahead of everyone else," he told the others. She didn't answer. She couldn't have told them what it was, that she was afraid to be alone out there, afraid her blood would draw something from the dark.

There was only one road into the Pareh. Driving on it would take her up, pausing at each turn as it angled back on itself to see where she had been. Earthfalls rolled, lingered in the valley. She saw the hillside farms that clung there, worn patches of corn suspended like squares of laundry in the sun. What she felt, angling there, rising, working her way, was that the hills didn't belong to the level forms below, the unobstructed plains, flat-topped acacia trees, and shallow lakes.

There were no towns or villages along the road. Dirt paths etched into the brush were the only signs that people lived here. She saw a few young women carrying water on their heads in plastic buckets or on their backs in clay jars. Then for a time she saw only children, unattended, busy with sticks and dogs. They would gather staring as she passed, then charge her moving car. In her rearview mirror, she saw ten or fifteen of them, an arch across the glass, diminishing, waving. She wondered how they would figure out intrusions like hers: loud, rough, exciting. Not unusual but never fully understood or explained.

More children were arranged ahead, like statues on the frayed edges of roadbed, among mud and rocks, a sepia monochrome, their skin, the stones, the terra-cotta earth. And more again until she thought there might not be anyone else. Apocalyptic, those children, as though all the adults had died in an epidemic.

She came to a tea stall of green metal siding and grass roof. She stopped there but found no one. Inside, the metal walls, waist high, proved to be a collage of flattened cooking-oil tins pressed together to form a sheet. She thought these were things she would have photographed had she been a tourist. It was swept clean, the mud floor as polished as tile. The tables, long planks on tree stumps, were rich with wear. In a corner there was a pot of water boiling on a bed of dying coals. A child appeared. Then another. And another, until there were ten or twelve. Some held hands. Antonia spoke. They didn't answer. The biggest one, a girl, wore a woman's dress that trailed the ground. The smallest was covered with white ash from the neck down, a standard treatment for rashes. Then, one by one, they went away. Still no one came to sell her tea.

There was a town not far from there, grown up around a gas station: a butcher stall, a tea kiosk, an Indian who sold whatever he could get his hands on. Kwavi warriors leaned against a tree, red-and-white checked cloths wrapped around their waists. One of them wore a baseball cap with a visor. A Swahili family from the coast sat on suitcases near a blue VW, painted so many times it had lost its definition. The car had two flat tires. A husband paced beside it in white *kanzu,* white cap, and leather sandals.

He recognized Antonia and called to her in greeting. His name was Abdullah. One of his children was brought forth, a girl she had operated on for a ruptured spleen three years before. The girl was shy, hid her face in her father's robe. The mother laughed.

"We are disabled," he told her. "They cannot patch us up." He had a black prayer mark, like a raised callus, on his forehead, the sign of devotion to Allah, of excessive worship.

"I'm not returning just now, or I would offer to take you all back down," she said.

"No, no, you are kind." Abdullah pressed his fingertips in an attitude of prayer. "Soon the bus will come. We have only now passed it in its progress. This is no worry. But, my car, you see. What can be done about it?" He began to laugh. So did his family. And so did she. "Perhaps in Sameh," he said, "they will patch my tires. Then I will return to this place. Then we will change them. Then we will be under way." He didn't quite believe that it would all go as smoothly as this and laughed again. His daughter bit at his finger, at the heavy gold ring he wore.

They heard the bus. Then saw it just above them barely moving. When it got to the bottom, Antonia talked to the driver. He was, he said, the only driver who went on that route, once every ten days. He had been driving for eight years. On the days when he didn't go up the mountain, he went to Iringa. This was how the company brought service to everyone. She asked him if he remembered bringing a young woman and a bearded man. The woman might have worn a red sweater. He said he remembered a woman in a red sweater but there was no man. She was alone, yes, alone. He couldn't say when it was, the last journey or the one before that. He was too busy going up and down, an absurdity that regaled him.

Stretching, talking, strolling around his bus, the driver complained that the road was getting very bad. His bus was not so nice as it had been and was now hard to steer. For this reason he drove slowly and the trip was getting longer even though his pay remained the same. He was a "safety's driver" he told her, and checked his brakes every time he began a run. But he showed her the worn tires and said it really wasn't safe with tires like that. Abdullah took it all in.

"What can we do?" he said.

Each year in the hot dry season, just after the New Year, the coffee farmers and their families had come up into these hills to play golf. At Sameh, they slept in tents. Next day there was a picnic lunch at Ndokaa, a waterfall and view point. The high range went up behind them to Lusutu, their destination. Up there were real alpine forests and a need to build fires at night to stay warm.

They brought their silver and crystal because they like to drag it out in the rough surroundings. The juxtaposition gave their enjoyments an ironic edge. It seemed to make them tougher, more sardonic, a little spiteful, laughing up their sleeves at the things they had left behind. No one ever thought of going home in those days; no one ever did. On these trips they drank continuously. The picnic at Ndokaa began with sack. Bill Redmond did his famous gin fizzes there—the only time he made them, the only place.

Diamond gin fizzes. Instead of seltzer, he fizzed them with champagne. As a kid, Antonia had been his assistant. She measured the gin, the cream, the sugar syrup while he did the rest, popping the champagne as everyone cheered. A medicine-man routine: his concoctions were all you needed for your heart, liver, kidneys, blood. Whatever ailed you. He used an accent and wore a ratty Indian headdress.

Driving up was to go out of Africa, as though, in addition to the horizontal, there were vertical boundaries. Africa was down there on the plains and the dry hills, in the villages and nomad camps. The mountains were for settlers from England where it was too cold at night, the slopes too steep for planting, the trees too big to cut for firewood, too far away from everything and everyone. Africans weren't mountain people; there was a distrust of those who had the means to live in such high, cool places. These were powerful witches or men who communed with evil spirits.

The Europeans had made a resort at the top, a hotel called The Lawns, with wide verandas and porches and tennis courts. The main attraction was the eighteen-hole golf course. There were hiking trails and a swimming pool. A ballroom. A bar. Each room had a fireplace that would be waiting, laid with logs when they arrived. At dark, old black men lit the fire as the heavy formal clothes worn each night to dinner were unpacked.

The drinking went on. It didn't seem unusual then to Antonia or nefarious, or even alcoholic. It was a routine, a thing as normal as eating and sleeping. There was ritual attached to it that had its own cycles of meaning—the preluncheon sherry, the wine with lunch, the port after. Beer was drunk in the afternoon, then tea, then Bill Redmond mixed up fancy cocktails in his room. Wine for dinner. Brandy after. Then whiskey through the night. Annual golf tournaments brought them all here. A man's game. The women played bridge and took their sherry earlier each day and the kids did anything they wanted to. Once someone got remarkably sick in the club bathroom. Breakfast jokes were made about the mess. The trouble was that none of the help would agree to clean it up.

"They draw the line at shit and vomit," the young McGeorge had whispered. He took his friends in to look at the disgusting pile, which he thought was hilarious. She saw bits of a dinner that she recognized and felt a nausea all her own. McGeorge wished it could stay there forever so they could watch it change as the years went by until it became a revolting fossil. Archaeologists, he said, would discover it in their efforts to trace man's evolution from apes on the dark continent. Homo sapiens: from the contents of a stomach. Later that day it was gone, but by then the subject had been hushed like a secret in the family.

Antonia reached Ndokaa at noon. The light was ruthless; shadows snapped in on themselves against it. There was no shade, no shelter. No one was around. Buildings were cramped tight against a turn that doubled back ascending. Packed in behind them was the waterfall where they had picnicked sampling diamond gin fizzes. She made the turn, crossed a creaking bridge, and saw a few women there getting water, their children near them washing, cooling off. She was aware of rounded stone shapes, black, polished, and as tumbled as the people kneeling on them, reaching, standing there like hieroglyphs, angular, engraved, eternal. She would have passed right by them, accelerating to make that first dash into the steeper climb ahead, but she saw a flash of red, arms and a torso.

She thought: Is it Esther? A strange feeling, to come on what you were looking for. Surprised, she almost wanted to turn away, because she didn't know what to say to her—what she would say. She wondered if it was possible to do the right thing. What did Esther think of her, after all? *Am I strong enough? Good enough? To listen. To say I understand the realness, the depth, the sad part of her feelings and her fear. To ask.*

She stopped and let the Peugeot roll back toward that wick of color as it flickered among the stones and falling mist. Her halting roll caught the attention of the crowd and they all stopped their work to look her way. The red sweater bounded to a wall beside the road and raised an arm to wave—a little boy, his hands hidden in the long sleeves.

Going up. Out of Africa. The horizon is above, domed. This is a mountain perspective. At the summit, there are blankets of moss and tall pines, the pillars of their dark trunks cutting light spaces from the sky. Here is the black-green of another hemisphere, a forest smell of pitch and sap, of fallen needles.

The resort had died, but the small town had remained. People lived in different seasons here, ate different fruits. Apples, which sometimes made it down to the coast, and peaches, which never did. Now there were peas in the market, like gems heaped in baskets. Earth treasures. These green shades: verdant beds of moss, wintery crowns of high pine, the wealth of emerald peas; colors describing more for her, an internal landscape, a knowledge deeper than the place. An aching for the north.

A Sikh trader was filling a small pickup with the peas. Women were lined in front of him balancing loads on their heads, bargaining wildly. At the car window, a young man tried to sell her a tea strainer. Another was selling a comb and a child's whistle on a chain. She passed slowly through.

The Lawns revealed itself in spaces between tree trunks, a strobe effect. Red tile roof, white pillars, dark squares of window, filigree of porches, back in there until, as she drew close beyond the barrier of the trees, she saw the building, low and attractive. There were the small stone-and-iron benches, the painted wicker, the small window panes and vines, the heavy set of an English country house.

At independence the name of the place had been changed to something African, a new sign nailed over the old one. Now both signs had fallen to the ground, but inside it was still The Lawns. The carpet insignia in the entry was barely legible, but still the registry book was clearly headed *The Lawns.* It was shabby but immaculately kept, more neat and scrubbed than she had ever seen it, almost as if the cleaning had eroded it, and not time, nor the lack of money, the loss of old days.

The manager spoke more to the air behind her than to Antonia. He knew her, had worked on the desk in the days when the coffee men came for their golf. He remembered her father. She told him he had died. And her mother? Living in America. And she? She was still here?

"I'm a doctor," she said.

It appeared the hotel was empty. So firmly placed, the chairs and tables and lamps and ashtrays all seemed as unused as museum displays, touched only to remove the dust that might have settled under another, less severe management.

He led her to her room past doors opened on still spaces: beds, dressers, shapes in the half light of drawn curtains. He was either proud or nervous, strict with his spine. A lord of vacancy.

"Are there any other guests?" she asked.

He answered, "No."

There were two small beds. She tested them, both bad, and sank exhausted, into ruined springs. A light, flat and unchanging, stayed fixed outside the room and the window barricade. The chintz curtains had surrendered to a process that was turning them to paper. She could remember that the faded prints had been of English scenes, roses and horse paddocks and dogs. Those hideous curtains at The Lawns! The room was still overburdened with drapery, a skirted dressing table with remnants of butterflies, a ruffled chair with sailing ships. Everything covered. Twenty years ago she had wanted to strip it all away and look at what was underneath, even the poor cypress they used to make these bits of furniture. Smoothing down her long skirt over tired legs, she felt a dampness in the worn cotton, thickening from loss like old skin. And the sheets beneath her, more starch than fiber, the simple sad messages of cloth.

What were her reasons for coming here? For finally seeking this out? For wanting to know?

An image: Esther carrying gourds of water from a spring, a source. Because she was finding herself dry? Reflections of Paul Luenga's hero. Nothing had ever happened on those operating tables or at those bedsides all those years to make her think that there were ways of healing that went beyond the disease itself. You repaired, you cut, you stitched, drew blood, swabbed samples that you bore away on slides, and under microscopes thought you saw the truth made visible at last. Those tiny answers. Nothing had ever made her think that this was not all there was to it. Or that stunned, staring at a child's rotting hand, she had watched an English woman cut it off and believed that somehow, in that violent act, she had taken charge against the chaos. An act Antonia had performed so many times herself since then.

That face: the face of a black cat. Was the girl awake? Breasts gently flattening over her chest, arms tied down, already on a drip. Who had done this? A knife? A broken bottle? Lips of skin and tissue, unfolding lily rose orchid.

When Antonia awoke, water was running in the bathroom at the end of the hall. It ran, then stopped, giving way to the fall of crisp steps, a sound so alone out there it gave Antonia the idea that she might have disappeared, not merely dozed. Whoever walked so briskly by didn't know she was inside, cupped in the weak springs of that sagging bed. Like the riddle of the tree falling in an empty forest. Was there a sound if no one heard it?

She went for tea on the porch. Rose beds radiated from it like spokes into the lawn. Remarkable, the roses had more than survived: they were thriving. A gardener must have caught the fanaticism of the stony memsaab who brought them here from England. He had learned to prune them, cut them, fertilize them. Had become a master at it. He must have been the one who walked in the gardens now with baskets of manure. But only for the roses. Everything else was let go. The peonies, the dahlias, the flowers she remembered from another world.

She saw there were other guests after all. Indians playing bridge, a woman who had filled her hair with the marvel of that rose garden. She was alone with three men and played the most vicious game. Her cards cracked on the table, the party's only sound, rhythmic enough to disturb, like hard wings of a fallen beetle slapping in distress.

A waitress brought the doctor a cup and saucer that didn't match, sugar in a plastic dish, a bent spoon. These broken, faded things depressed her; the flourishing roses seemed even more an omen, an old contradiction come to skewed justice, like the Indians who had not been allowed in The Lawns in other days—their brown skins, their turbans, their silks. An irony, this sorry place and their old desire to be admitted.

Behind the players, through French doors in the dark dining room, she could see a woman passing between two tables to the kitchen. She was carrying a tray, wearing a red sweater. Could she have been Esther? By now the phantoms Antonia chased mocked her. Red sweaters, purple jumpsuits, curling beards, and limps—they were like spite. She was startled only as long as it took to have the apparition disappear and then come again because she had been expecting, after all, that this time it would be Esther Moro.

EIGHTEEN

◁ ◇ ▷

When Esther saw the doctor drinking tea and facing her, she was not surprised. She had had a dream, a premonition: a man stuck through on a sisal. She could hear Nkosi weeping, calling her name. She found her way toward the voice and saw a Kwavi woman standing there. The woman had a mirror. When Esther looked into it, she saw Antonia's face answering hers.

She came up the mountain on the bus, unprepared for the transforming land, trees taller than she had ever imagined, their trunks enormous, the long red trunks and the earth turned red from their fallen needles—as if they were the whole of life pressing the air that was full of their smell.

Reaching Lusutu she asked everyone, "Where are these Africans from another country who came here in their trucks?"

In the market Hindis were buying peas and fruits to carry down. Boys who sold combs had surrounded her, trying to carry her things for wages, over stones and up hills.

A young woman knew. "Yes, they were soldiers. Even women soldiers." She was with a friend leaning against a kiosk drinking Coca-Cola. They offered Esther a drink.

"There is a hotel," the friend said. "Down there."

Below the market, where they pointed, she could see white buildings and rooftops deep in green.

And so she went, almost running, convinced that he was there. Walking in, she saw men, a few women, sitting at tables or on the grass. She walked among them like a spy but heard nothing and saw nothing. She finally said out loud, "Nkosi is my friend." More like a question so they would know she was looking for him.

He was inside. A woman called Nandi took her to him.

"He is not good," this Nandi said. She showed how bad he was, shaking her head in sorrow for him. But she only knew English and her own language and apologized, talking with her hands and face, fingers in her mouth because she couldn't help. They both looked down at him but he was asleep or pretending to be, in a room that was untouched.

"You know—this—" Nandi placed a hand on Esther because they all knew it: the yellow eyes, the tiredness, the swelling. Sickness of the liver. And other things. Perhaps his limping, a disease that had weakened him, speaking all this in English and making signs.

There was no doctor. There was no time. They had told him, before, in Sameh—she pointed down saying, "Sameh, Sameh," and shaking her head. No. No. But he didn't listen. She opened her palms.

Later, while Esther sat on the porch holding her red sweater around her chest in the cold, they all left, climbing into cars and trucks, moving at night in the dark with their secret war. Nandi was one of the last. She pressed Esther's hands. Esther saw then that they were really soldiers, dressed as soldiers and carrying guns.

Morning was the tray of tea she brought him. She was hoping for a sign, a command, but there was only the terrible dream image in the sisal, and for a moment, the image of his skull fallen to his bed. Too much like Musumbi on that footpath, crumpling. They had been sheltering near a rock. Masai with painted bodies came in the morning and gave them milk to drink from their cows. Then suddenly he was falling and she was running, afraid that she had done it, that her dream had been her wish, what she had seen, the shadows of his bones though his flesh, thinking, "I killed him," terrified to see him just that way as he fell, the shadows of his bones, as though she had made it happen. She was a girl running to a village calling for help. Men ran following her to the spot, and the women, bearing down to shield her.

In streaming images, time came unlocked and pouring. The voices were a turmoil like wind blowing sand.

Her memory wandered seeking pardon. She was stripping corn in her mother's house. She was the one who watched and waited for Musumbi's return, the spectacles and the coat, a form at the bottom of a hill. At night near the fire she stood between his knees, her elbows lifting to balance there. He was talking about sickness, about how germs came into the blood like malaria when mosquitoes bit you. Fevers from the water, from the dirt on your hands. He was a vibration behind her, her head against his chest. Faces fell away from the fire. In a breeze, women covered their heads with *kangas*, colors that came alive in the light, the pictures of the cloths like real fruits and flowers. They all let him listen, one by one, to the sounds of their hearts with his stethoscope, and she, with the silver horn pressed against his chest, carefully placing the tiny beads into her ears, felt her own body fill with the sound, more than love, listening to him beat there, taking it in like water, her thirst to know, until someone pulled her away, laughing, teasing her. It was her mother, close as this, her skin soft and red. She smelled of soap Musumbi had brought, lifting the child who was struggling to hold onto her father's neck.

What happened to Esther after he died? Somewhere feet braced against a slope, took her down a mountain, took her away. Skidding on rocks as fast as she could go. Crows broke into the air. She crouched in darkness hiding her blood on stones, in rags and papers. She unfolded in the smell of cloves and the weight of falling bones. A bed. A nightstand. Cats in the moon. The sound of breaking glass. The sailor's arm is even whiter under the sleeve of his shirt, and even more brutal where the flesh is underneath, white as a fish lifted from the sea.

The cluttering images hurt her as much as if she had been beaten. She couldn't separate what was making her sorrow for Nkosi and what she saw opening in her own life as a way to understand. Her innocence was there in that rush, taken in the sound of her father's poor beating heart.

She had to leave Nkosi then, to withdraw into her own sleep. Sleeping and sleeping. All she could do was sleep. Only sleep. There were no dreams, no messages, no images left. Alone, as if that flood of memory had torn her away from everything. Even Musumbi was out of reach. And she feared her gift was gone.

People at the hotel took Nkosi as their burden.

"He is a freedom fighter," the manager said.

Esther turned to real things she could touch, the blanket that covered him and the one she warmed under, the tray of teacups and the food she stirred behind the hotel with the people who lived there. The old gardener gave her flowers. The bottles she put them in were cold every morning and the flowers got wider each day until the petals began to fall. Rough needles from the trees pricked her hands as she knelt in them, digging and digging. She took refuge in this act—the pain, the feel of earth reminded her of goodness and the smell of God as if she could scratch His face there.

"Why do you dig?" the children asked her.

"Because my friend is sick," she said. They were the only ones who could understand and did. When they became adults they would think she had been mad.

She helped the women who cleaned the hotel. The manager wanted them to wax the floors so many times that they fell and slid like fools. Children slipped along the hall when no one looked or followed Esther as she balanced carefully, carrying the afternoon tray from the room they shared to the kitchen. Her feet took heat from the sun-warmed floors. She pressed her back against the wall and gathered more.

Some Hindi people came one night and slept there. Three men and a woman who played cards until the morning. The men smoked and the woman ate sweets from a small tin. She heard the sound of the cards, which made her think of counting the things you could lose. In the morning they washed and filled the hall with their perfumes. Clicking heels. The woman's bangles rang like bells. She had flowers in her hair at a table where the sun made shadows. They went on playing cards. The men wore black suits, one with a shirt that had blue dots. His glasses turned dark when he went outside.

The manager's daughter ran back and forth to empty their ashtrays and to tell everyone things: "The fat one has a watch that makes a sound. He has a wallet with too much money."

There were peas to eat but Nkosi said no. There were dishes on a tray, glasses of tea, old spoons. Esther saw a figure at the other table across from where the Hindis played. Her heart told her who it was. She began to weep.

Her face felt it before the tears came. Her friend was standing, offering her arms, a circle that promised protection. Approaching—surrendering—she was closer to her fears.

"Nkosi is so sick," she said, and, "I am here." Meaning that she was alone. There were things impossible to say. "I cannot help him." This was what it was: the signs were only inventions to prove what she knew—that skull hung against his face, his withering hands. She had told the visions to stop.

"I knew you would come," she said. "I had a dream," and she tried to tell it, wondering if the doctor would see the same thing in the image or if they would go on staring at each other without understanding. It was all coming too fast—"There was a girl in the Ruaha, in a shed where she had been cut and the others . . . "—to have an explanation confirmed. *Ambukizo*: infection. Something that was spreading like streams of water after rain. Hadn't they both, she and the doctor too, faced this same event? She was searching through the logic of parallels for an answer.

But the doctor understood, or seemed to, and said, "You thought of the time they brought you in to me, is that it?"

"That is it!" Eager because this might have been the way to absolution, as if both she and that girl in the shed had shared the same fate. Even now when it seemed impossible to change anything. Esther remembered the flaming tree and the accusing question of a dream. And waited. Silence seemed to confirm her innocence. "But the girl was dead," she added.

What she wanted to show the doctor had vanished before she could find it as language and say what it was. Her nails were full of the earth but nothing at all had been mended. Perhaps it was the price.

"I have seen pictures of Nkosi's children," was all Esther could say. Their talk had to take place in a way that silences could reveal what could not be said. Esther couldn't trust words, which were too precise and often confusing. Only the image of her father digging for medicines held together. The divided root: he looked for it wherever they went. It formed a man's shape, legs or fingers. Some said it was a serpent's tongue. It was the only way, Musumbi said, to heal a divided soul. The way a vine split and grew in all directions, far, far from the tap. The only water it could feel in its leaves came from tiny drops of rain that hit it. She was afraid for Nkosi, for the real sickness in him that could not be healed in time.

"Will you take me to him?" the doctor asked. Her hair was pulled back but other things about her were different as well. The way that trees smelled in this place clung to her breath—or pounded tea spices, or something else Esther could not identify.

Esther took the doctor to his room. There was no whispered, "You wait here," no quiet announcement of Antonia's advance. Suddenly Antonia was facing him, heart pounding like a hunter's, afraid because she anticipated the reaction he would have on being discovered like this by her. She could see how sick he was and that took her by surprise. No time to pull the incidentals in around him, to frame, to soften what she saw: only the head on a pillow, the angry hair.

He held his eyes open, on her, but without expression. She saw a mask, as if his spirit had been given hard form, as if he had conjured it, carved it, was showing it to bring her down. Right then she wished the forest was their context: a fire, drums, wild appearances, so she could stand protected, as a stranger, watching the dance.

Sarcastically he started listing his symptoms. "Terrible itching," he said, "dark urine, white shit."

"Yes, and you're jaundiced," she said. His color was green, muddy—horrid. His eyes yellow. "Have you been like this before?"

"It's chronic. My liver's full of bilharzia and malaria. We all have it. Like V.D."

She approached him but he stopped her hand which

had automatically started to peel the blankets to expose his abdomen.

"I didn't ask for a doctor," he said. He turned to his side, pulled the cover over his head.

She didn't know what she had expected to find here. Like visiting a new country, the image never matched the reality, and in retrospect could never recapture what had originally been imagined. Like quicksilver, dreamed shapes never held for memory.

Already, in her disappointment, she wondered why she had sought this out. She felt foolish, embarrassed. It irritated her that he was not pleased she was there. Did she have to plead with them? Esther was pressed into a small space between the wall and wardrobe like wood that might be turned to stone. It was too late and the wrong place to play at being a doctor, to be tough with him the way Mrs. Burton, Elsa Burton in that hotel room how many years ago, had sterilized her knife. There was no single stroke, nothing her competence and training could give her to let her know what she needed to do. She stood there wishing herself away, breathing deeply, rhythmically, and without thinking, turned from them to walk away. To defend what? The polished floor was her enemy now, pulling at her feet. Once outside she was able to run. Trees welcomed her, the long driveway and the cooling air. The smell of pine was like medicine, the purity of a high place. As if she could get away from them.

Across the road from the hotel there was a path, a gully really, that led up a very steep hill to a cliff, a balcony of rock. As kids, they used to climb up and sit, legs dangling, with snacks and flasks of tea. They liked to drop stones over the edge and bet on whose stone would roll closest to the bottom. They could see the hotel laid out there and the textured patterns of golf-course grasses, the rough swirling fairways and random disks of silky green.

"If you didn't know that was a golf course, Tony, what would you think it was?" Who had asked her that?

She remembered answering, "But I do know what it is."

Now the grasses had gone wild, yet those flat circles still remained, were, at last, even to her, mysterious, and she understood the question that had been asked so long ago.

She could see the Indians in the parking lot, an increased number. They were getting ready to leave, flowing around their car, carefully fitting themselves in. When they drove away, hers was the only car. There would be no dusk, only these hints that day would quickly end—the softened shadows of land, and a glazed hardness in the sky, porcelain shards of light along a low horizon. Threads of clouds.

At night she talked to Esther, who came shyly to her table in the empty dining room. The waitresses were two: they sat watching, eating their own portions of the bland food, peas in cream sauce poured over mashed potatoes. Antonia savored it. Warm, salty, it made no demands. She even asked for more. It came, the second time, on a piece of toasted bread, the residue of potato left around the plate.

"How long has he been sick like this, Esther?" knowing that time hardly mattered.

The answer was vague, "Since he left me in Sameh, to come here with his army, even after they told him no. But I knew even before this." She tried to explain how she had cast inside him looking for a way to release the sickness, a story of a root shaped like a man, fingers digging in the earth, a personality like his, that was divided or broken, was killing him.

"I put pictures of the children on a table. After that I opened the door so the light fell across them to show the message in them to him." Arranging outside things as confirmation. In the same way the mountain made it seem there were no places left to go: a way out, a way in, depending on your point of view. "The last place," Bill Redmond called it; his secret hope, where he would build his palace. Drawings of the dream house had appeared from time to time, something that went up and down a slope, huge porches, presumably with views of the cities he envisioned on the plain below, of airports, railways, schools. What do the trees and hills here say now except that he was wrong?

When the candle on the table went out, Esther got another one, placed it carefully in the center, then moved it slightly to the left. In a row: the candle, a shaker of salt, of pepper, an empty sugar bowl. Her nose, her mouth were stylized by the candlelight.

"We must try to bring him to the hospital," Antonia urged. "In my car." To which Esther seemed to agree, reluctantly.

Then she said, "I can't help him. Why do you hear *yes* sometimes and then you hear *no*? So that you are confused. I am only human, too." She moved the candle, salt, sugar bowl, pepper, into a ring. "Is this because of God?"

Waitresses, now that their work was done, were sitting at the table too, nostrils flaring in the light. No such thing as a private conversation here: one of them knitted, enthralled by this talk of God and photographs arranged in beams of light. She held an unfinished sweater to her breast each time she reached the end of a row.

"If you make sacrifices," the waitress told them, "God will watch over you."

Sleep made it possible for her to go to Nkosi in the morning. She found him alone. A blanket covered his head, sealing him off, but he was awake, yellow eyes set in ash. She hoped that without Esther there, she could make him listen.

"You really ought to let me look at you," she said.

"You really are a bitch. What do you think I am?"

"I think you're very ill."

"A sick African. Your favorite thing."

"Oh, yes, the racial issue—never very far from anything with you. Do you ever forget it?"

"Uh-uh, it's at the center of what I am, born into me along with the gene that makes my skin black. A chromosome created by evolutionary processes in my DNA—whatever it is that makes it possible for humans to adapt and survive. Genetic hate."

"Yes, I see."

She would have left but this time she couldn't. He held her with his eyes, slits in dark circling shadows, cast planes of forehead and nose, the tarnished skin, the deep fringe of his beard. She wanted to embrace him, wanted his embrace.

Finally he said, "Wait, what do you think? Will I get over this?"

"How long have you been down this time?" Again the

reflex to examine: she had moved and was standing by him, an angle of forty-five degrees, a doctor pose, her hand on the rough sheet that covered him. This time he didn't resist, merely flinched as she touched his flesh.

"Too long." He laughed. "I don't think I'll make it."

She found an abdomen swollen with fluid, a liver so enlarged it had no shape filling him.

"I want to take you down. You could hemorrhage. You'll need blood."

He waved his hands, then covered his head with them. "I wanted to go home," he said. "I was trying to make it back. You know that, don't you?" He turned his head away from her. He was puffy but the angle gave back to his face its monumentality.

He started talking then without looking at her. "So you'll know," he said. "I was a photographer in London for about ten years. Magazine work; not free lance, not advertising. I did fashion and features. Can you imagine?" He seemed to reach out. She was afraid of her instinct to take his hand and left it there. It made her sorry for them both.

"Then I joined the revolution. They wanted me to study economics so that when we came back home to tear the country down, we could rebuild it afterward. We'd have the right people for it. Trained people for it. I was already reading Marx and Lenin. I was already thinking about going home. There was a position to study in Sweden. We were a group there, a real group. A flat. Beer. People talking. More and more people were coming out. When a vision like that takes hold, you watch it forming, leaders come up. Ideas. Then things begin to change. Always changing. Time goes by and so does your innocence. Soon you know that it's been too long. You don't trust anyone anymore. Everybody's different. Everybody's been replaced. You're alone. No one knows who you are."

It was as though a rope they had been pulling against each other had been let go. He had dropped his end and she was letting go of hers, brushing the hair out of her face. This was a deathbed impulse, leaving everything else behind.

"Go on," she told him. "You came back here?"

"I was married to a Swede. We had three kids. They meant everything to me and that bothered me. I couldn't fit

them in with what I was coming to be. These are things
exiles feel: everything's hanging; you're always waiting to go
home even when you don't remember what home is. After a
while you start making the idea bigger and bigger until it's
like religion—Going Home. You get on your knees to it. You
make sacrifices. It's huge and you don't know what it means
anymore. You start to connect it with dreams and hope. You
understand what has been taken from you. You understand
hell and the terrible things that happen to black men. You
leave your children; you say you hate their whiteness. Then
Esther puts them in front of you. Pictures. Icons. If I live, I'll
go back to them. Fuck the rest."

After that he was silent. She looked past him through
a window on bands of changing green. She kept thinking
of Luenga's poem and buried gods. Nkosi almost looked
like one.

"I lost my blood mother, my blood father, my place. It
was easy to start thinking that each old black man was my
father, each old woman my mother, everyone else my
brothers and sisters because that's the way you get the
movement to work. That's the ideal. Funny how it was easy
to do that in Sweden where we were a few. Mother, father,
sister, brother—those were names we called each other. If
you didn't feel them, you pretended. You think I'm a
coward. You think I ran away."

He was exhausted but the language they shared pulled
him to her against his will. And she felt it too, his urge to
speak fluently and be understood was greater than his angry
posturing and excuses had been—exile, Zulu, victim—and
all the unmasked odor of his failure. A Londoner. White
children. Drinking beer and talking revolution in a flat in
Stockholm. What of Africa was left to him except that dark
hand he put on hers?

"Who was it," he asked softly, "that lived in London all
those years? And Sweden all those years? Who was it that
wore those clothes hanging there?"

He remembered his blood mother. He had been raised
in a black shantytown. "Like Soweto." The tin shacks and
foul water taps and piles of trash. There was always someone
around who had a gramophone playing scratchy records
over again and again so you learned about America because

you listened to jazz. You learned about black men there who conked their hair and led big orchestras. These were your dreams when you weren't fighting: husbands and wives, neighbors, kids—fighting, fighting. It was like a war zone in there: everyone battled everything. Even the weather. Everything was terrific: the heat, the cold, the filth, the noise. Everyone had rashes in the summer and pneumonia in the winter. They brewed illegal booze and drank it from tin cans. They went blind and crazy on it. The police would come down, checking the place, looking for the breweries, crashing into your house.

His father disappeared. He was three years old. As far as he could tell, this was when he had polio. So he limped. He wasn't alone, there were legions like him. Since most women lost their husbands from time to time, his mother waited until it wasn't reasonable any longer. Then she heard that her man had been picked up without a pass and taken to a farm in Rhodesia to pay off his fine in labor. She saved up the fine money and went away for a few weeks to get him and bring him back. But she came back without him.

That was when she began her search. To look for him she had to learn to read and write. She learned law, history, geography, government, the system. She came home from whatever job she might have and worked on her files, boxes of clippings, letters, interviews, photographs. She wrote constantly: notes and journals, records of where she had been and people that she had talked to. She wrote to everyone: magistrates, governors, wardens, farmers. She was the one who bought Nkosi the camera and taught him, from books, how to use it, even how to develop the film so no one else could see the pictures they had, the proof she needed that her husband had been taken as a slave.

She moved constantly, changed her name. Her files grew. Boxes and boxes. She interviewed miners, farm workers, men who had been in and out of prison, any prison. She kept names, addresses, pass numbers. She was convinced that there were many people who had seen her husband. Then she began to see him herself. The first time—Nkosi was twelve, perhaps thirteen—it was the middle of the night. She came and woke him and whispered, "Nkosi, your father has come back."

Down in Pretoria, Nkosi worked for an Indian who did photo portraits of blacks—their weddings and births and graduations. There were clothes kept at the shop for customers who felt their own things weren't good enough in which to go down to immortality. Nkosi's job was to print the pictures. In the chemical baths, he watched images emerge slowly; first the clothes, which he recognized, and then the faces, which he did not. The trick played on some deep element in his nature. He feared his mother's madness as he watched the pictures form, as each familiar shape focused—Is it? Is it at last? Until he saw the final outline of the face, the eyes, the nose, the lips. No, not his.

He had to leave South Africa. Even at nineteen he had no stomach for it and no hero's inclination to stay around and fight. All he wanted was peace. So what made him join up with the others, the home boys? Why had he become angry after all those years? It had to do with something in the nature of escape, which turned out to be psychological, not geographical. Then he came here and found out that what he'd been talking about in Sweden and what was going on were two different things.

His voice was thick, the cracks of his lips filled with chalky saliva his talk seemed to form. He was the first of his kind she had ever known—a guerrilla, a revolutionary—though the clothes he had pointed to seemed curiously part of the place, just another thing brought from far away. Empty on the hook.

"What happened?" she asked him.

"They let me teach. I wrote a few things. That's all."

"And Esther. How does she fit in?"

"Love," he said. "She's an incarnation of what I wanted, what I believed I could find. This thing about black men being closer to secret, supernatural things. It's physiological, a larger pineal gland." He smiled. "In your country the old niggers have a saying that black men have all the signs. Even though white men have all the cash." He laughed. "Like, if you have the signs, you ought to have the bucks. But it ain't that way."

"I never heard that." She was laughing too.

"Esther seemed like proof," he said. "I wanted proof."

"Tell me about her," she said, "about the cures. What you know."

"It's hard to say. I'm not a believer." His hands were all that was left of his energy. "But there have always been people like Esther. You must know. They read the signs. They see things. Dreams tell them. Shamans."

"What have you seen her cure?"

"A man covered with hives. Raw, itching. I watched them melt away. A boy, a woman . . . there have been many." He opened his palms to show his dismay or perhaps to offer his word.

"But she fails sometimes?"

"Sometimes the signs aren't there. Or the signs are bad. Like mine. My vital signs. Bad." He smiled.

She rocked slightly, her sigh almost a groan. She wanted him to live, holding his wrist against the gestures that were wearing him down. Without her tools, her medications, her knives, she was helpless as a doctor, stripped bare like the emperor in the children's story who had been tricked to nakedness. And he looked like someone who knew he wouldn't make it. As cancer victims knew: it's there somehow even before the death is certain, you see it in the faces. More than rampant cells—the cancer look—as though the illness had gone beyond the body. The Greeks understood it. They had a word, *cachexia,* the mysterious wasting away, a force outside, like weather.

"Why did you come here, now?" he asked.

"I followed Esther. From reports of where she was. To see for myself."

"Have you found out anything?" he said.

"Only that I did the right thing."

She saw how impossible it would be to move him, to do any of the things she thought she ought to do. A figure moved against the green backdrop that was his window: a woman with a vessel on her head. Not Esther: she was heavy, her walk solid.

"Where is she?" Antonia asked him.

"She'll come soon," he said.

NINETEEN

The figure in the mirror is her own. Her head is raised, features emerging from their own shadows. Her lips have caught the light, are rimmed with black. Her eyes stare. She has a long neck, a circle of red beads. Her shoulders are wide; the light finds their rounded shapes then breaks and spreads. She could be made of black wood, the core of a tree. Her breasts are gathered from her flesh, the nipples dark, hard in the cold. They are tender, fuller, heavy on her chest. She holds them in her hands. She tapers. Her belly swells. Her legs separate from her body and fall away like roots. She sees her feet flat below her. Now she offers her hands, palms out. Reaching toward the image, they become larger, more important, flat as wooden disks. She folds them against the cleft, where the sailor dragged across her. Sealed off. The ending of her shame.

She might have been beginning again, reeled back to another, purer time. Something strong informed her, beyond memory; she could see her own healing now that her friend had come, what she had been promised that morning when she woke receiving the stranger's blood. Parts had come together, easy to see there in the glass, her whole nakedness. She would not have dared to look before, but here the long mirror would not be refused, gave back the truth, though all truth was like that image, gone when you turned your head, flames that left ashes, djinns that rose like owls.

Her hands insisted. She let the fingers flare and open on the spot, grown back, the dark flower there. This was the way dreams repaired you, led you on. She was quick then, pulling on her gown, the chain and the green stone.

She appeared to them as if on cue, next to his bed. Priestess—Nkosi had called her shaman—in her robe and beads. A little hesitant.

Antonia drew away as the healer moved and sat, reaching out to place her hands over his chest. She moved them slightly, then held them just a few inches from his body as if she were feeling her way in the dark. He closed his eyes. Antonia was wary, nervous, backed up against the wall, waiting to be shown. She wanted the miracle. Lazarus brought back from the dead. She was ready to attest, to take the picture and tell the story in solemn tones to people who doubted, even though she knew, in the end, that if Nkosi got up healed and walked away from the room, her witness would mean nothing. There was nothing she could explain. There could be no explanations. She would only be able to say, "This is what I saw."

She wasn't ready for the change she felt in the room. Almost tactile, like humidity or heat; she flexed her own hands, would have used words like thickening or static or even bright, if you could think of touching brightness. So intense, pricking over the skin, this urge to mend, to pray, to offer, as if it were all within her reach. Perhaps it was her mood and the cold night she had spent, her first in so long, a dizzying change in the air and altitude.

She could have lived a whole existence in those moments at his bedside. In them the circumstances of her life were changed to something inevitable. She could have been connecting to all the shadowy things in her life that had never happened, like leaping into another universe in which it would be possible to deny time as she knew it, which once dissolved could surely dissolve all the rest—race and history and where it landed you on the globe—as if they all had become matter and electric forces that would not be destroyed by death. What would they all be then? Nkosi, whose flesh was fading, was not a black man even now. It wasn't what she had expected, and she saw how impossible it was for her to hold on to such ideas in the end. The sun

outside moving across the sky was making theory out of
what, for those split seconds, had been her belief. All she
could do was roll down her shirtsleeves, nervously, the only
protection she would ever have against its brilliant passage.

That night she didn't sleep well. It made no difference
which bed she lay on. There was a portion to the night when
people who lived in the quarters, but worked in town, grew
loud. It flared and subsided: one voice rose above the others,
pulling on a rope of laughs and shouts. An argument? A
joke? It was hard to tell. She tried fading into the noise in
yogic fashion, giving over to it the way you were supposed to
give over to pain or cold, until you found them to be
illusions, passing into deeper zones in the sound of your own
breath. It was possible to triumph this way, though when she
woke and heard the noise was still going on, she knew it was
her sleep that had been illusory. So she tried a less exotic
method and covered her head with a pillow.

She was awake next in total silence, crooked and
uncomfortable. Her eyes, adjusting to the dark, picked out
shapes along the wall—the lamp, the chairs. And her ears,
adjusting to the silence, picked up night sounds just as she
became slowly aware of a person sleeping in the other bed
and knew it was Esther.

In the morning the girl was gone, the bed carefully
covered. She found her with Nkosi, standing over him
almost in a trance, her hands against his skull. Antonia was
haunted by the vision of a cure, like an emotion now,
almost convincing her—despite all she knew—that he
could be saved. But he was worse. There was evidence of
internal hemorrhage.

They chopped firewood together. Digging at the wood
in easy rhythm, a deep **V** angling against itself to split apart
the log all in the last thrust of the wrist. There was nostalgia
in the perfume of the sap, the yellow chips, the arch and
swing of arm and back.

The two women laid a fire in his room. Coaxed him with
weak tea. With drops of sugary water on a spoon. He refused
to eat and drink. It was not what he intended, he told

Antonia: the faded English chintzes, the endless exile, the abandoned children, the white hand closed around his.

Antonia left them to go and stand in the lobby, looked at her idle car, thought nothing.

"You know them well?" the manager asked.

"Yes."

"And this South African man? He is going to die?"

"He won't let me move him."

"There is no trouble. They do not have to pay. We are not capitalists," he said.

She watched the old gardener working his own unpredictable hours among the roses, aereating the soil by sticking a metal prong beside the roots and rocking gently. He stroked the leaves, examined stems, checking and checking. He showed her there were aphids on the rosebuds, but he knew how to wash them with a soapy mixture made from certain flowers that grew wild along the road.

"A poison to bugs," he told her. He showed her a stem, crusted with tiny green colonies that quickly turned to liquid where he rubbed his finger, no traces of head or thorax, as though they had no anatomy at all. Burst droplets. "Apids," he called them.

She nodded. "Your roses are very beautiful."

He took a perfect bloom—tangerine, with flecks of gold and pink—and showed it off.

"My thumbs are green," he told her in English. He was finding one for her among his pinks, not too full, not too heavily opened. He nicked away the thorns with a knife and held it to her. He took her to the nursery nearby and explained how he started new root systems and then, so they wouldn't turn to bramble, he grafted them from the stock in his garden. There was an American woman from the capital who visited The Lawns sometimes and brought him stock. He showed her a red. Grafts that had taken amid new grafts, wrapped in muddy rags like bandages. *Memento mori.* She felt death all around, more so here in his attempts to hold it back. An old man, barefoot, dressed in rags.

She was walking fast, too fast for the altitude. The gully was like a staircase, the way the stones had placed themselves along the slope of the hill. And the cliff, a balcony of rock. Movements, then shapes, made themselves clear as her breath eased and she calmed. A line of children passed, open baskets of peas balanced on their heads. Their mothers followed carrying firewood and water jugs. A young man pulled sacks of charcoal on a low flat wagon made with salvaged wheels. He lifted and coaxed it over the damaged roadway, over stones, over potholes. There was a skinny dog.

Her vision was drawn back to the cluster of buildings and gardens that once had been The Lawns—the hotel an **E** shape, mowed spaces clinging to its outline, an anachronism of roses dotted around the porch. She could see the old gardener there, pruning, weeding. And a waitress moving tables. She was startled by a man who walked out from the rooms. The waitress didn't notice him, simply stepped off toward the kitchen. The man was wrapped in a blanket, limping, a full beard pressed against his chest. Then he looked up and scanned the hillside. No, not Nkosi—she caught her breath. But yes it was; she hadn't any doubt. He lifted his arm to shield his eyes, then went back inside.

She thought of the miracle—Lazarus.

She ran down then, over the road and up the driveway, through the lobby to his room. Esther was standing there.

"He has died," she said. *Amekufa.*

The manager was shaking his head saying, "Sorry, sorry."

She found it necessary to look away a moment to go over what she almost told them—*but I just saw him, outside.* Instead she held the wrist. There was no pulse.

Perhaps hallucination tells you more about yourself than about the world, though you'd rather the reverse were true. The waking dream. What was she to understand about the state of mind that made her ready to see things that weren't there? The picture of Nkosi looking toward her on the hillside remained even in the aftermath of his death.

"He was not a stranger." The manager of The Lawns talked about comrades and the revolutions in the world that made all Africans one.

Too real. Even if the ghost had been in her imagination, what emotions had called it up, in time to join her with his death? At the graveside, her mind, drifting, screened figures like him from an inner life, celluloid, transparent, laid across the landscape. Pictures too fast, too intense to be memory, superimposed there, the features and the gestures and her own life on that thin film. The hills surrounded. She drew a design from what she saw. Central was the prominent sun. Trees fanned out. Dark forms were arranged around the grave. The voices stopped.

Later, propped in her bed, Antonia waited. The hotel was empty around her, an echoing space, and the noise from the quarters outside the building, a solid, physical thing. It hugged the walls and windows. You could walk into it like a fog.

It was almost visible when the door opened, the pattern of sound, and Esther saying, "Will you go back down there?"

"Yes. Will you?"

"I want to stay here. To do my work."

"Healing the sick ones?"

"Yes." She was sitting on the other bed, her hands on her knees and her back straight, a perfect symmetry. Her hair had just been plaited and arranged into a low rich crown. Her eyes were wide. "When will you go?" she asked.

"Tomorrow."

"Back to your own hospital?" She was intuitive enough to know the answer and ironic enough to grin at her question and her own perception of how things were—*chini,* "down there"—for people like Antonia. Lids dropped over those eyes in alert response. It made Antonia think that irony was a true emotion, sometimes the only way to reconcile. They were both laughing now.

"No, no, I must go back to America."

"Because of the government." Esther had opened her eyes but lowered them, looking at her hands because it was a shame.

"That's right." Antonia stood up and stretched. She walked to the window. Her fingers touched the chintz curtains. The cloth was even thinner, more fragile than she had thought. She spread it open on the pattern: faded women in long dresses watched riders jump, dogs chase.

"But look," she told Esther, "Isn't it better for you to come with me, to return to Hadija and your friends?"

"I have no people," she said. There was still that sadness. Antonia recalled one of her first impressions on listening to Esther's story—of a child walking through a maze of events, a plastic purse in her hand, protected by nothing but her dream father.

"Nkosi belonged to the dead," Esther said after a minute. She seemed to be holding the tarnished light of the kerosene lamp as a shield, gathered in the oval of her arms. When she opened them it was liquid spread over the tops of things. "He belonged to the dead and I . . . inside where things made by God had closed . . . couldn't reach . . . rivers that will bend and join . . . "

Her words fell in syntax like a poem free in form so that what she didn't know, didn't understand, had weight even as it hindered what she wanted to say.

"I am," she began to try again. Antonia thought she would say "a tree" because that was the lingering image: I am a tree, my roots reach rain, my leaves touch wind. But instead she said, "I am the other one." She frowned. *Yule mwingine.* Perhaps she meant the sick one. Perhaps she meant all others.

"If I can be the other one . . . " she was correcting now, qualifying. It was her healing she would talk about. "My eyes see the rivers in your body, your whole body. These are my hands and they can grow out, longer. Very long." She held them palms up to show what it was. "If I can become the other one then we are together. Then I can reach . . . "

"Reach?"

"Yes, reach." She was stalled.

But Antonia knew what she was talking about. Another place. Too awkward to make clear to someone so firmly fixed in this place despite the ghosts that threatened her reason or the welling energy that she felt in Esther's trance. Too awkward, but she knew. Yes, another place. The other side of things.

The rest of it was what Esther could say. The other side of life was death. The other side of health was sickness. Of good, evil. Of light, dark. This was how she would take her strength, in balances like these, the most simple elemental things, a philosophy from which everything everywhere else had grown and overgrown until it was lost.

There was a lull in the noise out back, a kind of clearing in the dark. Other sounds became sharper, locusts signaling

the rain, a lone child singing, a hyena baying somewhere off
in the direction of the town.

When the rain came it was insistent and harder than
normal. The roof collapsed on several rooms out back.
Antonia woke to shouting, a sound like the weather itself, a
rising storm of voices. She dressed quickly and went out,
ducking into the first drops until she was soaked like the rest
of them. She saw Esther in the dark and wet, gathering and
counting children. The women were digging out their poor
things, dragging them to shelter. The men were carrying
broken furniture. Someone handed Antonia a basket of
soaked clothes. She stood wringing them and hanging them
on ropes that were already strung along the hallways in The
Lawns. They came into the hotel then. Lanterns appeared in
the dry empty space. Children ran trying the doors, all open,
choosing, shouting. The others came cautiously into the
polished rooms. This was how they moved into the
abandoned places, a natural invasion like grass growing in
the stones of a ruin. Years ago it would have seemed as
though everything had broken down; now it seemed right.

She thought of the Marina Club, heard voices in the
tapering rain, smelled smoke from the fireplaces. She
entered where they were brewing tea, turned in front of
the fire to warm her back. Someone handed her a cup so
sugary it coated her tongue. She relished it, let it linger in
her mouth.

It seemed to her that this could be an ending for
Luenga's poem, with the water falling as if it had been
hidden by the sky all along, and the metamorphosis a noisy
returning, a reclamation. Hardly noticeable, she could have
been anyone standing there. She could have been the
wanderer Luenga had imagined. There was a luxurious feel
to it, a kind of attachment.

She didn't want to look much harder, fearing that she'd
slip through time, but she found herself in girlhood, could
have slid along the overpolished floor into McGeorge's
back, buckling him at the knees, or heard along the
corridors her father's voice roused in anthem, or seen
Olivia's pinched face and stained skin. Or looked down from

the hill onto that absurd golf course where figures moved and swung and the black caddies waited. She heard her own voice then wishing it all would end, she and McGeorge and the others who thought of themselves as enlightened. They always took care, she thought, to reserve a place where they might stay on. As they were. Or even, in her case, altered, just so she could stay on. She had never considered that she would have to leave, too, and that the eviction had started right there at The Lawns all those years ago. She was only barely able now to understand why. Only barely able. There were no answers in the simple formulas of time or sin, or pasts and presents and lost futures, and what had to be paid as penance. Everything had risen to converge.

There only remained the journey down and then to be lifted in the plane and carried off. To leave at night and land in Europe in the morning so that there was no view behind but the strings of light that marked the land from the sea. Then the blur of taxis and the buses and the high, gray buildings, stone casting deep shadows, an alien language of steel and rock, of brick and glass and the cold.

She stayed with Esther through the night in the soft, relenting room. They moved around straightening things or stood to watch the rain that was still streaming windborne in angles that rose and fell. There was only emotion to share, which was quiet and had no form so that they drifted into it and out like people on the verge of sleep.

As the hotel settled, it seemed to be a ship put out to sea with the people unaware, except that they were here on a mountaintop and landed. There were soft cooing noises out beyond. Many things pressed together so that it felt like conversation, though the two women hardly spoke and sometimes slept.

From time to time they looked at each other. The light and smell of morning made Esther yawn and then they were both awake. One of the curtains had been torn by wind. Antonia held a strip of it like a ribbon in a dance. The impossibility of explanations had been made clear by the storm and their nightlong silence. Even more so now by something clean that had surfaced in the air. Antonia herself was someone who would have said there was too much room to be mistaken in matters that could never be expressed, but not this time when faith was as tangible as cloth and her hand a fist that tore it from its rod. And then another. Until nothing was left but shreds. And the stillness that comes.

"We will drink tea," Esther promised as soon as they both could laugh.

Outside white roses had opened in the garden. Somewhere a child was crying, a voice amplified in the forest overhead. There was no direction, even to the sound of running water—a ditch nearby? a stream?—as she worked the key into the Peugeot's door and got in. She leaned back in the seat. The leather resisted, stiff with the cold night. Dawn had been abrupt, switching on a livid sky and the mounting sun. Pines bent toward the center. Antonia enjoyed the moment, the radiant connections. And the sound of her engine coming to life. Children held fenders or pushed her from behind, trying to keep pace as the car rolled. And then they stopped, suddenly, arms extended, stunned, as if they didn't believe any of it, not the car, not their own speed, not their loss. And Esther behind them waving and waving.

It was raining in Kinondoni and green, greener than when she had left it; too green. Termites had risen in clouds to search for each other in the light, a rocketing flight and then a fall, dropping their wings as they came into a feathery carpet. On the ground they were not more than worms pulsing toward the dark places where they lived. Children ran gathering them in baskets to be fried and salted and eaten around fires throughout the night.

Antonia found Charles sweeping them up, fussing; the wings were everywhere. Her house otherwise was neat, tidied over and over while she was away. He told her that Mr. Laxmanbhai had somehow got a paper and was leaving the country. He had left a folder for her containing everything she needed. She didn't look at it. Instead she drove out to find him, or tried to. He had moved, down to one small room someplace in another man's house; she couldn't find him. So she gave the car up to its own will and took directions as they came, a left, a right, letting it find the way for her. It was still early enough for vendors to be out roasting cassava. She saw the last kites of the Asian boys riding down into the alleys. Some of the whores had come out to stand in doorways with their beaded falls of hair and glass bracelets, holding the cigarettes they couldn't afford to light. In small bars, where men drank beer brewed from anything that was around, curtains parted for the evening trade.

There were so few cars that the streets easily became her own, around the crescent beach, the waiting crane, where the Indian girls had sent their wishes out to sea, across the bridge, up onto the cliffs of Oyster Bay. The houses were strangely darkened that night, but she could imagine a party there set in the future, if Armstrong's predictions came true and there was a second wave of colonialists back to repair the ruins or finish it off like vultures on a corpse. Patios strung with colored light, luminaria around a driveway, men in Filipino shirts. Would the women be wearing soft caftans and negligees that doubled for formals in the heat?

She traveled around the half-moon bay, all the way to the cusp, to the highest point where the wind unfurled in the distance and there were no boundaries. There was not even a moon to line the horizon. Then back down along the dirt track that ran along the other side, where Makonde had started to pitch makeshift huts of cardboard and plastic bags. Women appeared in doorways, squinting as she passed, and men, seated around small fires, nodded or blew on their pipes of *bhang* like *shetani,* smiling through their filed teeth. On and on, her light skimming a backwater swamp held together by webs of mangrove root, until she surfaced and could see the red tile roof of the hospital, the bulky walls and waiting patients. Lights from the windows in the wards fell on the nurses who had come out on break to stand near the fence that faced the sea, taking whatever coolness they could from the breeze before it died.